"Get close together, ~~the~~ ~~Lady~~ ~~with~~ ~~the~~ weapons to the fight!" A ragged cheer went up, though several of the men were unable at first to fight free of Mathkkra.

Ylia stood where she'd bridged, irresolute. Still dangerous to use the Baelfyr, and the sword—that terrified her. She caught at the sword hilts, hesitated, pushed the blade back firmly into its sheath and stepped forward . . .

There: she brought up her hands and cried out the ancient words. Flame tore down the road; five fell dead. Beyond them a man cried out.

"Draw *back*, I *told* ye, come away from the creatures and hold together, that's your Lady with the fire!"

Ace books by Ru Emerson

THE PRINCESS OF FLAMES

THE FIRST TALE OF NEDAO: TO THE HAUNTED MOUNTAINS
THE SECOND TALE OF NEDAO: IN THE CAVES OF EXILE

THE SECOND TALE OF NEDAO

IN THE CAVES OF EXILE

RU EMERSON

ACE BOOKS, NEW YORK

This book is an Ace
original edition, and has never
been previously published.

THE SECOND TALE OF NEDAO:
IN THE CAVES OF EXILE

An Ace Book/published by arrangement with
the author

PRINTING HISTORY
Ace edition / January 1988

ISBN: 0-441-37050-0

Ace Books are published by The Berkley Publishing Group,
200 Madison Avenue, New York, New York 10016.
The name "ACE" and the "A" logo are
trademarks belonging to Charter Communications, Inc.
PRINTED IN THE UNITED STATES OF AMERICA

10   9   8   7   6   5   4   3   2   1

Acknowledgments

Sometimes, even when the plot flows and the characters cooperate, there's something not quite complete about it all. Often the idea needed is simply buried. When that happens, sometimes you can work it loose yourself; occasionally it needs to be coaxed free with outside help.

Doug, you've helped that way more than once: having a roommate with taste you can trust is better than just nice. Thanks from me and from Mal Brit Arren.

Ginjer, there have been so many times we've sat and talked, and something truly exciting has come of it: an idea, a twist, something about a character's personality I hadn't realized. It's been help above and beyond the call of, and I deeply appreciate it.

To Doug, with purple hearts and flowers
and the triple cross for conspicuous bravery
in the presence of
Wicked Rewrites

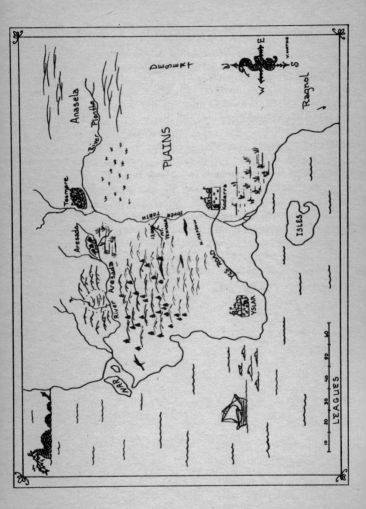

Prologue

It was cold; the stars were a frost of light from tree-lined high horizon to cliff-edged high horizon. Rock shone a faint blue; the shadows under the trees were impenetrable to normal eyes. Across the bowl-like valley, there was a deep silence. Stone lay in crazy piles, slabs of rock slanted against rare, intact walls, chunks and shards flung wide as though by a giant hand covered an expanse of close-cropped field.

Elsewhere in the mountains, nightbirds flew and uttered muted calls, small beasts crackled through the brush. Creatures hunted or were hunted and not in silence. Here, had any man stood and listened, he would have heard nothing but the thin scree in his own ears—or the overloud thump of his heart, for there was fear here, an ancient fear, as old as the shaping of the stones themselves. And, perhaps, he might have seen the faintest glow of sullen red light within a row of tall, shattered windows.

There was nothing else.

It is my tale, as it was from the first, and so I shall continue: I, Nisana, the only AEldra of cat-kind to journey east of the Foessa Mountains and dwell among the Nedao.

You who have heard me speak before know of that: how the Lady Scythia of the Second Ylsan House came to Nedao to wed its King, Brandt. And so I went preforce to the walled City Koderra, for where my Scythia was, I had to be.

I have spoken already at length—greater length than is normally my wont—of the journey north from shattered Koderra, after the barbarous Tehlatt swooped down across Nedao and slew 8 parts of the folk. Of 2,000 Koderrans, only 9 of us escaped the final battle. My sweet Scythia died there to avenge her Lord, King Brandt, leaving young Ylia orphaned and in my keeping.

As much as such a one could be in anyone's keeping. She was strong-willed even then, Ylia, though scarcely able to use her AEldra Power at all, for she was only half AEldran and the block of her Nedaoan blood was such that even I could not break it; weapons-trained, Ylia, but not skilled in true fighting. On that journey, she came into battle strength like her father's, into full use of the Power, like her mother's.

For once in the Foessa, we were beset by such things as even children do not deem real: Mathkkra, the blood-drinking terrors which stalked Nedao's Plain 500 years before; evil

2

seemings, *set to snare the inner being of any
foolish enough to dare the haunted mountains;
Thullen, great flying creatures of such horrid
aspect I shall say no more of them, until I must.
Lyiadd, who exiled himself from kin and hearth,
who turned his back on the wealth of AEldra
Power to seek that which was more—and
other—and dread dark. He, who sought my Ylia
herself, though in the end, he had only the point
of her blade.*

But not only evils inhabit the Foessa—though
Nedaoan legend certainly held it to be so. We
found allies and friends there: The Nasath, the
Ylsan Guardians who first gave the AEldra Power;
and the Folk, who still dwell deep in the northern
woods.

She dealt with both sides of the coin, my Ylia,
both fair and not, and so it was no wonder to us,
her companions, to see the strength in her when
we came finally to Aresada and she challenged
and deposed her foul cousin Vess.

My second tale, which I begin here, is mainly
of Nedao and its young Queen. But there were
others who had a hand in shaping the story as it
finally came to be, and as I tell it now. And
though often I did not know of those folk until
long past the event, those I learned of are part of
my telling now, as though I had known them at
the time.

1

It was cold and rainy, the sun a chancy and sometime thing. And on the upper ledges before the main entrance to the Caves of Aresada, the wind was definitely chill. But those who passed the young woman huddled in her torn soldier's cloak, her grey-green eyes fixed on a spot far down-river, felt none of the cold, and little of the hunger that had been theirs for a full month. Ylia—the King's daughter and heir, now their Queen—had returned to them beyond all hope and against impossible odds; the House of Ettel again properly ruled. Things had been bad, since the fall of the Plain. No one doubted that now they would improve.

Ylia for the moment saw none of them, was aware of none of the movement around her: She was concentrating on two widely diverse things. The first, probably more important, was the Search she was making of the River, both banks, as far as her sense could reach. All very well for Marhan and Levren to assure her Vess would not return to the Caves! He would not, at the very least, because if he attempted such a thing and she became aware of him, she'd have the breath out of him. Forever.

Vess: Hated cousin, so hungry for Nedao's crown, for its power, he'd dared the return to Teshmor, up-river and North, avoiding the barbarous Tehlatt by staying to the foothills. There he had pledged his aid to the beleagered Corlin of Planthe—*aid!* A lie, all of it, spoken only so Corlin would accept him, so the folk still within Teshmor's walls would. So that he could thereafter slide from the City at the last, reach Aresada and take the ruling he wanted.

He'd planned it well, too, and under extreme pressure of time and circumstance: but he'd known, as any would, that once he'd announced Brandt, his Queen, his daughter all dead—*liar, bastard and liar!*—that Corlin would refuse his aid, force him to leave Teshmor as the last of the House of Ettel, to hasten to the Caves and lead the people. He'd miscalculated his safety, and nearly lost his life. Only chance had spared him death at the hands of the Tehlatt.

Had it been that important to him, Brandt's crown? But she knew the answer to that. Yes. To Vess, any power was preferable to none. Easy to piece together, given enough of the facts and sufficient hindsight: He'd taken the Caves and those within, knowing the King and all those with him must have perished in their desperate last stand before Koderra's gates. Later, he'd seal to him the folk who'd escaped Koderra by Sea. Yes, he'd planned.

And she'd not forgotten the thing her mother told her, that last night in the King's City: Sea-Raiders. Vess had thought to sway Brandt to seek aid from the fierce Southern pirates against the Tehlatt. Doubtless he'd still held to that thought, hoping to retake the Plain. She shook her head. Yet another thing to ask Erken, or another of her council.

The second thing she concentrated on, a thing much more difficult for her, was a determination to stay her ground and neither faint nor become ill, since at the moment she looked down to the River a full ten lengths below. Nearly impossible for one with her irrational terror of heights. To be sure, the ledge wasn't overhung and rock was visible below her all the way down to the bridge. It didn't help.

All right, enough. It was; she'd held to the guard's height a sufficient time to please herself, and hadn't been caught out by Malaeth (who'd fuss or panic), or Nisana (those who said cats had no sense of humor had never been laughed at by *this* cat). She stretched warily, dropped back down to solid ground, and turned then to gaze out south.

There, the narrow gorge through which they'd come—Mothers, could it have been only three days before? At the moment, it felt more like three months, with a hard-worked Planting Month in their midst. From this height, she could see the pale greens of the Marshes, and beyond them, near the edge of sight, the dark green Forest of the Folk, a faint line of purple distant mountain capping them.

We did it. She felt a flush of pride, looking back down their trail. Pride and astonishment, that any of them had lived to tell of that month of cold, short commons, terror and loss. *Brendan.* It smote hard, catching her, once again, by surprise. *He* hadn't reached Aresada, her brave Brendan.

She fought the sudden grief aside; there was no time for it. Too much to worry. Food. True shelter, for the Caves were scarcely more than very temporary. A pasture for the tattered little herd that was all Nedao's flocks. The goats, of course, could eat anywhere and they were fine among the trees, but the sheep were another matter, as were the horses and the very few remaining cattle. Golsat had been gone since daybreak, searching for grassland near the Caves, that for the safety of the orphaned children who'd been given the task of keeping the animals.

Nisana was gone, too. The cat had located a few cattle and sheep abandoned just within the mountains, had taken Lisabetha—who could still, with the senses she gained on their journey, sense if faintly what the cat wanted—and Lus, the woman they'd rescued in the Foessa, for she had been raised in a herder's village. Ylia worried, but finally let them go. *No choice.* There wasn't. They needed any animals they could find, short of raiding the Plain and taking their own back from the Tehlatt. But to send Lord Corry's daughter afoot into these mountains after a lost cow . . . it didn't bear thinking about. *Nisana,* she reminded herself tartly, *can bridge them out of any trouble they might step into.*

And—*poor Lisabetha.* There was a wonder all its own, one Ylia would never have believed possible: Lisabetha had begun the journey from Koderra in terror of the mountains and a worse fear of the magic of her AEldra companions, a fear still worse of her own ability to *dream* true. She'd grown, Lisabetha, over that journey. So much so that when she gained fleeting ability to hear AEldra mind-speech, she'd taken her ability to hear Ylia and the cat with honest pleasure, had grieved at its rapid loss.

Ylia shivered. The sun was gone again, lost behind dark, ragged-edged clouds. The ledges were deserted, except for herself and the guard. By her stomach, it was past noon-hour, there'd be a thin soup which would at least be hot. And after that, yet another meeting.

She strode into the darkness of the outer chambers. No warmer here, but at least the wind was gone. And down in the Great Temple, on past and through two wide corridors of stone to the Vast Hall, the temperature remained constant. In the chambers where the people gathered, it was actually warm, a combination of so many bodies and the cook fires. Fortunately there were enough openings in the limestone overhead that it wasn't particularly stuffy.

The food was indeed, as she'd suspected, thin soup, bland enough that it had to be rabbit again. There was also a flat rolled up pancake of sour cattail meal. Dipped in the soup, it lost some of its unpleasant flavor, and it was more filling than only the soup. With luck, Marhan and Levren, and Erken's lads they'd taken with them, would come up with deer, or enough of *something* for stew.

They didn't dare sacrifice any of the sheep or goats to the pot. There simply weren't enough of them to spare.

She ate quickly, aware of the eyes on her, the undercurrent of approval. She'd needed no one to tell her Vess had not eaten with her folk. She turned a little aside, though, when she caught whispers she wasn't intended to hear: the women were talking about her scar again. *It barely shows!* She kept her fingers away from her cheek by main determination. The fact was, it *did* show, if only as a thin white line against a tanned face. It ran from temple to chin in a straight line. It had mates, too, though none but her companions on the northward journey knew of the cross between her breasts, the short mark below her belt that looked like a scratch and had been the worst of them all, or the ragged cut from elbow to wrist. Likely, there wouldn't have been fuss about *those* anyway, it was the mark on her face that upset them. *I don't care,* she told herself. *Alive matters more. I'm alive.* But she turned her face aside when the older women looked at her too closely.

Erken had managed to put together a rough council chamber not far from the main entrance to the Caves, in a small room originally cut from the rock as a storehouse. It adjoined the natural pocket that had served Vess as a bedroom, and now served Ylia. From somewhere, the Duke of Anasela had garnered a trestle, two short benches and a number of sawn logs for seats, and had raided the household goods of Nedao's remaining northern Baron for pens, ink and a flat packet of thick Narran paper. Her candles came from the main store.

The little room was only half-filled: Levren, Marhan and Golsat were hunting; Lisabetha away with Nisana. Those five she'd included in her council, half expecting argument from the others, somewhat surprised when she got none. For the rest: two minor lords of the sort who served under the Baronry, one to every four or five villages; Bnorn, a Baron who'd been traveling with his family from Teshmor to his manor in the western foothills when the Tehlatt struck. He had thereby brought in his wife and son, his grandson, household men and many of his servants.

And Erken, Duke of Anasela. Exiled, it was true; Erken had ruled no land since he'd lost his eastern holdings to the barbarians ten years before, keeping instead his title and pledging himself and his following to Corlin of Planthe, father to Lisabetha. He had fought at Corlin's side until the outer gates of Teshmor fell, and only at Corlin's order had he and his remaining men fled through one of the City's tunnels.

Ifney of Sern and Marckl of Broad Heath, the Lords Holder, had been difficult for Ylia to tell apart at first. They were short, even for Nedaoans, and she stood on eye level with both of them; they were plainly clad, as simply dressed as the peasants who'd worked their lands. But she was learning to distinguish them finally: Marckl was darker and clean-shaven. Ifney wore a touch of moustache across his lip, a faint brownness against a dark face. There was more grey in his hair, more snap to his speech.

The Baron Bnorn was elderly, as old as Malaeth, Ylia's childhood nurse, and she was rapidly nearing 80. But he carried his winters well. His hair and beard were white shocks against a skin darkened by sun and wind, his eyes weather-narrowed. He sat to one side and at first made no contributions, so abashed was he by his presence at the Queen's Council.

Ylia inclined her head gravely as her young door-warder announced her. Erken had been busy with *that* sort of thing, too. And though she still found it a bit disconcerting after so long in the mountains as simply one of an armed company to have attendants everywhere, she had to admit the Duke had the right of such things: her Nedaoans wanted and expected her to be properly surrounded and were proud that they could at least provide that much for her. And it gave purpose to such as young Merreven, who had lost all his family when his village was razed, but who now had a task—and an important one—he could accomplish.

Erken sat at the far end of the table, turning his hat in his hands, eyes fixed on it. She bit back a sudden smile. The folk of Teshmor were known ever as Nedao's dandies. The best Narran silk and Oversea velvet and jeweled satins went always to the northern City and not to the King's halls. But even among Teshmorans, Erken had stood out. And notwithstanding he'd fought a hard siege and that he'd been at Aresada for all of Planting Month, he had managed somehow to keep his garb faultless: the deep blue shirt, the fine-woven Osneran breeches of a matching shade might have just come from his tailor's, if one ignored a little fraying around the hems and at the throat. But the hat which was Erken's mark and his pride had not fared so well: the wide brim was notched and dirty, the jaunty ochre-dyed feathers that trailed from the lace-cut leather band were matted and grey. Erken studied it with evident distaste.

They'd already explained the situation to her, the first night. No worse than she'd expected, who'd not really dared to expect at all. Nearly three thousand had reached Aresada so far; another few hundreds no doubt still wandered the edges of the mountains, afraid to penetrate them or lost, though after so long they could not be certain of finding such folk. But that was Nisana's chore, along with locating scattered cattle and sheep, goats and chickens.

Food was critical. Those who had fled the Plain when the Tehlatt came upon them had for the most part come with only the few things they could grab before they ran, which was seldom much. Particularly among the villages to the east, there had been little warning. Few even had spare clothing or food.

And now three thousand folk lived in the vast caves and sought to hold their lives together, until matters improved. A difficult situation, at best: Nedao's people were settled, farmers and herders, fishermen from the villages along the banks of the Torth. Those who lived such lives had followed in the steps of their parents, and their parents' parents for nearly five hundred years. Hunters—there were some who hunted in the foothills of western Nedao, but not many. There would have been mass starvation already, had the Foessa not been thick with game.

Even so, those who had spent the Planting Month at Aresada had gone hungry most of the time.

"Any word from the hunting parties?" Ifney wanted to know as soon as she settled in. Ylia shook her head.

"They've had to go farther afield, of course. Tonight or tomorrow. We've more beasts coming, though."

"Mmm," Marckl grunted. "Something, that."

"Can't eat them," Ifney reminded him.

" 'Course not! But next year—"

"Aye." Ifney sighed heavily, resettled himself on the hard wood. He and Marckl exchanged a brief look. Ylia knew that look, and sighed quietly. Nisana again; it was nearly impossible for these men to accept that a cat could carry the years and hold the Power she did. Lisabetha had helped considerably: the Lords Holder knew her and because of what she'd told them, Marckl had at least quit making horns at the cat.

Fortunately, Nisana preferred to avoid council meetings, saying she had more important matters to deal with and that she had no desire to sit with arguing humans unless urgently necessary. Also fortunately, Nisana was more than used to such treatment and had been merely amused, though not so amused as to have her idea of fun with any of them.

"You"—Ylia gazed down the table—"were going to tell me what chanced when you arrived." Erken frowned, jolted out of some dark thought. "Vess," she prompted.

"Vess. Mmm." Erken dropped the hat on the table, shoved it over the edge and out of his sight. "If you want to take the time for that *now,* though."

"After all, he's gone—," Ifney began. Ylia shook her head. "Gone, yes. But I need to know."

"Well—," Erken began slowly. "With so much else to discuss, are you certain there's point to it?"

"Yes." Ylia nodded. "And we keep pressing it to the end, and then we're one and all too tired to talk about it. Now, Erken. Please."

"Well—," Erken repeated. "These men came before I did."

"Aye." Ifney turned his sharp glance from one to the other of them. "And if you'll not say it, Erken, I will. I never held with Vess nor his ways, ever, and I never swore to him, as you all know!" He recollected himself, swallowed. "Um. I know he's kin of yours, Lady."

"One cannot choose kin," Ylia replied dryly. "You do not upset me by straight speech concerning Vess. And how often must I tell you, I need you to speak freely. What good is a council such as this if you do not council?"

The Northerner considered this. Smiled briefly. "Just so, Lady. Well, then. I got here the middle of the twenty-fifth of First Flowers. There was a fair pack of us. I'd taken my folk, sent my women ahead and gone for Marckl's holdings. He and I roused three villages between Sern and Teshmor. We met up with Bnorn just within the Pass. So we were—what, Marckl?"

"Mmm. Perhaps four hundred, all told."

"Well." Ifney cleared his throat. "We got to Aresada a full day later. The herds held us back and we didn't dare leave the herders and their beasts behind us, even if we'd wanted or if they would have let us. So by the time we reached the bridge, we found Vess in power. There were over a thousand folk here by then, they'd all sworn to him, worse luck!"

"Well?" Marckl demanded. "What did you want of 'em? So far as any knew, the whole South was gone! Vess had been there, he was the only one who knew anything about Koderra. Remember? Remember too what he told us? He was the last of the House of Ettel! If there was anyone alive—yourself, Lady, or the King—we couldn't know. And you weren't here."

"No."

"Between us, we had more armed than Vess," Ifney said. "But we talked it over, and we couldn't see any other choice. No one *liked* Vess. But he was what we had." A gloomy silence settled over the three men.

"And—?" Ylia prompted.

Ifney shrugged. "Well, it wasn't good when we got here. It got worse. Vess wasn't much interested in food, save what went in his mouth. Bnorn's men, mine, and Erken's boys did what hunting there was. The fishers have kept busy. We weren't good at it, though we got better because we hadn't choice."

Erken finally spoke, but his reluctance was evident in his face and the slowness of his speech. "Vess was not content with remaining here, with ruling the pittance of folk at Aresada. Between us, as you've seen, Lady, we have perhaps five hundred armed. Not, mind, skilled armed!"

"I have seen that." She had. Green boys, still years from their first moustaches, white-haired old men who in better days would have been sitting in the sun spinning tales for any who'd listen. Anything and everything between.

"Not soldiers." Marckl growled. "Nor likely to be, most of them, to my way of seeing it. But Vess harped ever that we must retake the Plain, particularly we must regain the South, must hold Koderra once again."

"By means of a bargain," Ylia said flatly, "with the Sea-Raiders." Dead astonished silence greeted this remark. "He said as much to—to my father, the night before Koderra was attacked. Had he sent for their aid, or did he just talk of it?"

"He didn't say anything to me," Erken replied. "I was not particularly in his confidence," he added with a brief grin that erased fully twenty years from his lean face. "But I think he had persuaded—I think that is the word—certain folk of village Keldan to build rafts. The work wasn't yet begun when you arrived."

"Rafts." Ylia considered this in silence for some moments. She laughed then. "Thanks, sweet cousin! I had not considered rafts as a means of reaching Yls. But the river itself—do any of you know it?"

"It turns west," Erken said doubtfully.

"That much I've *seen*," Ylia replied, a faint emphasis on her words. Erken considered this.

"Seen. Yes." *Magic*. His dislike wasn't as strong as old

Marhan's, but he clearly hadn't much more use for it than the Swordmaster did. "Well. They say it widens perhaps 30 leagues from here and empties out into the Bay of Nessea. Now, I *have* seen that Bay and two rivers do indeed empty into it. If one of them is ours, then we could very likely reach Nar. And take passage to Yls aboard one of their ships."

"We haven't true shipwrights, Lady," Marckl said. He leaned across the table, suddenly eager with thought of something useful he could do. "But I think we could locate those who've built the sort of light, narrow-hulled boats that were used on the Planthe—market-boats. They'd be safer than rafts."

"Yes." She thought. "We'd need only one or two—"

"Three," Erken broke in gravely, "for safety."

"All right. If you will then, Marckl, see to the building of three boats. We don't need much room, only for men to carry messages to Nar and Yls. I want to bring the folk there north as soon as possible. If they'll come," she added doubtfully.

"They'll come," Marckl said decidedly.

"Then—the boats needn't be large, just good enough for two men each to go down river and return." *Gods and Mothers, messages. That will take thought.* "One last thing," she said finally. "Lord Corry provisioned Aresada for a safety in the event of such a thing as befell us. What do any of you know of this?"

Erken shrugged. "What most men know. Rumor, largely. Corry intended to send his clerks before him. If he did, they never arrived here. In any event, the lists are gone that tallied where things were hidden, and how much of what things. Grain was sent, I know that much."

"So do I," Bnorn put in his first comment of the evening. "A lot of it came from my fields, along with seed and tools."

"It would not have been left in any of the outer chambers," Marckl said flatly. "Because of beasts and—well, Nedao can trust her mountain-hunters, I hope, they wouldn't simply steal things left here, but in need men might use up food left in plain sight."

"Mmmm." Ylia considered briefly. "This is a task for the women who are not as useful at gathering. Lisabetha may well know something of Corlin's plans. I'll ask when she returns; perhaps she can organize the search." *And remain safer here.* It suddenly shook her: *Inniva guard me, speaking as I am, making decisions, appointing tasks—as though I knew what I did!*

They went on to other things, and still others: It was dark by the time the meeting broke. Ylia staggered to her feet as Erken, the last of them, bowed and left her. She stretched. "Father, if you'd known how I'd take the ruling—," she whispered. She pulled the thin gold band from her brow—it had been Vess's, the smith had refused to simply cut it down for her and had reworked the metal. She stared at it gloomily.

It would have been hard enough simply to follow the footsteps of one so beloved as Brandt, and she'd always thought to do it with more years and experience. And now—the work before them terrified her as much as anything they'd faced on the journey north from Koderra: Food they needed, a source of food that did not depend upon what the hunters could catch, what the women could forage. Clothing, shoes and boots. And desperately, a place to live. She must search, must bring Nisana back and set her to that task. Because if they didn't get seed in the ground soon, they'd be as good as dead.

None of the folk wanted to leave, which had mildly surprised her. Considering what hardship they lived under, she'd expected some at least would want to seek out sanctuary in Yls or Nar. No. They were Nedao and they were hers to care for. *Mothers grant me the strength, that I not fail them.*

She stretched hard, doused the candles. It was near time for evening meal. More thin soup no doubt. And then, after that, a *search*, and a serious one.

To those who have never lost all in disaster, it is incomprehensible, as it had been to me all my life. Of a sudden, there is little or nothing, even of those things that were taken for granted: food and water. Bedding. Warm clothing (though that and footgear had for obvious reasons not ever been among my needs). Among those who had followed the ways of their forbears for a 10 of generations—not only such basics as food and clothing and fire, but seed and ground to plant it in; grazing lands for their herds. I did all I could to aid the child Ylia in her efforts to succor her folk, and yet I know the weight of it lay squarely across her slender shoulders.

2

Cloud cover was holding the smoke from the cook-fires low and spreading the smell of it through the Caverns again. She brought her head up wearily, watched as grey tendrils drifted across the lantern-light, swirled about the narrow openings in the rock across the chamber. *Ugh.* Too wet to work out of doors, unpleasant inside. There was a faint scent of cooking meat, teasing at her empty stomach. The last of the venison, and so yet another soup. It made one hungry for the stew of the first night, when Golsat and his boys had staggered in with four spring-thin deer, though a year ago scarce a Nedaoan now living at Aresada would have considered that watery and vegetable-poor mess to be food at all.

Their situation still wasn't good, though it was a little better: the hunters were supplying what meat they could; the fishers had moved downstream and the catch was larger; two of the orphaned girls who were herding had located wild onion in veritable thickets on the hillsides.

And the Caves had finally yielded the first of the caches: waterproofed bags containing two dragweight of wheat-meal. Enough to thicken soups and stews, enough for flat bread once a 5-day, at least for present. They didn't dare save it; there was already a thin layer of green across the top of the bag and in another season it would probably have been completely inedible. In the same chamber they had located a dragweight of wheat seed, and a clutch of smaller bags of seed from someone's kitchen gardens. Beans, cress, melon and several kinds of squashes— good eating, all of it, *if there is a place to plant*.

She worried that, constantly. Without proper land, they might as well resign themselves all to begging, to a home in exile and poverty, in Yls or Nar.

And within another generation—*that* pulled at her also, though only when she woke, middle night, and could not readily return to sleep: *I am the last of the House, save only Vess. If I die without an heir there is no House.* Never before had she been so aware of how fragile a thing life was, how light the grasp of any upon it. During the day, it seldom bothered her, save as a passing, impatient thought: *Take reasonable care; you cannot wed and get children here and now. Take thought for who can be named successor, if you die.* That, of course, was easy: who better than Erken?

In the meantime, she turned back to the task at hand, sternly banishing extraneous thought, the nostril-tickling smoke, the growling of her stomach. *Messages.* The boats were well under way, they'd be done in a full 5-day. Ifney and Marckl wasted no time, and there were plenty of men from the Torth to do the actual building. She'd discussed the Narran messages with her council: the request for aid which Nedao would repay as soon as possible. Another message to the Nedaoans who had—*must* have!— reached Yls.

She'd spoken only with her original companions regarding the third message, the one to be directed to the Sirdar himself, warning of Lyiadd. It would need tact, that the proud old man not take offense. A half-blood had found the Valley of the Night Serpent and its inhabitants, and he had not. She knew where his eldest child, Marrita, housed, and with whom—or what. It would need careful framing, indeed. And, of course, that message would need to be cast into High AEldran, for though the Sirdar spoke all the languages of the Peopled Lands, he would take great offense indeed if any message addressed to him were not in the ancient language.

Ylia *knew* High AEldran: her mother and Nisana had both instructed her. And she'd used it recently enough, when she'd challenged Lyiadd to the fight that ended in his death. But this was a matter more complex than a duel-challenge.

Nisana would have done the translation, if she'd asked. But the cat would not have let her forget for a moment it was her own desire to be anywhere but stuck inside with a text that caused her present difficulties.

There—finally!—it was done. Her hand ached from clutching the pen, and, as usual, she'd somehow managed to get ink across the web of skin between thumb and forefinger. She eyed the result critically: Her lettering still sloped uphill but other than that the letters were well formed and no one could fault them. The text itself: "Twelfth of Spring Floods. The thanks of Ylia, daughter to Scythia of the Second House of Yls, heir to King Brandt of Nedao, and now Queen to Nedao in its exile, to those that have cared for our folk in their hour of need. For such food and shelter as has been provided by our Mother's land, we shall pay, when the ability is again granted to us.

"Know that our beloved and honored parents were slain in the fall of the King's City Koderra the Twenty-third of First Flowers." Unnecessary as a matter of information, the Sirdar had no doubt *known* of Scythia's death long since: he'd have *seen* it, or *dreamed* it. "We do not ask for ourselves, or for our folk, that these deaths be avenged, or that aid be given us to drive the barbarians from the Plain. The attack was too great, and we are perhaps a tenth of our original numbers.

"To us it seems best, therefore, that we remain within the Foessa, for the Mountains offer us sanctuary from the Tehlatt as nothing else might, and here we shall rebuild as best we may. Those of our kind who may have reached Yslar and who wish to rejoin their own are welcome and a place will be made in our midst for them. Those who wish to remain among the Ylsans are free to do so, and with our blessing, for the way before us here will not be an easy one."

So much—easy. Now for the difficult part: "A matter for the eyes of the Sirdar, and those in his trust only. On our journey northwards through the Foessa, we came upon a great, deep valley well within the mountains. A fuller description of this place should not be necessary, as it is doubtless in every ancient scroll dealing with the First War fought by the AEldra a thousand years ago. There are torn and burnt buildings in the depths of that place and a presence of Power that is ancient and evil.

"Those walls are again inhabited, by one of the Fifth House called Lyiadd, his household armsmen, his servants and"—she'd hesitated long here—"his woman. One of our number was slain by his following. I in turn fought him, blade to blade, doing him such great injury that he may be dead.

"But it is possible he is not. I was not able to ascertain whether he breathed before I was bridged to safety.

"I perhaps speak of things already known to the Sirdar. They are of sufficient urgency, certainly, that I warn of them now, that those stronger in the Power than I may deal with them, lest the Night-Serpent Lammior find a successor to unleash war across the entirety of the Lands.

"Nedao has no army remaining and little strength at present save to protect herself. Should there come a day, however, when Yls has need of us, send."

She sighed. It was the best she could do, she'd agonized most of a day over it already. If the Sirdar was offended by any of it—well then, anything else she could say would offend him also. The proper forms were all there, no one could say she hadn't been formally, exactingly polite. She lifted the pen again, inked it and signed her name across the bottom: "Ylia hra'da Brandt, Coreas Nedao". "Ylia, Brandt's daughter, Queen of Nedao." Now, if Erken had got that colored wax from Bnorn's clerk—there, at the bottom of the box of quills. Not much of it, but enough for now. Likely there'd be no need for more messages such as this one until year's end. She pulled at the thong around her neck, fished out the rough seal the smith had cast for her and folded the paper. A lanolined sheath for it, a pale green ribbon (one of Lisabetha's last) around that. A splash of wax at the joining, seal—quickly—on that. She leaned back against the wall, closed her eyes. *Mothers, who'd have thought a few lines on paper to be such a task?*

It wouldn't always be, of course, providing her father's household chose to come north. Among them were Brandt's scribes and clerks. With their aid, she'd only need frame the idea of any such future messages, the rest, save the signature and seal, would be done for her. She smiled briefly. There was something, after all, to be said for household folk.

If there was need for such messages again, she decided, the old

Chosen Grewl would aid her. He'd already been an invaluable
ally, when Vess had refused to fight her according to Nedaoan
custom, and it had been Grewl who had found the loophole that
allowed a champion to take her place; Grewl who had taken a firm
stand when two of the more fanatic young Chosen had tried to
start trouble among the people because of Ylia's AEldran blood.
He was at something of a loose end at present, for he was an
Oversea scholar who had been studying Nedaoan histories when
the Tehlatt attacked. He had no official standing among the
Nedaoan Chosen, and had reluctantly taken temporary leadership
of them pending confirmation from Osnera. But there was little for
him to do, save lead the few services and ceremonies the Chosen
had: all of the written histories and tales had been lost to the
Tehlatt, and there wasn't enough ink or parchment to spare him.
He was too elderly and frail to hunt or gather. But he wanted to be
of use.

And he'd remain silent on the matters Ylia and her original
companions felt best kept from the people: there were enough
causes for discomfort and panic, without adding others. Lyiadd.
Mathkkra. No mention of those unless—*until*—it became absolutely necessary.

She stretched, pushed to her feet. Enough smoke for a while,
whether it rained or not, it was time to get some *air*. And, if it was
bearable out on the ramparts, she could attempt another *search*.
Somewhere, *somewhere* in these mountains, there had to be a
refuge!

But if there were such a thing, it didn't reveal itself this time,
either. She finally gave it up as the wind howled down across wet
rock from the north, bringing a squall of rain that by the feel of it
was half ice. She ducked back inside the narrow rock portal and
went in search of Lisabetha.

It wasn't a particularly difficult search, once one of the old men
in the Grand Temple pointed her in the proper direction. At the
rear of the chamber just behind the Grand Temple was a half-
hidden opening, leading back and away into darkness. Near this,
she found clear sign of Lisabetha: a length of the thin twine used
by herders to make temporary pens was wound around a
stalagmite, tied off with several hard knots. The free end vanished
into rockbound dark.

The second level of sight would have guided her easily enough.

Ylia took a torch anyway. She didn't like being underground; she couldn't bear it without some kind of light.

These caves were unlike the Mathkkra caves, where she'd rescued Lisabetha and nearly lost Brelian, younger brother to her beloved Brendan. There she'd gained the full use of the AEldra Powers previously denied her, and won free of those horrid crumbling tunnels. She still never felt truly comfortable in such stony halls and was acutely aware how much rock and dirt weighed over the passageway where she walked.

Lisabetha apparently remembered little or nothing of her experiences that night, for she showed no discomfort even when nearly a league from the Grand Temple and the outside world. She *was* extremely careful with her guide rope, even more careful with chalk-markings when the rope ran out and she explored further.

"Ylia!" The girl straightened, wiped grubby hands on the cloth torn from her underskirt and fastened to the belt of her worn travel-skirt. Unnecessary for her to ask the identity of the one still hidden behind the torch, for few others came after her beyond the length of rope, and none else alone.

"Myself. You've come far." Ylia had counted seven joins in the length of rope before it gave out and the arrows on the walls, shoulder high, began.

"Aye. There's so little in the near chambers and halls, though. I can't imagine *why* things would be placed this far back, but the alternative isn't pretty."

"No. But the caches are here. Must be."

"I think so." Lisabetha eyed her hands dispassionately in the doubled torchlight, sighed and scrubbed them down again. "I did find more planting tools, about two hundred steps back, in a chamber to the right. A few. Not many, though."

"Where you put the double crosses?" Lisabetha nodded. "Good. However few they are, we'll need them." Ylia's voice echoed: The chamber was enormous, its ceiling lost in the gloom. Here and there, she could see tiny points of light that marked holes far above. The air was cool, fresh. "Astonishing, how vast these caverns are. You'd never know it from the entrance."

"No." Lisabetha sighed again. "I saw Father's maps, just once and long ago. It must have been not long after Anasela fell, I couldn't have been above six or seven. Too long for me to remember much of them. The size, of course. But seeing's different. And searching them—!"

Ylia patted her arm. "We'll find what's here. We know it was brought, and there's been no one hereabouts for long, save mountain-hunters. Hunters might have taken the grain, but never farming things."

"No. Well. What's the hour?"

"Two till evening meal. I thought I'd come aid you. You should have someone with you, anyway, remember?"

"I know. Usually Annes comes, or Janneh, or both. Malaeth set them to grinding dried chickory root for her. They knew which way I went, and when," Lisabetha added with a smile, "so that if I broke my neck, they could come for the body."

"Nice," Ylia laughed. "All right, I'm fussing. I'm sorry."

"Another Malaeth," Lisabetha replied primly, and laughed herself. "Well, then. Two hours, but we'll need part of that time to return and wash. Which way? Your choice is as good as mine."

"Perhaps. All right, then, that way." She gestured with the torch. Lisabetha draped her hand-rag across a low point of stone, mid-chamber, marked an arrow on the stone itself and two on the floor. They moved on.

"Drier back there, it's all I can suppose," Ifney said. The evening meeting was a busy one, the small chamber nearly packed: All the council was present save Levren. "And three more caches, that's good."

"Enough to start with?" Marckl wanted to know. Ylia shrugged.

"I'm no judge of that. I'd say yes, if only because we *must* start, and that soon."

"But not here," Ifney put in.

"No." No need to add to that, they'd all done so, at least once a night, since she'd arrived.

"If we sent men—" Erken began tentatively.

"We're already sending men," Ylia reminded him. "Hunters have eyes, like the rest of us. Otherwise—pointless. We need our full force here, near the Caves, for protection." She bit her lip. *Damn!* Marhan scowled at her. But the Lords Holder and Bnorn took her words at face value. After all, they'd lived with fear for over a month, it was reasonable to take sensible precautions even though the Tehlatt showed no sign of coming for them.

Erken cast her a shrewd glance, but fell back to brooding on his hat: the greyed and muddy feathers were gone and the hat looked much the worse without them.

"We're looking," she went on. "I am spending what free time I have in search; Nisana searches also. If there is anything within safe distance for the finding, we'll have it. I know it must be soon, lest we starve this coming winter."

"I—" Whatever Erken intended to say, he shrugged off. He looked dubious, though, and Marhan's expression was one of open distaste: for all he'd learned of AEldra Power and its usefulness on their journey north, he still didn't like it.

"Brelian, how goes the training?" That was Golsat, diplomatically changing the subject.

Ylia's Champion spread his hands wide. "As well as you might expect, considering our lack of swords. The smithy Bos from village Eydrass is taking what metal can be scrapped and making points for spears and arrowpoints. It isn't much. There *are* some good bowmen. Not enough of them. Or enough weapons for them, or enough arrows. Lev could tell you more about that, when he gets back."

"I would like to say a thing, if I may." Golsat rose to his feet. Ylia eyed him in surprise: since the first night, when he'd accepted her appointment, he'd stayed well back in the shadows and seldom spoke, unless it was to take the edge from a heated discussion, or to redirect one headed for trouble, as he'd just done. At first she'd feared trouble, for her new councilers were one and all Northerners, and Golsat's half-Tehlatt blood had caused him considerable difficulties in the North. But there was no sign that even the decidedly narrow-minded Ifney looked down on Golsat for his heritage.

"Whatever you choose."

"There may be those who disagree with what I say, though my companions from our journey may recall I broached the matter before. I do not put this forth without long thought, know that! In Anasela, before the Tehlatt finally overwhelmed us, we lived for many years in fear of that attack. We therefore put aside Nedaoan common use and custom and began to train girl-children with bow. And, for those who wished it thereafter, with light sword and shield." His eyes glazed briefly and his face darkened with memory of that last attack. "As Duke Erken knows, we began such training over-late and we were too few, the barbarians drove us forth, such as they did not slay outright.

"Well. We are now a tenth, perhaps, of what we were. And while the Tehlatt no longer hover over us, who is to say what threat will descend upon us next? Do we sit, as we did before Anasela, before the end of First Flowers this year, and wait for yet another enemy to fall upon us and wipe us all from the Peopled Lands? How often have we thought ourselves safe from all threat, to our sorrow?" He paused. Silence. "I say we must *all* be prepared to fight—or resign ourselves to eventual death, individually and as Nedao. And I know which I choose!

"There are perhaps seven hundred males here who can hold a sword at all, and I count among them boys of the age I had when Anasela fell, and men who have earned the right to a comfortable old age before the fire. There are at least as many women and girls who can be taught weaponry, if only for self-defense." He gazed around the table, meeting the eyes of each of his fellows squarely. "I found on our journey north from Koderra that it is easier to fight knowing those I defend also defend themselves."

Erken nodded. "I agree with you, my friend. I agreed ten years ago. My own Lady was among those trained by my armsmaster."

"Even the old are not completely helpless," Golsat went on. "Dame Malaeth is among the oldest here, man or woman. She can use a staff for more than aid to her feet."

Marhan shook his head unhappily. "I must think on this," he said. He twisted his moustaches, resettled himself on the hard stool. "You all know how I feel. I trained Lady Ylia at her father's command, else I had never done so! To me, it is still not right."

Erken stirred. "But, Marhan, after all you've seen—"

The Swordmaster waved a hand, silencing him. "Oh, I see the logic of what you want, you and Golsat. Just let me think on it. I'm old and set in my ways, I admit that. Give me a little time."

"Yours, Swordmaster." Brelian stood and leaned across the table to clasp Golsat's hand. "Golsat, you have my aid. After all, there is precedent for this, even in our day. Lev has trained not only Ylia but his own daughter. If we arm the women among us, we double the number of our armed. If there is need for armed." *When*, he might as well have said; it was clear in his voice.

"There will be resistance," Ifney warned. "And not just from the Swordmaster. You know Nedaoan villagers, their lives change slowly if at all, and they are not folk to take to new ideas readily."

"Well, but," Marckl cut in, "all our lives have changed rather sharply of recent, haven't they? And Nedaoan women once fought amongst their men, or so the tales tell us."

"I will do what I can also," Lisabetha spoke up from her place beyond Brelian. "But there will be less resistance than you might think, Ifney. Women who have seen their loved ones slain while they stood by helpless—do you think they will hesitate? I would not. I do not. And—" she smiled across the table—"many of the younger women would leap at a chance to use sword as Ylia does. You can see it in their eyes."

"Well!" Ifney pondered what were clearly new ideas to him. "I'm not against it, you know! Only uncertain there's to be many interested. But I'll do what I can among my own women."

"Good enough," Ylia said. "Now. About the boats."

"Ready in another two days, at most," Marckl said. "So we'd better decide soon who's to be sent."

"I'd thought to ask you. We'll need men who've navigated the Torth in spring flood. What we can see of the Anasela isn't gentle."

"No more it is. Well, then. I've two men, my guardsmen, from one of my villages. They're older but they know how to read a stream. They can find others. You'll need mostly such men, I'd think, but perhaps one or two to carry messages?"

"Mmmm. Erken? That's more your knowledge."

"Depends on what you want," he returned. "Ambassador quality? We haven't anyone."

"Not necessary. We've written messages for Yls and Nar. Letting them know what has chanced among us, warning of Vess. We'll want to start trade with Nar, I'd think, and that right away."

"They're closest," Erken agreed. "Nar has a reputation as tight-fisted, but they're good men to aid folk in difficulty. They'll give no charity, which," he added mildly, overriding Marckl's intended sharp retort, "we in no case want, do we? But they'll give us credit. Osnera is too far away, and less known to us. Less friendly as well."

"So we'll need someone who's dealt with the Narrans, if we've such a man among us. Someone who can talk trading language and not sell us short."

"I've a man," Bnorn spoke up quietly, "who sailed with a Narran cog, three summers ago. He was one of Lord Corry's go-bys before that."

"Good. We can decide tomorrow what we might have to offer in exchange for what we need most desperately, and what we *do* need most desperately. Think on it, will you, and let me know tomorrow, so we can set things down. Lord Bnorn, bring your man with you then." The old man inclined his head, faded back into his chair.

"We'll need someone to deliver the messages to the Sirdar. For that, we need one who can bow prettily and not be left open-mouthed by the Ylsan great-halls. They're fussy about protocol, the Ylsans, so even though we're few and rough at present, we should present ourselves with what grace and dignity we can muster.''

"I'll see to that," Erken said. "Someone who knows proper forms of address or can learn quickly. *And* a good change of clothing for him. The last," he added ruefully, "will be difficult, but I daresay we'll manage."

"Good, I'll leave that to you, Erken." She stifled a yawn: the chamber was smokier than ever, and there was an underlying unpleasant odor of damp, warm woolen clothing, and indifferently washed bodies. The scent of wax and whatever flowery oil Malaeth had laced into the candles lay incongruously over all. "Enough for tonight then, we're all tired, and tomorrow will be another long hard day."

"Yes." Erken pushed to his feet, clamped his tattered hat firmly to his head. "The latest hunt—any word?"

"Only rabbits and thin birds so far. There was sign of deer, though. They may have something tomorrow. Lev will probably send some of the younger boys back with what they got today." So much she'd seen from the upper ledges while it was still light.

"Rabbits and thin birds," Marckl mumbled. "If," he added as he stood, "we can't find plantable fields and dwelling land soon, we'd better move the herds on and use that ground to plant what seed we have. It's the best bit of dirt anywhere near. At least it would be something."

"We'll think on that, Marckl." Ylia stifled another yawn. "Do so, all of you. Here again tomorrow, same hour. Ifney, let me know about the boats, if there's change or anything you need."

"And so I shall." A few more minutes, they were all gone. Her young door warder snuffed the candles behind her, slipped past her to serve as escort to the Grand Temple and thence to the outer chamber. She dismissed him there, wandered out into the open, sparing a smile and a wave for the guard. 'Nisana?'

'Here.' The cat was perched on a rubble of fallen tree, high above the main entrance.

'Anything?'

'No.' And, with a rub against the girl's arm—'Nothing yet.'

'Perhaps the Folk could—' Ylia hesitated. It was difficult for her to speak of the Folk, even to Nisana. 'Perhaps if we spoke to them, asked for their aid, they could help us.'

'Perhaps. I will go out South later tonight, perhaps Eya will speak with me.'

'Good. Near the River, if possible.'

'Want a little, don't you?' the cat grumbled. She eyed the girl critically. 'Are you eating and sleeping at all?'

Ylia shrugged. 'Enough.'

'See that you do! You are no good to these folk worn to nothing, remember that!'

'Of course.'

'Of course,' the cat mocked. 'I see I must find this refuge for you soon, to get you the rest you deserve.'

Ylia laughed, ran a hand across dark ears. 'As if the labor will stop there, cat! Don't fuss, I daresay I sleep better than most here. I can always use the Power to sleep, or to set aside worry.'

'You *can*,' Nisana replied tartly. 'You never do.' The wind soughed over them; the few visible stars vanished behind a ragged, fast moving cloud. Drops of rain splashed Ylia's upturned face, sending them both hurrying for shelter.

Odd, that reticence between us when we spoke of Eya and her kind, or of the Nasath we had met, deep within the Foessa. Seldom could either of us speak to the other of them without stammering, as though it was a thing to hold close, a thing incapable of being shared, the experience we had had with Eya's Folk, that wondrous meeting with the Guardians. Certainly Ylia could not speak aloud of the experience, and of course I was not capable of such a thing, had I wanted to. On thought, I doubt I would have.

But there was no such hesitancy between us regarding the renegade Lyiadd, though Ylia perversely clung to her insistence he must be dead. So human, that: that he must be dead, because she dared not think otherwise. I knew there was still an edge of madness in her that Lyiadd, dead or alive, could trigger, and so I did not fuss at her for her stubbornness. And at least she could speak of him with others, such as her Duke, if need pressed.

3

It was an hour she'd have foregone, two months before, an hour she'd still have been deeply asleep: the chill hour of first daylight. The sun was not yet above the eastern ridges and would not rise for many a while. For a mercy there was yet no wind, though it doubtless would come with the sun. She stood, her council about her, the folk, filling the bridge and the narrow pathway from the Caves, lining the cliff walls, huddled on the riverbanks. Before her, in a deep, eddying pool, were the boats: Three narrow, shallow-drafted boats and nine men in the warmest and best lanolined cloaks they had been able to find. Ylia handed the waterproofed packets to Erken's man, who stowed them in the pouch around his neck. "We'll return as soon as we can." He had to shout to be heard above the roar of the water. "If there is delay, we will somehow send messages."

"Mind you do, Kalann!" Erken shouted back. "Leave Jersary in Nalda in any event, your decision whether to leave Hever with him. Right?"

"Sir!" They'd had it out five times the night before; poor Kalann would repeat the orders in his sleep the next month running. There was nothing to add. Grewl, temporarily at least Father to the Nedaoan Chosen, stepped forward to bless the boats and give a short prayer. Ylia blessed them after her own fashion. And then the ropes were cast off and they were swiftly gone.

The folk disbursed rapidly as the last of them vanished around the point: it was too cold to remain outside, and there was a watery porridge in the kitchens. Scarce filling, but at least hot. Ylia stared down river; she was barely aware of Marhan's rumbling assurances, Erken's hand against her shoulder.

"They will return." Lisabetha spoke in her ear; she jumped. "Don't fret what you can't alter, *you* told me that. There is food and Malaeth is fussing. You've lost weight."

"I can afford it."

"Nonsense. You can't afford the argument with Malaeth, in any event."

"I—well—"

Lisabetha frowned. "You look unwell this morning, are you sleeping?"

"Sleeping? Mmmm. Yes. Enough."

The girl hesitated. "Not—dreaming, by chance?"

"No." Ylia searched Lisabetha's face then. "*You're* not, are you?"

"Once. Nothing much. Only the once." Lisabetha shook herself, shook Ylia's shoulders. "You need food, go on now! Wait—" She stepped forward, straightened the thin gold band across her Lady's forehead. "*Now* go!"

"You," Ylia grinned suddenly, "are spending entirely too much time with Malaeth, you sound more like her than anyone has the right to!"

"I got a dose of it myself just now, for letting you go outside without food," Lisabetha replied tartly, but her eyes sparkled, "and I see no reason not to share. Go on, now, did you ever eat anything worse than wheat gruel *cold?"*

"Yes." Ylia nodded energetically. "Golsat's smoked fish, remember it?" Lisabetha grimaced. "All right, then," Ylia added, with a sidelong eye at the cliff, "I'll race you, come on!" And she took off at top speed for the bridge.

There was an indignant shriek behind her, and footsteps pounding the path. Ylia sped across the bridge, drew a deep breath and plunged up the steep trail. Left—right—left and the trail took a brief dip, pointed even more sharply upward. The breath was burning her throat and lungs, but the upper ledge was almost in reach. Lisabetha passed her moments later and stood waiting as she staggered up the last few steps. Both of them were red-faced, gasping for air and giggling like children. It was several minutes before they could help each other back across open rock into the Caves. Ylia fell back against the stone wall; Lisabetha collapsed onto a flat shelf.

"Haaa!" She brushed the damp hair from her brow and grinned. "You forgot, didn't you? I can even beat Brelian!"

"I shall never—forget it again!" Ylia gasped. She was still laughing. "But anyone else would have let me win, which of us is Lady here, after all?"

"Good for you," Lisabetha giggled. "You begin to give yourself airs."

"Hah. We'd better go, my food is congealing."

'Ylia.'

'Nisana?' Ylia shoved aside the near empty bowl. It was absolutely impossible, hunger notwithstanding, to finish the stuff. Nisana sniffed at it gingerly, stepped back with a look of distaste on her dark face.

'Search. You will lose your edge, do you not keep at it.'

'I know, cat.' She sighed. 'Time! There just isn't enough of it—'

'There won't be, if things come upon us unseen,' Nisana remarked pointedly. 'And you create time for practice, you do not wait for time to present itself, you know that!'

'All right. Here, or where?'

'Well.' Nisana considered her gravely. 'At least in *that* much you improve! I recall a time, and not so long ago, when you would no more do search among your Nedaoans than—'

'Circumstances change, cat,' Ylia remarked dryly. 'Ledges. The sun's up by now, it may be warm.'

'A wager on that?'

'No. Come on!' She scooped the cat into her arms, slid the dish in a pile so Malaeth might not mark it as hers and slipped from the chamber.

'Have you seen anything, Nisana? Sensed anything?'

'Anything? You mean of course Mathkkra or Thullen, or other of Lyiadd's sendings?' Direct—however unpleasantly—as ever, Nisana. 'No. Nothing of that sort. But it is a vast place, this, and a tiresome search.'

"I know, cat. I'm sorry."

'Don't be, it gives me a task. I am no longer a kitten, interested merely in a ball of twine or the hunt, you know.' And as Ylia opened her mouth, 'No insult intended, either way. Now. Search. Far vision first. A tight circle, all around us. Good. You've stopped closing your eyes to initiate a search, that's even better. I still think you need to use much less of your strength. However, we will *not* argue about it! All right. The touch now, try for more distance.' Silence. 'More than that, this is not far vision, you should have *much* greater range with touch!' She shifted. 'Better.'

'Nothing, cat. Save ourselves, our herds, our kind. Odd, though. As much trouble as we had coming North, it seems unlikely we should not be attacked. Consider the herds, if nothing else.'

'That's so. The Folk said they were in-gathered to the south. If that is the case, even if Lyiadd is dead, and his creatures scattered, it would take them time to return North to harry us.'

'I—I'd think so.' She would not argue *that* matter with Nisana again, she kept the thought locked firmly away. Lyiadd was *dead*, damn his soul to the Black Well! She was aware of the cat's gaze on her, kept her eyes closed. Nisana caught considerable of her thought at inopportune moments, but if she'd done so this time, she made no comment.

'Which might account,' the cat went on, 'for our temporary safety here.'

'So it might.' "Enough," she said aloud. "There is nothing here. And no," she added sharply, "I see your next thought as clear as I see the rocks around us, I have not tried to bridge, and I will not!"

Nisana sighed. 'If you only—'

"No."

'But you could—'

"*No!*"

'All *right!*' The cat scowled at her. 'Just remember, though, all the other times you said no, and were proven wrong!'

"Hah! They were different. And you know how it affects me, it makes me ill and faint. There are enough things in this world to make me ill, I need not add to them deliberately."

'All right.' Silence. 'I am taking a look out East this morning.'

"Why? We can't live that way."

'Probably not.'

"And you have brought in all the animals that were abandoned along the road."

'Perhaps. I'm not certain. I want to check the foothills, between the Planthe, say, and the Citadel. It will not take long, and it will cause me no danger. Besides, if folk still are lost in the Foessa, where is it most likely they would be?'

"Foothills, of course. But—Nisana, it's over a month!"

'It's no danger to me, no great cost in time,' the cat reiterated patiently, 'and it comes to me to do it.'

"All right, then." It wasn't particularly sense, but if Nisana felt the need in that way, she'd do it, whatever Ylia said. And she was coming to trust that odd sixth sense the cat occasionally had.

"Lady?" One of the ledge guard stood below them.

"Imbrus?"

"Duke Erken wishes to speak with you. No matter of great urgency, he says, but as soon as you are free."

"Ah." 'Nisana?'

'I'll see you after your night meal, before council.'

'Luck, cat.'

'Hah.' Nisana bounded away from her, bridged out of sight mid-leap. Ylia scowled at the place she'd been. *Swaggerer!*

"Imbrus, tell Duke Erken I'm free now, and unless he has a reason to meet indoors, I'd greatly prefer him here."

"My Lady." Fortunately, Imbrus's line of vision hadn't included the rock behind her; Nisana's vanishing trick would have left him glassy-eyed.

Ylia was well aware how many folk, like Erken's young guardsman, were unnerved by the magic Nisana used, and were thereby uncertain who to believe: the Chosen who called her evil, or their young Queen, who by strict Chosen standards was also a servant of their Dark One. Fortunately, the cat's continued presence was easing the tension; Nedao-like, people simply were becoming used to her. As long as she made no show of her Power. And show was not Nisana's way.

The tall Lord of Anasela, Exiled, climbed nimbly up from the ledge, bowed most correctly before taking a seat beside her. Erken was a stickler for such formalities, and it was only with the gravest of misgivings he'd taken her order and so addressed her, rather than using her full formal title. "You're right, Lady Ylia, it's quite nice here. How goes your search?"

Astonishing. Erken had been one of the most sceptical, when she'd first explained her method of searching. "Slowly. Not so slowly as if we'd only foot and horse for it, but not fast. Not," she added, "fast enough to suit *me*, either. But I haven't Nisana's particular talent, to think myself elsewhere in the space of half a breath. At least we've only two directions for serious search. That simplifies things a little."

"Why?" Erken frowned. "You've dropped such hints before. East: anyone could understand why the East is closed to us, and I daresay the North wouldn't be much use; the farther north one goes, the colder and shorter the growing season, but—"

"Not north. South."

The Duke gazed at her thoughtfully. "It's not just *you* either. Golsat said something yesterday afternoon, and Lev shushed him, strongly I thought for a mere misstep of the tongue. I could perhaps be of more aid, if you saw fit," he added pointedly, "to tell me."

Ylia swallowed past a suddenly tight throat, blinked rapidly. Almost Brendan's very words. *Do I kill another—friend—by taking him into my confidence?* But that was stupid; Erken needed to know, and it wasn't fair to keep him unaware of knowledge he might desperately need, and that soon. "All right, I'll tell you. When I've done so, though, you may wish I'd kept silent." She met his eyes, managed a faint smile. "Last chance, Erken."

"What, for blessed ignorance? I'll chance it, tell me."

"Your choice, then. Remember that." And she plunged into the tale of the journey north after Koderra's fall. A much shortened one, of necessity, but leaving in every odd occurrence, every scent of fear, the growing knowledge that they were not alone and unmarked, that their path was foreshadowed and perhaps fore-destined, and that evil lay in wait for them.

"We suspected, Nisana and I, long before we had proof, that someone or something was aware of us, that the cat and I both were recognized as AEldra and therefore at the least an impediment, at most a danger. Either way, something to be—removed."

"Killed, you mean," Erken put in quietly.

"Killed. We were two 5-days, a little more, on our way, when we were attacked by Mathkkra."

Erken's hands tightened briefly on the brim of his hat. "You know this for certain, do you?"

"By their own admission. You would not recognize them as Mathkkra, we did not. I was told so by those who would have taken me for a blood sacrifice." She shivered. "I was fortunate."

"Indeed, since you live."

"The AEldra Power was stronger than theirs, and so I escaped. None of *that* tribe did. But there are more of them. Many more."

Silence. Erken moistened his lips. "I know of the Cave-Folk, of course." His voice was steady, matter-of-fact. "All Nedao do, if only from the figures at Harvest-Fest. But they were evil only by their habits and their mein. They had no magic, that any of the tales tell us."

"They *had* none," Ylia replied grimly. Her inflection was not lost on him; he studied her. "There is—there *was* a man, an AEldra, of their Fifth House of nobility. A man named Lyiadd. Like most of his House, he was—magician, you would say."

"Say, if you choose, of the Power," Erken replied. "I am not so Northern as *that!*"

She smiled briefly. "He was like most from the lower Houses, not greatly skilled. Unlike most of his class, it bothered him. So Nisana tells me, and she knew him."

"Nisana. But—"

"Another time." *One odd thing at a time, though I doubt he'll accept as easily as did Golsat that Nisana is twice his age.* "He sought marriage with women of the upper Houses, to improve his standing, among them Scythia, my mother. Apparently, such rejection added more fuel to his—whatever was unbalanced about him to begin became even more unbalanced. My mother refused him, of course. Nisana says rudely, at the last, for she'd already pledged to my father." She drew a deep breath, let it out slowly. Her eyes caught at a small tuft of black cloud drifting across an otherwise brilliantly blue sky, followed it. "He left Yls—at this point, I speak conjecture only, Erken, no one knows for certain save Lyiadd. He left Yls, vowing vengeance on all who had slighted him. Taking with him the Sirdar's daughter, Marrita, who for some reason found in Lyiadd what she wanted in a man. She also nursed a grudge against her House, though just what and why I do not know.

"Again, I speak only what I suppose. They went in active search of an ancient place of evil in the Foessa and they found it: the home, a thousand years ago, of the Lammior."

"The Night-Serpent." Erken caught his hand half-way through the Northern warding sign. "My dear Lady Ylia, no! Mathkkra, all right, if you insist, but the Night-Serpent is nothing but legend!"

"He is only myth to Nedao, Erken. In Yls, there is written history to substantiate *him!* And there is other, more recent proof of the tale, listen! They found the object of their search. A valley, to all appearances only another deep, tree-lined bowl in the midst of great peaks. They settled in, they and Lyiadd's friends and arms-sworn, and he began to work to wrest the Lammior's secrets from the ancient walls."

Erken shook his head in stunned wonder. "No, I do not disbelieve you. I *think* I don't. Continue."

"As you wish. When we came into the mountains, my companions and I, he became aware of us. Not impossible, for one of great Power: he could search with his mind at distance, and Nisana and I made no secret of ourselves, we used the AEldra Power to search, to protect those with us, to ward against evils. For whatever reason, he saw us, Nisana and me, as a threat, and so determined to take us captive."

"Mothers guard us," Erken whispered.

"And so he did." Ylia's throat was dry, her voice scratchy, but she spoke with a sense of detachment: It was almost as though the thing had happened to another, as though she had memorized a tale—a terrifying tale, true, but only a tale—and now spoke it from memory. "Brendan—died on the ledges, trying to aid us, but it was no good, Lyiadd's Power was stronger, and he had men and Mathkkra to outnumber us. He sent the others away. That was when I challenged him, and fought him."

"Brandt's daughter." A brief smile quirked Erken's face. "So much we'd expect of his heir."

"Well, Lyiadd did not. I—I killed him. At least, if he was not dead when Nisana pulled me to safety, he was near it." She drew another deep breath. "But his woman, his armsmen, his Mathkkra, his other creatures still live. The South is closed to us, Erken."

"Aye. And now a man sees why. But, is there no way you

could—that is, no way you could perhaps look to see if he is dead? Or if the others plan against us?" Erken, clearly a man bewildered, fumbled to a halt.

"I dare not search that place myself, it is unsafe. If he does live, I might be snared once again."

"Not, then, a good idea," Erken replied gravely. "After all, you are the last of your House and heirless."

"Not entirely," she replied as she jumped to her feet.

"Well, there is Vess, of course." Erken rose as she did. "But for all practical purposes, you're Ettel's last." He sighed, turned away from the lower ledge and the guard there. They strode slowly across the rough, mossy rock toward a stand of scrubby fir. "And I know it's early days, but you need to begin to consider those qualified as, well—" He paused. Ylia laughed.

"As Royal blood stock. I'm sorry, Erken, I've shocked you."

"Not at all," he replied stiffly, but his color was unusually high. "I'm acutely aware of the need for heirs. But that hadn't come up, two months ago."

"No. I'm sorry, I hadn't meant to offend, or to remind you."

"It's all right, Erken. If you've lists in that mind of yours, set them down and give them to me. I know the Sirdar has a grandson, but he's scarcely Lisabetha's age and I doubt they'd have *me,* even if I'd have *him.*"

"Well—"

"As to an heir in the meantime, I'll speak it to the council tonight but you'd better know now, my Lord Duke. I'm afraid you're for it."

Erken stopped cold, stared at her blankly. She laughed again. "Who did you think I'd name? Weren't you next in line to Father after Ettel and then Lord Corry?"

"I—but, Lady Ylia, you can't—"

"If he'd lived, I'd have named Corlin. Since he didn't, you're next, Erken. And after you, Bnorn: he's old, but next logical. And then his son, and his grandson. If you'd had a son, of course, *he*—" She stopped. Erken looked like he'd been hit. "Oh, Mothers, Erken, I'm *sorry!* I—there's no excuse, I forgot!"

"It's all right, Lady Ylia." He brought up a weak smile. "I forget, myself, sometimes."

Not true, anyone could have seen that. Erken's son Galdan, his only child, gone these past four years after a terrible argument with his father, and no one had heard from him since. She moved to his side, clasped his arms. "Perhaps—"

"Perhaps," Erken said and nodded. "Perhaps anything." A genuine smile, then. "Nevermind. You," he said, "had better take very good care of yourself, I have no intention to try to fill Brandt's shoes!"

"You," she replied feelingly.

Erken clapped her across the shoulders. "You're doing an excellent job of it, don't fish for compliments! Look at that," he added in a deliberate change of subject. He drew her near the edge—nearer than she liked, but she couldn't bring herself to say so. "There's a terrible job for you." Far below, foreshortened by distance and the height, Golsat and Marhan stood with eight young Nedaoans, swords gleaned from Erken's men in their inexperienced hands. The boys were working determinedly on first lunges, and Ylia could hear Marhan bellowing the changes. "He'll have no voice at all by mid-day." Erken shook his head. "Better him than me."

"Mmmm. I'd say the same, but likely I'll have a similar group of my own before long."

"Wager it?"

"Whatever—within reason," she amended cautiously, "you like."

"Within reason," Erken snorted. "As if anything was reasonable anymore. What I came to tell you, by the way, I nearly forgot. We're off, me and five of my lads. Word just came in, the hunters found a herd of elk and brought down three. We may be back before dark, but don't worry if we're not." He bowed, turned and slid down the rock ledge, was gone. Ylia spared a last look after him, another for Marhan, now bellowing fiercely as he demonstrated for clearly at least the tenth time, the pattern to be followed, and set her self determinedly to a search. Touch, at least. If she followed the River down, and if it was working well, and if—if, if, if—but if the Touch was responding properly, perhaps she could locate side streams. It chanced, along the Torth, that some of the feeder streams went back through hills and into valleys, if nothing so large as what they now needed. Perhaps it would be so with the Aresada. In any case, it was a starting place.

4

The coast was wild at this northernmost edge of Yls, the surfline a rock-strewn and treacherous thing to cross. The slender black boat went through it to gather in the five humans and back out again to the waiting ship as though it were any surfline and not a soup of swirling water, hard-crashing waves and a muddy rip current five lengths wide. The four young Sea-Raiders took the trip impassively: the same could not be said for their passengers.

They were guant and worn, all five, and something of the shock of the past days still hovered around their eyes. One wore the pale grey of the Osneran Chosen, three wore swords and the colors of the fourth. Vess alone of the five seemed to note little of their nerve-wracking journey across the rough water to the *Vitra*—his nerves had not yet recovered from the sudden and unexpected arrival of his most hated cousin, his defeat at the hands of a sword-wielding child, and his expulsion from Aresada.

Every night had taken its toll in desertions; at least he could feel certain of these remaining three armsmen. The rest had left him without a word, had merely vanished—into the trees, downstream toward Nar—well, who knew or cared?

Ylia, though: *Your life in my hands, cousin, the threads of it warped by my fingers. We'll meet again, and mine will be the choice of time and place*. He brought his attention back to the moment as the Chosen Tevvro touched his knee and met his eyes with warning in his own: *Caution. We're there*.

No, Tevvro wasn't pleased with their present placing. But Vess wasn't going to simply sail off in the Chosen's company, in search of aid in Osnera. He'd go, but *after* he'd sealed this Nod Bri H'Larn to him, and through their battle-chosen leader, all the Sea-Raiders. A dangerous ally, Tevvro had said: in such times, in his situation, a man needed dangerous allies! Tevvro wasn't all the man of grey cloth and peace he presented to the world. He'd been a nobleman's second son and seen war on Osnera's northern borders. He'd bloodied his sword more than once. He'd sat in on lords' councils. And *still* the fool thought that a paper from the Osneran Chosen, from their Heirocracy, would change matters in Nedao! Tevvro had been too long from the real world, that was what. *If he remains in my company long enough, he'll learn,* Vess thought grimly as he stood, spraddle-legged to keep from falling in the wildly rocking boat, and caught at the ladder.

The *Vitra* rocked, but not as dreadfully as the smaller boat had. He could stand straight here and not lose quite so much face, though he knew there wasn't a cabin boy among them who wasn't laughing at all of them—at *him*, damn their hides!—for their lack of sea legs. His hair was plastered to his forehead by the thin, driving rain, water was seeping down his neck through the rents in his cloak, and the smell of fish, wine, ale and cooking fires threatened to make him ill. He swallowed hard, ran a sodden sleeve over his eyes.

Nod Bri H'Larn crossed the wet deck with a cat's ease and gripped his forearm, added the briefest of bows—more an inclining of his great shaggy head. Teeth gleamed deep inside the thicket of his red-grey beard. "When we saw the fire and the signal, we thought it was one of your men, not you yourself, Lord Vess." Vess nodded once, curtly. "Rumor is true, then: the barbarians have taken back your Plain and your ruling house is gone."

"Partly so," Vess replied evenly. The words threatened to stick in his throat, and Bri H'Larn's breath left his stomach reeling. He detached himelf, stepped back to lean against one of the inner railings. "My cousin, Brandt's daughter, rules what is left of Nedao. They are holed up in Caves north and east of what was Teshmor."

"Ah." Another gleam of very white, strong teeth. "Then our usefulness to you, and the bargain you proposed, are of no point, are they?"

Vess shook his head. "Not so. The Plain—I want it back. *And* the people."

"The Plain." Shaggy grey brows went up; Bri H'Larn contemplated him with suddenly shrewd eyes. "What, all of it?"

"No." Galling to have to face that truth. "There aren't enough of us to hold it. The South—we can handle the South. We will, if it's ours again. Your side of that bargain: you'll get all I originally promised, I'm taking less."

"There's less of you to offer it, also," the Sea-Raider remarked with a brief grin. Several of the men behind him laughed; he silenced them with an imperious chopping gesture. "Let me talk it over with my commanders, those I have with me. There's hot ale in my cabin, if you like."

Vess didn't like, particularly: didn't want to go below decks in a

heaving Sea-Raider's ship, didn't want to be cut off from the
outdoors, however wet and cold it was. He was too tired and cold
to argue, and Nod Bri H'Larn might take offense if they didn't. He
cast a glance over his shoulder: the land was too far away to reach,
unless Nod wanted to send him back to it. Small matter if they
went below or not.

It might have been an hour; he and his armsmen and the Chosen
Tevvro sat close together in the small, warm cabin, drinking hot
mulled ale, eating an oddly herbed stew and listening to the
muttered voices, and the occasional flare of temper outside. They
couldn't make out words, or even the gist of the argument. But it
was Nod himself came to get them, and Nod who led them out
onto the deck.

The atmosphere was charged, and one or two of the men stood
stiff-legged, hands on hilts. A few looked, worriedly, from their
leader to the holdouts across deck, then back again. But as Nod
took his place mid-deck and held up a hand for silence, the nearest
of the holdouts turned and walked away, and the other few
followed him. "The bargain is set!" Uneasy silence. "This man,
Vess of the House of Ettel, is known henceforth to us as King of
the Nedaoans! At such time as he asks it, we shall aid him in his
venture to retake his own, and in return, he will aid us in any
ventures we make against the sea-merchants of Nar!" A brief,
ragged cheer at that. Doubtful looks among others of them.

Nod Bri H'Larn extended a hand, then, and aided Vess up onto
the hatch. From that slight advantage of height, Vess gazed across
the men there, memorizing faces, stowing them in his capacious
memory. Across the bared heads he met pale blue eyes under a
wide freckled forehead, and a mass of red curls. *Wild.* The Sea-
Raider stared back at him arrogantly. *I'll remember you,* that look
said. Vess met it with one of his own.

"Who is that, Bri H'Larn?" he asked. Nod Bri H'Larn
followed the direction of his gaze, shrugged.

"Mal Brit Arren, captain of the *Fury.* Don't let him worry you;
he opposed me bitterly, but he won't live to see next winter's
storms."

"He doesn't worry *me,*" Vess said coldly. "He's *your* worry,
not mine." He gathered his men together for the return trip
through the surf. Appraising, chill blue followed him until he
vanished into the woods.

They were creatures of the Plain, so the tale of the Nedaoans has it. Mathkkra preyed upon their flocks and upon the herders, until the last of them was slain by Merreven Wergenson. Of course, by the Nedaoan tale, they were an upright people, two-legged, two-armed, nothing like the creatures in truth are. Properly nosed, where in reality they have only an opening midface to serve. They were also said to be a hairy folk and they are not. Nor are they of the Plain originally, as even they believe.

Did the Lammior create them, or find them? The latter, most likely, for his Power was great but not that of the One. Though he thought it so. No, I believe—and so do many who have given the matter thought—that he found an underground nest of foul and noxious creatures, and he raised them to a level something higher than they had been. Gave them a portion of intellect— sufficient for his needs. And set them to harry his enemy, hoping to so wear them down. It must have done that, for I remember all too well my horror at sight of such an endless enemy— mindless, without number—Mathkkra.

But it was Lyiadd who conferred upon them use of the Fear, and their ability to hide that Fear and themselves when they chose. For they had not had that ability before he found them and in his turn raised them from their skulking places among the rocks and night to serve him.

5

Two days, a third. They faded into one another, difficult to separate: it was cool and drizzly without, smoky within Aresada. The search for seed caches went on, as did the nightly meetings. During one of them—she could not, after the fact, separate *those* one from another—she named a reluctant Erken her temporary heir, an even more reluctant and thoroughly abashed Bnorn as Erken's successor, should need arise. Sometime—not, as she recalled, the same night—Erken had brought her a list of suitable consorts. *Ugh.* They'd been few, and few among those listed she knew by face. Not that such a thing mattered, not for Nedao's sake. *I always hoped to wed as Father did, when he found Mother. I knew it wasn't likely.* But since Nedao was in no position to bargain for a Lord to wed its Lady, she put the list in her sleep chamber and forgot about it.

Nisana had returned late one evening with astonishing news: She'd found the village Telean, intact. They'd had luck: they were so near the Foessa, so far within the foothills, the Tehlatt had missed them. And they had stores: winter-depleted, but stores nonetheless, and tools, seed, fencing.

Levren and a dozen of Erken's men had gone out at daybreak the next day with two heavy bullock carts. They'd be a 5-day or more, for many of Telean's people were old and unused to travel of any kind, let alone across such rugged terrain.

Nisana set out with them, though she didn't intend to travel the entire distance either direction. It was her intention instead to bridge to Levren once a day so she could advise Ylia and Erken if problems arose, but otherwise to continue her westerly search.

Ylia, who was learning of necessity to worry only one matter at a time, and that as it presented itself, let Telean and a future home for Nedao both fade from her mind in the cat's absence. In the meantime, things settled into a comfortable pattern: She spent most of her mornings helping prepare hides for the one shoemaker they had left, for shoes were nearly as critical a need as food. Many of the women were going out to forage in shifts, sharing boots between them, and fully half the children were barefoot, or

40

wrapped their feet in rags. But even such bits of cloth were at a premium.

Afternoons, she made search of her own, more for enemy than a valley, and she kept half a sense tuned down River even though it was far too soon for the boats to return.

And evenings: meetings, meetings and more meetings. Every cache they found had to be studied, portioned to the kitchens for later if it was meal or grain, assigned and set aside if seed or tools. And there were always new matters to discuss: the sword-training and its progress, warm clothing for the herder-children, particularly the older ones who kept night-guard, an extra turn of guardsmen for the herds and the children. Then, cloth for Nedao's Queen: Ylia had protested but in vain, and found herself in possession of a near-new cloak of rich blue, newly lined in soft grey rabbit fur, with a thick hood to match.

Erken had flatly cut through her arguments, finally: "The folk are poor, yes! And cold and hungry. But they have you, and they love you. Do you dare refuse them that right, to be proud of what they *do* have?" So put, she hadn't dared refuse, though she felt guilty and uncomfortable, sleeping and walking the ledges so warm, when so many weren't.

Fourth night—fifth? She came awake with a start. 'Nisana?' The cat butted hard against her shoulder, pressed at her thought.

'Come alert, Lev was attacked, not an hour past.'

Gods and Mothers. "How many hurt?"

'None. But we've trouble. Look!'

Trouble indeed. Ylia threw back her cloak. She slept, as most did, fully clad, save boots and sword-belt. She began pulling on her boots as she joined, sharing the cat's inner vision.

Dark: it was a black night, the moon near full but hidden in thick cloud and now low behind the trees. There, not a league from Aresada and next to the track leading from the foothills to the Caves, fires, perhaps a dozen. Sleeping villagers: many white-haired, a few children, a young woman, a middle-aged couple. A drove of sheep, dogs keeping them effectively penned, horses circled by ribbon-draped twine, a similar pen for half-a-dozen cattle. From the carts, the whispery, soothing sound of the penned drakes, an occasional answering raucous quack from a she-duck. Armsmen moved in and out of the light: they were taking no chances, even so near their goal.

And well they hadn't. There was sudden bedlam among the carts: the birds scented it first, but the dogs weren't far behind.

The sheep milled, panicked and several broke free. Levren snapped orders, and one of Erken's men, a boy short of his first beard, ran to cut them off, spear out sideways at knee height to block them. Sheep hit the pole, nearly bowling him over.

It was too dark for shadows, but one moved across the ground, dimming the fires. It rolled over the young guardsman, who cried out in terror; the spear fell from nerveless fingers and he threw himself to one side. The Thullen ignored him, caught a sheep between enormous long-taloned feet and was gone.

"Guard the beasts! You folk, away from the fires, get under the trees! No, not that way, get with the cattle! We are not enough to protect in two directions!" The Bowmaster's shout reverberated through her mind. He roused his comrades, shouting, jostling them, and they, in turn, got the fear-frozen villagers out from under open sky. The village boys and the dogs got the rest of the sheep under cover.

Just in time: A Thullen—the same or another—circled the clearing, sailed low across the road and came straight for them. "Stay back, he's mine!" Lev took two long strides into the open, dropped to one knee and braced the short horseman's spear against the rocky ground as the thing dropped for him, claws out and ready. The spear was torn from his hands; Levren caught up his bow as the Thullen, with a shriek that burned Ylia's AEldra sense, as it had Nisana's, flailed away and flapped for altitude. Two of the Bowmaster's red-fletched arrows caught it at the tops of the trees and brought it down.

The vision faded.

'There have been no others.'

"Mathkkra?" Ylia slapped the dagger into its forearm sheath. 'None.'

'Wait.' Ylia crossed the tiny chamber, shoved the thin curtain aside. Door-warder: at this hour of night, he'd be walking the hallway worn between the main rooms and this small side cavern. She ran him down halfway to the Grand Temple. "Merreven, find Erken, Marhan. Brelian if he's back. Council Chambers, at once. There's an emergency. No, not here. Near enough, but we're safe for now."

Nisana bridged back to Levren as Marhan—the last of them—staggered into the narrow chamber. Brelian wasn't back yet, but Lisabetha, her hair half plaited and hanging down her back in a black ripple, took his place. Bnorn, Bnolon. Erken. Marhan, still blinking and yawning, at the far end. It was a grimly silent audience she told of the attack.

"The Thullen are spoken of nowhere, that I know, Nedaoan tale or Ylsan. They are deadly. The scent of evil precedes them; their eyes paralyze you with fear, and the thing can carry away a grown sheep—or a man."

"They—no." Bnolon protested faintly. Marhan stirred.

"Know how you feel, steda-Baron," he said. "Magic." The word still fell from his lips like an epithet. "But I've seen 'em, I've *felt* 'em. These creatures—but you'll see, I don't doubt that at all." Bnolon cast him an unhappy glance. Marhan stifled a yawn, scowled at his hands. "Damn. But it wasn't likely we could keep it all quiet, was it?"

Ylia rubbed her eyes. "No. But I hoped for a little time, that was all. Well, we *had* a little." She started as Merreven pulled the curtain aside to admit Marckl and Ifney. "Sorry to wake you."

"Weren't sleeping," Marckl replied shortly as he dropped onto the cushionless smoothed stump that served him for a seat. "We were trying to devise some source of iron for plows."

"Might as *well* have been sleeping," Ifney grumbled, "for all we accomplished. What's to do?"

"The incoming village, your Telean, was attacked tonight."

"What! Tehlatt so near the Caves?" Ifney's eyes went wide.

"No," Ylia began. Erken laid a hand on her arm.

"Is it," he asked quietly, "a good idea to spread this particular tale, Lady Ylia?"

"No," Ylia replied grimly. She became aware her right fingers were drumming at the table, stilled them. "But we have no choice." She briefly told the tale again for the two Holders. "There will be no keeping Telean quiet. What, a hundred folk, many of them so elderly or so young they'd never remember a vow of silence? And the rest of them? They'll be singing Levren's praises so loud tomorrow the River itself couldn't drown the noise!"

"And well they should," Marhan mumbled. "Man's done well."

"There's more," Ylia said. Her mouth was dry. Hard, so hard to speak it. "Each time we met with Thullen, on our way north, there were Mathkkra." A babble of noise, silenced abruptly as she held up a hand. "With them, or nearby. If Thullen attacked Telean, so near the Caves—well, my friends, from now on, no one walks abroad alone after dark."

"I—no." Marckl shook his head firmly indeed. "I'm sorry, I

simply can't believe *that!* Mathkkra?"

"You had better." Lisabetha leaned forward. "They're as real as you are. Ylia? May I?"

"Go ahead." Ylia studied her hands, drew her finely balanced dagger and studied it gloomily as Lisabetha spoke of her capture by Mathkkra, her subsequent rescue.

"I know my repute, Marckl. Lord Corry's high-strung, inventive daughter. These creatures I did *not* imagine. No one could. Doubt the look of them, if you will, for they resemble nothing we think of as Mathkkra, but do not dare doubt they exist. For the sake of all our lives."

"I—well." Ifney cleared his throat. He looked worried and unhappy indeed. "After all, a man can prepare for the worst, whether he believes in its form or not." Silence, which he again broke. "Now, the folk themselves, you aren't suggesting we tell *them*, are you?"

"I don't know." Ylia returned the dagger—Brendan's dagger, Brelian's gift—to its sheath. "I need your help with that, all of you. I hoped to avoid panic, and needless fear. And so I held my companions on the journey north to silence, and kept silence myself. Now—now that the threat comes near again—perhaps we have no choice. *I* can see no choice. If any of you can, tell me now!"

They talked: together, one at a time, argued and fought it. But she was right, there *was* no choice. Telean would spread the tale from one end of Aresada to the other. Or Erken's armsmen would. No choice.

"Better, if the tale comes from you, Lady," Bnorn said finally. Ylia sighed, bowed her head in reluctant assent.

"At evening-meal tomorrow. All right." She met Erken's eyes, shook her head minutely. Nothing of Lyiadd, nothing of the rest of it, the vowed vengeance against her personally, unless it became absolutely necessary. He caught her message, looked rather relieved.

"Keep in mind, all of you," Marhan said as they rose to seek what little sleep might be left them, "they can be slain, and by men bearing plain steel. A thing to remember, I own I forgot it often enough. The Fear is merely an additional shield for them. Think of it so, and they become less deadly an adversary."

"You reassure me," Marckl replied dryly. Clearly Marhan's words did no such thing.

• • •

'Nisana?' Ylia sank back into her chair as the last of her council left the chamber and sought the cat with urgent mind-touch.

'I'm all right, these people are. No further worries so far.' Ylia caught at the cat's thought for distance and direction, turned to the far vision. Fires burned high out along the narrow trail that led from Teshmor to Aresada: the dark was no protection against Thullen *or* Mathkkra, and that being so, the folk had as well stay warm. The beasts were even more well guarded and Erken's armsmen patrolled ceaselessly. Nisana had settled down near the fire; one of the old women was stroking her fur with a shaking hand. But even as Ylia watched, the tremors slowed. Nisana's way with fear: so she'd dealt with Lisabetha when the girl's terror had threatened to drive her into madness. The old woman would sleep soon—more, she'd never know why she'd had such a pleasant night's rest.

'Nisana, where's Lev?'

'Mmmm? Oh. He took two of the guard and two of the village boys who use bow to make a wide circuit about the camp. Lest there be anything else abroad.'

'Damn. He knows the Mathkkra can hide from a normal search!'

'Or any other sort. Of course. He's taking reasonable care. You know the man! But there may be prints. Besides, it gives the others something to do, and a sense of worth that they are doing it.'

'I—well—his choice, of course. I don't like it.'

'No.' The cat arched her back, let a limp old hand slide away as she moved. The granddame was snoring gently, her head fallen onto her chest. 'Like me, you like none of it. I'll remain here the night, and if there is need, I'll rouse you. Otherwise, look for us before noon-meal. We will waste no more time, I'll wager you.'

'No take on that. Have care!'

'Hah. Go sleep, girl, and don't fuss at me.'

She *was* fussing, she who'd sworn she'd never fuss anyone, not after all she'd endured of it. Levren had all the experience of the journey north to guide them. They could fend for Telean, he and Erken's armsmen. "Go sleep," she ordered herself, and pushed away from the table with determination. "Worry tomorrow when it gets here." She doused the candles, stumbled across to the smaller chamber. Her bedding was rumpled and cold again. She kicked off her boots, set aside the sword sheath, unstrapped the dagger but laid it near her hand, and pulled the furry cloak across her shoulders.

Sleep she did, finally. But the branches under her crackled as she tossed and turned, and she dreamed, as she had so often since entering the Foessa. Lyiadd's halls, as she'd seen them, shadowed, blood-red shadows edging the firepit, a sense of someone—*something*—occupying the great chair upon the dais. Lyiadd or the Lammior? Or, perhaps, Marrita? But—was it now, or the future, or a time long past she saw?

A blackness, an inner blindness; she was disoriented and frightened, keenly aware of the path her feet unwillingly followed, knowing surely she went to face Marrita. Not the pampered, silk-clad noblewoman she'd once confronted, no. She had changed, Marrita, for there was a chill certainty about her, an assurance, and her very shadow was a horror. Only the eyes remained the same: enormous in that fragile-looking face, a dark brooding blue, filled with chill hatred for the swordswoman before her. But was this a thing of the future, or—*Mothers grant it*— merely bad dream?

But she was drawn, drawn back and away, and Marrita faded, merged with shadow, was gone. Drawn—it was as though twine was looped about her wrist. She walked, her boots falling loud against stone floors, scuffling at fallen rubble. Aresada? She could not tell, for the dark was absolute, the second level of sight denied her. A faint music teased at her ear, pulling at her. She nearly ran, hands sliding along rough walls for balance, and her breath came short.

Light, then, faint but increasing by the moment even as the music did, until it filled her, the golden light of spring dawn on the northern Plain and in the air a battle anthem to draw the very dead to life again. She scarcely dared breath.

Three things hung suspended before her: a narrow shield, bronzed and carven, inlaid with polished stone and one golden topaz. A horn: silver, delicately turned, with a tattered silken banner hanging from its length. So rent and stained was this, she could not see the design of it, any more than she could make out the patterning on the shield. And lastly—

The sword.

Inniva, *such* a sword! She could have wept of sheer hunger for it, and yet she dared not reach though she surely could have touched it. It lay upon the air itself and light cushioned it. *Mine, it must be, it must be! Ah, no!* For the light was fading, the sword scarcely visible, and now she did reach, but her hand encountered only air and still darkness. The air shuddered into her.

Her eyes were suddenly dazzled: She stood upon a stone ledge, the setting sun level in her eyes; it blazed on the copper-hilted dagger in her left hand, and in her right—the sword itself, pulsing with light as though it were a living thing, possessed of the same pure joy that suddenly flooded her. *Mine!* she exulted, and could not doubt. Only then did she become aware of the Mathkkra— thirty or more of them—facing her. Facing her, and an unseen ally, who stood shoulder to shoulder with her. Wounded; he was hurt, she knew that; it was hard to block his pain to concentrate on the fight before her. Who? She turned, but the sun was a red glare in her eyes, she could not see his face, and the Mathkkra were drawing near. She *sensed* him, sensed the inner strength of him— *not Brendan, then, who had none of the Power. And yet, not AEldra. Who?*

A faint music touched the edge of hearing once again; battle- cry, a battle-song that brought strength back into the bleeding man at her side. Whoever it was, she knew surely that they would win out. The sword blazed in her hand.

She was tired the next morning. A night of odd dreams took much from her and she'd had little enough sleep to begin with. Levren, Erken's men, Nisana (she was carried by village children in turns the whole distance) and village Telean came in not long after sunrise.

The Caves were ablaze with the news: the daring rescue, the Bowmaster's slaying of the Thullen, the evil creatures themselves. No, there would have been no way to keep the matter secret.

"As well," Levren said, when he was finally able to break free of an overjoyed folk. "Too many here were treating this as a midsummer picnic. They'll be more careful now. And I counseled from the start the gatherers and the fishers at the very least should have armed guard. Perhaps *now* they will listen!"

"To you?" Golsat laughed. "To anything you say, from now on, a wager on it!"

Levren laughed, shook his head. "Well, Telean, anyway—at least for the moment."

How often it is, that in the search for a thing, we find another—unexpected, and because unexpected, not recognized for something every bit as essential. But so it proved, though it was long indeed before the entirety of what we found was realized.

6

'*YLIA!!!*' The mind-speech reverberated through her, jerking her away from Lisabetha's side. They were far down a side branch and some distance from the main entrance. So strong was Nisana's call, though, that Lisabetha caught the faintest edge of it.

'Mothers, cat, don't *do* that! Where are you? What is it?' After the first startled moment, her heart lurched—Mathkkra attacking? Or some other and worse thing?

'Come now, I've *found* it, I have it!'

"Gods and Mothers," Ylia muttered. "Nisana needs me."

"So I gathered. Why?"

"Anyone's guess, she's found something." But at that, she knew what it was. "By all the Nasath at once, she's *done* it, she's found our refuge. Come on!"

"But—the cache," Lisabetha protested.

"Leave it, come *on!*" They didn't run, it was too far, too dark, and their twine had run out five chambers previously. They had to hunt out two of the arrows. "Next time, we leave a stack of stone to mark the location of the arrows," Ylia said firmly as she caught at the end of the thin rope and began rolling it into a ball.

"No argument from *me*," Lisabetha replied. "If she *has* found it—!" But neither of them really doubted.

Nisana was awaiting them impatiently in Ylia's council-chamber. 'Took you long enough. If you'd bridge, girl.'

'No. You know better. But particularly not *inside* the Caves!'

'There's no danger. You locate where you want to be with the

48

vision, *feel* what you would touch when you arrive, and—there you are.'

'No, there *you* might be, not I!' And, aloud for Lisabetha's benefit: "You found it? The refuge? Where is it?"

The small, darkly furred body radiated satisfaction, and for once Nisana would not be rushed. 'I have searched every stream, every rivulet that pours into the Aresada, for days now. Every gully leading back from the River banks—'

'*Where*, cat?"

'—I'm not finished, be still! This morning, I found a large pool to the north of the river, perhaps seven leagues downriver. I almost passed it by, for it seemed nothing but a catch in the River's flow.'

'And it is not?'

'No. It marks the end of a stream nearly as broad as the Aresada, but shallower and hidden amongst willow and trees. It goes back some distance through low hills and heavy brush and forest, and it comes out—but see for yourself!' They joined.

"Oh, Mothers, look at that, *look* at it," Ylia whispered. It was enormous: It could have been no less than five leagues from side to side, at least seven in length, and it was surrounded by high peaks, rounded barren foothills. Such trees as dotted the landscape were similar to those growing near the Torth, the trees of lower altitudes. She turned to Lisabetha. "I am sorry, that was rude of me. But Nisana *has* found it."

"Where?"

"Downriver, a little north. I—I wish I could show you what I see."

"I," Lisabetha replied quietly, and with a little sigh for what she'd had so short a time, and lost, "wish you could, too."

Nisana rubbed against the girl's arm. Ylia shook herself. "What hour is it, do you know?"

Lisabetha shrugged. "Not mid-day, perhaps two hours short. The kitchen smells haven't come this far yet."

"Ah. Good." And, as Lisabetha eyed her warily: "Get Annes or one of the other of your friends to go with you, back down the way we came. Get two of the boys to carry. If Malaeth asks where I am, if anyone does—"

"You're waiting with the cache, or otherwise not available," the girl said resignedly. Ylia laughed.

"Exactly. Nisana, let's go."

'I just returned—,' the cat began indignantly.

'And you want to show off your find properly, don't you? Let's go!'

'You could go by yourself if you weren't so stubborn.'

'*No*, I couldn't! Let's go, before I lose my nerve.' The cat closed her eyes briefly—*Just once, if the girl would listen to me, as though she has not put forward the same stupid argument for everything she now does!* And, with a touch of self-directed dry humor, *And each time I react to her in the same manner, she is not the only one doomed to repeat stupidity.* 'Join,' Ylia prodded. She loosened the dagger and let it fall into her hand as Nisana bridged them away. Lisabetha stared at the place they had been.

They stood well within the valley, nearer its southern end; on three sides were mountains, glorious, snow-capped mountains that recalled her childhood view from Koderra. Hills, covered for the most part with low scrubby brush, edged the mountains, and dotted the northern end of the valley. There was a heady scent of sage and sun-warmèd earth, an underlying, teasing breath of clover born on an occasional breeze. Tough, wiry grass covered the ground under their feet, interspersed with yellow bell-flower, early lupine. Wild rose brambles pushed against berry bushes, their flat white waxen flowers just beginning to open. She tilted her head back as a whistling scree cut the air, and a hawk soared just above her head, and disappeared into the trees that lined the southern end of the valley.

Groves of oak and fir, grasses already knee- and waist-high there; to the west, a line of white-trunked willow, aspen and stands of reeds that marked the passage of the stream.

"Oh, Mothers, it's warm, it's *warm*." It was. She'd felt no such air since the previous fall in Koderra. She'd come without her cloak, intending not to stay long, but would not have needed it in any case. She pushed sleeves to her elbows, tilted her head back to catch the warmth of sun on her face—sun that was not marred by icy wind! A tingling along the inner sense roused her: not fear, for once, not warning, but a bubbling joy that burst forth in a laugh.

She knelt, dug a handful of dirt and let it slide between her fingers. And caught her breath sharply: "Nisana!"

'What's wrong?'

"Nothing. But I dreamed this place, I *saw* it! I remember I was kneeling in a warm and sunny place, and there was a sweet scent to the air, and the dirt was warm and crumbly in my hands." Her voice died away.

'It's nothing to fear,' the cat assured her tartly.

'No.' She let the last of the dirt slide, dusted her hand against her worn breeches. 'It's not that. It's just—if that were all I dreamed, these past days—'

'You never *dreamed* before.' Nisana's thought was suddenly concerned.

"There are many things I never did before. The soil seems good to me," she added in a deliberate change of topic. The excitement was building again. "We can grow what we need here! And there is room and to spare for us."

Nisana seemed to have caught her mood. She rose up on her hind feet to bat gravely at a butterfly. "There is little game for you humans down here, but much in the mountains. There is enough room for those at the Caves, those in Y1s—" She was prattling like a kitten. Ylia bent down and hugged her hard.

"Your reward for this—"

'I'll have it if we come here. The Caves do not suit me. This does. But it *will* need work!'

"Mmmm. We'll need to place it on the maps, Nisana, so Erken can come here at once, perhaps bring one or two of the herders and the farmers with him. The planting must go forward as soon as possible. If we return soon Erken could set out yet today. I wish we need not, it's so *nice* here!"

'And so no doubt he shall. But just look, you see how that stream bends, and the ground on the far side is higher—not unlike the way Koderra was placed.'

"So much work, thank the Mothers for my council, I could never decide all that faces us alone, cat! But, as it is, I see in this place—"

"*I* see in this place," a loud male voice broke in, "a man-clad girl and a housepet, and by all the creatures of the Black Well at once, why? I have not been drunk since midwinter!"

An airless little cry caught in her throat and she whirled. The dagger was still in her fingers. She pulled her sword free. 'Cat, *where?* Where is he?'

'There. Those three little cottonwood? The shade hides him.'

'I—all right, I have him.' She couldn't really see much, just the shape of a man.

"Show yourself!" she shouted. Her voice echoed across the valley, back again.

"Why?" he demanded. "The girl has a blade! By Lel'San, she

has *two,* like any proper armsman! Might she not slay me out of hand? Perhaps I'll remain here!"

'I'll cut him in two for that scare, Nisana!'

'If I leave any of him for you,' the cat replied flatly. 'A lesson to us both, it might have been anything behind, not merely one impertinent mountain-hunter!'

"I said show yourself!" Ylia bellowed furiously. "If I must come for you, by the Mothers, you'll regret it!"

"Ah!" He laughed. "Well, then! Either way I bleed, that it? Peace for the moment, then, so please you—and here I am." He strode forward, arms spread wide, hands empty and an impudent, mocking grin on his face.

He was tall, lean, and dark. Moustache and beard were heavy but cut short; dark heavy brows hooded near-black eyes. By that much alone, he was of Nedao, though his accent had already given that away. His long dark hair had been caught in a plait and wrapped in leather thongs; his breeches were tanned leather hides, sewn together with thongs. A cloak of serviceably dark Nedaoan wool—a peasant's cloak—hung from one shoulder; his blue shirt had more the look of Nar to it and the boots were Narran beyond doubt.

An ash long-bow was slung across his left arm at the elbow, and an arrow pouch hung low on his right leg, balancing the sword that lay against his left.

He was still laughing as he came close. When another step would have overrun her, he stopped. He towered over her. "The Mothers damn me for a fool if I know where you come from, child, but if you play costume games, this is scarcely the place for them. Besides, Leffna wore two swords, you know, not sword and dagger."

Ylia tilted her head back and scowled up at him. "If you're finished—"

"Aye. All right, it was a bad jest, but all I had for the moment, and under such a circumstance. Where *did* you come from, you and—and that—?"

" 'That' is Nisana. And you?"

"Wait." He'd gone, suddenly, wary and he took a step away from her. "Wait." He peered at her, cast the cat another doubtful look. Shook his head. "She's the Queen's cat, the witch-cat, isn't she? But, then—. You're *not* the Lady Princess," he said flatly. "You're a grown girl, and the Princess Royal is—"

"She's passed her twentieth summer," Ylia cut in, as flatly, "and she carries sword and dagger she earned honestly and by hard work."

"Ah, seven hells," the man shook his head, laughed ruefully. "The first Nedaoan I encounter in a clutch of years, and it's Brandt's daughter. And I insult her! He'll have my ears for it! But if you're Ylia, what are you doing *here?* You can't think it's safe!" He squinted, took another step forward. "Look at the child's face, *gods and Mothers!*" She winced. "Dropped your guard, just the once, eh, girl?" His lips twitched; his eyes had gone cool.

"What matter to *you?*" Ylia demanded flatly. *Why should I care what he thinks, why should I care whether he thinks me comely?* But she could feel the blood hot in her face and her hands twitched into hard fists.

"Indeed." He smirked. "What matter if the King's heir marks herself and renders her sweet face unpalatable, the rights and honors that go with marrying Brandt's daughter render those unimportant."

'I'll kill him!'

Hold off, girl, there's no point, is there?'

Not much, cat!'

"First Nedaoan in a clutch of years," Ylia said finally, her voice nearly quivering with her determination to keep it level. "How many?"

He shrugged. "Who counts them? Five—maybe seven. Maybe even more than that. Why? And what?"

"Wait, I'll answer your queries all together. Let your arms down," she added dryly, "you might need them later." She sobered. "It's bad, be warned."

"I gather that." He was suddenly apprehensive.

"Nedao's fallen to the Tehlatt, we've lost the Plain." Silence. She glanced up, half expecting another jest, but he'd gone white; his eyes were shut hard. "Here, you'll fall, sit down!" She grabbed his arm, shook it. He staggered, clutched at air and dropped. Ylia dropped down beside him.

"D'ye mean it?" His voice was a ragged whisper.

"The Tehlatt set upon us. Teshmor fell, Koderra was lost on the twenty-fifth of First Flowers."

"Brandt—the King——?"

"Dead. He and the southern armed held Koderra to allow the folk to escape by boat down-river. My mother died there, too; only nine of us escaped at the last, and we came north through the mountains."

"Tehlatt." He was following his own thought; whether he'd heard her last words, she couldn't tell. "We knew they would, and yet—" He gazed at his hands. A bird-shadow fell briefly across them. Ylia glanced up in alarm, but it was only a spotted lark. It warbled, vanished into the tangle of berry-bush. "How—how many left?"

"At Aresada, there are perhaps three thousand of us. Three or four more thousands in Yslar."

"By the Black Well. *Gods, Inniva's weft!* But—but Teshmor, of the City—" He seemed to recall himself then, shook his head hard. "No. *No.*"

"Very few escaped from Teshmor's walls, Lord Corry and his Lady were both slain. If—if there was anyone in particular, any name, a person, perhaps I'd know. Perhaps I could tell you."

"*No.*" The sharpness of his reply surprised them both. He looked up; tears stood in his eyes. "There was no one! No one in the North, who would remember *me*. None I remember." A lie, it stood out all over him. But she could not push the matter, his sudden grief was too strong and she could not bring herself to intrude upon it. *A woman, someone he left and now regrets.*

"But, wait." He pulled himself together. "The King—you said—" He leaped to his feet as though stung. "You might have *said!*"

"Said what?" She stared at him in confusion, let him pull her in that stunned state unresisting to her feet.

"Here I sit, talking with Nedao's Lady as though she were some peasant girl! Blast you, you might have said!"

"It wasn't important. It still isn't. Don't do that!" she added furiously as he knelt and bent his head. "I didn't say, because there are things more important than form and protocol at present! One of them is a place for my folk to live. This place, unless you know a reason against it."

"Reason? Other than that *I* like it, and if it's cluttered with stodgy Nedaoan herders and farmers I'll need to find me another? No."

"Or," she went on, ignoring his comment, "unless you know a better, close to hand."

"Close, no." He shrugged, tugged at his beard. "Twenty leagues to the south, there's a good place. It's near the Ylsan border, but not too near."

"No, not south."

"It's nice," he said persuasively, "nicer than this. Larger, too."

"And *you* don't like it so well, no doubt," she cut in dryly. "Nevermind. The South is closed to us."

"Why? May I see that?" he added, holding out a hand as she made to resheath her blades. She dropped the dagger into his palm. "Thank you."

"Of course. Have you not been south of late? I came north through the Foessa myself. There are dangers there, such as I would not expose my 'stodgy farmers and herders' to. That is all."

"Well. Perhaps. There *are* odd places near the Pass."

"More than odd, and not only so far south as that, either."

"True enough." He was turning the dagger over in his hands. "Was this made for you?"

She took it back, bent to sheath it carefully, and with more care than such an action would normally take. "No, it was a gift. Why?"

He shrugged. "I thought I recognized the cut of it. Perhaps not. But what is this of the South? You need only avoid the odd places, and there aren't so many as all that!"

"No? Have you never heard of the Fear-Which-Follows? So I am told you hunters call it." He gazed at her in wide-eyed astonishment, and broke into loud laughter. "It's no laughing matter," she overrode him. "I have *seen* the Fear, I *and* my companions, among them the Swordmaster Marhan, and he's no man for wild imaginings! Mathkkra, we called them on a time, and so they still call themselves! And have you never felt a shadow cut across you at sunset and thought it a large hunting-bird, save that your spine crawled with a sudden chill?"

He sobered instantly; she had apparently reminded him of a thing he'd rather not remember. "I have never seen the Fear, though I felt it once. And as for the other—nevermind. Mathkkra!" He laughed shortly and without humor. "Aye, it would be, wouldn't it? You take much on your shoulders, holding superstitious Nedao within the Foessa, even so far as Aresada! And to bring them here. Well! *My* mind boggles, I'd make no attempt at it for any coin!"

"There hasn't been choice. A Tehlatt sword, a fired cottage, or flight into the unknown mountains? But *you* ill speak Nedao."

"Do I?" he returned, mildly enough, and cast a glance at Nisana, now balanced on Ylia's shoulder so she could gaze out to the west. "And how many of them horn *her*, when her back is turned?'' Nisana turned, gave him an unfathomable look and went back to her study of the valley floor and the mountains beyond it.

Ylia laughed, shook her head. "All right, I'll grant you that! But they're a gallant people overall, and brave. Superstition and Chosen religion alike notwithstanding. No one has left us, though they've been given the chance. Perhaps you've never seen them put to the test before—what is it?" He'd gone grim-faced at her last words. *What did I say, or was it what I said?*

"Nothing. I simply haven't your faith in them. Stodgy," he reiterated firmly.

"Well," Ylia replied loftily, "you need not worry about them. I am certain your tracking abilities are such that you can avoid this place after it is populated!"

"Well answered!" he grinned. "I swear! I take back my first words, if there *was* a woman who could rule such a folk in such a setting, you've at least the tongue for it. Perhaps someday after you're a new Nedao here, and a City, and a Midsummer Fest, I'll come to see if you've earned those blades honestly! In the meantime," he added with a mockingly grand Teshmoran bow, "I freely give this valley to my Queen and my folk. Live here and prosper!"

"The thanks," she replied dryly, "of your Lady *and* your folk. Come to Midsummer *this* year, and test my blade against your own. You owe me that for the scare you gave me."

"Hah." He was still grinning broadly. "If a man used it for anything save to swat at his pack-mules, you'll get no such challenge from *me!* Good day and good luck to you," he added, and with another bow, turned and strode away. Ylia stared after him until Nisana butted against her ear.

'Join, we've been overlong.'

'Mmmm. So we have. But who thought to encounter a mountain-hunter here?'

'Why not?' Nisana demanded reasonably. 'But one so young and handsome?'

Ylia laughed outright. 'Handsome? *Handsome?* Cat, are you serious? He's all hair and smelly hides, and if he's handsome— Gods and Mothers, Marhan has better looks!'

'And better manners,' the cat observed, with one last glance after the retreating hunter. 'Lisabetha will not be able to cover for you much longer. Join.'

* * *

There were still skeptics, and many still made horns at my back as I passed, thinking me then unable to note it—though if I were half the witch they thought, surely they'd have deemed me capable of behind-sight. But from the day I found what was to become, again, Nedao, there were many also who accorded me a little respect.

7

The cabin was small and dark: dark wood, dark hangings. An enormous bed took one entire corner. Rich velvets spilled down the side, hung twisted and rumpled from the corner posts. A brass lantern over an ornately carved table spread with Osneran lace shone ruddy on the plain silver wine jug, and two matching cups. Charts covered most of the surface; wine had dribbled onto them, and been wiped clear, if not clean, with an impatient hand. The lamp swayed, casting long shadows as the ship rocked at anchor. Two large, square glass ports were open, shutters fastened against the inner walls. An occasional warm breeze brought sea-scent with it. Moonlight on the water beyond revealed a new moon-shaped cove between out-thrust stone arms of a calderalike island. The harbor was nearly empty.

Two men hunched over the table, talking in low, earnest voices. The cups were empty, and though neither man was notably drunk, clearly the containers had been emptied more than once. One was an older man, though most of the weight on his shoulders was not years. Ban Brit Unliss had aged ten years since Nod Bri H'Larn had deposed him a mere six months before.

The other man was, by contrast, young, and fit. Life burned with a terrible heat that shone from his pale blue eyes. The same man, this, who had looked challenge at the blade-thin and worn Nedaoan on Nod Bri H'Larn's command ship.

"Well, I flat out told Nod Bri H'Larn he dare not treat with this Northerner *or* these fool religious, *and* told him so straightly." Mal Brit Arren's teeth were bared in a fierce grin that had nothing of humor in it, unless it was at the thought of the discomforture of his chief, the exchange of low remarks and laughter among the other captains and Nod's crew.

"But—"

"No, Ban. Nod rules, but he has no right to make such a decision without vote by all the captains, and so I told him, before his entire crew *and* half the council." Brit Arren's hands balled into large, red-freckled fists. "He absolutely will never again dare to put *me* in such a position! Or dare to promise my support where he does not have it!"

"Unwise, Mal. Unless you intend to move against him soon."

"I do. Sooner than I had originally thought to, but Nod needs stopping, now. And if my plans go right, the *Fury* will be lead ship before summer is high."

Ban Brit Unliss shrugged; his red hair was more than half gray, receded from a high, lined and sun-darkened forehead. His blue, watery eyes were fixed on the map, on the dagger pinning it in place. One hand clutched at his winecup; the other—once his swordhand—lay at the table's edge. He glanced at it as it twitched involuntarily. Twisted, withered, permanently reddened by the fire that had nearly taken his ship, it was and had been useless the past five summers. And so he had lost the ruling, he, Ban Brit Unliss, who had led the Sea-Raiders for nearly twenty years. He had not even been able to take the challenge when Nod spoke it, could not have held sword in that puckered claw. It still shamed him. "Nod knows you will challenge him, Mal. *I* knew, long before he ever moved against me. He knows."

Mal Brit Arren ran square, capable hands through his close-cropped hair. "I planned it that he would. When I am ready, at the time *I* choose, I will take him."

"It matters so much to you, Mal? The ruling?" Ban Brit Unliss drained his cup. Foolish question. It had mattered to *him*, more than sense or reason, when it was his.

"Perhaps." Brit Arren shrugged. "But Nod is not the man for us, not in these times, you know that, man! A Sea-Raider depends on *no* outsider for aid, no one! And Nod had us pledge support to this Nedaoan bastard for aid against the Tehlatt savages. And why? A pittance of gold, the Narran trade routes we already know ourselves—and for *his* aid to us, against Yls and Nar, as though we could not deal with both ourselves!" He laughed; the sound echoed across the water and was given back by the high rock of the island peak. "Or, at least, those were the reasons he gave us. You know Nod, he's so devious he'll meet himself one day coming onto the *Vitra*'s deck." The smile faded, but his eyes continued to gleam. "If I do not gut him first. As I fully intend, for what he did to me, shaming me and the *Fury*'s crew before— ah, to the black depths with it! Drink up, man. We celebrate tonight, my coming victory. Young Jon will bring more, when this is gone."

While I have many traits not shared with Nedaoans, one of the most curious is that I have raised both my own young and human young: young Ylia and before that, her mother, my sweet Scythia—her mother's sister Ysian. And so, while many another might conjecture upon the differences between child and kitten, I can state with knowledge. In many ways they are similar: demanding, self-centered for much too long, prone to an astonishing amount of trouble when they begin to toddle. Kittens grow, gain independence and leave sooner—a relief, frankly, since they come in greater numbers than human children do. Then again, kittens learn more, and faster, and are seldom—as certain human children I could name—arbitrary, stubborn and mind-set merely for the exercise of the thing. Nor will a young cat nurse a grudge or wrong for so long as a day. Though now and again it is this holding onto a wrong until it can be righted that is the proving of a young human.

8

There was a feast that night, with good, plain meat for everyone and true bread, for though there was still cause to conserve what they had, there was an end to that in plain sight. Only Erken and fifteen of his men did not attend, for they were already well on their way west.

There was even an attempt at berry tarts, but the pastry had an odd taste and the fruit was over-sour.

Ylia's council met after—though it was difficult to free her from the cheering people—and did not conclude until well past middle night. "Lists," Marckl moaned, late on. "If I hear that word much more!"

"Mmm. Agreed." Levren yawned. He'd led a hunt out as soon as Telean was safely delivered, and he'd had little sleep the past 5-day. "However. We have Telean, and what—? Seven other villages near intact. Ifney and Marckl, you'd be the ones to put to them if they'll remain whole. If there's room," he added doubtfully.

Ylia shrugged. "Erken will have a better idea of that. Marckl, if you and Ifney would broach the matter with the village elders, just in case. It might spread us too thin, beyond a point where the armed among us can protect the helpless."

"Well, those last will be fewer by this winter," Brelian said. "Though it's not easy work, teaching young farmers to wield sword. Lev, there's work for you. Many of them know bow-use."

The Bowmaster nodded. "It's a matter, at present, of materials. And the hunters among us still need me. But there's a man of the Baron's here who has good skills. If you can spare young Olon, sir, he could at least start lessoning for me, until I can spare the time."

"I'll send him to you, first light."

"Good. I'll do what I can about bows. Rumor has it," he turned back to Ylia, "that you've more women to train than Brelian has boys."

She laughed. "Twice as many, at least! We scared together ten light swords and the smith recast four more from unstable heavier weapons. If I had all the hours of the day to teach, the hilts would stay warm. Lisabetha did too good a job, I fear." She continued. "I've started twenty, first patterns for now. There's no time for anything else. Now, if Marhan would only relent, and give me some help—" she added with a wicked grin in his direction.

"You know it's not that," the old man began huffily.

"No, I know it, Marhan, you've no time either. We'll sort it out, eventually. Now." *Everything that's against us is moving at such speed, I know it is, and we sit here, for hours! Wrangling matters we can't even yet do anything about!* She swallowed sudden irritation and an equally strong desire to be back out of doors. "Erken's got two men with him who've helped parcel hides of land. They'll give us a more accurate measure of the valley, how it can best be split up. This first year, it may well be we'll make no divisions."

"It may be easier to provide for everyone if the land is kept in trust for all." Bnorn made his first remark of the evening. "Like the herds."

"Perhaps," Ifney said. He didn't look convinced, not by half. "Men work harder for a thing theirs. And if we could divide the land and *then* divide efforts: You know, set some folk to the planting, others to building houses, some to the herding."

"We *have* herders," Marckl reminded him.

"So we have. Are we intending to keep using those children the way we have, once we leave Aresada? I'd not think it wise to leave them homeless." His mouth twitched. "Or particularly kind."

Levren leaned forward. "They will take warding-families, of course, those still young enough, and those older ones who wish it. This hasn't been quite the place for that. But the children who needed the support of family have found families. Haven't you noticed?"

Ifney waved a hand, dismissing the subject as settled. "Well, then. There'll need to be a market-place, and a town for those who lived in Teshmor and Koderra."

"A matter that can be put in the hands of the arrivals from Yslar," Ylia said. "But I have already found what may well be the site: close to the stream, not in a position to be flooded. And the stream—it is nearly a river, at that point, looks to be navigable, at least by small boats and barges. It flows down through trees to the Aresada, and though I did not see it myself, it seems a good means of reaching the River, and so staying in close contact with Nar."

"Well, then." Marckl ran a dark, short-fingered hand through his hair, wincing as he caught a snarl. He was as direct as his friend Ifney, as quick to force things from settled subject to unsettled one. "I will start the lists for the folk who were mine, their exact numbers, what they had on the Plain, their needs at this time."

"And I for mine," Ifney added. "And for those few of Teshmor, if there's no objection."

"None, here. I'll see to my folk and those south to the Citadel," Bnorn said.

"Grewl. If you'd give me a list of your needs, I'll put them with the rest." The elderly Chosen looked up from his place near her

right hand—she'd taken him as scribe as an aid to both of them—
and nodded.

"They won't be long," he began tentatively. Ylia shook her
head.

"A complete list, please. We've plenty of room for your
housing and fields, and your people are useful." They were: those
of the North who had taken to the Chosen religion found much-
needed comfort in it, and Grewl was tireless in his efforts to help
them. And they had accomplished so much of the task her
grandsire had set them. Though the written histories and tales
were lost when the Tehlatt attacked, that was scarcely their fault.
Setting them down was a task they could accomplish again. She
turned to Marhan and Levren. "If you'd make lists for the South
I'd be grateful. I'll need your help regarding Koderra. I'll prepare
those lists, but I know I won't remember everything."

"I'd say a thing," Ifney put in. "I had a fair-sized holding of
my own, before the Tehlatt took it. And folk under me. Well, now
we all share something with Duke Erken, and like him, I'd just
want to say, now, that I make no claim on the lands the Lady and
her—and Nisana found. This isn't the time, though I'll continue to
aid the folk who were my responsibility, if they want it."

"You've said what I think, friend," Marckl said.

"What we all think," Bnolon murmured.

"There is land in plenty all around the valley," Ylia said. "And
doubtless there will come a day when we can spread out, as much
as we wish. You have my word that you'll none of you lose by
your offer." She stifled a yawn. "It's late. I'll go at first sight
tomorrow and bring back a pouch of the dirt for some of the
farmers to examine. And I'll have a closer look at that stream, to
see how shallow it runs."

"I'd rather you didn't go alone," Marhan said, mildly indeed
for him. She shook her head.

"It's safe. Remember Nisana can bridge me away before
anything can touch me." *And this time, I'll pay closer heed to my
back!*

The minor lords left together, Bnorn and his son close behind.
Marhan had to shake Levren; the Bowmaster was half-asleep. The
old man stopped at the entrance. "You *swear* you'll be careful?
You worry me sometimes. Remember where we are: the Foessa.
Not someplace safe."

"I won't forget." He seldom made it so clear, how deeply he
cared for her, and despite irritation at being coddled, she was

touched. "If you're *really* worried about me, you can come with us," she added; her eyes sparkled with a held-back smile.

"Huh. *Magic.*" The old man nearly spat, only just remembered where he was. "Not much! *You* watch your back, boy!"

"Mmmm." He was at it again, his old pet name for her from the time when he refused to acknowledge it was a girl he was teaching. "Of course I will, old man. I promise." Marhan scowled at her, an expression that failed to hide his concern and love for her, and he turned to go. The door-warder pushed past him. "Swordmaster, your pardon, Lady. The—one of Lord Marckl's men—" The curtain was ripped from his fingers and one of the northern swordsmen strode past him. He was wide-eyed, gasping for air.

"Lady, the herds are attacked, we need aid!"

"Marhan, Brelian, go!" Marhan was already gone, Brel close on his heels. She caught Marckl's man by the shoulders. "What is there? Speak, man!"

The man shook his head, hard, rubbed sweat from his eyes. "They—they came down from the hills, there's a ground fog, hard to see much but the tops of the trees, can't see anything low at all—"

"Never *mind* that, what are they?"

"They—they're small, pale grey, near white. Like—spiders but armed. Swords. And—and I was so afraid, we all were, of a sudden—"

"Mathkkra," Ylia said grimly. The man paled even more and she thrust him onto a stool lest he faint. "How many?"

"I—perhaps two dozens. More than we."

"Lisabetha? Never mind, Menfred, get this man something to drink." The door-warder nodded, was gone. "'Betha, get my cloak, will you?" 'Nisana where are you, I can't go without you!' But the cat was already at her feet, and jumped to the table as Lisabetha slung the heavy blue cloak across her shoulders. "Nisana, join, bridge me there." She closed her eyes as the cat leaped to her shoulder, swallowed as the solid rock seemed to dissolve from under her feet, leaving her to fall, helplessly—.

It was, suddenly, bone-chillingly cold, and the cries of frightened children, terrified beasts, the wounded, and the scree of swords replaced Lisabetha's cry of luck and the guard's shout of surprise.

"For the House of Ettel—to me!" she cried out, and fell upon the Mathkkra from behind. She drew on the Power, and Baelfyr split the air, turning the fog blood-red. Several of the creatures fell dead, and those nearest fled from the horrid light and flame, onto Nedaoan swords. The herd-guard cheered and lunged forward. Suddenly there were only five Mathkkra where there had been twenty, and these were running, bounding toward the northern rocks and safety.

"Do not let them escape!" Ylia shouted. Baelfyr crackled from her hands, an arrow sliced through the ball of flame and caught fire. One of the Mathkkra shrieked and fell, and did not move. Flames licked at its rough garments. The remaining creatures were cut down moments later by Erken's swordsmen.

"Search! There may have been more, hiding!" their captain shouted.

"The herds, how are they?" Ylia demanded. The animals were milling. It was impossible to tell much, for their fear drenched her mind nearly as strongly as the Mathkkra-fear had. She cast a search loose: nothing. They were gone. But—let the guard look, she thought. It gave them something to do. At the moment, the herds needed her, and so did the herders.

There were fifteen of them, orphaned children ranging in age from six years to nearly seventeen. The two oldest boys were armed with bows and village-forged swords: no serious fighting man's weapons, not made of such soft iron. She made a mental note of that for later: Nold and Kereden needed proper blades. The younger children were huddled just inside the shelter where they slept.

"What happened? No, don't bow, Nold, we were arms-mates tonight, you don't have to be so formal." She gripped the oldest boy's arm. "And we were arms-mates before this, anyway, weren't we?"

"Lady." He smiled; thrilled that she remembered him. *Of course she does, silly,* he thought, *that's how she is.* It hadn't been that long since her company found him and the other children lost in the Foessa with those Chosen and that poor burned old man, and she'd spoken to him like a friend then, too. "We bunched the animals for the night and the guard settled in around us. We'd seen nothing, heard nothing, but the goats were nervous. Terribly jumpy, for some reason. We thought, perhaps there'd be thunder tonight, they sense such things. But there was no sign of a weather change. It was odd."

What isn't, around her? he thought. One of those Chosen had tried to tell him, recently: one or two of the City kids had, to keep his distance from her and from all she did. *Evil, ho, they don't know the half of it!* He thought indignantly. That lady he'd seen in the woods, a dryad, she'd said. It burned at him, that he couldn't say it, he'd sworn secrecy with her. *It's not all evil, the magic. What she did here tonight killed those things, not us. Only a stupid priest or a City kid would think magic is all bad.*

Kereden leaned forward to take up the tale then. "We chose lots, who'd take the first half of night-guard and who the second," he said. He had reached grown height but was still boy-thin. "It was just after change. Nold woke me, and I woke Danila, Meron and Vorey. Just as Nold's lot came in and we headed out, we saw—Mothers, it was horrible! I—there was fog, knee-high in places, over the guard's shoulders in others, and no moon yet, you could just see where it was coming up, and—" He swallowed, exchanged looks with Nold, went on with reluctance. It clearly galled him to have been so scared, galled him more to have to admit it. "Suddenly I was so frightened, my knees buckled and I fell flat. I heard Vorey cry out and Dani scream. I made myself stand, then, somehow, and they—they were coming down the slope at us, not running, sort of—sort of jumping, hopping. I saw swords. By then the guard was coming toward us. They'd heard Dani and Vorey, and I think they saw those things, too."

"It wasn't just you, you know that," Nold reminded him soberly. "We all felt it. Just, all of a sudden, it was like the fog had turned to fear, you breathed it in and—" He shrugged. "I know I did, I was almost too scared to move."

The guardsman strode through hip-high mist to her side. "There's none about the valley now, Lady. We slew the last of them. But—they came upon us so easily. They should not have come through the guard. If someone was sleeping, I'll know it."

"No. Not your fault, they are more than simply quiet. They have a cover that allows them access to any place, and they spread a fear to chill the bones, as these boys can attest. But they *can* be killed, as I said two days ago. You have slain Mathkkra, captain."

"Mathkkra," he echoed dazedly.

"Mathkkra!" Nold exclaimed. "Kerry, gods, Kerry! Did you *hear* that, you killed Mathkkra!" The horror of it wouldn't stay with the older boys. Excitement had effectively banished any remnants of fear.

Marckl's captain shook his head unhappily. "Mothers guard us. We need more men, Lady. If such as *that* come upon us again, it is too dark tonight, and we are too wide spread, even with the herd bunched.''

"You'll have reinforcements," she assured him. "You should—I think they're here." Horses clattered across rock, tore into the valley. Marhan reined in and glared down at her.

"I might have known," he said.

"Yes, you might," she replied evenly.

"Huh. The Mathkkra?"

"Dead. All."

"All? Do you say so? Still, there may be more, you know that. Brelian, choose fifteen from those with us. Leave them until morning. We'll move the herds back to the Caves at first light. Lady Ylia," he added, all stiff formality, "if you'd be pleased to ride back to the Caves with us, there'll be a spare horse for you."

"So you can warm me with a glare all the way? No. I'll return the way I came. It's faster."

Nisana rubbed against her leg; she positively radiated smugness. 'I *told* you that you'd adjust to it.'

'Don't count on that just yet, cat. I have no desire to put up with that grouchy old man, that's all.'

'Hmmph,' Nisana snorted. 'Your silly reason doesn't matter. What matters is that you'll do it. In case you forget, not long ago, you wouldn't. Now, if you'd only try to initiate—''

'No.'

No. Always no, and in such a tone of voice or thought that said flatly she would not even discuss it. And yet, already, she took a bridging nearly in stride, she was so far from the terrified girl of a month before, the one who wept at the very thought of a bridging. She had it in her, the ability to bridge, I knew full well she did, stubborn child. But I also knew her well enough to know it would take some event, some terrible urgency, to push her to that point. As it always did.

I watched the burgeoning trade between the two peoples with great interest: such things have always held a fascination for me—much like swordplay. For what, and with what would a cat, even an AEldra cat, trade? But to watch the humans at trade: it is like their swordplay, like their formal dancing. It creates patterns, as one sets forth a need or a want and the worth of the thing, and the other counters with a different worth, and so they weave patterns often pre-set, take steps already foreseen by each other, until the thing is done and the bargain set.

9

At first light, the herds were brought back down before the Caves and the guard on them kept high. All the children save the eldest were temporarily relieved of night duty: Nold, Kereden, and because she would not be denied, young Danila, though Nold had to promise, many times over, that he would keep her close to him.

Brelian was out with the sun, and by the time it struck the lower ledges, was instructing four of the orphans with the small bows he could get together. Several of the other children were seated on the river bank, binding points to long shafts for spears. It was already warm; Ylia had left cloak and jerkin both behind, and Brelian mopped his forehead as he came to meet her.

"Keep your front arm level, Danila!" he shouted over his shoulder. "Better. But work on your release! Try again!" He turned away, closed his eyes briefly. "Gods and Mothers. Kereden and Nold have used bow before. At least there is *that!* As to the rest—" He shook his head.

"They're not so terrible." Ylia watched as the girl Danila

68

concentrated on her shot and actually caught the edge of the colored target. "Practice only, that's all."

"Aye," Brelian replied gloomily. "I suppose. Do the Mothers grant us time for practice. I took that upon myself," he added, with a wave of hand toward the spear-makers. "As we did for Malaeth."

"Sensible of you. We came off well, last night."

"Better than we deserved; *some* of us knew better than to leave the herds so far away after dark and so ill-tended. Neag now has a guard of thirty regular, with extra men for windy or moonless nights."

"Good. We dare not lose any of the herds. Absolutely we must not lose people. In another 5-day or so, perhaps we can send the herds on to the valley."

"That isn't guaranteed safer, you know," Brelian said. "And the children—would you send them on as well?"

She shook her head. "I don't know. The youngest of them—I'd rather not send the little children. Guarded or not. Perhaps we'd better hold them all back."

"I'd rather—Nold! Bow straight up and down, you're canted too far to the side! Better!" Brelian sighed. "I don't know either. But even the little ones would feel shamed if their herds left without them. That's how they see the animals."

"I know." Ylia gazed across his shoulder. A girl—she couldn't have been above seven, her hair roughly plaited, her feet bare— sat nearby, carefully winding strips of leather around her spear for a grip. With such a sweet face, it wouldn't be long before some family took her in. In the meantime, they *were* her herds. She'd lost mother, father, all her family, her village. Marckl had found her dazed alongside the road, dressed only in a shift. If she had a name, they still didn't know it, for she didn't speak, and no one at Aresada knew her. But now she had a task, a cause, a way to earn her bedding and the thin stew that was most of their food. To take that from her, who'd lost everything else— "Gods, Brelian. Let's leave it as is for now; we can decide later." Ylia gripped his arm. "I can't thank you properly for all you've done—"

He shook his head. "Only such aid as you ask, and likely not all of that," he replied. "And—and I prefer it. Staying busy." His face went carefully blank, he gazed out across the river with sudden intensity, though it was doubtful he saw anything there at all. *Brendan. Brother.* All the family he'd had left, after Teshmor fell. Now a pile of rock on a lonely ledge. And a thought, that

came at times and tore at him. *My Brendan*—She let the thought
slide away, blinked hard.

"Look at that." Brelian broke her thought. She gazed along the
line of his arm. He cleared his throat. "Marhan, there. How can
he stand it?" The Swordmaster had moved his group of boys
farther down-river, but they could hear him as he bellowed out the
changes or corrected someone's poor work. Twenty young men
were valiantly trying to follow the first pattern of change that was
every armsman's preliminary chore. Most of them were failing
lamentably. Ylia laughed.

"I'm not saying a thing. It will come against me with my
women. Though I don't think they're as bad as *that!*" Brelian
grinned briefly, shook his head. "Well, luck with your own class,
I've got lists to study, and a map to rough out so Grewl can copy it
properly." She waved encouragement at the herders and went
back up the ledge.

It was an hour past noon-meal when a shout came from the
Outer Guard, and Merreven burst into the chamber to convey the
news. A boat had come up the Aresada: Nar had sent aid.

Ylia sprinted for the outer ledges, waded through a press of
excited Nedaoans to reach the guard platform. A shallow-drafted,
flat-decked boat was drawn up against the bank. Poles floated
back down the current and men were loosing long tow-ropes from
five sturdy ponies. The captain was on his way up, though he was
going to be a time at it, through so many cheering people. Ylia
reluctantly allowed Malaeth and Lisabetha to drag her back inside
so the Narran could be formally presented.

"Malaeth, don't fuss, *please!*" she implored as the old woman
shoved her into her place at the council table and brought out a
comb. "He's not expecting Koderran splendor!"

"He *is* expecting Nedao's Lady and Queen. Sit still!" Malaeth
pulled the leather ties from all four plaits, slapped Ylia's hands
away as one caught on a snag. "Leave be. I'll be done all the more
quickly if you hold still. 'Betha, undo those, please, and
quickly!" Ylia closed her eyes, bit her lip and gave in. Malaeth
got the ends combed down a scant moment before Merreven came
into sight.

"M'Lady. Tr'Harsen, captain of the Narran *Merman,* seeks
audience with you."

Ylia swallowed a smile that was half amusement, half embarrassment. Such formality—M'Lady, yet!—and all directed at her!

It felt like a child's game, it felt so out of place in this rough stone chamber. But Merreven clearly considered it no game, nor did Marhan and Brelian, who were at his back. *Your job, M'Lady*, she urged herself dryly. "Let him enter."

She'd met Tr'Harsen before. The *Merman* had called twice a year in Koderra. He was in Koderra when word came of the Tehlatt attack, and had taken a load of refugees to Yslar. Ylia was to have been among them; she wondered what he had thought when he realized she was not. "Lady." His bow was a neat, economical inclination of his upper body. Very Narran. "We came as soon as we could, after your men reached us. We've goods for you. My men are unloading now. And I have written messages here from the Lord Mayor and from various Narran trading companies, my own among them."

"If we need to deal with those now, I'll take them." Ylia stifled a sigh: Paperwork, and more paperwork. Tr'Harsen pulled a thick, waxed packet from his belt and handed it to Marhan, who frowned at it. Lisabetha ushered Grewl in and got him settled in his place at Ylia's left hand. Marhan passed the messages across the table; the old man began breaking seals and unfolding a sea of heavy paper. Tiny bits of hard wax colored his sleeves, his fingers.

Tr'Harsen shook his head. "Let your man sort them out. We can talk about them later. They all say the same thing, more or less. Nar's folk have sent aid. I've brought flour and grain, dried corn, what I could gather together at once and would fit in a river-boat. Food as would not spoil. Your man said you'd a desperate need for iron for swords and arrows. We've a very little with us, but there's more coming. Two other boats were loading when I left. They'll be about a 5-day behind us. Perhaps less."

"For your aid, our thanks," Ylia replied formally. She hoped she didn't look as uncomfortable as she felt. She'd never done this before, only stood at her father's shoulder while *he* did. "But we ask no charity. We'll pay as soon as we can for what you've brought."

Tr'Harsen waved that aside. "You'd do as much for us, if we had need. And there may yet *be* need, if the Sea-Raiders continue to harry us." He ran a dark, rough hand through close-cropped dark red hair. "However. Your man said as much, that you'd pay. And so, we can make it a trade, goods you need now and later, in exchange for something of yours. The Lord Mayor asks the same thing in one of those messages."

"Something of ours?" What, possibly, could Nedao have that

the Narrans would want? Nar traded with Osnera and other, highly sophisticated lands across the sea. What Nedaoan goods would *they* want?

"Something indeed," Tr'Harsen replied warmly. "Your wool. Many of us wear Nedaoan cloaks we've traded for in the Koderran and Teshmoran markets. Or in the villages between, where prices were better. But we've never been able to work a deal for the cloth in quantity. Frankly, until recently we hadn't created a market for it, not a decent enough one to let us meet the price your father wanted for the cloth. Now we have one. And we no longer have to round the Ylsan peninsula to get it, which makes the deal all the better for us."

"Our wool?" Ylia stared at him blankly. Heavy, rough Nedaoan wool?

Tr'Harsen smiled, pressed what he saw as an advantage. "Now, your man said you intend to remain within the mountains, Lady. The Aresada is a hard river to travel, but it could be made navigable, and it's safer even as it is than the sea route."

"Closer, too," Marhan said. He nudged Ylia's foot with his, under cover of the table, cast her a warning look and sent a brief one in the Narran's direction. She brought her face under control.

"We've found a place for ourselves, near the River, about fifteen leagues downstream. We'll be nearer yet," she said.

Tr'Harsen smiled. "That's good. The most treacherous water is here and just downstream. Some ugly rapids. However. Pleasure before other business. There's wine aboard my boat; if I may, I'll have it brought up."

He took Merreven with him. "Gods," Ylia breathed, "if Nar wants our wool!"

"If we've any to spare this year," Marhan reminded her sourly. "And don't look so eager, this is a Narran, remember? He'll have an eye to an edge in his trade, however much he wants to aid us. Mind that!"

"I'll try," she said. "We probably won't have any to spare, anyway. Or women enough to weave it. But if they want wool, it's something we *can* provide, eventually. If they'd wanted coin or the sheep themselves, we couldn't possibly have provided either."

Tr'Harsen returned with two of his crewmen, one carrying a small wooden cask, the other bearing a box of heavy-bottomed wooden cups.

"I took the liberty of asking your boy to have water brought. It wasn't sense to transport the best wine on such a rough journey;

this is good stuff, but it's strong." He adroitly parceled out cups, wine and—when it arrived—a generous dipper of water to each. "To the beginnings of a new and prosperous trading union between our countries."

"I'll drink to that," Ylia replied. Tr'Harsen was right: Even mixed, the stuff was strong, still a dark red, and much sweeter than her taste. It was her first wine in over a month, and it was absolutely wonderful.

"Now!" The trader set his cup down, dropped into the seat at Ylia's right, and crossed his arms on the table, leaning forward. "Could we arrange a trade for your wool—well! The Osnerans in two port cities have taken a liking to it. Someone apparently got hold of a Nedaoan cloak—traded it off a Narran, probably—and set a local fashion. The embroidery has taken their fancy, too: Osnerans take whims, and they have more money than sense, some of them." He considered this last statement gravely, shrugged. "Though in this case, and knowing what their winters can be like, it's more likely someone was showing sense for a change."

"If it profits us, we can't condemn them," Brelian put in. Tr'Harsen laughed.

"That's good! I like that!"

"The trade sounds proper: aid from you now for wool when Nedao can provide it," Grewl said diffidently. "But if it's merely fad, you won't have a long-lived market for the cloth, sir."

The trader shook his head. "Not 'sir,' I'm Tr'Harsen, don't know how to answer to anything else. But the market will hold. At least for the wool, for the cloaks. The embroidery—well, they want it, and not just on the heavy wool, *that* might not be wanted a year hence. But even if Osnera loses interest in the wool, there are folk farther north who won't. The winters in Geheran are terrible. Why, we've even traded Ragnolan wool to them, and inferior as it is to yours, they snap it up."

Ylia set her cup aside. "Unfortunately, our wool harvest this spring may not be sufficient to provide anything beyond our own needs. We lost too great a portion of our herds, and few of us have even a change of clothing at present."

"We can supply you with raw wool, as much as you need. For your own needs, as well as for trade. Geheran wool, wonderful stuff. Poorly woven when Geherans do it, unfortunately. But take your time over a decision," he added. "Study the Lord Mayor's offers, consider my own. There will be others in that packet, I'm certain you'll want to at least think on them. And let me know on my next journey up-river."

"We'll do that." She smiled, raised the cup to him. "Thank you for this. It's the first wine I've tasted in much too long."

Tr'Harsen grinned. "It *was* forethought, you know. Any trader's act is. But I have a special reason: Nedao likes its wine and we Narrans love a good malty ale. We've a few beermakers in Nar, but no one who can copy your dark, heavy brown. Now, if we could arrange another trade, wine for ale? This one, though, is strictly *my* idea, and if anyone else brings it up I'd ask you to remember who made first mention of it. We could of course supply whatever grains and such you needed, down to the very casks."

"I'll do that—my council will. I doubt many Nedaoans would take such a trade amiss. Certainly we'll have no grape harvest this season, whatever else we have, and I personally don't care for wild berry wines. Too sweet."

"Well, then." Tr'Harsen drained his cup at a swallow and stood. "I should get back to my boat, to oversee the unloading. I'll have invoices for your stewards, Lady."

Stewards? "Marhan, go with him, would you? Foodstuffs should be sent to the kitchens, anything metal to Bos, and the rest—you'll know." The Swordmaster rose and followed the trader out. "Gods, real wine. Grewl, your cup's empty, would you like a little more?"

The Chosen nodded absently; he was deeply engrossed in a multi-paged document. Tiny flecks of red, green and gold wax were in his beard, where he'd tugged on it with chip-covered hands. He broke yet another seal, dropped the waterproofed outer wrapping to the floor, began comparing the two. Ylia watched him. Grewl was useful: more useful than she'd have thought when she'd pitied a desperately burned old man and restored him to health with the AEldran healing. Nor had he reproached her for using what most Chosen saw as black sorcery on him; that was not Grewl's way, and not only because it had been *his* life. An intellectual, this Grewl; unlike certain others of his kind she could name, a man who applied common sense, logic, and an active brain to the Chosen teachings.

It was too bad he wouldn't accept the leadership of them all: but that Grewl refused to do, despite urgings from many of his people, despite Ylia's own urgings. He wanted nothing beyond his books, the scholar's life he'd sought in the first place when he'd taken the grey cloth. And only evil chance and the Tehlatt had made him part of the Nedaoan Chosen, for he'd only been visiting from some house Oversea when they'd attacked.

She supposed there was good sense to his attitude. Jers still remained at the Caves—fanatic Jers, narrow-minded Jers, ambitious Jers. And he had followers among the Chosen, if not so many as he'd originally counted upon. Grewl was technically still a guest of the Nedaoan Chosen. The Heirocracy would have to confirm the transfer before he would be properly Nedaoan. And Jers looked to be named Father by Osnera. For Grewl to merely assume leadership would foment problems, notwithstanding that more of the Chosen wanted Grewl than Jers.

If we could simply send Jers down-river after his friend Tevvro! Unfortunate he *hadn't* left with his close colleague and her beloved cousin. Oh, he had reasons, she never doubted *that!* And she was not certain that all of them had to do with his personal ambitions. She was keenly aware of his black gaze on her at odd times. Unfortunately, there was nothing she could do about Jers unless he actively threatened her and that he most carefully did not do.

Grewl looked up, blinked himself back to the present. "If there is enough to spare, I indeed wouldn't mind just a little. More water this time, please. Thank you, sir," he added as Brelian handed him the cup. Brelian mumbled something and went back to his place at Lisabetha's side, his color high. He was having a hard time indeed adapting to being addressed as noble, and since he was Ylia's Champion and the vanquisher of the traitorous Vess, folk did. Grewl set the cup aside after a bare taste, buried himself in the first of the messages once again.

"What do you think, Brel?" Ylia asked finally. She gazed at her palm in annoyance: it was black from the charcoaled map she'd drawn on the table. Someone had wiped it off just before Tr'Harsen's entrance, but there was still plenty of soot smeared across the wood. She rubbed the hand down her trousers: *They* were so awful, a little more black wouldn't even show.

Brelian shrugged. "I think we have more fortune than anyone could hope for. Not that I question it!"

Lisabetha gripped his near hand. "I can't believe they want our wool. Who'd have thought?"

"Not I," Ylia said. "It's not pattern-woven. It's plain-colored, not even dyed to fine patterns. The embroidery—well, that's fine-work and elaborate, but I'd think folk like the Osnerans would call it primitive, from all I've heard of them. Grewl? You know Osnerans better than we do."

The Chosen looked up. "Nedaoan wool? There's nothing warmer, or better wearing. I've a Nedaoan cloak I'd not trade for any pretty Osneran bit of fashion, and my robes are that same wool. Most of our women are Nedaoan, you know," he added. "I will speak with them, if you like. Certainly we will want to be of use in this trade."

"I am sure you will be." They were a useful people, she couldn't deny that. They certainly had been at the Caves. The women were among the most ardent of gatherers, many of the men good fishers, though none hunted. If they were not so narrow-minded! She didn't demand belief in what *she* had, no AEldran did. "All weavers we have will be kept busy, if this trade works out. Now, what of those messages? Should we send replies back with Tr'Harsen? Because the framing of them may take awhile."

It did, though considerably less time than it had taken her to prepare the letters that had gone to the Sirdar and the Narran Lord Mayor. There were various offers of assistance, and requests for trade of astonishing variety, plus many offers for Nedaoan wool.

A number of the proposed trades would need to be discussed with the crafters from Koderra, when they came north, for they concerned Koderran fine-work. Silverwork, finework pieced fur, blown glass, carved bone and horn buttons: such craft the Narrans assured her had ready markets, and could be exchanged for coin, for Oversea cloth, for fish and shellfish, and for seed and grain.

The Narrans ate with Ylia and her ladies—Malaeth insisted that Nedao's Lady be properly attended this once, if only by herself, Lisabetha, and Lisabetha's friend Annes—in the main chamber. There was a thick stew, a light sour-rise bread and a bit of tart berry spread to go on it. And for everyone, a little wine. That last brought such clear pleasure, it was no sacrifice at all, though it reduced Tr'Harsen's gift to one very small cask.

"You were speaking of the Sea-Raiders earlier," Ylia prompted Tr'Harsen as the meal neared an end. The trader wiped his mouth on a dark, rough-woven handkerchief, tucked it back in his belt, nodded.

"We had a breather of sorts, two years ago. Your Lord Corry, rest him, was part responsible for that. He got one of their captains and sent his boat to the bottom."

"Dros Bri Hadran," Ylia nodded. "I remember that! They must have been sorry they set on that particular Nedaoan ship! And I remember *him:* red-haired as a Narran but wild."

"Even so. There are those who hold we may be kin at a distance. Myself, I doubt that, but nevermind. We sank two of their ships ourselves, not long after, and the Osnerans had another that came too far west: blown off course by a winter storm, perhaps, but they wound up in the wrong shipping lanes when it blew itself out. It was a tiny portion of their might, of course: three, four ships. They can fill that harbor of theirs, it's said, and that takes a hundred or more ships. But you'll know that."

"Aye." Not from having seen it, but Nedaoan histories described. *Nedao that was.* The huge crescent of a harbor that lay jewel-like between outspread arms of rock. She could have drawn it. "They stopped harassing you, then," she prompted.

"Awhile. We cost them too much, and there's other game, farther south. I hear the Ragnolers and their neighbors in Holth had a bad year of it. It's said they used land routes for a time, they lost so many ships. They're secretive folk, both, they haven't said much to us. But we've seen precious few of their ships on that stretch of water, of late." He set his empty cup aside; people were wandering out and women from the kitchens were beginning to collect Nedao's odd assortment of trays, bowls, wooden rough-turned cups, fine china and glassware, and flat, sanded slices of hardwood that served to hold their rough meals.

"We've lived with the sea for many lives," he went on finally. "My grandsire's grandsire had a house near the sea in Southern Osnera. We Narrans were not happy living amongst such soft and settled folk, and we were traders even then. The rougher life of the Great Isles, with the mouth of the Aresada on our one side and the sea upon the other, and ourselves our own masters suits us. No man owns a trader, not even another Narran. And we sail back and forth between the Peopled Lands and the Western ones, bringing silk and velvet and filigree-set stones, spice and rare liquors from Osnera to Yls and the southern lands, returning with clove and pepper from Ragnol, coffee and oranges from Holth, sen-fruit from Yls and what crafts we could coax from Nedao. It is a dangerous life, and hard, often cut short by the sea. But we love it.

"The Sea-Raiders have been a problem to us, always. By the

nature of our ways of life, it was inevitable we should attract them. And in the space of a year, we'd lose the best parts of four or five cargos. Of recent, however, they've increased their raids. Already this spring, they've taken four ships and stripped them clean. And sent one to the bottom.''

"That's worrying."

"So it is." Tr'Harsen mopped the last of his stew with a bit of bread. "This is excellent, by the way, but I'm not familiar with the meat."

"Elk."

"Ah. It's good," he reiterated. "We now send armed men— such as we have—with the ships. So far, we've lost none since we've begun that practice, though another was attacked not long before I started this voyage. It *is* a worrying change in such a fierce enemy. If they chose, they could wipe us from the face of the sea."

"I wish we could help you," Ylia said. She let Malaeth take her plate and cup, tucked her spoon back into her belt-pouch. "If there comes a time when we can—"

"Thanks for the thought, anyway," the trader replied. "In truth I wouldn't mind a session or two with your Swordmaster. There are some among us who fight Nedaoan style, with sword and dagger. It's well suited to close fighting. A man could use that if his ship was boarded."

"Yours." She stood, shook crumbs from her lap. "Tomorrow, if you like. Marhan's teaching a beginners group, but I know he'd be glad to take the time for you."

"If I have time," Tr'Harsen said doubtfully. He smiled, then, bowed. Ylia held out a hand while he clasped hard. "I have papers to draft, the holds still aren't empty. I'll see you tomorrow, before I leave."

"Please. But there's one other thing." She started back toward the council-room and Tr'Harsen fell in beside her. Lisabetha and Annes rather self-consciously followed them. "A cousin of mine, one Vess, and a dozen men in his colors, left us, twelve days ago. There was a Chosen among them, too. I thought perhaps he'd have stopped in Nalda, that you might know something of him and where he went."

Tr'Harsen held the curtain for them, took the chair at Ylia's right hand again. "There *was* a ship, the *Orchys* I think, left the day before I did. She was headed west, though. I seem to remember a rather ragged-looking Chosen on the decks, and—

wait. Thin man, brown hair?" She nodded. "Then I think so. I didn't really pay close heed. The *Orchys* goes about her own business. She's Osneran, a ship the Chosen hire. She's of the few ships this side of the sea where a Chosen could call in his grey and take free passage."

"Ah."

"You're worried for him, perhaps?" Tr'Harsen asked. "If so, I'm sorry I can't tell you any more. I can ask, if you like."

"Please. It's not worry, not that kind," she added grimly. "He's ambitious, my cousin, and thinks himself better qualified than I to lead Nedao. I had difficulty persuading him otherwise, when I finally reached Aresada. And I'd like to know his whereabouts."

"I'll find out what I can, then. They tell me," Tr'Harsen added blandly, "there's a tale in your travels, but I know nothing of it since it was not the route your father arranged for you. Was it?"

Ylia laughed. "I thought I could be of more aid to him in Koderra." She sobered abruptly. "I think I was. A little."

"A *little!*" Malaeth snorted under her breath. She came out of Ylia's sleep-chamber, Ylia's spare shirt over her arm. She continued as the Narran turned to eye her inquiringly. "She saved my life, mine and young Lady Lisabetha's both; brought us from Koderra cool as you please, not a moment before the walls fell. And hauled us both from death more than once on the journey here! A little, indeed!"

Ylia shook her head, cast Malaeth a warning and repressive glance; the old woman ignored her, which was no more than she'd expected. Ylia winked gravely at Lisabetha, who smothered a smile. "She exaggerates, Tr'Harsen. We *did* come north together, the three of us, *that* much is true anyway. Not a journey I'd repeat willingly."

"Understatement, from all I got of your Swordmaster," Tr'Harsen said. His eyes fixed briefly on her face. "You didn't have *that* before."

"No." She was all too aware of Malaeth's disapproving glower, resolutely kept her fingers away from the scar. *It'll fade, old woman. Leave it be.* "But you're in serious trouble if you listen to Marhan; he takes advantage of his years and grey hairs, don't trust what he says, either."

"Mmmm. Even so." But she could see he was far from convinced and she quailed at the thought of the tale he was going to take down-river. "Well. The hour grows late, and I've your trading papers to prepare before we leave tomorrow. I'd like to pass the first rapids downstream while the sun is still on them and a man can see where he aims the boat!"

"I'll see you at morning meal, if you can face it." Ylia rose, extended her hand. He touched it lightly to his lips before gripping it as he had her father's. "It's a hot one, a wheat and rye porridge, but like glue and there's seldom any milk for it, except for the children."

"I'm warned then," Tr'Harsen laughed. "But it sounds no worse than many a fast-breaker I've had running my ship before a storm. At least it won't be covered with cold salt water. I'll see you then."

"That's a good man." Malaeth gazed after him. She was puttering around the table, putting small things to rights, neatening Grewl's writing materials. Ylia kept a resolute silence, though she knew the long-suffering Chosen would be put to the work of resettling them to his own taste the next day.

"So he is," Lisabetha said. She was drowsing where she sat. She forced her eyes open with an effort, shook herself. "I was up at all hours this morning, long before the sun, searching down that way we went two days ago. I think I'll rest until Brelian returns from herd-watch."

"Wise idea. If you'd like to borrow my bedding, go ahead. I've plenty to do, and I know the single women's area isn't too quiet at this hour."

"No, I'm back against the wall, I've more or less a niche to myself. And right now, I could sleep through anything. But if Brel comes here, will you let him know where I went?" Annes left with her. It was quiet in the small chamber for several long minutes.

Malaeth finished her tidying. "Child's done well, hasn't she? But she needs company, she and the boy."

Yiia grinned. "After so long in the Foessa, practically sleeping in each other's arms, you want to—well, really Malaeth!" she added as the old woman turned a scandalized glare on her. "There's hardly a place in Aresada they could be alone, anyway. The place is simply stiff with people. You can't seriously mean to sit with them to guard the girl's virtue?"

"Some thing are important, no matter where you are," Malaeth said primly. "It's not proper for a young girl to sit alone with her young man, and they're not even acceptably trothed. It's no more proper than those breeches of yours are without a tabard to cover your legs!"

"Which," Ylia said repressively, "I absolutely refuse to wear. And I do not care what anyone here thinks of my legs. If they're offended, they'll have to look another direction!" Malaeth scowled at her. Ylia sighed heavily. "Malaeth, by all the Mothers at once, be sensible! If I'd worn that stupid tabard the other night, I'd probably have tripped and the Mathkkra would have cut my throat!" Silence. "I haven't argued with you about anything since we came to Aresada, though the Mothers know once or twice I've wanted to! I won't argue this, either. *We* won't. Because it's not open to argument *or* discussion."

"It's not *seemly!*" Malaeth folded her arms and set her mouth in a thin line.

"Why isn't it seemly? Marhan wears breeches, Brelian does."

"They're not maids!" Malaeth snapped.

"Aha! So we finally come to it! Malaeth, that's *really* stupid! I'm a swordswoman! A person who uses a sword. Persons who use swords wear breeches. That's all."

"It's just not—"

"I know," Ylia sighed. "Not proper." Argument was absolutely pointless when Malaeth's mind was set.

"It's not! Look at you! With a body like yours! A blind man could see you're female from a league away!"

"So? I can tell by a man's beard he's male at the same distance, Malaeth!"

"That's different!" the old nurse stormed.

"No, it's *not!*" Silence. Stubborn silence. The air was thick with annoyance. "It doesn't matter, Malaeth. Because I'm not changing my mind, or my clothing. I have to fight in what I wear. I'll wear a tabard as I used to in Korderra if you insist. Waist or hip length *only.*" Fiercely angry old eyes met mildly irritated young ones. Malaeth capitulated suddenly, and with at least a glimmer of good grace.

"All right! Stubborn like your mother, aren't you? It's that cat, she did you both proud!" Ylia merely laughed and shook her head. "But I'm going to make certain 'Betha has company tonight when Brelian comes back from guard," she grumbled as she pushed past the curtain. She stuck her head back in for one parting remark. "It'll be hip length, not waist! Mind!"

"All right, all *right!* But no longer, or you'll find it hacked off like the last one was, I promise you that!" Malaeth rolled her eyes again and disappeared. The curtain flopped back into place behind her.

A gift and a burden both, the Power, have I not said so often enough? It is not always the answer, nor is it always enough. There are trades, little bargains, always, and often so simple an action as healing drains strength from the body of even the most skilled AEldra. And there are the other burdens of Power, the subtle knowledge that comes with experience and with age.

It was no great surprise to me, then, that I knew nothing of the Tehlatt prisoners until I found them by merest chance, or that my beloved Ysian was safely within the Caves before I sensed her.

10

Her dreams were formless but unpleasant, waking from them, momentarily at least, a great relief. The hair was plastered to her brow, her body chilled where she'd sweated through jerkin and shirt. She flailed at covers, caught at the arm that had shaken her. "Who—'Betha? What are you doing here, it must be middle night!"

"I was mending your shirt when I heard you. You were talking in your sleep. It didn't sound pleasant."

"My thanks." She shook her head. "What's the hour?"

Lisabetha shrugged. "Early. They've just built up the kitchen fires and the guard's not changed yet." She hesitated. "What did you dream?"

Ylia pulled the cloak close to her. It was cool in her chamber, with the stream of outside air blowing through and across her covers. "I don't know. Nothing *real*, nothing I could see or sense. Just—fear."

"That's not agreeable," Lisabetha replied feelingly. "I know."

Ylia reached between the folds of the fur-lined cloak to grip her hand. "I know you do. Thanks for waking me. I'd wager you'd like sleep, though. Why not go and get some? Whatever you're doing out there can wait that long, can't it?"

"I—" Lisabetha smothered a yawn. "I suppose it can. There's an hour before the sun's up. You'd better rest yourself."

"I intend to." Ylia lay back down, closed her eyes determinedly. It had been another late night, one of several in a row, and she needed all the sleep she could get.

A surge of power, sudden and near to hand, brought her up onto one elbow again. Nisana leaped to her side. She was taut, nearly vibrating with the need for haste, and her ears were flat against her skull. "What's wrong, cat?"

'Shhh, don't speak aloud, your guardsman will hear. Sound carries!'

'All right, but what's wrong? We're not attacked, are we?' Ylia began to push free of the confining cloak.

'No, not so immediate as that. Lie back down, you'll catch chill,' the cat added tartly. 'I found more cattle yesterday.'

'I swear, if you woke me over a cow, however necessary—!' Ylia began warningly, but her inner sense was tingling. Not just a cow, not with that look to her.

'There are Plain-folk still alive, not far from Teshmor. The Tehlatt hold them imprisoned in a woven fence, well guarded, and I warrant by all the Nasath at once for no good purpose.'

"Black hells," Ylia whispered. 'How many, how large a guard. And,' worriedly, 'what is our chance of rescue?'

'That last, I don't know. You look!' Nisana laid her thought open for reply.

Early afternoon. The sun came from between masses of dirty-edged rain clouds to set the Planthe shining, and across that golden ribbon stood what was left of Teshmor: blackened towers, the gate and the walls around it now piles of rubble. Rooks, crows and vultures lined the inner walls, and darkened the sky.

To the opposite direction, a Tehlatt temporary camp: of that she was certain, even from a distance and with the vision—diluted as it was by transference. Warriors camp, none of the colorful women's tents, no herd enclosures, none of the broad-shouldered hairy oxen that carried the burdens of each family from pasture to pasture. No children in sight: only two long, hayroll-shaped black warriors' tents, and a third that by the smoke hole at its peak was a shaman's. A chief tent just beyond that—black like the others, but square-cut, flat-roofed, and before it a blue greeting-blanket. A branch-woven corral filled with sturdy white or grey hill ponies. Twenty-seven ponies. No more Tehlatt than that, then. Perhaps fewer, since some must be used for the baggage.

Across the camp there was another corral, but this was larger and higher: It towered above the guard who stood before the sole gate. It was densely woven of heavy branch, laced liberally with thorn-bush. Wicked points edged the top, all the inner walls.

And within that compound, seventeen Nedaoan men, women and children. Gaunt, haggard folk. "Gods and Mothers, cat," she whispered, aghast as two faces stood out from the others. "*It's Lord Corry and his Lady!*"

'I know.'

'That you thought to look at all—!'

'I seldom do; remember Lyiadd's words! When he set the Tehlatt against the Plain, he gave Power to at least one of their shamen. It is dangerous to search, it might betray us, and I do not want to discover first-hand if they could do anything about me! I am not certain *why* I did search, this time. Well that I did. At least,' the cat amended dubiously, 'well, if we are able to rescue them. They're not in a good position for such an attempt.'

'No. Oh, *no*.'

'Since the Tehlatt have kept them alive, so far—why would they? They do not take slaves, do they?'

'Midsummer. Longest Day Fest,' Ylia replied grimly. The cat eyes her curiously. 'It's no mere contest of arms and crafters, as ours is. They make sacrifices to Chezad, their god of war and fire, to make certain that once the days dwindle down to winter, they lengthen once again. They burn folk alive.' Nisana's eyes went wide with horror, her ears went, if possible, even flatter.

'How certain are you of this?' she demanded.

'Certain enough. Wait, though, there's one can tell us better.' She wrapped the cloak around her shoulders again, strode through the council-room and into the hall. Variel or one of the other very young and unpolished of her door-warders would be on duty at such an hour. It was Variel; he saw her from far down the hall and came running when she motioned to him, quietly, gods, that was good. But when he came near she saw that was only because he'd no soles left to his boots. "Variel, get Golsat for me, as quickly as you can, please. He's in the men's dormitory. I think he sleeps near the back."

"I know where, apart from the others," Variel began eagerly, and then realized whom he'd interrupted; he clapped a hand across his mouth.

"Nevermind, just bring him. Don't wake anyone else, if you can help."

"I won't." The lad set his tall spear against the wall and sprinted off toward the main entrance. Ylia drew back into the council-room, lit two of the near-gutted candles stuck to the table-top by enormous puddles of wax, and settled into her chair. She caught her fingers as they started to drum the wood, stilled them against the rough surfaces. Nisana jumped to her lap.

Variel was quick, indeed; he was back with Golsat before she could begin fretting. Golsat mumbled something she couldn't catch as he dropped into the chair nearest hers. Sleep clouded his eyes, his loose shirt was wrong side out. Ylia handed him a mug of cold water flavored with a little of Tr'Harsen's wine.

"Danger to Aresada?" he asked, cup suspended halfway to his lips. Ylia shook her head.

"No. Drink." Golsat drank, dipped his fingers in the icy liquid and rubbed them across his eyes. "Awake?" He nodded. "Plain-folk are still alive out there." She gestured roughly eastward. "The Tehlatt hold them prisoner. Why?"

Golsat closed his eyes, considered briefly. Candle flame bent against the cold air flowing through the chamber, casting strange shadows across the Tehlatt planes of his dark face.

"They consider slaves useless, since they have women. Prisoners are merely something to be guarded and fed, and so a drag on a moving tribe, a drain on its supplies. You've *seen* them?" She nodded. "They would be keeping them for Longest Day Fest. They used to burn women accused of witchery or unclean acts, men who stole horses or other men's wives." Or those who left the tribes to mate with non-Tehlatt, or the offspring of such women. He didn't need to add that; he and Ylia both knew the Tehlatt would have burned him before Koderra's gates, if they had had the chance. That they still would, given an opportunity. He spread his hands. Shrugged. "Any Nedaoans not killed during the attack two months ago, anyone they kept alive—they'll burn them at sunrise, Midsummer day." Ylia gripped the edge of the table; the color drained from her face and Golsat reached for her shoulder in sudden concern.

"I'm all right; thanks, friend. It was what *I* feared, but it's different to hear you say it. There are nearly twenty people, they're in a camp near Teshmor. Lord Corry is one of them."

Golsat started. He withdrew into himself for some moments, his eyes hooded. He worried a piece of wax from the table, ran it absently through his fingers. "So. We cannot leave them there." He met her eyes; his were black with purpose. "Lord Corry was my first liege, before King Brandt. He took us in—me, my mother and my sisters—when others would not have because of our blood. And he is Father to our 'Betha." Golsat had grown as fiercely protective of Lisabetha as if he'd been her older brother. He brooded in an intense silence. "She must not know of this, unless we succeed."

"She won't. But we need an idea, a plan. Something, anything!"

"Let me think. Perhaps I have the beginnings of an idea or two." He rubbed his forehead, hard. "Let me think some more. But at the very least, I will need—"

"*We* will need," Ylia corrected him gently; her eyes and her jaw were set. "I will be part of any plan you make, don't dare doubt it."

Golsat met her level gaze. "We. I don't doubt. And you'd solve a problem or two I can see already. But if you intend to leap into a Tehlatt warrior's camp, I'd keep it from Marhan!"

"Done," Ylia said flatly. "What will we need?"

"They doubtless abandoned Teshmor once they looted it. They do not like walled cities. And we know they fear the Foessa. If we could reach the City in secret—late at night, a few of us might be able to do that—and if you could then bridge us into that prison-keep. If you could bridge them out." He shrugged, spread his hands. "I don't know, can you?"

"It's Nisana that can bridge, not I," Ylia said finally. "But we'd need her anyway, my strength alone would never suffice, even if I *could* bridge. And we would not dare bridge directly into the midst of the prisoners. Someone might cry out, or there may be someone in that camp who could sense the use of Power, especially so near."

"Well, let me think on it," Golsat said. "You *saw* the camp?" She nodded. "Can you draw it for me?"

"I can try. Well enough that you can tell where things are."

"Good." He pushed himself up, leaned against the table. He was still thinking hard. "We'll need Brelian; he knows how to keep his mouth shut, and he's good. He and I can choose the others; they won't be many since this will be stealth, not fight. Whatever our plan."

"I'll leave that to you."

"All right. Midsummer's a distance off. The Tehlatt won't harm them between now and then. But we'll free them as soon as we can."

"My oath on it," Ylia replied grimly. They shook hands on that, and Golsat was gone.

'I like that man,' Nisana remarked. 'He has sense, and a good head on his shoulders. I'm gone again. I left ten cows milled on the main road. They had better still be there! Send someone for them at full light. We should be within two leagues by then.' And, as she jumped down, 'Go back and sleep. You have need of it, and you'll aid no one by sitting here worrying!'

'I know.' Ylia went back to her covers. She settled the cloak around her shoulders as Nisana bridged out, closed her eyes determinedly. She was tired, *gods* she was tired! But in the end, she had to will herself back to sleep.

The upper ledges were deserted: it was raining fitfully, the air chill, and fog drifted up from the river, down across the heights, occasionally obscuring everything beyond arm's reach. Extra guard was posted with the herds. Not far away, Brelian was teaching basic sword use to a few of the herder children. He'd managed better blades for both Nold and Kereden, though they still weren't proper quality.

Golsat had had a few of the older women out earlier, but they'd gone in when the weather turned nasty. Marhan's boys were at second and third-level passes, and the irascible old Swordmaster wasn't allowing them to quit for a little foul weather.

She searched: touched briefly on two boats coming up-river. At the rate they were making, they'd likely arrive before day's end. An AEldran aboard, too, she sensed Power; personal messages from the Sirdar in response to her own, no doubt. There, not far from the river but much farther west was Erken. She couldn't *see* him, not at such a distance, but the touch identified him as surely.

She was fidgeting, realized it and forced herself to be still. But the inaction still ate at her, and there was nothing to be done about it. She didn't dare let it show, either: Malaeth could still read her, now and again. Lisabetha was extremely sensitive to mood.

Avoid them both, until you can control this. She went down to borrow one of the horses and two of Erken's guardsmen, two of

Telean's young herders. She'd go meet Nisana, bring back the cattle. That should keep her busy, and distracted, for at least awhile.

The day passed: the cattle were tractable, easily driven to join the rest, and though she'd seldom ridden since the previous fall, the mount Erken's boy had chosen for her was small, and smooth-gaited. The rain cleared off, the fog lifted, and the return journey was actually pleasant. Nisana, to the amusement of those with her, elected to ride back draped across her lap, on the horse's shoulder. Fortunately the animal was also placid of temper.

The Narran boats were already pulled ashore, their captains stripped down to breeches and jerkins like their crewmen to unload. Bags of grain, fruit and rice, blankets, bundled clothing were being handed up the cliff-face. Kre'Darst, who was captain of the sea-going *Blue Conch,* hailed her. "An Ylsan lady came with us. She went up not long ago. We'll come ourselves, Tre'Bern and I, when we've finished here. The inventory itself though"—he fished into a damp leather pouch at his belt, pulled out a waxed roll of paper—"you'd as well have it now."

"Lady? An Ylsan lady?" That wasn't like the Sirdar at all, to risk a noblewoman on a sea-voyage, let alone the one from Nalda to the Caves!

"Aye." The Narran grinned. "She asked I not give her away."

'Lady.' She crossed the bridge, slid past the press of onlookers at its far end. 'Nisana, who'd come here, who would they send?' But the cat, with a sudden twist, scrambled free of her arms and sprang up the winding path, leaving Ylia to stare after her. 'Cat?' Nothing was making sense!

But it did make sense when she pushed into the council-chamber to find a tall, radiant AEldran woman sitting next to her place at the long table. She was dressed plainly, in a dark, serviceable travel gown, but her golden hair was loose and fell in a heavy wave down her back; Malaeth was brushing it for her. A heavy red cloak, lined in black fur, lay across the table. Nisana was in her arms, dark paws twined around her neck, her hard little head pressed against the woman's chin. Ylia stopped dead. For half a heart-lurching moment, she had nearly cried her mother's name, but this was not Scythia, though the resemblance was strong.

The woman looked up and smiled cheerfully. "Well, niece, haven't you a greeting for me, after I've come so far?"

"By all the gods at once, Aunt Ysian, *what* are you doing here?"

"Your eyes are good. That's nice to know." Ysian smiled, ran a hand through Nisana's fur. "I've *missed* you, precious!" she murmured to the cat and planted a kiss on an adoring, upturned face. "What am I doing here? Ah. Well, you sent such a nice young man with your messages, I thought it impolite we send back only paper."

"Messenger," Ylia echoed blankly as she dropped into her chair. It rustled and prickled against her legs: Malaeth had gleaned a little cloth for cushions, but the dry leaves weren't the most comfortable of stuffing. "The Sirdar sent *you?* Here? As a messenger?" She shook her head. "I don't believe that!"

"Of course he didn't." Ysian laughed. "It was *my* idea, and he wasn't pleased with it. But then, he wasn't best pleased with *me*, either, by the time your messages were chewn up. I'd have come anyway, sweetest," she added to Nisana, and kissed her furry brow once again. "I really *missed* you, cat!"

"Aunt Ysian—!"

"If you'll please," Ysian broke in crisply, "*not* call me Aunt, I won't call you Little Ylia. Fair trade? Which," she added, eyeing her niece critically, "you certainly are. Scythia didn't give you much height, did she?"

"No, Au—no, she didn't, Ysian. You're avoiding my question: why *are* you here?"

Ysian shrugged, became suddenly quite businesslike. "I'm postponing unpleasantness. Bear with me. I was on the Sirdar's Council, you know, after Father retired. He'd nominated your uncle Ardyel to replace him, my oldest brother, but Ard's such a fool even the Sirdar wouldn't have him. Father didn't like it, but I went over his head and was approved.

"So I was there when your man came in on that Narran cog. Your people, by the way," she added, "are doing all right. Homesick, of course. The crafters have a market going, they're paying their own way."

"I'm glad to hear it. We've charity coming from Nar and it's appreciated, but we pay our debts."

"Well, you won't have any debts in Yslar. And you should be pleased with that boy of yours. One could see he wasn't Embassy-trained, but his manners were impeccable."

"Erken, my Duke, will be glad to know that," Ylia said. "He

made the choice and briefed the boy. You're postponing again. Go on."

"Well." Ysian sighed. "The council accepted your thanks, which I thought large of them. I was getting irritated, by then. It was as though they'd found a monkey playing the viol: you know the old joke, no surprise that it played so well, just that it could play at all."

"Oh." Ylia bit back a grin. She *hadn't* heard that before, but Ysian might misunderstand if she laughed. "Honestly, I didn't expect much else. I know how they look on Nedao."

"I suppose you would, wouldn't you, girl? But it's not as though Nedaoans are savages, is it?" Ysian demanded irritably. "Well, I managed to keep my peace until they got down to—ah, does Malaeth know what we're about here?" Ysian asked. Ylia nodded. "Good. Didn't want to spring any surprises. I gathered from the tone of that personal message that you weren't exactly making Lyiadd general knowledge."

"We're not. She already knew."

"Ah—of course. Unfortunately, *I* remember Lyiadd all too well. After all I was there when he was pressuring Scythia. I was only eleven or so, but he left me feeling unclean even then. I had a *feeling* about him. When I read that paper of yours, I didn't doubt a word of it."

"*You* didn't."

"Clever rascal, aren't you? The Sirdar got his back up immediately, and of course all the senior members of the council went right along with him: the Senile Seven, the more sensible of us call them. They're ancient as the docks and stubborn, arrogant, proud—so narrow-minded I swear most of 'em have room for only one eye each!" She scowled as Ylia laughed, but finally grinned and went on in a much lighter mood. "So the old men got all lordy and absolutely refused to believe any of it."

"Any?"

"Any," Ysian said darkly, "Oh, we've all learned our history, you know. It's expected, and probably most of them can recite The Conferring—Shelagn's death and the Gifts of the Guardians, *you* know. That doesn't mean they believe what they repeat, though, does it?"

"It's a common failing," Ylia said. "My own people are much the same. If you can't touch it, or see it, how real can it be?"

"That sounds odd, 'my' people coming from my sister's daughter and not speaking of Ylsans. I'll adjust, girl. It took every last one of the rest of us united—and that's not a common thing, believe me!—generally shaking the rafters to get the old men to agree to search."

Silence. "The Sirdar," Ysian said finally, "of course has his own reasons for digging in his heels, since Lyiadd's whore is his baby daughter." She glanced up. "You did a fine job, the way you put it, but—well, there wasn't anything you could have said, about Lyiadd *or* Marrita, that wouldn't have put him out. He hasn't mentioned either of them in seven years, and it's my belief he'd die that way if they walked into the council-room tomorrow."

"That's a very ill thing to say," Malaeth admonished. "It's not so far wrong as you might think!"

"You needn't convince *me*, ma'am."

"Ma'am, indeed! Ye make me sound aged, and I was that child's nurse since I was yours!"

"All right, Malaeth," Ysian laughed. She straightened around again as Malaeth tugged impatiently at her hair. She murmured something against Nisana's dark ears, Ylia cast her eyes up as Nisana stretched up to rub her cheek against Ysian's. She *had* forgotten how sickening the two of them were together.

"So what did you find, did you find any trace of him?" Ysian looked at her oddly. "He is dead. I know it. But Marrita is there. There must be some trace." Ylia's voice faded to nothing as Ysian shook her head gravely. "There has to be!" Ylia insisted. "He had two full companies of men, a hoard of Mathkkra! Thullen all over the place! The stink of Lyiadd's Power alone will contaminate that valley for years, Ysian!" Silence. "Look, they *did* search, didn't they?"

"Told you so, didn't I?" Ysian replied. "We insisted, and there were enough of us to get what we wanted. We found the valley. There was no doubting what the place was. There aren't as many on the council who doubt the truth of the Lammior, not after that search. Nothing else could account for that place.

"But—for the rest, there's no recent trace of anyone there. No trace of Lyiadd, absolutely. Nothing of the kind."

"That *can't* be!" Ylia shouted. Her door-warder, concerned, stuck his head in; she waved him back. "That simply cannot be," she reiterated flatly, but more quietly. "He was *there*. I'm *not* the only one who saw him, saw Marrita. Malaeth—others who were with me did." She swallowed. "I didn't imagine *this*, you know!" She traced the scar with a shaking finger. Ysian shuddered, closed her eyes.

"Malaeth warned me. I'm—sorry. Maybe I can—never mind. Later. I'll tell you what *I* think, though. I think Lyiadd—be he alive or dead—must be changed indeed, to be able to remove all trace of himself and his from a place."

"What *you* think," Ylia caught at the nuance again. "No one else believes me, though. Is that it?"

"Near enough. A lot of them agree you could have run afoul of him, somewhere in the Foessa. They'll agree that he could be alive, that he could still be living in the mountains. They see no reason why his Powers should be other than AEldra, *or* greater, to subdue you and your companions. They flatly don't believe he has followers, other than his sweet Lady and the men he took with him. No Mathkkra, no Thullen. They ignored your warnings."

"Seven hells." Ylia ground her teeth, became aware of it, closed her eyes and let her mother's calming charm wash across her mind. It didn't help much.

"No," Ysian retorted acidly, "seven ancient fools! Well, I got tired of listening to their insults and finally decided to take no more of it." Ylia eyed her in sudden alarm. "You *are* clever, aren't you? Right in one, girl. I told them just what I thought, and why. *And* what they could do with their precious council and my empty seat." She considered this with some satisfaction.

"Ysian—"

"Of course they didn't like that, and I daresay I can't blame them, *I* wouldn't have put up with it either. Particularly if I were a damned old fool. And then I let your man escort me out of the Tower, and went home to pack."

"You—went—" It was difficult to catch up. Ylia shook her head to clear it. "You haven't—you didn't—"

"Have, went, and did," Ysian replied. She still looked exceedingly pleased with herself. "Father was apoplectic, but he's no better than the Sirdar and I told him plainly what I thought of a man who'd disown his daughter and then refuse to back his grandchild against the opinions of doddering old fools. He'll have what he wants, now: me out of his house, and no more need to apologize for an unwed, middle-aged daughter. And a seat for Ardyel on the council. They'll have to give it to him now. Poor stupid Ard, he's the last eligible member of the Second House."

"Ysian, you can't!"

"Can't what?" Ysian looked up in alarm. "Don't say that after I exiled myself like that, you won't have me!"

Ylia laughed helplessly. "Gods and Mothers, no! But, Ysian,

you've never lived outside Yls at all. Where we are is so primitive, you'll be shocked by it, I promise you."

"Hardly ever been outside the City," Ysian replied cheerfully. "But the journey here was wonderful!"

"It's truly not easy here, just now, Ysian. We've not much to eat, you'll be stuck with the rest of us on watery stew—Malaeth, for pity sakes, tell her!"

"Wretched food," the old woman said.

"But *you're* making do, aren't you, Malaeth? And if you can do it, I certainly can!"

"The bedding: well, there just isn't any," Ylia went on unhappily. "Rock with a few branches or grass under your hip to keep it from bruising, that's the best any of us have. I sleep in breeches and shirt. And I'm still not warm."

Malaeth held up a finger for her attention. "I'm reminded, you choose hours tomorrow to be inside. I'm washing those things of yours at first light."

"No, you're not, I haven't hours to spare. Ysian, it's not—I don't meant to offend you, but it isn't just adventure. It's hard, it's rough, the smoke gets into everything, you can't bathe properly. Even those who lived rough lives on the Plain are living rougher ones here, and finding it difficult."

"I'm staying," Ysian said firmly before Ylia could go on. "And a little hardship won't hurt me. I can't go back to Yls without apology to a dozen people. I'd choke on the words and die. I won't go back to Nar. I'm tougher than I look, I promise you. Besides, I can be useful, my girl."

"Useful," Ylia echoed blankly.

"Of course. I have the Power, remember? You can't tell me it'll come amiss to have another with the family abilities among you, not with troubles such as you've got."

"Ysian—!"

"You *need* me. Malaeth's told me about the seed and grain you can't find because no one has maps of these caves. Malaeth, tell her."

"She finds things," Malaeth spoke over the newly plaited head. "It's her own special ability, like Scythia's to calm."

"I find things, lost things," Ysian said. "I don't even need to have ever seen them, and I can find them. I think about them, and I know where they are. You need that," Ysian said persuasively. "You need me."

"Ysian, you can't do this to yourself, please! Nisana, tell her, will you? *Show* her what it's like!" Ylia implored.

'I have. She knows. She's right, we can use her. What she can do, who she is.'

"Cat, you're no more sensible than she is! Seriously. Think, will you?"

'I *have!* I love Ysian, I'd want her to stay for that alone, but she's right. We can use her. We need her. She's strong and stubborn as you. She'll manage. *You* manage, after all.'

"I'm a swordswoman. I've been trained—!"

'You were as unprepared as any of us when we took the Hunter's Crossing into the Mountains,' the cat retorted.

Ylia scowled; Nisana scowled back at her. Ysian smiled gently across the cat's head. Ylia closed her eyes, shook her head. "I swear—! I give up, I know when I'm outnumbered. Nisana, you're not fooling me in the least, I know why you're siding with Ysian! But—all right. Ysian, you're welcome to stay with us. If it becomes more than you can bear, though, *swear* you'll tell me!"

"I will," her aunt promised. "But it won't."

"We'll see," Ylia replied grimly.

*How long has it been since our kind gauged
their acts by the moon and stars, and the paths
and actions of each? And were our long kin once
so barbarous as the Tehlatt in their efforts to
control events? Though I am not human but
animal in nature, even I was chilled at what we
learned of them.*

11

It was late, past middle night and she was elbow-deep in Ifney's
lists when Golsat burst into the chamber. "Eclipse," Golsat said
tersely, adding as an afterthought, "did I startle you? My
apologies."

"You did; it's all right." His first word caught up with her and
she pushed the lists aside. They fell unnoticed to the floor.
"Eclipse?"

"Of the moon, two nights away. One of the Chosen—I was
speaking with him just now and he mentioned it. There's a
ceremony among their kind, apparently. He was talking about a
song he'd written for it." Golsat recalled himself. "The Tehlatt
have another way to call the moon back."

"Mothers, no. *Gods* and Mothers, if you'd not found that out,
Golsat, and we'd—"

"Well, I did," he cut in sharply, "do not dwell on it. I've put
more shape to my plan. Enough, I hope, because we'll have to set
it into motion tonight."

"At once. Now," Ylia said grimly, and sent a mental, 'Nisana!
I need you, fast!'

"I'll go for Brelian."

"No. Variel's on guard, send him. Talk to me, tell me your
plan." *Give me something to do besides worry!*

"All right. It's still rough, though." Golsat strode to the
curtain, spoke to the door-warder and sent him on his way. He

stepped back, then, in sudden surprise, and bowed as Ysian and Nisana came in. *Lel'San's spindle,* Ylia thought savagely, *I forgot Ysian!* Golsat gazed after her, wide-eyed.

"You keep late hours. I've been asleep for ages."

"Fairly late," Ylia said and cast Nisana a brief, dark look. Ysian caught it and laughed.

"Don't blame her, I heard you too. You hauled me awake." She glanced from cat to niece, up at Golsat. "What's wrong?"

"Nothing, Ysian. Go back to bed. Sorry I woke you."

"Nothing? Of course, you *always* wake Nisana like that in the middle of the night, just to test her reflexes," Ysian replied dryly. "It's me, girl, I can tell. And your man here—you *might* introduce me—your man's got a grim face like I never saw."

"All right, it's nothing, to worry you," Ylia amended soothingly, and as her aunt opened her mouth to protest, added, "Golsat, may I present the Lady Ysian, my mother's sister. Ysian, this is Golsat, one of my companions from Koderra."

"Honored Lady," Golsat said correctly, and bowed gravely over her hand. Ysian raised her eyebrows, visibly surprised by his manners. She brought her face under control before he could catch her in such a breach of her own manners. "You've much of the Lady Scythia to you."

"You've a good eye," Ysian replied with a smile. "And I've heard a good deal of *you,*" she added. "Malaeth and Lisabetha were more forthcoming than you were, girl."

"I didn't want to distress you, Ysian," Ylia replied equably. Inwardly she was stewing: how to get her aunt back to the women's quarters, quickly. And where was Brelian? Ysian snorted in the most unladylike fashion.

"Don't worry about distressing me. That's very irritating, you know! I'm not blown glass, after all! I'm here to help you. You've obviously got some kind of problem, and you're trying to keep me out of it, aren't you?"

"I—all right, yes, I am," Ylia said flatly as Brelian came in. "Why? I can help!"

'She might indeed be able to help,' Nisana added.

"Nisana," Ylia began warningly.

"Another AEldra," Ysian said. "Keep that in mind. Also keep in mind that if I want to know what you're hiding, I can find out. You're Lisabetha's Brelian, aren't you?" She turned away and held out a hand, which Brelian self-consciously bowed over. "Another AEldra," Ysian went on, glancing from him to Golsat.

"I know you men have seen AEldra Power used. If I can help you, tell me how."

"Ysian, you're suborning my men," Ylia cut in tiredly.

"Well, then?"

"You'll regret you ever asked. Nisana, go ahead, *you* tell her." Ysian laid a hand against the cat's side and closed her eyes. "Brel, I'm sorry if we woke you."

"You didn't. I just got in from helping the herd-guard, and your lad found me throwing wager-sticks with Marhan." Ylia groaned. "What?"

"Marhan. Mothers, is he still there?"

"Well—there were about six of us, he probably is," Brelian replied warily. "Why?"

"Why?" Golsat grinned briefly. "Ylia's about to do something he won't like, and so she plans behind his back. Honored Lady?" he added in some concern, for Ysian had gone white to the lips. Nisana rubbed against her arm. Ysian blinked. Her eyes were all pupil. "Honored Lady, are you all right?"

"Oh, *I'm* fine," Ysian managed, "don't mind *me*. Set your plans."

"I warned you!" Ylia said flatly. "Golsat, if you'd escort the Lady to the door and get Variel to take her back to the women's quarters, I'd be grateful."

"No," Ysian said. She was pale and trembling, her eyes still wide, horrified black pools, but her mouth was set. "Find a use for me. This thing can't be allowed to be! Barbaric," she whispered under her breath. She drew in air, let it out slowly, and Ylia caught the backwash from Scythia's calming charm. "I'm all right, I swear it. Go *on!*"

"Brelian, we need you and two men you can trust."

"Trust—well." Berlian thought. "That's every man here. How, trust?"

"With your life," Golsat replied grimly, "with total secrecy, until the thing is done. And with innocent lives. We need someone who can accept AEldra Power. What say you," he added as Brelian pondered this, "to a raid on the Tehlatt?"

Brelian gazed at him, stunned. He bared his teeth in a mirthless grin. "Lead me to them. When? And—why?" Golsat told him why. "By the Black Well," he whispered finally. "Golsat—my poor Lisabetha! If—she can't know of this!"

"She doesn't, and she won't, until we return with them. On that we all agree," Golsat said. "Two men. Do you know two who'll serve?"

"Readily. Do you want them now?" The dark man nodded. "Wait, then. Pereden was on guard with me. He won't be asleep yet. Faric may be sleeping, but his blankets aren't far from mine."

"Good, go." Golsat turned back to the table. "Have you managed that map for us, Lady Ylia?"

"Ylia, Golsat," she reminded him absently. "This is private, remember?" She fished through the pile of lists at her elbow, finally found the tattered paper on the floor, wrong side up, one of Bnolon's now useless breeding-sheets for his sheep on its back. "Here. I'm not good at maps or drawing, but it shows everything."

"Good. We need nothing else." He drew it to him, took the seat across from Ysian and hunched over it. Silence. They could hear Variel's spear scraping the rock floor, down the hall. Ylia's nose twitched: whatever had been used to scent the new candles was cloying, and she was acutely aware that she needed hot water and a clean shirt. Golsat spoke only once while they waited for Brelian and his friends. "How accurate are your distances?"

"They're rough, but not off by much."

"Accurate to within half a league?" She nodded. "Good." He lapsed into silence again. Ylia glanced at Ysian: her aunt had herself under control but she was ghastly pale. Ysian wet her lips, attempted a smile.

"How many of them to a camp? Because if you're taking only four men, that's bad odds, isn't it?"

"We don't intend to fight them, Ysian. With luck, we won't even see any of them. Besides, if we tried to take our own back by force, the Tehlatt would fire that compound before we could free anyone." Ysian swallowed hard, closed her eyes. Nisana rubbed against her; Ysian caught her close.

Brelian had both men with him. They were both northern, both Erken's men, perhaps, though she wasn't certain. Too like so many others: young, tall and slender, their faces scruffy with boys' first beards. "Lady, these are Pereden," Brelian introduced them, "and Faric. I've known them since I was a boy, they'll aid us."

"Any aid you desire, Your Majesty," Pereden said formally as he went to one knee, "you need only ask." Faric knelt beside him.

"Rise, both," Ylia replied gravely, but she could feel the heat in her face. "And 'Lady' is sufficient, for present. We've a dangerous task ahead of us tonight, and I do need you. The Tehlatt have several of our people they've kept alive for burnt sacrifice two nights hence. They're outside Teshmor, in a compound. We go to rescue them."

Pereden glanced at his friend, at Brelian for confirmation, dubiously, but without animosity, at Golsat, who still sat hunched over his map. Curiously at Nisana, who gazed openly back at him, and briefly at Ysian. He laughed then in a sudden surge of joy, and clapped his hands together. "Mothers, I prayed for this! Tell us what we do, we'll do it!"

"Good. This is Golsat's venture, his plan. We'll follow him tonight, all of us." Golsat looked up as she spoke his name, held out a hand. There was no hesitation on the part of either man to clasp it. "His mother was Tehlatt. He knows their customs."

"Well," Golsat replied doubtfully, "a little. I hope enough. It's been long years since my mother spoke of her people." He tapped the map. "If the Honored Lady Ysian meant what she said," he added formally, inclining his head as he gazed across the table. Ysian nodded firmly. Golsat transferred the look to Ylia, who set aside heavy misgivings, shrugged. "Good. Honored Lady, if I may—"

"It's Ysian, to my friends," she said with a faint smile. *That* cost her, Ylia knew, but she warmed to her aunt for the effort.

"Ysian," Golsat said gravely. His face seemed darker than usual. "If I may? You're Ylsan. AEldra." Ysian nodded both times. "And so you've talents like Ylia's, or Nisana's?" She nodded again. "And—like them," Golsat went on, a glance including Brelian's friends, "there are certain things you can and cannot do with this Power?"

"Just so."

"Good. I know," Golsat went on, another glance at Pereden and Faric, "that Nisana can bridge—that is," he qualified for the two newcomers, "she can move from one place to another in less time than it takes to breathe. But Ylia cannot."

'Won't.'

'Silence, cat!'

'Hah.'

"Can *you* bridge?" Golsat finished.

Ysian nodded. "I don't much; it isn't called for. But—I can."

"Good. And—your pardon, but how strong is what you have?"

"Mmmm. Good question." Ysian considered. "Strong. I'm

Second House. But I don't really know. As compared to Ylia or
Nisana? Ylia?"

"As strong as my mother's was, Golsat," Ylia said finally.
Ysian *was* strong, that wasn't hard to tell. As to how much
sustained strength she had—well, that might be another thing
entirely, and they'd only find that out the hard way. "If you're still
thinking of the same notion, I'd say she's strong enough. The
three of us are."

"So. Good. You bridge us all to a place near the camp. Then
you and I go in, afoot. If anyone is about at that hour, they'll think
me a warrior from another camp, you another prisoner. We'll deal
with the compound guard, and I'll take his place while you go
inside and—black hell, I forgot," he slammed a fist into the table.
"You can't bridge."

"No. And we can't take Ysian into that camp," Ylia said. "She
couldn't handle that."

"I wouldn't suggest it," Golsat said.

"It's not necessary, anyway," Ysian said. "If Ylia's—if she
goes in, she and I can join, we can bridge them out. You did it
before, Ylia, when you and the Bowmaster used Nisana's strength
to bridge away from your companions, to help the old Chosen.
Both your strengths, her use of the bridging." She dredged up a
faint smile. "Nisana and I can remain well outside the camp, you
can be *inside* the compound and bridge your people to safety."
She looked across the table. "Will that work into your plan?"

Golsat nodded. "I've both the bridging, and the strength for it,
particularly if Nisana backs and if we're fairly close. A league or
less."

"We'll get you that close," Golsat assured her. "But there'll be
no danger to you." Ysian waved that away. "Give me another
minute." He retreated into his map again, ran a square finger back
and forth across it.

"Thank you, Ysian," Ylia said in the ensuing silence.

Ysian shook her head. "Thank me when I've earned it. I hope I
will. I intend to," she finished grimly.

"I'd rather prefer it, though, if you'd stay in the foothills,
instead of coming down onto the Plain."

"No. A thing like this is tricky, and even though I've never
done it before, I know the theory of it. There's a knack to bridging
this way. Touch, of course: you have to physically touch those you
move. But the rest is proximity. The nearer I am to you, the more
people we can move at a time, the faster we get you out of there."

She paused. "I don't want to bridge the last of your people out and find there isn't enough left in me to bring you and your man back."

"I just don't like it. I'll worry about you."

"You'd better not," Ysian said tartly. "I can bridge myself away, if I have to, and don't doubt I will!"

'Your words to Marhan, not long ago, as I recall,' Nisana put in.

"Cat, you're *not* helping. But it's no good, is it?" she demanded of both of them. "You're in league against me. I'd never win!"

"No," Ysian said quietly. "But we're not against you. We're trying to *help* you. Fair enough?"

"I—oh, all right," she capitulated with a little sigh. "Fair enough." It wasn't, really. And if her mother's sister came so far to die—Golsat's voice brought her back to the moment.

"All right." He stood, pushed the map to the center of the table, lit another candle. "We strike just before first light, when the camp will be quietest. Now that's not too many hours off," he added. "So we must reach the Plain as soon as possible. This hill just to the north of that camp. Brelian, you should remember it, it's got a spring near the top and water runs down deep clefts. There are a dozen places to hide, gullies and thickets of aspen near the bottom."

Brelian nodded. "One of the safest places to hide thereabouts, though I daresay the Tehlatt took it for the good water."

"I know it, too," Faric said. "But if you think to reach it still *tonight*, you'll need wings!"

"And we'll have them. In a way," Golsat said. "As you'll see. Now. We bridge from the hills to Teshmor's shadow. From there to one of the gullies on that hill."

"Bridge. You keep talking about bridging. What *is* it?" Faric asked.

"Magic," Golsat replied. "Lady Ylia can explain it to you. But don't think of it as magic, consider it another weapon—"

"I don't care," Pereden cut in. "We both don't," he added, and Faric nodded warily. "Just give us a cut at the Tehlatt, that's all!"

"Good. Though I hope, for the sake of all of us, that no one gets a cut at them. This is a raid, a very secret one. Got that?" Nods all around. "All right. We reach that hill. The moon's near full, but clouds are coming from the south, so it should be obscured. It won't matter much. We'll just need extra caution if it's bright. Brel, you, Faric and Pereden will come as far as the edge of the horse-pickets—here." He pointed. "And wait, in case anything goes wrong. Ylia and I will go alone from there. The guard will be drowsy and bored, and we may not be seen at all if we're careful. If we are—well, my mother gave me her looks for good cause after all. They'll believe I'm from another camp, and that Ylia's a prisoner for the fires. I can distract the compound guard while our folk are being bridged out of there." He looked at each of them in turn. "Or, if it's necessary, kill him." Silence. "If there's a flaw any of you can see, anything I haven't considered, tell me now, so we can correct it."

"Clothing," Brelian said immediately. "Your face is fine, but the rest of you is very much Nedao."

Golsat shrugged. "Most of the warriors in that camp will be wearing at least Nedaoan armor. It's taking the bravery of your enemy to yourself, to wear the things of the man you killed."

'Nisana,' Ylia sent to her urgently, 'you can *screen* us, you once said you could, outside Koderra!'

'That was different, the Tehlatt were half a league away. So close to so many of them, it would never work. And even the simplest of shamen could sense us.' Ylia shrugged. 'Sorry, girl.'

'A thought, that's all. We'll do without. Golsat's plan is good.' She met the cat's eyes, her thought carefully shuttered. Ysian was intent upon the map and missed the look. Nisana closed her eyes briefly, non-thought received. Ysian would be well guarded and pulled from the spot instantly if there was any trouble.

"Why do you have to go through the camp?" Faric wanted to know. "I mean, if this bridging can take you anywhere, why not just in with the prisoners and back out again?"

"Because someone might cry out," Ylia said. "Or one of their shamen might feel it. We'll have part of that hill between us and the camp. That and distance will shield us. There may be no one there who could sense us, but we don't dare chance that."

There was a silence. Golsat slapped the map. "Then we'll do it?"

"Aye." Brelian dropped his own hand to cover Golsat's, the other two men covered his, and Ylia and Ysian laid theirs on top. Pereden smothered a grin as Nisana gravely placed a paw over all.

"Good. I need my hair done warrior-style, that I can't forego. Brelian, can you plait?"

"I? No!"

"Don't look at me," Ylia said quickly. "I've no talent beyond a 3-part braid, and even those are indifferent."

"Fancy plaiting? I can," Ysian said.

"Good. My hair's too short for a proper job, but the hood of a Nedaoan cloak will hide that. I can describe what I need, if you think you can work from that."

"I've a better idea. Ylia, *show* me how they do it."

"All right. Golsat, what do you want, plain horseman?"

"I think so. Unwed horseman, but with previous battles and several kills. Someone with sufficient war-strength to be trusted with a prisoner, someone still unimportant enough to be saddled with a female one, late at night when senior warriors sleep."

"Well," she began doubtfully; but she remembered the previous fall, Kanatan's retinue, his messengers, Marhan pointing out the arm colorings, tattoos, what the various elaborate hair plaiting signified. Warrior, plain horse: she thought so.

"I see." From the look in her eyes, Ysian didn't care much for what she saw, but she was trying to take things in stride. She expelled a long breath in one fast gust, and was suddenly briskly efficient. "I can manage that. We'll need things. Can any of you supply me with some feathers, dark ones? We could coat them in soot, I suppose, if not. But long." She measured with her hands.

Faric nodded. "I'll go down to the kitchens, there was a bird and onion mess for dinner two nights ago. There might still be feathers, I'll see what I can find."

"Good. And a bit of pale leather or fur. I don't suppose," she added dubiously, "there'd be ribbon anywhere. I never wear such things, so I brought none with me."

"I don't know who has any except 'Betha."

"Well, then, nevermind. The hood will hide that, too. And the dark." She moved over behind Golsat, who'd resumed his seat, and deftly separated a section of his hair. "Ylia, that tabard of yours is dark and it's already frayed, work me loose half a dozen threads to tie these."

Golsat fixed his eyes on the map. He was extremely ill at ease and could only hope no one noticed. This Lady, he thought—she was too fine by half to handle his hair as though they were equals. Not as though she were arms-mate, like Ylia: He'd taken practice with *her* almost from his first day in Koderra, had long since adjusted to the fact that, though she was then Princess Royal, now Queen, she was also his companion and his friend. It hadn't ever been difficult to name-speak Ylia. The Honored Lady Ysian, with her fair face, she was different. He reminded himself she was AEldra and that the AEldra Power would play as much part in their venture as sword-skill. More, please all the gods at once, if it went right. Reminded himself also that she'd asked it, name-speaking, and as if she'd meant it.

Difficult. He felt, as he often did, very much out of place, and he wondered if his father knew what company his black-haired son kept.

He closed his eyes, sat still, jerking only once as Ysian's fingers caught a snarl. She worked it loose gently and swiftly, worked the 4-strand plait, wrapped the end with a twisted doubled thread. She next gathered the hair that normally fell from a center parting, ran it down beside his face. Her nose wrinkled as she worked two of the long feathers into its end: they reeked of damp ash and other things not as pleasant as that. A third braid, behind his left ear then.

"You've wonderful hair," Ysian remarked. Brelian turned away to hide a grin. Golsat opened his mouth twice but no sound came. Ysian finished off the plait, instructed Pereden to cut an opening in the ragged bit of black worn leather he'd produced, pulled the remaining loose hair through it, twisted and wound it down into a knot which she fastened with a wide splinter Brelian worked from the edge of the table. The leather lay across his right ear, more feathers worked over that. Ylia produced a worn bit of edging from the neck of her tabard; Ysian bound that into the fore plait and stood back to admire the result.

"Mothers," Pereden breathed. Golsat was scarcely recognizable.

"Right enough," Brelian said. "You *look* Tehlatt; I never realized before how Nedaoan you really are."

"It's a shock," Faric agreed.

"Well, then, I'd better make certain no one sees me like this before we reach that camp, hadn't I?" Golsat stood. "My hood will cover my head when we leave the Caves, fortunately." He turned to Ysian, who still stood close behind him. "Thanks, L— Ysian."

"My pleasure." She inclined her head gravely. If she'd guessed at or sensed his discomfort, she gave no indication. "If we're to go soon, Ylia, I'd better return to my bedding. I took off my warm stockings tonight, and I want my dark cloak. Is what I wear acceptable, or should I change—or is there time?"

"There's time, get your stockings, and if you have heavier

boots, put them on. The ground is rocky where we go. Your slippers would be cut to bits." Ylia eyed her critically. "Otherwise, you'll be all right."

"You mean," Ysian said shrewdly, "you won't let me where anyone might see me. That's fair enough. I won't be long. Come on, cat."

Ylia turned to the armsmen. "Get arrows. All you can but don't rouse attention, and by the Black Well, stay clear of my Swordmaster! If he finds out—!"

"I know. He won't. I'll go with them," Brelian said. "What else?"

"Spare knives," Golsat said. "If you can find them without asking. No one else must know what we're doing until it's done. And if we fail, *no* one must know. *Ever.*" He paused. "A last thing. Pray that we come in good time, and that our luck not fail us!"

12

The wind was chill, salt; it cut through her heavy winter cloak. Her fingers were tucked into fur pockets, but they were numb, her cheeks burned. She gazed with weary distaste across the pale green marshes, over a long, flat expanse of sand to a roiling grey sea. There was a tang of sea in the air; an undercurrent of the sour odor of marsh; now and again, when the wind died for a brief moment, the unpleasant smell of burned wood and things long dead slipped up from behind her.

She turned away from the dreary southern view. The northern one wasn't much better. A shamble of wall there, in its midst a single gate hung still by one twisted hinge. Beyond that, disaster: the Baron who'd had these holdings had not gotten his goods free in time, nor most of his folk. Paper, burned hangings, a rubble of furnishings littered the courtyard. The men she'd brought with her were out behind the walls, somewhere, digging an enormous pit for the rest.

For this—for this I gave up my father's wealth, the man he wished me to marry, the splendor of Court, the music, the beauty of Yls—? For the first time in long years, her resolve faltered. *I'm tired, that's all,* she told herself. *Tired. I couldn't have stayed in Yls. Never. Not without him. Whatever it cost me.*

And it had cost her: She had the clothes she stood in, a second pair of stockings. Her household women, Lyiadd's armsmen. Lyiadd would want all his armsmen, when he was better. Her hair was uncombed, there were lines around her eyes and mouth. Her hands trembled; she did.

Lyiadd. He caught at her every breath. He'd hovered at the brink of death for so long, every heartbeat so fragile it might have been his last. She'd brought him back from that edge, the first thing she'd done once she'd harnessed the Power sufficiently to use it at all. He breathed more easily now.

But when he looked at her his eyes were a child's; they held no knowledge of himself, and none of her. And his inner sense might never have been.

She'd bring him back, she could—if she could tame this new Power, bring it under control, learn to *use* it! In the meantime, the Foessa were no longer safe; *she* had reached the Caves, doubtless her first act was to warn Yls. And Yls would act—what, such a chance for her father?—they'd act at once, and even if she could save herself, she might lose everything else.

And Lyiadd—what he wanted had to remain paramount: He'd fought for it for too long, he'd nearly died for it. They must not find him!

She'd cast about for a likely safety, finally settled on this southernmost tip of the Plain. The Tehlatt had withdrawn from the sea and the mouth of the Torth alike, but that didn't matter because they'd never approach *her*. She'd bridged a handful of her people first, brought the rest two days later. Returned the valley to the state they'd found it, though *that* cost her; she retained barely sufficient wit and skill to bridge herself back to this temporary safety.

This wasn't the best of all possible safeties, no. It was better than most. And from here, she could signal those who would shelter her and hers properly. What better sanctuary than the Great Isles, for who would dare approach those barren rocks save the Sea-Raiders who held them?

And it would give her a great deal of pleasure, negotiating the bargain with them, watching their faces as they smirked at her, woman and alone—knowing that in the end, it would be they who took her orders and later Lyiadd's. They who cringed from her, if she wanted that.

She tilted her head back. Above the reek of the outer courtyard, there was a whiff of woodsmoke. It would be warm up there. She pulled the cloak closer, started across blackened cobbles.

*I have said it before, often enough, and I
myself merely quote others of reasonable wit,
who hold that need brings out quality in some
people, and a realization of that quality by
others who perhaps had seen no good in that
person before. So Brendan and the xenophobic
Bowmaster Levren had learned of Golsat on our
journey north. So, in fact, I learned myself, for
even I could not have known the inner strength
the man had, or the coolness of his wits in evil
placing, until need brought it out in him. But I
learned; Levren did. Young Brendan. And so,
even the folk of Nedao. And, my beloved Ysian.*

13

Six people and a cat huddled in a deep, crumpling cut at the
base of a bald hill. There was a trickle of water at its center,
though fortunately there was also room on each side of that for
folk to stand dry. There was rock, too, and Ysian was grateful for
Ylia's foresight: even her boots weren't thick-soled enough, she'd
have bruises to show for the night's work.

She shivered. The wind was fierce and blew down from the
north, sighed through willow brush and setting the aspen grove
around them to a continuous whispery clatter. Nisana pressed
against her, concerned; she stooped to rub the dark fur, sent back
reassurance. The cat relaxed, moved back to Ylia's side.

Ysian slid one foot before the other, cautiously, crouched down
behind her niece. "All right." Ylia's voice would not have carried
five paces, even on a still night. The armsmen leaned close, heads
nearly touching, so they could hear her. "Ysian, you and Nisana
stay right here. You'll be safe, you can see anyone coming long
before they see you. If there's trouble"—she eyed them in turn—

"swear you'll bridge." And, as Ysian hesitated: "We cannot concentrate properly on what we do out there otherwise, Ysian. That could be very dangerous. Swear."

"By the Guardians and the One," Ysian whispered. "But remember I came to aid you!" Her voice shook; all of her did. *How can she? She's still a child, and she's going into that camp as though it were a garden walk!* It hadn't felt real in the Caves, whatever she'd *seen*, how could it? It was; and it threatened to make her ill. Golsat touched her arm, smiled at her; she managed a faint smile in reply, and somehow felt a little better.

"Good." Ylia slipped the dagger from its arm-sheath, slid it up her sleeve where she could reach it in need. Another made an uncomfortable lump against her ankle, down her boot. Golsat tapped Brelian's arm, pointed toward the dimly lit camp. "Brel, the horse line's just there—no, this side of the fire. See it?" He nodded. "Get back under the trees, well in shadow and don't move unless it's absolutely necessary. The guards won't be looking for trouble, but they've good eyes. Remember that!" Golsat cast an expert eye overhead. "The cloud cover will hold. We've that in our favor. For the rest—the Mothers aid us!" He kissed his fingers in blessing, the others followed suit: Only Ylia caught the superstitious warding sign he made after. "Well." He let his air out with a quiet sigh, held out a hand. "Ylia, if you're ready?"

"As I'll get." There was the least of tremors in her voice; only Golsat heard it, but when he looked at her she nodded. She extended her arms, let him bind her wrists with thick rope. He caught up the loose end in one hand, drew his sword.

"Let's go. Take care, all of you. Lady." They were all gone. Ysian wrapped her arms around herself, hard, to stop the shaking. Nisana stared after them.

'It's well, they'll come through. Courage, Ysian!'

"Courage," she whispered.

The two reached the horse lines in silence. Golsat stopped, pulled Ylia close to his side and gave her a reassuring hug as Brelian and his two companions slipped out of sight among the trees. Golsat nodded. Ylia swallowed, rubbed her damp, bound hands against her breeches and stepped into the open. Into the Tehlatt camp.

It was gloomy here; there were few fires and all but one had burned to coals. There were no fires near the prison compound, only an occasional torch shoved into soft turf a length from the fence. They skirted a pile of weapons, moved in total silence around the end of one of the warrior tents. Faint snores drifted through the open flap; the stench of male sweat wrinkled her nose. Golsat grinned mirthlessly and pulled her on.

Five paces to that woven fence; three—two. Golsat gripped her arm in warning. A muffled clink of ring mail, a grunt as someone tripped and caught himself before he fell. The guard came into sight, saw them, sauntered toward them. He was half asleep, probably half-witted from the look of him.

"What man are you, and why here with this woman?" His voice was low. Ylia understood sufficient Tehlatt for that, but lost much of Golsat's swift reply, save "prisoner," and perhaps, "orders." The guard lost what little interest he'd had in the matter and was yawning as he pointed. "There." She understood nothing of his next remark, until he asked, "Do you remain here?"

"No. We come north, all, for the celebration," Golsat replied. The guard nodded, yawned and moved on.

"Good." Golsat breathed against her ear. "Trusting fellow; he believed us. And he told me there's another guard at the gate itself, we're forewarned."

Ylia nodded. The encounter had unnerved her badly and she was trying to keep that from her companion. The inner sense was badly disoriented, despite Nisana's reassuring touch, and she couldn't place any individual Tehlatt for the overwhelming sense of so many, all around her. *I could die here. Now. Tonight.* The fence seemed to go on forever, though she knew it couldn't be more then ten lengths, less than that across. A torch, a second, nearly gutted. A third, and just beyond it, the indented section that served to protect the guard from north and south wind. The gate was in the back of that black alcove. The gate. And its guard.

Golsat's fingers dug briefly into her arm: warning. She lowered her eyes, let her shoulders sag. The gate-guard came into the light, twigs falling from his fingers: he'd been weaving them into small shapes, the ground all about the alcove was littered with them. He scowled at Golsat, sharp eyes taking in the man from hair to Nedaoan boots before moving to his prisoner. Golsat's fingers twitched involuntarily; he released her then, pulled at the rope and she staggered forward.

Again that harsh question and Golsat's rapid answer. The guard slung the remaining twigs aside, grabbed the rope and yanked. She nearly fell into him, and the sudden reek of oiled leathers, heavily scented hair oil, the stale musk of his body was overwhelming. The guard snatched her plaits, yanked hard. She gasped as her head snapped back, hard, stared glassily into suspicious eyes. The guard searched her face for what seemed forever, turned to bark another question at Golsat. Golsat began an answer; the guard waved an impatient hand, said something that brought Golsat up sharply.

His face was still so near hers, they nearly touched. She felt slowly, so slowly for the hilt of her dagger, let it slide down into her hand, shifted her grip to a two-handed one, the blade between them. The guard's attention came back to her abruptly as she dropped; too late: her knife rebounded from the stiffened leather breastplate, went in just below his ribs. She pushed up, threw her weight into it; Golsat's arm was around his throat, hand across his mouth, but the guard fell with the least of sounds. Ylia went down with him.

Golsat dragged the dead man back into the shadows. Ylia rolled out of the faint light, worked at the ropes with trembling hands. Her sleeves were wet to the elbow, she didn't dare think with what. The rope wasn't responding to her tugging, Golsat finally had to cut it for her. He held out the dagger; she wiped it on the grass, pushed it hard into the arm-sheath.

Golsat caught at her arm. "You all right?" he breathed against her ear.

She nodded. "Him or me. I remember." He studied her briefly: She was upset, but she wasn't giving in to it, as she had at the Hunter's Crossing, the first time she'd killed. She'd be all right. He nodded, pulled her back farther into the alcove, pulled the gate open and pushed it shut behind her.

It was black as a pit inside: the moon was not even the blur of white against cloud cover it had been earlier. No light from without penetrated the fence. 'Nisana?'

'What chanced? What went wrong? Are you all right?'

'The guard was suspicious, he's dead. It's all right, I'm inside. Are you ready?'

'Both ready.' That was Ysian. Her thought was still erratic but her determination was strong, and the bond between the three of them reassuringly steady. Ylia brought up the second level of sight, used that curious blend of AEldra-enhanced night vision to find the prisoners.

Most slept, stretched out on the hard, damp ground or in huddles of two or three. There was no shelter from the weather, the cold. But someone was keeping watch: *Corlin—Lord Corry himself*. She breathed a sigh of relief. Their luck held.

Corlin started, peered anxiously at her as she knelt beside him. Someone nearby stirred; he put out a reassuring hand, murmured something Ylia could not hear. She did hear the startled gasp as she leaned close so he could see her face.

"Lady Ylia—Princess. Gods, you're—how did you—?"

"I'm not a prisoner, it's all right, we're getting you all out of here," she whispered against his ear. His fingers caught hers in a painful grip as the words and the sense of them penetrated.

"We'll—we'll not burn—!"

"Shhh. There's no time to talk now. We must work quickly to save you all. Day comes soon." It was hard to recognize Corlin, Lord of Teshmor, in this fragile, thin, terrified and ragged creature. The Tehlatt had nearly destroyed him before they killed him.

But only nearly. He drew a deep breath, let it out slowly, and the trembling in his hand eased; his grip on her fingers let up. He nodded. "What must we do? Have you secured the camp?"

"No. We came by stealth, we're using AEldra Power to bridge you from here. It's fast, but it may frighten some of these people. You'll find yourselves in the hills yonder," she gestured, "with my mother's sister Ysian. Keep everyone quiet, don't let anyone panic. Stay close together and close to Ysian. That's all."

"We'll do that." He bent down to whisper to the cloak-covered bundle nearest him. His Lady, Lossana, sat up, blinked. She'd gone gaunt and old, even more fragile than Corlin, but she'd still an inner core of strength.

Ylia glanced over her shoulder. Silence in the camp, silence within the compound. "Corlin, you go with the first of them. Take my hand, touch anyone you can reach. Lady Lossana, I need you here. It won't be long."

"Hurry," was all she whispered in reply.

"We will." 'Nisana, now!' The sudden, sharp drain on her strength left her momentarily blind, as the second level of sight was wrenched from her. Corlin and four others were gone. Lossana stared blankly at the place they'd been. Beyond her, someone moaned and rolled over, sat up in sudden fear. "Keep them quiet!" Ylia hissed. Lossana scrambled on hands and knees across the bare ground as Ylia drew a deep breath and reached again.

It took time—it took too much time, she could feel it slipping away, feel her blood pulsing hard through her hands and the edge of a terrible headache. They had to rest after the first four, between each thereafter, and after the first could bridge only two at a time. Even so it was exhausting almost beyond bearing. Ysian was worn thin, her breath coming in little gasps. And then there was no one in the compound but Ylia.

She staggered to her feet, nearly fell. Black dark, and she was too worn to force the second level of sight. *Crawl, if you can't walk, go.* 'Cat, keep it quiet out there!'

'Lord Corry's managing them. Don't worry about us.'

'I'm fine, too,' Ysian said. She clearly wasn't. She was strung right to the breaking point. 'Get out of there!'

'I'm on my way. We'll be a few minutes getting back to Brelian, don't worry. If I need you, I'll yell.'

'Go!' Nisana snapped. She went, blindly, groping along the wall. She caught splinters and a thorn, swore under her breath, worried them free with her teeth as she went on. *Mothers, was it this far when I came in?* But the exhaustion was beginning to wear off; another few minutes, she'd be all right. *Good. I might need the Power, crossing the open again.* She shivered.

The gate loomed before her, suddenly; she caught at the edge of it, tugged. No response. Silence. A pause—long enough that her heart lurched. And then it swung in and Golsat caught her hands. "Done?" She nodded. "Ready to go?" Another nod. "I'm going to move him inside, out of sight. If he's found before we get away, there'll be trouble."

"Golsat, don't bother. Lets just go," she whispered, but he already had the man by the wrists and was dragging him farther into shadow. She edged out to keep watch, brought her breathing back to normal. A fire burned low a few paces away, the nearest torch flared in a gust of wind. The gate creaked faintly; the sound brought her around, heart in her mouth. Golsat suddenly froze, his face went still with shock.

She whirled back, sword in hand. The other guard blinked at them stupidly. "I heard odd noises inside there—," he began, and broke off in astonishment as he saw the prisoner free and armed where his fellow should be, the stranger from the southern camp behind her, his blade reflecting red firelight. The guard snatched his short blades out, leaped for Ylia with a bone-chilling cry. She pivoted, and brought her sword around on a flat slashing plane. The barbarian's cry towered into a shriek and he fell, clutching his belly and wailing in agony.

The night air was rent: shouts echoed across the camp.

"Golsat!" But she couldn't reach him. Already there were two men between them, forcing them apart. More ran from the warrior tents, half-clad, half awake. "Get to me!" she cried out.

"Can't, I'm trying!" he shouted back, and then swore viciously. "Get back!" he bellowed. "Get *back,* damn thee all for fools!"

"Ah, gods, *no!*" Three figures were sprinting through the open camp, dodging firepits, weapons, tent-ropes and poles, running at dead tilt straight for them. Brelian, Pereden and Faric pushed through a confused clutch of old men, gained the minimal safety of the woven fence.

"Gods of the Black Well," she swore, "is that how you obey orders? We had a chance!"

"Could we just stay out there and watch you die?" Brelian yelled back furiously.

"Get closer to me!" She lunged, drove back one of those fronting her, cut another. She didn't dare look anywhere else. "Get close. If we can all touch, we can get out of here alive. Nisana, watch your chance and get us *out* of here!"

'Ylia—!'

'Ysian, don't argue with me, you'll be my death!' She was briefly aware of fierce argument between Ysian and Nisana before she severed the distracting joining.

Golsat managed to work his way back to her side and set himself at her shoulder. But Brelian and his friends were two full lengths or more away; it might as well have been twenty.

"Take them!" Someone shouted that; a wild cheer answered. The Tehlatt pressed forward.

"Nedao!" Brelian cried out, ripped the torch from the ground, and thrust it into the dry branch and bracken behind him. Flame leaped skyward and a hideous wall of heat assaulted them. One of those Ylia fought threw an arm across his eyes and died so; Brelian killed another, and he and Golsat turned to force their way through the Tehlatt separating them. "Golsat!" Ylia's back was against his, her dagger hand caught in his cloak; she had to shout above the roar of the fire.

"Got them!" he yelled back and she pivoted around him. "Grab my arm, Faric, do it now, come on! Nisana, get us out of here!" Her hands caught other hands, someone's fingers dug painfully into her bicep; the Power surged around them and tore them from the camp.

• • •

It was achingly cold after the sudden heat of the fire. Brelian picked himself up, felt his arms cautiously. Pereden was half under him, mumbling to himself and wincing as he stood. Ysian caught at Ylia's shoulder. "There's only three of you. Ylia?"

Pereden gazed around, caught his head between his hands. "Where's Faric?"

"Brel," Ylia hissed against his ear. "Brelian, did you see Golsat? I had him, I swear I did!"

Brelian coughed, shook his head. "I saw him just as you caught my shoulder," he said. "He twisted offside to avoid a sword, I tried to say but too late. Faric—he fell, I don't know if he was dead or not."

"Oh, *Gods.*" Ysian drew a ragged breath; Brelian was at her side, a hand clapped over her mouth before she could cry out. She was trembling all over when he let her down; Nisana leaped to her side. 'Ysian! Control yourself, Ysian, *listen to me!*'

"Take care of her, keep her quiet." 'Ylia, wait—' Nisana barely glanced at her; Ysian needed all her attention.

'There's no time, they'll kill him.' *Golsat—my friend, my armsmate, they'll play him for the pleasure of it, then burn him alive when they tire of the game. Unless I can reach him.* Nausea twisted her stomach as she tried to bridge, went light-headed and nearly blind as it refused her and she tore at the Power, dredging up nearly all she had. *I can't* grappled with *I must;* she closed her eyes. *Golsat.* Despair, pity and terror were balanced, all at once, and in that sudden calm she found the focus and bridged.

Intense, searing heat beat down on her back. She staggered to her feet, took the three steps that brought her to Golsat's side.

He cast her a brief, startled glance, all he dared. Two fell to their assault. A third. The Tehlatt withdrew.

"You were supposed to stay with me," Ylia said breathlessly.

"I tried," Golsat replied. His eyes, like hers, remained fixed on those before them. "A sword came between us. My apologies. You should not have returned. It's not safe."

"I'm not leaving without you, you and Faric."

"I think Faric is dead."

'Nisana? What are you doing? Get us out of here!'

'I can't, not by myself. Ysian was hysterical. I had to send her sleep. I barely had strength enough to do *that*. I'm sorry, you'll have to hold them off. A little. Can you?'

'We'd better be able to, hadn't we?' "Golsat, I'm sorry, it went all wrong."

"Not your fault. Can we get out of here?"

"Not yet. I used all the Power in me just now. Nisana's weak. We'll have to wait."

"All right." He eyed those who stood just out of reach, cast a swift glance at the burning fence. The wind had shifted, was blowing the flames away from them. Sparks touched one of the tents; the flap smoldered and the flame licked at it. Someone shouted; a few of the warriors scrambled to deal with this new danger. "We can do that, can't we?"

Silence. She was almost shivering, reaction as much as anything. "What are they *doing?* Why don't they attack?"

"Why should they?" Golsat shrugged. "They have us pinned here, they need only wait. We dare not go after them, and sooner or later, the wind will shift and the fire will drive us into the open. Stay alert." His gaze shifted. "Ylia, 'ware!"

She sensed what he saw, stealthy movement on her left. She pivoted, brought up her sword. It caught one of them a glancing blow. Nedaoan armor foiled that and it threw her off balance, worn as she was. A spear-end glance off her shoulder, slammed across her back and she fell, stunned.

The world around her dimmed, briefly. She was vaguely aware of a clash of blades over her head. Hands caught at her wrists, tried to drag her away. *No!* She twisted, tried to free herself. No good.

Power surged over her, blazed red against her eyelids. The Tehlatt shouted something and ran; she rolled to her hands and knees, blinked. The ground tilted ominously. AEldra Power washed through her, carrying strength with it. Golsat caught at her shoulders, pulled her up and steadied her until she could stand alone. He pressed the sword back in her hand, closed her fingers around it.

She rubbed sweat from her eyes. Who—? A small dark shape pressed against her leg. 'Nisana? You shouldn't be here!'

'Nor should you! It's a little late to worry about that, isn't it?' The cat leaped into Golsat's arms, clambered nimbly to his shoulder and balanced against his ear. The Tehlatt whispered nervously, took a collective step back. Nisana gazed cooly over them, let the Power form silvered rainbows around her ears. Dead silence as she stepped lightly onto Ylia's shoulder.

Someone spoke, then, far back in the crowd, and the warriors parted. The man's clothing and mail was Nedaoan, but the red on his eyelids and hands, the plaiting-pattern of his hair, marked him as chief. He was short, stocky. A thin moustache trailed down past his chin to mingle with a sparse beard.

Ylia tensed. "I know him, I *know* him—!"

"Kaltassa," Golsat said grimly. "Kanatan's son and heir. Here for the ceremony, of course. I'd wager Kanatan's expected, but his tent's not here."

"We would bargain with you!" Ylia shouted. "I know you speak my language, Kaltassa!" The Tehlatt stirred. How did this witch know his name? And from where had the familiar come?

"We do not bargain," Kaltassa said flatly.

'Faric's alive,' Nisana put in suddenly. 'I sense him.'

'Gods of the Black Well.' "We took your prisoners, Kaltassa! There will be no sacrifice of Nedaoans!"

"There will be no bargain! You owe me blood for the deaths of my warriors!"

Ylia laughed. "I am owed more blood than you! And I will have it this night!" At her side, Golsat made a protesting movement, stilled it. He knew her; knew her mood. Knew, too, what she sought: the moment had filled her, caught her up and there would be no turning back from it. "I am Ylia, King Brandt's daughter, come to take kin-price and blood for *my* deaths!" She set her sword upright before her.

There was a babble of speech: The Tehlatt gesturing now to her, now to Kaltassa. *Tanea-a-Les. The Witch Warrior.* The Tehlatt embassy had called her that, the year before. It heated her blood, urged her past common sense and caution both. "Golsat?"

"Ylia?"

"Nisana could bridge you back to the others. But I need you here."

"You wouldn't shame me by offering me a choice, would you?" he demanded sharply. "At your back or your side, whichever you need, and you know it!"

She nodded. Her color was high. "I know it. I had to ask. Nisana—"

'Don't think it. Think about what you're doing.'

"I am. I have."

*The Power is an aid, often a trial and an
exhausting burden, on occasion the means of
saving a life and on other occasion the means of
destroying one. It gives no more clue to the
workings of one's mind than the lack of it does.
And there are often unsuspected layers to it,
depths even its wielder does not suspect to exist:
Such depths I found in myself that night, as did
my poor unfortunate Ysian. Ylia: Who can say?
But in one or two things, she was older than I.*

14

The Tehlatt subsided, watched them in silence as Kaltassa
spoke to one of his warriors. The compound still burned, but less
furiously now, and in the distance they could hear shouts as some
of the barbarians fought to keep the flames contained, the shrill
cry of a terrified horse.

'Now what?' Nisana demanded. 'You plot something, anyone
can see that! Are you bothering to tell us?' Ylia cast her one dark
glance. The cat stared at her through narrowed eyes. 'Be that way.
But you came back for Golsat and the boy. Golsat's here, bridge
him.'

'No. We can do that whenever we must, but I need him. If this
works, we'll leave together, all of us. But—black hells, I wish we
could—it really is impossible to bridge a non-AEldra without
actual touch, is it?'

'*You* know that,' Nisana retorted. 'Why else would we have let
you risk your life in there? And when you and Lev bridged to the
Chosen, didn't you keep hold of him?'

'I didn't know, how should I, you never told me! I held Lev to
reassure him he'd survive it. The matter never came up!'

'Well, now you know,' the cat replied shortly.

'Look, it doesn't matter, we have to get Faric out of here, and that means my plan, or your reach or mine. All right?'

'Don't get angry, it clouds your thinking. You'll have a better chance of reaching him. They won't come near *me*,' the cat replied shrewdly. And then, very seriously indeed, 'It may come to choice, Nedao's Queen or a young armsman. You know that, don't you?'

Ylia nodded grimly. 'I know it. But I have to know I tried. One last attempt. And then—could you kill him? Could I?'

'The Nasath aid me.' Nisana's eyes went black, the hair between her shoulder blades stood. She forced it flat. 'I—if I must.'

'I can't force it upon you, cat. But if it's all we can offer the boy, a clean and swift death, against what he faces from them—I'll do it and hope another does the same for me, in my need. Think of Faric!' she implored. Aloud, she shouted: "Listen to me!" The murmur of speech faded. "I have said I will bargain with you! Give the Tanea-a-Les her other armsman, and we will do no further harm in this place!"

Kaltassa stared at her, long enough for her to wonder just how good his grasp of Plains-speech might be. He turned his back on her again. He spoke with two old men, argued fiercely with a younger one who sought to restrain him, then took a step toward her. The light of the fire from the blazing compound shone red in his eyes, glinted off the Nedaoan mail shirt thrown unlaced across his breast. "A bargain," he repeated. The vowels were flattened, his accent hard to understand. "You want back this man?"

"I want him."

"You will fight for him?"

Ylia gaped at him in stunned silence. A disapproving rumble of speech behind the chief was silenced as he shouted an order. So. She pulled her mouth shut with an effort. *I wanted this; wanted it so badly I did not dare expect it. It's like a gift of the gods, you don't reject them.* "Golsat. Advise me."

"What," he laughed grimly. "Whether to fight Kaltassa? You want it. Any man could see as much. What do you want of me?"

"Your eyes to my back." She kept her eyes on Kaltassa, gripped Golsat's arm. "Thanks, friend." She ignored Nisana's dismayed protest, Ysian's weak, frightened and wordless cry. 'Nisana, Ysian will distract me, deal with her. Please.' The cat cast her a displeased look, shuttered her thought away; Ysian's as suddenly left her.

"Who is this traitor at the arm of the Tanea-a-Les?" One of Kaltassa's advisors stepped forward, leveled a hand at Golsat. Golsat shifted so the camp fire lit his face clearly. "I am Golsat," he replied in Plains-speech, "son of the Plains armsman Noldan and the woman Goyes of the hill tribes. Nedaoan armsman to this Lady, to Nedao's Queen."

"Mongrel bastard," the old man spat. He said more, but Golsat would never translate it. He hadn't needed to: the look in the old man's eyes said enough. Kaltassa shoved him impatiently aside; the old man staggered.

"Silence! *I* speak here!" the young chief shouted. "You, mongrel. Tell my words to the woman. I will fight her for the man we took."

"You have already told her," Golsat replied. "Ylia—? He wants an answer to his challenge."

"I will fight for my liegeman," she said. "Let me see the man first, so that I know he lives!"

Kaltassa gestured; two men came through the crowd, dragging Faric with them. He was half-conscious, and blood from a long cut ran into his eyes. His arms were bound. *If I could just reach him!* She took one step forward, Kaltassa shouted another order and they hauled him back.

"The Tanea-a-Les can see her man lives," Kaltassa said flatly. "If she tries to touch him, he dies. We have seen how men vanish when she touches them!"

"I am satisfied."

"Then I will fight," Kaltassa said. One of his advisors was waving his arms, expostulating vainly; Kaltassa sent him staggering back into the crowd. "There is no shame in this, and there will be honor to the tribe when she dies! And we will take the beast, and the mongrel, and burn them all!" This met with loud approval among the younger warriors.

"You must kill me first," Ylia shouted after Golsat translated for her. This brought another loud outcry, and heavy jeering. "Golsat, I wish you'd—"

"Don't!"

"All right, nevermind, I'm sorry, I didn't mean insult."

He laughed, but his eyes were flatly black. "I know what you meant. Thanks, but no. You need me, and you know it. Tehlatt don't fight the way you learned, you need a sword at your back that's your own." He shouted over the noise. "We want Kaltassa's honor, that the man of the Tanea-a-Les is ours, when she wins."

"Honor!" She understood that much Tehlatt, the Mothers knew how often she'd heard the word the year before. "Honor from *these?*"

"In their own light," Golsat replied. "But not for you, that's why I'm staying. And—I can take care of young Faric, if I have a chance."

"You won't. Think of yourself, how I'll feel if they burn you after all I went through to get you out of here. Look how they're watching you! Stay close to Nisana. She'll get you out fast if things go wrong."

"If things go wrong," Golsat replied grimly, "they won't have him alive. Or me."

'If it goes against you,' the cat warned flatly, 'you'll find yourself away from here! Not for your own stupid self, for poor Duke Erken, who must suffer in your place if you desert it! Do you forget you are Queen of Nedao?' There was no answer she could make to that. And Kaltassa, who had been again consulting with his old men, turned back to them.

"See! A bargain!" He turned as he spoke, taking in all those who crowded around the fire pit. "If the Tanea-a-Les defeats me, the man is hers! If I defeat her, she is ours, and the man, and *that* man, who is only half true man! They and that creature!" he pointed at Nisana. A low disapproving murmur: none of the warriors liked the thought of attempting to take the cat-shaped demon prisoner. "There will be no faulting in this bargain, I swear by Chezad, who gave us the victory here!"

"Golsat—Nisana, keep ready!" she warned, and, as she took a step forward, added: "I will take my family blood and that of all my people from your skin!"

Kaltassa roared out a laugh, clearly pleased by the response; the warriors sniggered. They moved back as she stepped forward, formed a loose circle around the firepit, away from the still burning compound. Ylia shifted her grip on her blades, stretched the muscles across her neck and shoulders to loosen them and began a slow stalk to the left.

Nisana's thought suddenly rocked her: 'Ylia, beware! One of Power comes!' Her concentration was shattered. But the Tehlatt scrambled aside to make a wide path to the fire. Kaltassa turned abruptly away from her. Whatever came, he feared, and she wondered at that. 'He has true Power—he was shielded!' The cat's thought echoed, was abruptly gone as she broke contact.

Shaman. A man so old, it seemed a wonder he could walk, his

hair and beard were sparsely white. But there was a ruddy glow around him, clear to AEldra sight. And there was reason for that, wasn't there? "Mine," Lyiadd had assured her, "the urgings to the Tehlatt which set them to the conquest of the Plain—" And this ancient, doddering creature in his fine-woven robe, and filthy grey leather leggings: *This* had been Lyiadd's link between himself and the barbarians?

The old man moved suddenly, quickly, caught Kaltassa's arm in a hard grip. "Hold!" He spoke in thick Tehlatt, mumbling his words for he was missing most of his teeth. Golsat pulled her back a pace, translated against her ear. "This is not right!" The shaman was shaking with fury and indignation. "We must take these," he pointed, "and this man we keep! We were told to make sacrifice to Chezad on the night when the moon hid its face. Was it not for this that we kept those misbegotten City folk alive? Did not Chezad himself speak to me when he set his sign upon me and gave his word that the Plain should again be ours? You and your father had victory by those words, Kaltassa, and now you will call Chezad's vengeance upon us with your fool ways! The day for fighting is past. If you must use your sword, wield it in practice against your own kind! You are old enough for more sense, and you are your father's heir! This female is a peril to you."

"She cannot defeat me," Kaltassa replied angrily.

"You shame the honor of the tribe to fight a female!" One of the other advisors, heartened by the appearance of the shaman, stepped from the crowd. Kaltassa struck him with the back of his hand, sent him sprawling.

"She is not female like our women! She is the child of the Nedaoan King Brandt and the Pale Witch, she is warrior and witch! And she has invoked the spilled blood of her ancestors. There is no shame to this fight!"

"No," the shaman's voice rose to a shrill, furious pitch. "No shame, only stupidity! And danger! This female despoiled Chezad's very temple! Do you think I do not know her?" Kaltassa eyed him with forebearance. Clearly, he didn't believe much of the gods, and less of this new tale. And the old man was no fool to miss that. "As you will, then. I have warned you, the god himself warns you. If she could wield so against Chezad—!"

"Then the god has less strength in his sword arm than I," Kaltassa said loudly, but he suddenly didn't look as certain of himself. The old man paled and caught at a handful of bones, bells, beads and other charms, hanging from his neck, then turned away to mutter over them.

"No!" Ylia clashed her blades together, brought the attention of the watchers back to her. The old man must *not* change Kaltassa's mind! "A vow was spoken here! Does Kaltassa hide behind an old man's dirty robes, fearing that the Tanea-a-Les shall slay him as easily as she would a rabbit?" Nisana looked at her dubiously, gave a mental shrug that reverberated through the girl's mind and padded forward stiff-legged, the Power playing openly across her shoulders. The shaman turned to stare at the small cat. "If he wins, Kaltassa has us all, as a true sign his gods smile upon him! Why does he need this old fool's word for the god's pleasure?" Kaltassa eyed them in turn once again, but the shaman's attention was all for Nisana, and still the warrior hesitated. "Shall the Tanea-a-Les then return to her own kind and say that Kaltassa broke his word because he feared to fight her?"

With a visible effort, the old man turned his attention from the cat. The charms jangled against the shaman's chest as he laid a restraining hand on his chief's arm. Kaltassa shook it off savagely and began a light-footed stalk around the fire. The old man fished a length of feather-wrapped bone from among his ornaments and brought it to his lips. It fell away, unnoticed, as Nisana leaped for him. The air around her shimmered, Baelfyr flared, and a mountain-cat stood snarling where she had been.

Shape-change! The Tehlatt scrambled frantically out of the way, the guards abandoned their prisoner and ran. Faric fell heavily to his side and lay still. The shaman wet his lips nervously, but he brought the bone whistle to his lips again. It shattered, the pieces fell smoking about his feet. 'Kill Kaltassa!' Nisana snapped, 'I am worn and the old one is powerful!'

'I will.' Ylia shut her mind to Ysian's wordless cry of fear, the power-struggle that suddenly raged between radiant were-cat and Tehlatt shaman. She lunged across the guttering fire, struck Kaltassa's sword up with her own and laughed. The Tehlatt hurtled across the firepit and brought his short broad blade down with murderous intent.

She flung herself to the side, skittered back out of his reach. Kaltassa pursued her around the fire, backed her in a circle twice before she found any kind of pattern to his fighting. It was unlike any she'd ever encountered: Even Lyiadd had had form similar enough to her own; this man was wild, his blows relied on strength rather than subtlety to break her guard. *Caution,* she warned herself. The battle over her shoulder blazed into her mind, faded as she shut off her thought once again.

She jumped back as he leaped at her, knowing he'd win if he once caught her in a clutch, then jumped again as his bare foot snaked out to trip her. Attack: He gave ground, a slow step at a time, as she wove a web of steel around him, but still neither had touched the other. He swore at her as she retreated toward the fire, leaped for her again. She caught her heel on a rock, lost her balance and fell. Kaltassa almost had her then but she rolled even as she hit, regained her feet and pulled a slashing cut as she pivoted. The point sliced up the back of his bare arm.

Silence, save for the burning compound, the crack and scree of blade on blade. Kaltassa's swings were still wild and heavy. But he was wearing down: blood ran in a steady stream from his elbow.

She was again, all at once, aware of her surroundings: the battle that raged and flared not far from her, the Tehlatt warriors who watched her and Kaltassa, the gap where none would stand, lest were-cat or shaman strike them dead. And Faric, who had managed, through infinitely cautious movement, to work his way into the open, until he lay not two lengths from her.

She sidestepped a savage overhand, caught her point in the mail-ringed shirt and for one heart-stopping moment thought she'd lost it. But the shirt was not properly laced; it slid with the sword and she tore a deep furrow along his ribs. Kaltassa hissed, tried again to kick the feet from under her. This time he nearly succeeded: the night's labors were telling on her badly and her legs felt leaden. She dragged the blade free of the barbarian's mail, hauled it back, forced shaking arm muscles to hold it up and steady. He retreated but when she went after him he stopped, dropped his sword and caught her shoulders in a crushing bear-hug.

The breath was driven from her, her sword and dagger were pinned to her sides. She nearly panicked. But Marhan had driven his lessons in well—too well for her to forget the way out of such a hold. She brought a knee up, dropped onto her back and rolled. Kaltassa was laughing breathily; he had expected struggle only, no such trick as this and nothing so swift: Before he realized he was falling, she was already down, thrusting hard with both feet, throwing the badly overbalanced man over her head. He landed with a thud.

"A good trick." He caught up his sword, came up with it at the ready. Air labored into his lungs. "I shall remember it!"

"No," she panted. "You won't live to remember it!" Painfully bright, blue-white light flared over them, blinding. A gust of horror—the old shaman's—and a gust of raw power—Nisana's—shook her. There was bedlam among the warriors; many of them simply turned and fled. Kaltassa lunged but his guard was wide and he fell onto her sword. She nearly went down with him; the hilts were torn from her hand.

Nisana—the cat herself, once again—stood ten paces away, staring at a ragged, motionless bundle on the ground before her. A dark red haze hung over it, but it was already fading.

"Take them!" One of the old men shouted. The Tehlatt moved as one, hesitated as they looked from Warrior Witch to Shape-Changing Demon. In that moment, both acted. *'Join!'* the thought came from three directions at once. Ylia grabbed Golsat's arm, launched both of them across the intervening distance and fell full length on Faric as the bridging enfolded them and pulled them to safety.

Poor Ysian. It wasn't fair, no one could have taken such an introduction to Nedao. For such as she, with my fair Scythia's beauty and courage, but with no knowledge of how harsh things can be outside Yslar, it was a horror and a nightmare. And I was sorry I'd done my share to push for her remaining. Though I'd done it from good motive: that she could indeed be of use, and that I always loved her, and wanted her company. And now, I could only hope that what she had learned about Nedao, and herself, she would take away to think upon, and that she would return, some day.

15

Light filtered into the sleep chamber from the niches in the rock. Ylia blinked at it sleepily. *Same day, or another?* No way to tell. She levered herself onto an elbow, pushed to her feet. *Ugh.* There was a flat taste in her mouth and the smell of smoke to her clothes and hair. Her hands were clean, but she thought she remembered an extremely angry Malaeth sponging blood and soot and mud from them, expostulating with her the while. Her shirt was gone. It had been stiff with the guard's blood. She shuddered.

Marhan, after he'd finally realized what she'd done, had refused to speak to her at all. At the moment, remembering their return to the Caves, she couldn't think which of them was more irritating. Marhan wouldn't let her, or anyone else, explain what had happened because he wouldn't listen, and Malaeth hadn't let her get a word in the entire time she'd been with her.

One thing, at least: There wasn't a man, woman or child at Aresada who would look askance at Golsat ever again. Doubtless they were still singing his praises out there. But Golsat—she wiped a sudden tear aside, swallowed others. Golsat's mother and one of his sisters had been among those rescued, and he and they hadn't even seen each other until they reached the safety of the Caves.

Nisana leaped to the table as she moved into the conference chamber. 'You look better,' the cat observed.

"I should, I slept like the dead. What hour is it?"

'Seventh. You woke for evening meal but not by much.'

"Ah. That explains why I feel so slept out. How is Ysian?"

'Better. Still sleeping. I think the circumstances were harder on her than the use of so much Power. Malaeth was furious with us, but I convinced her to leave Ysian alone; Ysian couldn't have taken it.'

"She took it all out on me, anyway, there wasn't anything left over for Ysian. You think she'll be all right when she wakes?" Ysian had recovered by the time she and Nisana bridged back to the hill, and she'd held together with grim resolution through the return to Aresada. But by the time they reached the River, Golsat was carrying her. And once she was within the women's quarters and safely flat on her own blankets, once the dark man was gone, she'd burst into tears. Ylia's attempts to soothe her proved useless and she'd left her in Nisana's care.

The people had been wild for her to come back anyway. By then they'd heard Corlin's story of the rescue, and Golsat's, the gods help her, and they'd wanted *her*. She'd spoken, tried to tell her own side of it, unvarnished and plain, but she knew it was no good. They'd already chosen what to believe, her people.

And then she'd let Malaeth, a very angry Malaeth, snatch her from their midst and drag her like a truant child back to her sleeping chamber. In truth, she was too tired by then to care how it looked.

'Malaeth's not so angry either, now.' Nisana broke in on her thought. 'Ysian explained things to her.'

"Oh. Good. I think."

She found Merreven in the hall and sent him in search of warm washing water. Lisabetha pushed through the curtain moments later, a steaming copper bowl in her hands.

"I had them keep this warm, I thought you'd want it soon." Her eyes were overbright. She set the bowl on the table. "I wanted—I didn't get a chance to say anything last night."

"It's all right, 'Betha. I know."

Lisabetha dipped a cloth in the warm water and set to work on Ylia's face. "It's the best thing anyone ever did for me."

"I'm just glad we succeeded. But you know it wasn't all *me*, not by half. Golsat planned it. Without him we'd have gotten nowhere."

"I know that. He's wonderful. But you'd have thought of something," Lisabetha added loyally. "We'll have to wash your hair, it's *awful*. Malaeth has you a change of things. She's washed the shirt you wore last night three times and it's still not clean. She wants your breeches."

"If she has me a dress of Ysian's," Ylia warned, "I refuse it."

"She knows better than to even try," the girl laughed. "No, the last boatload of things the Narrans brought—there was cloth, remember?"

"That's for the children!" Ylia said indignantly.

"Most of it. Some was set aside for you. The people aren't pleased that you must dress as poorly as they. Don't you know that?" Silence. Ylia rolled her eyes. "Well, *I* do, I spend more time among the women, and they talk to me a way they wouldn't to you. You aren't supposed to look like a peasant. Anyway," Lisabetha went on cheerfully, "it's too late to complain, you've breeches and a plain shirt to match. It'll keep you decently covered while the rest of this is washed. And," she added as she redid one of the badly tangled plaits, "Malaeth's working that tabard, and it's waist length. Thought you'd like to know, after all the fuss she made."

"You jest—ow!"

"Don't turn your head like that, I have your hair in my hand."

"I noticed!"

"Frankly, it's more because she couldn't do a proper job on any more length. There wasn't enough of what she thought decent stuff."

"Decent stuff," Ylia repeated. "I'm afraid to ask what that might be."

"Not pale pink silk, if you feared it," Lisabetha laughed and started on the other plait. "No, it's dark and actually practical, but she wanted your arms on the front of it, and the proper patterning down the sides. Ysian lent her colored thread, but she hadn't much, and so Malaeth has resigned herself to the inevitable. I'm so happy for Golsat," she went on after a small silence. "He couldn't have had a better reward for what he did."

"I suppose we shouldn't have been surprised to find them there, considering," Ylia said. The girl finished her braiding, began to rub Ylia's shoulders.

"I—no, we shouldn't have. One doesn't like to think about it. You're tense."

"No, stiff. And bruised. I had a full-grown Tehlatt warrior fall on top of me, remember?"

"Ugh." Lisabetha shivered. "How you did that, just went in there like that, I'll never understand."

"And yet you want sword-training?"

Lisabetha sighed. "I do. Whether it'll make me any braver—or if you just don't *think* when it comes to the point, I don't know. But I'm not going to be caught helpless as I was the once. Not ever again."

"Good. That's part of it, you know. It's not bravery like—well, like Bren used to think of it. Something you are, something you do. At least, I don't think it is," Ylia qualified. "A thing has to be done, you have to do it. You *don't* think, you don't think about what might happen to you. I don't. The moment comes, you have to take that one step forward, and you just do it. That's all." She smiled up at her young friend—more like a sister, anymore, than Lady *or* friend. "But you know that."

"I?"

"On the ledges. Remember?"

Lisabetha shook her head. "That was different."

"No. Think about it. I hope you never have to face such a thing again, but if you do, I'm not afraid for you. Not for your courage." She stood and stretched, very slowly and cautiously indeed, and with full awareness of her aching muscles. "How long til evening-meal?"

"It's all confused out there, but there's food now, if you're hungry. They're just starting to set things out."

"I can wait, then. Ask your father and mother if they'll eat with me, I'll be out shortly. And do you know if Erken's back yet?"

"I don't think so. And I'll find Father." She scooped up the copper on her way out. Ylia stretched again. Water and fresh air, and a little sky overhead presented themselves as definite needs, suddenly. She was limping slightly. She'd turned her ankle somehow last night, probably when she fell. But she was otherwise unhurt. *Stiff. But luckier than anyone deserves*, she thought and followed the thought up with Golsat's warding gesture.

. . .

Erken hadn't returned yet, though she found him with a mind-search from the outer ledges. He was on his way back, and would no doubt arrive by the next afternoon. She just sat awhile after that, for the sun was warm, the wind almost nothing.

Shielding—Lyiadd had been generous with his instruments. If Nisana had been much more tired, or if the old man had been a little younger and more skilled with what he had, the cat might have come off second—she couldn't think *dead*.

But it had come back, as all things did: or so the old ways said, the pattern was never lost, and what of it went out of sight was merely hiding on the back side of the loom, to emerge later. She'd revenged Bren, when she killed Lyiadd. She'd revenged Father, Mother—her people—on Kaltassa. Kanatan must look to his second or third wife for an heir now, and must find himself another shaman. One without a mantle of blood-red light for eyes that could see it, one without a means of speech with their likewise-dead war god. Golsat had gone to rescue the man who'd first taken his armsman's vows and had found his mother, a sister.

But poor Ysian. Well, she'd learned, though in a way Ylia'd never meant. *Not my choosing, that.* She'd return to safety, to Yslar; she'd patch up her quarrel with the Sirdar and his council, with her family. Nisana would miss her—*I'll miss her myself*, Ylia realized in sudden surprise. But Aresada was no place for a true lady, and the valley wouldn't be either, at least not yet.

Besides, Ylia wondered, what would Ysian think when she realized how many of the younger men watched her with heart in eyes? Including, the Mothers aid him, Golsat?

The council-meeting the next night was a very short one, set originally to brief Lord Corry and Lady Lossana on their situation. But Erken rode in partway through the meeting and came straight down before meal or a wash: he reeked of horse, smoke and garlic in equal parts.

So quickly did he travel from the horse-lines near the bridge to Ylia's council-chamber, in fact, that he had no news of the rescue, and he gaped like a boy when his eyes adjusted to the dimly lit room. "Mothers' justice," he breathed finally, "it's my Lord Corlin!" Corlin pushed to his feet—he was still weak and painfully thin—and embraced the Duke. "And the Lady," Erken went on, still stunned. Lossana smiled up at him. Even the least speech tired her, but she no longer looked as haggard, or as old.

"They found us and brought us here," Corlin said. He smiled at

Erken, pounded his back. "Gods and Mothers, but it's good to see you again!"

"Found you?" Erken caught at that much. "Where?"

"It's a long tale, too long for council. One you'll hear all too often the next few days," Marhan said. "Ask your men, Faric and Pereden. They were in on it."

"Ask anyone," Brelian laughed. "Including Redoran, Bnolon's minstrel. *He's* already made a song of it." Erken turned back to Corlin.

"You're worn, my good friend, and much too thin: You should be resting."

"Not just yet," Corlin said, though he resumed his seat gratefully. Lossana took his hand in hers and he clutched her fingers tightly. "We wanted to know how things went, what aid we can give. And they tell me we've already another place to live, now that the Plain has been taken from us. And that you've just come from there, Erken." And, as Erken continued to eye him with concern, "We've slept, and such minor harms as we had have been cared for. Worry over things not properly known or understood gnaw at us both now. You know how that is, Erken."

"If you say so," Erken said, but he resumed his own seat. "My news should wait for last. Pride of place," he added with a faint smile.

"Fine," Marckl said. He was practically twitching in his impatience to get things moving. "Lord Corlin, if I may, your men never came to Aresada, and we've none of your maps for the caches you sent here."

"I know they never came. They never made it out of my halls. I have an imperfect memory, but I daresay I can be of more aid than a blind search. We used back chambers, where beasts and men wouldn't be as likely to go, and where it was drier. And there were pits, man-dug, one or two, if I recall correctly. We made good use of those."

"They must be well disguised or far back indeed," Ifney said. "We've found nothing like a pit so far, and no sign of human tampering farther back, save the chalk-marks your daughter's left to guide her when her rope runs out."

"Good girl," Corlin said warmly. "I knew she'd prove useful, Lady Ylia." Lisabetha stirred, embarrassed; subsided as Brelian touched her hand and smiled.

"She has indeed, and I'll tell you how much someday when there's time," Ylia replied. "Well. You've seen how many people we have here. But most of Koderra is in Yslar, waiting for transport."

"You got them out, then. Good." The smile faded; his son had carried the warning and died bringing it. Lossana tightened her hold on his fingers, and he patted her hand.

"Mostly. It's been hard here, and there hasn't been much to eat, but we've managed. We sent to Nar for aid and they've already made contract with us for woolen cloth. You'll be invaluable in setting that up, and arranging other trade."

"Good. I'd hoped to be of some use."

"I can set up the weaving," Lossana said. "Unless it's already organized. I can help."

"We've arranged for raw wool from Nar to supplement our own, but nothing else. I'd be grateful if I could leave that to you."

"Of course."

"We've something of a herd, all massed at present. Enough to start with. We've hunters and fishers."

"Seed we'll have, when more of the caches come to light," Ifney said. "And we've received iron from the Narrans for our smith to supplement what tools and swords we have."

"We'll survive, then," Corlin said.

"No doubt of it, sir." Marckl nodded. He turned to Erken. "What've you found, then?"

"It's just as described to us. Warmer than here. I'm assured the soil is workable and that the land itself is good. The size is enough and to spare for present, but eventually we'll be able to spread out: there's a series of interconnected valleys and dells to the north, another valley not far west that's similar to the main one but half the size.

"The main stream that flows through the valley is something short of a river, but smaller transport—rafts and the like—will do well. It flows straight into the Aresada, and there's a stillwater at the mouth, almost a natural harbor. It won't be difficult at all to make docks there, and warehousing for storage.

"There's plenty of wood for building, and stone. Game is as plentiful there as here. Have I left out anything?"

"Gold in the river and gems in the foothills," Ifney retorted readily, but he was grinning.

"I wanted to leave half my men and the three farmers I had with me, but sense and caution prevailed. We'll gather everything together we can, though, and start back—" he thought hard—"in two days' time. Sooner, if we can."

"You'll have my aid," Marckl replied. "I've got men already picked for you, if you'll take 'em."

"And I've got those who know how to build fast and sturdy," Ifney added.

"Good. I'll take anyone you've got." Erken yawned, smothered it with a grubby hand.

"Go get a wash and some food," Ylia urged him. "And sleep. You can't have had much."

"I haven't." He smiled as he turned at the curtained entrance. "Nearly forgot: we found wild garlic and onion all over the hillsides."

"We guessed," Ylia replied dryly. "It even overcomes two days of horse. Lord Corry, unless you and Lady Lossana have anything to ask, or if there's anything we didn't mention, you might as well go get some rest, too."

"You've reassured us. I think I can sleep now." Corlin stood. "I'll meet with you tomorrow, when you have time, to go over what the Narrans want, and what they've offered in return. And I'll think on those caches. Though it's a pity Davica and Hordic didn't leave Teshmor in good time."

"We'll manage, sir," Brelian put in diffidently. "We have, so far."

"So we will. My Lady?" And, as Lisabetha came around to go with them, "You needn't come, sweet. We're going directly back to sleep. And I think your young man might welcome your company. You've neglected him shamefully the past day or so."

"Father!" Lisabetha protested weakly. Brelian opened his mouth, stared blankly and shut it again. Corlin tipped his wife a wink and led her away. Ylia bit back a laugh, aware that Marckl and Ifney, both terribly sharp-eyed, had caught that wink also. Corlin was well aware how things stood between his only child and Brelian. Given Brelian's new status, it was a suitable match for any nobleman's daughter. Not that Corlin would have forbidden them. He had a soft spot for his daughter, and Brelian had saved her life more than once.

But Corlin was following a time-honored pattern: he'd make the young man sweat before he finally gave his consent.

Ifney and Marckl gave Ylia their promised lists after Corlin left.

"That was quick work. Thank you. There'll be a lot of parceling to do." Ylia fought a yawn, stifled it behind her lips. Her ears popped. "What I'd like, if you'll do it, you and Marckl, is for you to ride out with Erken. You've done a lot here, but you'll be more use there."

"I'd like that," Ifney said. "I'd like to see this stillwater firsthand. There's bound to be a lot of work to it, but we'll need that wharf early, and I'd like to get started at it."

"I've a good eye for laying roads," Marckl put in with surprising modesty. "We'll need those soon, too."

She shook her head. "I'm leaving that all to you, Marckl. You, Ifney and Erken. I've already got my hands full here."

They were gone, finally. She fought another yawn, stretched. Pulled, tired muscles ached. The healing had helped them. Doubtless she'd have stayed flat on her back without it, but she was still stiff. At least the ankle was a normal size again. *That* had hurt bad, and she hadn't even been aware when she did it.

The curtain rippled, and Ysian pushed through, Nisana in her arms.

"You shouldn't be here," Ylia began. Ysian shook her head, but gratefully sank into one of the chairs. There were now four around the table, counting her own, thanks to Ifney's woodworkers. Ysian was still pale, and her eyes were haunted. Ylia dropped into the chair next to her, ruffled Nisana's fur. The cat opened one eye, closed it again and rumbled herself back to sleep.

"I'm fine," Ysian insisted. She visibly wasn't. She brought up a weak smile. "I—I just can't believe how you lied to those men, telling them my strength was equal to yours!"

"It is. You just haven't had to use it recently like I have."

"Not ever," Ysian whispered. "Don't look like that. You didn't kill me. I went into it with all your warnings echoing in my ears, it wasn't as though you hadn't told me. I just—I couldn't *imagine* things as horrible as that, that's all. It—it would take getting used to, wouldn't it?"

"It's not always like that. That *was* bad. Look at me! But we have other enemy in the mountains. Mathkkra. Thullen. You know, it could be that bad again. It's been worse." Ylia laid a hand on her arm. "I'm not trying to upset you, honestly, Ysian. I just want you to know."

Ysian smiled wanly. "Well—I guess I know. It's—do you know what surprises me most, thinking about it? I'm ashamed."

"Ashamed? Why? You have nothing to feel shame for, Ysian! You held out as well as any of us."

"I didn't. But that's not why. I'm taking your advice, your *first* advice. I'm going to crawl back to Court and make the Sirdar put me back on the council." A brief grin touched her face. "Ardyel will be properly furious, and Father will probably try to disown me. That promises to be amusing." She sobered again. "It's the fact that I'm quitting, that I'm giving up. That's what's shaming."

"You're not quitting, you're showing sense. Ysian, it's not that we don't want you. You know that we do!"

"I know." One slender hand stroked dark fur, bringing up a purr that filled the room, slowly faded and died away.

"It's not what it would have been, if we'd still had the Plain. And you weren't prepared."

"Next time, I will be." There was grim promise in her voice. She met Ylia's eyes. "There will be a next time, you know that."

"I don't doubt it. I'm glad that's how you feel. I want you back."

"Good. It's an astonishing thing, to learn so much about yourself, so fast. I found out I'm not brave at all. And I did things anyway, just as though it didn't matter. I'm proud of that, anyway." Ysian shook her head. The long plait she'd persuaded Malaeth to work flew across her shoulder.

Ylia took her hand. "I'm proud of you, too. You did well, don't forget that. Without you, we might not all have made it back." She hesitated. "Before you go, talk to Golsat. He helped me sort things like this out, and not very long ago. He'll help you."

"I'd like that. If he doesn't mind." Ysian sighed. "When I come back it will be for good. I mean that, Ylia."

"Then talk to Golsat."

"I can help you with your trade, from Yslar."

"We'd appreciate that."

"Don't go all formal on me, girl! You make me feel old and already gone."

"Sorry."

"And I know you'd appreciate it. You need it and I can help. It's something I'm good at. If I stayed—I can't picture me in one of your sword classes, can you?"

Ylia laughed. "You never saw Lisabetha before *she* began!"

"I wager she's not afraid of knives like I am, though. I hurt myself on sharp things, always have. Don't like them. I can't think why you still use knives and swords. You don't need to anymore, girl."

"You always had your Powers. *I* didn't. I needed sword for protection and also because I was heir, after my brother died. I had to have weapon-training then. I'd have wanted it anyway. Something Father and I had in common; Mother never understood either of us."

"She wouldn't." Ysian shifted Nisana and stood. The cat resettled herself to the curve of Ysian's shoulder, purred softly. "I don't understand how I can still be so tired. It's not sense."

"Reaction."

"Perhaps. I'm hungrier than tired, though, at the moment. I'd better go. Malaeth said to come down to the kitchens and she'd find me food. I missed evening meal."

"It wasn't worth waking up for, there was an odd flavor to the stew and it put my appetite off. But Malaeth never, ever would send *you* to the kitchens. You must have misunderstood."

"Well," Ysian smiled from the entrance, "she said she'd bring it here, but I thought you might like to avoid her. Until she runs out of things to blame on you. At least until your shirt comes clean!"

"That's a thought."

"So I told her I would go there when I was done talking with you. There's a trick to it," Ysian said sweetly. "You just have to know how to manage her."

"Teach *me* that," Ylia demanded. Ysian laughed, shook her head.

"It took me years to learn, and I don't think my methods would work for you. Besides, anyone who'd challenge a barbarian the way you did can't possibly be afraid of one old lady."

"They aren't even on the same level," Ylia began, but Ysian laughed again and left her. She sought out Golsat, then, as she had been advised, but what passed between them Ylia never knew for certain.

The next morning Ysian left with the Narrans, traveling this time only in what she wore: She left the rest of her clothing for Malaeth to distribute; her colored threads and needles, a length of pale green silk went to Lisabetha for her bride-box, and a curiously woven shawl of Holthan goat-hair to Lossana.

She'd gone down to the Narran boat alone, allowing neither Ylia nor Nisana to see her off, lest she cry. She kept herself resolutely under the canvas shelter and dabbed at her eyes with a serviceable dark kerchief as the sturdy little boat moved to midstream and caught the current. The Caves, the horse pickets, Marhan's practice ground—gone. The last thing she saw before the river swept them around the bend was first sun touching the foot-bridge. She blinked: was someone standing there? She couldn't be certain.

Golsat leaned against the railing, high above the roar of the Aresada, and gazed down-River long after the boat vanished beyond tall fir and crumbling ledges.

One cannot know all the histories—there is too much that has gone before, even for so young a land as the Nedao of the Plains, with its 500 years. How much more difficult to know even a portion of our histories, who have dwelt against the sea for over a thousand years—or to know which of the tales we have of the Nasath are just telling and which are true histories? Even so, such knowledge as I have would have denied that either folk ever dwelt in or near the Caves of Aresada. Though, if they had, that would still not explain what we found.

16

She missed Ysian, even though she'd been there so short a time. Not that it wasn't for the best. She didn't brood; there wasn't time for that.

Her fledgling swordswomen were still painfully novice, all twenty of them. It was all she'd time and blades for at the moment, though there were at least five times that many who wanted lessoning. Mindful of the remarks among Erken's younger armed, among Marhan's second level novices, she decided to brazen the thing out and keep them in plain view, just as Marhan did his. And however much anyone could fault skill, balance or ability in any of them, they couldn't deny the women's determination. The number of onlookers halved by the second session, fell away to near none by the fourth.

And then suddenly, as such things always happened there were one or two who showed true potential. Lisabetha was one. Another was Eveya, daughter of a village mayor, who'd spent most of her eighteen years guarding her father's goats. She'd strength from that, more than others, like 'Betha's friend Annes.

Ylia was working the girl personally, both of them sweating under the hot sun, the rest gathered in tight circle to watch. Third level passes: some of them wouldn't reach that point for months, but it was good for them to see what they had to face, and Eveya was more than ready. "That was good, you've got a quick eye." The farm girl smiled, pleased. "But did the rest of you catch the one thing she did wrong?" Silence. "All right. When you lunge, don't come so far forward. It puts you off balance, right on your enemy's sword, if he's paying attention. And what did I tell you of that?"

"He's always paying attention," they chorused raggedly.

"Good. If I'd wanted, I'd have had her. Now," she demonstrated, "if you take another step, *then* lunge—see the difference? Take two or three, if you have to, don't overstep your lunge."

"I—extra step, then lunge," Eveya mumbled to herself.

"Go ahead, try it." The girl brought up her borrowed sword, sought another opening. Ylia parried wide, stepped back and blocked. "See the difference? You can pull back from there, attack again."

"I see it." The girl mopped her forehead. "Thank you."

"Good work. You've got a talent. Is your father still—?"

"Displeased, Lady?" She shrugged. "Some. He'd rather I didn't, but he's made no order that I not."

"I'll speak to him. In a group with some of the other men, so he doesn't feel singled out."

"Thank you."

"We need skill like yours. All right!" She turned to the rest of her group. "Change pairs, and do two sets of full pattern, then that's it for today." A moan of disappointment swept them and she laughed. "Half of you won't be able to raise your arms above your heads tomorrow, and anyway, Marhan's waiting for those blades." There were still disappointed looks on most of the young faces, but they obediently moved about, settled into the formal stance of two wide-spread lines and began the formal set of crossings. Ylia walked up and down behind them. "Rialla, get that elbow *in!* Lisabetha, you've shifted your grip again, that won't serve in the long run, shift it back! One more time, good! All right!"

She left them to return the swords to Marhan, who was impatiently waiting with his own class—the younger and less skilled—and started back up-river. Just short of the bridge she stopped to dip her sleeve in the chill water. She rubbed it across her forehead, held it against the back of her neck as she climbed.

Lisabetha caught up with her just within the entrance. "Still want to explore this afternoon?"

"I've the time for it, and anything's better than that sun just now. Is Brelian coming with us?"

Lisabetha grinned, shrugged. "He thought he might. Protection, or something. And he can carry more than we can—"

"I'm not Corlin, you needn't justify to me," Ylia replied dryly, and then laughed. "Glad to have him. Maybe he can suggest something we haven't tried yet."

Brelian lost track of their direction, wasn't too pleased about it, even with the length of twine in his one hand, the torch reassuringly bright in the other. He didn't like being so far from an immediate exit to the outside, with no idea how to find one. *I never feared caves before—before I went into that one after 'Betha. How either of them takes it so well, I'll never understand. But then, 'Betha remembers almost nothing of that night, and Ylia: even if she feared the way I do, she'd never show it, he thought.* He considered that as the two women consulted over one of Lisabetha's old chalk marks. *She'd do what I'm doing, she'd go straight back into Aresada, and fight the fear until it gave way. Pray the Mothers it does, and soon.*

"We came through here, what, a 5-day ago?"

Lisabetha shrugged. "I think so. And one other time before, but I can't remember, it was pretty far back." She turned slowly, gazing at the gloom-shrouded walls, at the silky looking flows of stone, like frozen, opaque waterfalls, that kept them from seeing far in this large chamber. "We never tried that way, that I recall—" She pointed off into heavy darkness.

Ylia frowned. "No. The marks would show, and besides, I think I'd remember. Brel?"

"Want my vote?" To his relief, his voice was steady. *Outside, now!* the inner voice urged. "Let's try it." He stepped forward, held the torch out. "There's plenty of room here, and it opens out even more once you get through." He stopped to let Lisabetha tie the twine off as they reached the narrow opening between two damp pillars of greenish tan stone.

He went on through, Lisabetha followed and Ylia, bearing a second lit torch and two spare unlit ones, came up at the rear.

It was a narrow opening, not tight for her, though from the sound of things, it had been snug for Brelian. Fortunately, it wasn't a long passage, and it came out into a smooth-floored area.

Two blue pools covered most of it. Hundreds of delicate, clear icicles hung in clusters from the ceiling. She touched one, uncertainly. Rock. Water beaded on her fingertip.

"Well, what do you think?" Her voice echoed.

"There's a passageway here. A big one, see?" Lisabetha caught at Brelian's hand, started forward again.

It was high-arched, like a tunnel, the floor was sandy and in places strewn with rock fallen from the ceiling. It went on some distance, then opened out into another chamber. This one might have been as enormous as the Grand Temple, but with only the two torches, they couldn't tell.

"Wait." Brelian stopped, turned back. Ylia was standing still, one hand clutching rock for balance. Her eyes were closed. "Wait. There's—"

"Are you all right?"

"Fine—but, wait, let me think—" She drew a deep breath, let it out slowly, took in another. Her companions watched in anxious silence. She gazed out into darkness, seeing neither of them. "There's something here."

"Mathkkra?"

"Not like that. Not bad. Something—I can sense it." Without another word, she started forward. Brelian grabbed her arm, pulled her around.

"Are you *really* all right?"

"Ylia?" Lisabetha broke in, worried indeed. Ylia blinked, met her eyes with sudden recognition and nodded.

"It's all right. I've felt this before. Once. It's—there's something or someone here, I don't know which. I—I *have* to go to it. I'm sorry I can't explain better than that. I don't know anything else."

"Well, then," Brelian replied lightly, but he loosened his sword and let the dagger drop from its arm sheath down into his hand, "we'd better come with you, hadn't we?" If he expected argument, he got none; Ylia was too preoccupied with whatever was tugging at her inner sense to waste the time. She turned again and started toward what looked like a solid wall. Brelian eyed Lisabetha dubiously, shrugged, put her in front of him and they followed.

Ylia peered uncertainly ahead, thrust the torch into the low, narrow opening.

"What now?" Brelian whispered. "Ylia?"

"It's down there. I still can't tell what."

"Good, though; you're certain of that." *Gods and Mothers, assure me of that, the look of you isn't reassuring at all.*

"Not bad, not evil. Keep yourself aware, though."

"I always do, now," he replied grimly.

"Good man." She clapped his shoulder, rather absently, went back to her study of the narrow way. "It's a chute, it drops down, comes out into a small room and there's real light beyond that. I'll go first." And before he could more than open his mouth to protest, she crawled into the opening, sat down, pulled the torch in close and pushed off. She slid out of sight, around a corner, and was gone. They could hear her a very short moment later.

"All right, I'm here! Keep the torches low, you've room beside you but not much above! Brel, you're taller than either of us, keep your head down!"

"All right, we're coming!" He helped Lisabetha in, kissed her cheek and gave her a shove. She let out a startled gasp but he could hear her giggling as she reached Ylia. He joined them moments later. "Children's games. What next?" But he felt better already, even though the distance to the Aresada was greater than it had been, for he could see clear daylight not far off, and the air was filled with the sound of falling water.

They crossed the tiny chamber, stepped out into midday sun. "Mothers! Look at this!" Ylia breathed. They stood near the bottom of an immense chute; thick-bladed fern and bright green mosses covered the walls from top to bottom where it wasn't wet black rock. Across from them and to their right water fell in long thin streams from high above. Spray feathered about them.

"It's beautiful. But—is this what you sought?"

Ylia shook her head. "No. But it's near—there." She pointed directly across, to a hole similar to the one where they stood, half in and half out of the opposite fall.

Brelian squatted on his heels, doused the one torch and surveyed the ground. "All right. It's damp all around here, but there's plenty of handholds." And he stood to catch at Ylia's arm as she moved forward. "I'm supposed to protect you, by all the Mothers at once, and I can't do that if you go before me." She smiled ruefully, shrugged and stepped back. He handed her the torch, stepped down onto wet greenery and caught at rock.

It was treacherously wet, but as he'd thought there were enough holds, enough places for their feet that it wasn't dangerous. They made it across, now thoroughly wet, ducked inside. "That would have felt good after practice," Lisabetha said. "It's too cool in here for it."

"Mmmm." Ylia bent over to wring out her plaits. Straightened up and took two steps, stopped again. "Brelian. Give me your torch. Now." Her voice had gone flat again.

He relit one, handed it to her. She started forward again, but slowly now, almost reluctantly. It was all around her, calling at her, picking at her, almost so near she could touch it. *By all the Guardians at once, what is it, and why does it pluck at me so?*

Torchlight caught at a million crystal facets, clear and amethyst, filling the chamber with a dazzling radiance. Lisabetha cried out; she and Brelian crowded forward.

Ylia swallowed. She was visited by the intense feeling that she did not, could not, belong here. She'd had *that* before, too, though this had none of the feeling of the Folk about it. And Bendesevorian—she'd thought him, when she'd first sensed the *drawing* that had pulled her halfway across Aresada, but *he* wasn't here. Power filled the chamber, the far wall with its geod-like brilliance the source. It filled her, dizzying in its strength, burying the last traces of fear and uncertainty. She swallowed again, went to it.

There was an inlay in the midst of that glittering wall, a thin slab of onyx; it was covered with etched lines of fine writing. She didn't recognize the lettering, could read none of it. She ran a hand across the surface and it shifted against her hand, came away in her fingers as she caught at it to steady it.

Lisabetha came to her side. "Those aren't Nedaoan letters. I've never seen writing like that! And—Mothers, what are these?" There were three chests, almost at their feet: one the size of a wardrobe chest, the other two smaller, like jewel-boxes. They were all three plain unfigured wood, bound in figured copper bands that gleamed like mirrors: Ancient, they had to be truly ancient. But there was no greening on the copper, no rust on the iron hasps, and the wood itself was sound. "Where did they come from?"

Ylia didn't hear her. She knelt, reached for the hasp on the large chest. Her fingers rested there. *Take it, it is yours.* The words tolled through her. Her hand tightened, she lifted the lid before sense and awe and failing courage could prevent her. It creaked faintly. There was a shallow tray, lined in deep green silk. Centered on the silk, alone, lay a bundle of an even darker green deep-napped velvet. She touched it, starting as the Power vibrated up her arm and set her heart to thudding. She drew a deep breath, let it out slowly as both hands caught at the soft fabric.

The chamber, the crystal wall, her companions faded from her sight. Dark: night and swirling fogs surrounded the woman who stood before her. She was young, or so it seemed; her face was hidden, and she was either ill or in great pain. *Take what you find here, heir of mine. I sent it across the years to you, it is yours by birth and by right.* And the woman was gone, the vision was gone, the chamber again real and solid around her. Power warmed her, urged her on, left her giddy and reckless. She pressed the velvet wrap aside.

Silence, but for the sound of her own breathing. A shield, a small diamond of hardened leather: the patterning along its edges was smooth to the touch, somehow soothing. Arms had been worked into its center; around an enormous golden topaz. Her vision was too blurred with excess Power to make it out. Shield. It would cover, protect a forearm; the grips on the back were sized small—it was no man's guard.

Music teased her ears, rippled through her in a shiver. Under the shield, wrapped in its own soft suede case, was a battle-horn. She set the shield upright against the raised lid, slid the horn free. A worn banner hung long from its lower tube: the metal was battered, it had seen hard use before it was placed in its case and then in the trunk. The banner was torn and stained with soot, what might be dried blood, smeared with mud. The device might have been a ship, the colors were near her own.

And under that—

She was shaking. She caught at the plain leather scabbard, felt blindly for the silver rope hilts. The music was gone, buried under the hurtling of her blood, the heavy thump of her heart. *Take it up, take the burden that is yours. I leave it to you, but you must take it freely, and with it all else I have left you. Take up the sword, knowing nothing will remain as it was. All life brings change, and responsibility, but not always such responsibility as this single act presents you. Do you dare? Are you truly the heir I foresaw?*

She cast a startled glance at her companions, but they could have heard nothing: Lisabetha knelt before one of the smaller boxes, and Brelian was staring blankly over her shoulder.

Fear and anger: She drew her hand back, though it cost her. *I am myself, Ylia!* she railed silently. *No heir to these riddles of yours, whoever you are, no mindless slave to foreseeing or drawing!*

No answer. The box and its contents waited, as they had waited for so long. Waiting for her. She knew it, knew deep down where the Power sat, and she knew she could not walk away from that challenge, or from what was here. She gazed down at it. Silence still. She reached with a hand now steady, her fingers tightened on the hilts and she drew the sword from its sheath.

It was a slender blade, long and true-shaped, a joy of a blade. The hilts were cool and fit her small hand; the guard came up in a narrow twist of silver bands across the backs of her fingers, covering to her wrist as though it had been crafted for her alone. A pang stopped her breath as she turned the blade: it was marred, near the end, by a splotch of black, a thin line, as though it had not been properly cleaned before it was stored. But that was wrong, she knew before she touched it to rub it clear: something had touched there and wounded the blade.

Joy stabbed at her, catching the breath in an already tight throat. Her eyes blurred: the blade caught torch-light and gave it back as silver and gem-light. *Mine!* she exulted fiercely, and knew it for truth. "Mine," she whispered.

The return journey was a merry one and went much more quickly than the trip in had. Ylia was still light-headed, the tri-fold Power of the things she carried filled her, temporarily at least setting aside doubt and a faint but growing realization she'd been manipulated into finding and taking the weapons. Lisabetha and Brelian were like children, and small wonder. They'd found coin: ancient, and of a kind never seen in Nedao, but honest gold and silver. And in a small carved box, deep in the same chest, cut loose gems.

The second chest held a thread-of-gold embroidered edging that had been carefully picked from someone's robes: It was stiff with pearls; a tiny brocaded box held two slender needles and more of the pearls. There was a length of pale silver gauzy stuff, a rope of the rare grey pearls from the seas south of Ragnol, an ornamental dagger, two knotted silver and opal broaches, a pair of gold ear-hoops. A short, soft leather jerkin lined the bottom. This last had a tracery of fine-work at the square cut arms, and high on the right shoulder someone had worked a crest: ship on a stormy sea, an osprey circling the mast. It matched the crest at the upper edge of the scabbard, and what could be seen of the banner hanging from the battle-horn.

The largest chest had revealed a different trove: a short-sleeved mail shirt of rings stitched to doubled leather, a pair of soft leather boots, an osprey burned into the toes. A length of unfigured dark velvet, two leather belts and a number of hand-braided straps. All cut for a woman unnervingly near the size of Nedao's Queen.

A bride-box, or a series of them; Lisabetha'd thought that, and Ylia tended to agree with her. A bride-box for a woman pledged but not ready to wed. A swordswoman.

The wealth exulted her companions, but she couldn't feel it. There was nothing for her, had been nothing for her since she'd drawn the sword and taken that challenge straight on.

Whose the challenge, and whose the sword? And whose the writing, of what kind, this stone Lisabetha carried for her? 'Nisana.' No response. The cat had gone off on her own a good deal since Ysian left, and was probably prowling the valley.

They were nearly back to the occupied portion of the Caves. She must have walked a league blind and deaf. " 'Betha, can you find Grewl for me? I need him. If anyone can read that thing, he can."

"I'll find him." Lisabetha pushed her ball of twine and the stone page into Brelian's hands, took one of the torches and ran ahead of them.

"That coin—" Brelian began.

"You brought some, didn't you? I didn't think."

"I noticed that," he replied dryly. "Yes, several of each. It looks like proper gold and silver, for all the cut of it's odd."

"So it does. It'll help. The council will like that."

"It's—" He hesitated. "You think it's—that we can—that it's ours?" Silence. "It's old, really old. Whoever left it there—they couldn't be still around to claim it, could they?"

"I don't know what to think. I hope Grewl can decipher that thing. I hope it tells us what we want to know." *What I need to know. What do I have in my hands, what are they, and what have I done?*

Brelian left her at her quarters, went to find food and to alert the council to a meeting after late meal. Ylia washed down from the tepid bowl of water left from her morning bathing, and ate what Malaeth had left her, but she scarcely tasted the food. Perhaps as well, since it had been heavily herbed to conceal the gamey flavor of old buck and even the over-application of sage hadn't been wholly successful. And it was cold. The bread had gone hard, but at least there was nothing wrong with the flavor of it: the Narrans had brought leaven, salt and more grain on their last trip.

Grewl arrived just as she finished the last of it. "I'm glad you came. I need your aid."

"Yours, if I can give it." Ylia waited until he settled into his place, rearranged his writing materials to suit himself. She pushed the onyx slab across to him. Grewl's eyes lit with pleasure; he ran his hands lightly across the etched surface.

"Where did you find this?" he asked finally.

"Back. Well into the Caves. It wasn't alone."

"No, I see that, by what's written here."

"You *can* read it?"

"By all that's blessed," the old man breathed, "I *know* it. By the heart and soul of the One, I thought I'd seen the only copy of this." He was nearly as shaken as she; his fingers trembled, slid down the stone and to his lap. "Arms and armatures, there should have been—" His voice faded away to a stunned silence as Ylia slid the sword, the shield, the horn toward him. He touched one, another. "I thought—"

"What is it?"

"It—ah?" He came back from a long distance, blinking hard, and finally took in her question. "This?" His hand was lovingly rubbing at the incised writing once again. Ylia swallowed impatience and nodded. "Those are Shelagn's weapons. And this is Shelagn's Will."

In truth, I did feel sorry for her as the old Chosen told his tale—and what she saw as its meaning came clear to her. To be used, in such a manner? For she had been used, drawn and caught off balance, caught up in matters before she could think them through. I would have felt violated, indeed I felt it for her. But there was more to Shelagn's tale than Ylia knew, more that I had had from my own long kin. For there is another tale, which tells that Shelagn had those things—sword, shield, horn—from another before her, that she was drawn, coaxed to the sword, overwhelmed by desire for it, and that her choice was made in that same manner. And only then, only when she knew she must have it, it warned. And whom it took, it used. Shelagn was strong, sword-arm, shield-arm, Power all alike. Not, in the end, strong enough.

Then, too, she had not had strength at her side such as Ylia had in me. Perhaps that smacks of vauntage—but it is not so intended. I saw myself then in no special light, no part of any great prophecy, no being of greatness and perfection surpassing that of the Guardians, no. But—if Shelagn had had assistance, any at all, to her side, she might not have died on that battlefield.

And I was to be a brace in hour of need. Though not the only.

17

Ylia stared at him, stunned into silence. She shook herself, then; shook her head. "No."

"I've *seen* it, Lady," Grewl replied earnestly. One hand still stroked the roughened stone, lovingly traced the lines graven into its black surface. "A copy, on parchment, that was a copy of another, older parchment. And that, they said, was copy of copy of copy."

"They—they?" she whispered.

"The Ylsans. In Yslar, in the Sirdar's palace, they have a room where old writings are kept. When I first came to the Peopled Lands from my own, I brought requests from our Heirocracy, asking that I be allowed to study them. The Sirdar and his council were gracious enough to permit that. That was where I first heard the tales of the wars of a thousand years ago, and those who fought them. And where I first learned what a man might learn of Shelagn." He took the stone gently in both hands, brought it closer to him and lit candles. "You are part Ylsan. I am certain you know those histories."

"I know them. How the Lammior made war against the Nasath and the Folk and drove them across the Foessa, and how the Sea-Folk came in response to their call for aid. Shelagn died there."

"Not at once. She brought down the Lammior, at the last, but she was wounded and even those with the Power could not save her. She lived awhile: long enough to see her folk settled, to see the Gifts conferred upon them."

"Long enough," Ylia said, "to write *that*." Silence. Grewl transferred his attention to the other things, picked them up one at a time, handling them with reverent hands. He drew the sword, examined it minutely, laid it sheathless on the table between them.

"There, if you needed proof beyond this document, beyond the graven arms on the shield and what can be seen of those on the horn." He touched the blade, let his fingers slide across the stained point. "The Lammior's blood did that." Silence again. Ylia wrapped her hand around the hilts and brought the tip close. The metal was cool, silk-smooth under a trembling hand. She snatched her hand back as it slipped across the marred finish: it sent a shock up her arm, white-hot and for one brief instant horrifying. *Gods and Mothers*.

"The Will," she said finally. "It—what does it say?"

"Ah. A moment, Lady." He rearranged the candles, bent over the stone. " 'I, Shelagn, go young and unwed, heirless to the home of my ancestors, leaving behind all but my inner being, there to reap the harvest I sowed in life.

" 'I leave to my father and my folk the lands we won, my share of all the reward we gained as a result of that winning, the Gift that would have been mine.

" 'But wars such as this one do not end, though it may seem for long lives that they have. The Lammior is dead, and by my hand, but the things that fought for him have fled, and the evil that was his is not a thing that can be killed. Someday, one will rise to take his place, take his Power, and again subdue these lands. I will not be there to oppose him. I therefore give into the hands of she who is my heir my sword, my shield, the horn that brings aid, and all other things which were mine, for all of them may be of aid to her in some way.

" 'She will know herself to be my heir, beyond all doubt, for like me, she will be a catalyst. Like me, she will be a leader of a driven people and because of her, through her, events and many folk will come together.

" 'The sword will find her, she will wield it against evils great and small. And she will know, by these gifts, by her allies, by the Power that is hers, when the time and where the place that evil must again be confronted and destroyed.' "

Silence. Grewl cleared his throat again and went on. "Strange words. No one in Yslar has given meaning to them, though I asked those who scribe in the Sirdar's halls and who know the tales."

"Mine," Ylia whispered. "I dreamed of this blade. It was in my hand—" Her gaze went, half-unwilling, back to the sword. "But that it was *hers*—"

"And now yours," Grewl said gravely.

"An hour of need, when it shall slay evil." *I? Why did it draw me? There are Nasath, there are the Folk—who am I that I should be drawn to that ancient cache, that these things should be mine? Is the blade given to me to slay the remaining Mathkkra and Thullen in the Foessa, or will I destroy Lyiadd with it, if I did not before? And who is the man I saw in that dream, the one who fights at my side?* Dread vied with joy, pulling her asunder, and she was all too aware that desire had played her, had set her hand to those hilts when common sense would have sent her flying from that wonderful crystal wall. She was scarcely aware when the Grewl left.

'Ylia?' Nisana leaped to the table. Ylia blinked at her.

'How long have you been here, cat?'

'Long enough. I heard the old man read. I should not have left you alone. You needed me with you.'

'I—would that have helped me?'

Nisana leaned against her shoulder. 'To avoid these things, this blade? No. To accept what is now yours—I could have prepared you for it. You would have realized what it was and taken it in that realization.'

'No.'

The cat eyed her with mild irritation. 'No? Easy to say, in your mood. You're afraid and not thinking properly.'

'Cat, I *am* afraid.' She was. Her thought shook, her hands did. She let go the hilts and stuffed her hands between her knees. 'To be part of a prophecy, *any* prophecy—no. It can't be, I won't!'

'Why?' Nisana demanded tartly. 'Because it has nothing to do with eating and spinning wool and planting seed and the other things of daily Nedaoan life? Because its source is a parchment copied many times from this stone, buried in the Sirdar's towers? Remember the tales of Nedao! Do you doubt that Queen Leffna was real, or Wergn her King?' Ylia shook her head. 'Or Merreven, who slew Mathkkra?' She shook her head again. 'Then do not doubt, merely because you are part of it.'

"I don't, cat," she whispered. "I don't think I do. Shelagn's sword in my hand, her bridal-box, her dowry to our need, her mail for my protection. By the feel of the blade, I should have known it, I *knew,* gut deep, when Grewl read that—her Will. But—to feel her hand, to hear her words, Shelagn's words, cat! Over a thousand years! And to know what they mean, what they portend for me. I'm afraid, yes. Anyone of sense would be."

'You—' the cat began tartly. Ylia laid a hand on her ears.

'Is there any alternaive? You know what they said. I went back through those rock chambers, gained a sword and lost myself.'

'Why?'

Ylia pushed away from the table, paced the small chamber. The sword lay in full view, in reach. Her fingers ached for it; at this moment, she dared not touch it. "Well? I wanted it, I've wanted it since the first time I dreamed it, Gods and Mothers, I still do! But was it really *me* that wanted it, or is another—the Guardians, Shelagn herself—playing with my thought, twisting it to their own ends! And to have taken another's burden—!''

'No!' Nisana interrupted her sharply. Ylia turned to stare at her. 'Not *their* ends! The battle is yours, the enemy yours and these people's. No longer Shelagn's, who has been dead ten lifetimes or more! You are her heir, not her slave!'

"Can *you* sift through her words to see that?"

'Yes. I have read the ancient books, and I knew of the Will the priest read. I have seen the copy he spoke of. The words are hers, and by them, you are indeed Shelagn's heir. The things, the sword found you. They do not control you.'

"Words, cat. You're trying to help me, I appreciate that. But—"

'Catalyst.'

The word dropped into her thought, brought her up short and around to lean against the table, face to face with Nisana. 'Catalyst,' the cat repeated. 'Did *he* not tell you?'

"Bendesevorian?" she whispered. The Nasath who had given her aid against the Mathkkra, such aid as he dared against Lyiadd, who had spoken with her not long after while his sister Nesrevera had communed with Nisana. "He told me many things, cat. About Lyiadd, mostly. A very little about their own kind. Nothing of a catalyst. For what? And *why?*"

'*She* did not tell me much of these things. The sword itself, the horn, the histories I know are aiding me to piece it together.' The cat eyed her gravely. 'There are things, sometimes people, and sometimes both, which come at certain times, and because they are what or who they are, events are torn from their paths and reset in others.'

"I *know* what the word means, cat," Ylia snapped as she hesitated. The cat lifted a corner of her lip in delicately phrased irritation.

'Good. Pay attention! Because Shelagn was *who* she was, because she alone was able to rally folk to fight for her; because her blade was forged in a certain place and time, and with certain spells upon it; because she had the Power to use the horn and the sense of proper moment for its use; because she was a wise woman as well as a fighter and could therefore control all three things: sword, shield and horn; because she understood the uses of each and was not afraid of consequence from their use. Because of all these things, the Guardians and the Folk and the Sea-Folk who were hers won that last battle, and the Lammior was slain. Had the leader of those forces been other than that woman at that time, with that blade, there would be no AEldra, there would be nothing but the Lammior's realm. *Now* do you understand?'

'No.'

'Because you don't want to, stubborn child!'

"I *don't* understand! And why me? Why should I be special, why of all the folk between here and the Sea should I be singled out?" The sword was calling to her, and a faint music was touching her, raising the hair along her nape. She moved away from the table, but her eyes brooded on it.

'You're not thinking, and you're doing it on purpose. Stop being so silly! Who else, in all the Peopled Lands, in this time when Lyiadd stands ready to fall upon us all with death, is both sorceress and swordswoman? Who else in all the lands has met with the Folk and made a pact of mutual support with them, when no other human has seen them in over five hundred years? Who was there, with the Power *and* a sword, to slay Kaltassa *and* the old shaman who spoke to them with Lyiadd's voice?'

"You killed the old shaman, I didn't. And Lyiadd is *dead*."

'Don't be so foolish,' the cat retorted sharply. 'Think on what I have said. And don't keep trying to deny Shelagh's legacy. It will haunt you to no purpose, and you've already taken its burden. You did that when you first grasped the sword. Why torment yourself with thoughts of "if I had"? You didn't, and it's too late to change that!'

"Too late," Ylia whispered, and bowed her head. She was silent, withdrawn for some time. Finally, with a little catch in her breath, she reached for the buckle to her own scabbard, slowly undid it, fastened the other in its place. She closed her eyes briefly, wrapped her hands around the hilts, slowly slid the blade home. "The Nasath grant I not fail you, long-kinswoman. *Or* your bequest." And, in an even quieter voice, "My poor people! How long have we, to rebuild before evil falls upon us again?" Nisana rubbed against her arm but for that she had no answer.

She had a handful of coin, two faceted blue stones, sitting in a bowl on the table when her council came in, and had the fun of watching each of them gape at the loose, ancient wealth. The weapons could not go unnoted, either, and she laid them in the center of the table again. "It is ours, trust to that. That stone tablet dates it, and gives it to us who found it. The sword, the shield, the horn are mine; the coin and the jewels we will use for the good of all."

Corlin took up a gold piece, bit at it gingerly, examined it in the candlelight. "This is like none I've seen before. Word's out, though, that you and my daughter and Brelian found something truly ancient, back there."

"Someone else apparently used the Caves for storage," she said.

"Not unlikely, I suppose. There've been folk in the Foessa long before us. This is proper gold even if the coinage is not valid. How much is there?"

Ylia shrugged. "Upwards of two hundred pieces, gold. More of silver. But Brelian and Lisabetha had a better look at it."

"I didn't count," Brelian said. "But I'd say there was much more than that; more silver than gold, too. And gems: many like those two. And there were some emerald, some darker blue. I don't know what they are. Pale smoky brown ones. Two small bags. We opened them, took out those two, we didn't pour them out, though."

"Gods," Bnorn breathed.

"Mothers," his son whispered. "If a man had known there was such wealth in these Caves! What chance of more?"

"We can look," Ylia said. "This was special. It's not likely there's another like it. But we've still corn and seed to find, so there's no harm in looking."

"This *is* special," Marhan said. "We've needs enough. This should come to good use." He dropped a piece of silver to the table; it rang, and he touched it with a fingertip to silence it.

"One of Erken's men just came in," Corlin said. "I sent him to get food and sleep; he must have burned the grass between the valley and here. The planting's started, and when Larig came away, they'd finished rough-roofing two houses. There's been rain the past days, enough to keep everyone damp. They'll use the houses to shelter the planters and guard for now. Larig said they measured out a pelt of land around each. Ifney sent word there's land and to spare for the numbers of us. There'll be a pelt of land per household and land left for the herds, up-valley. They're leaving the parameters of the valley, north and east, unparceled so Telean and the other villages can stay together.

"Marckl sent word that they're hard at work on the docks. Erken says Nar will be able to use them long before we're all moved, and the warehouses are marked out. Marckl wants more of his men—he gave Larig the names—who helped him box and drain river bottom land. That way he says there won't be flooding down there every spring."

"Whoever and whatever he needs," Ylia said. "And we'll send word back that we have this coin, if they have needs they can't otherwise meet. We won't need to be totally dependent on future trade or alms now."

"No," Corlin said. "And we can afford to get our exiles brought north and up-river. We'll be able to afford to feed them, once they're here."

"It's progressing, Mothers grant it continue so," Golsat said, and warded himself covertly. He flushed as he glanced up and Ylia winked at him. But his eyes were drawn back, as were everyone else's, to the coins in the center of the table.

Levren laughed; he'd seen the superstitious gesture, too. "They will. But we should keep in mind the Narrans want our wool and they're willing to pay well for it." He smiled, his gaze went distant. "Blessed Mothers, I'll have my family here. Soon." He looked up then, aware he'd spoken aloud, and the smile became rueful. But no one laughed, and the only smiles were understanding ones: Everyone knew how much Levren loved his large family and how keenly he missed them, though he seldom said so. *It'll be lively for certain, when his Lennett comes here,* Ylia thought, and bit back a grin. She could almost see the same thought running through Golsat's mind, by the suddenly wary look in his eyes. Levren's eldest daughter adored her father, patterned herself as much after him as one of her flamboyant temperament could—and passionately fought Ilderian, her harassed mother, for sword training, "Like Ylia!" She'd unintentionally alienated Golsat—and many others—early on with her outspoken ways. No, there wasn't much chance of things being dull, not with Lennett about.

"We won't forget," Lossana said. She was turning one of the silver coins over, rubbing her fingers against the raised lettering around its edge. "And if the Narrans want our cloth, they'll have it, all we can spare. And best quality. They'll get nothing we would not wear ourselves." She let the coin drop with a faint click, touched her daughter's shoulder. "Wake up, child."

"I wasn't sleeping, Mother." Lisabetha was drooping, though: swordwork was more wearing than she would ever have thought, and she was spreading herself too thin: afternoon hours helping the kitchen women gather greens or grind flour for bread, in

addition to long and arduous searches in the distant recesses of
Aresada. Evenings, they carded wool the Narrans had brought,
that sheared from Nedaoan sheep, and the wonderfully long and
silky wild goat hair Lossana had discovered clinging to the bushes
high above the caves. There was stuff to find for dyes, pots of
color to tend, wool to spin—some of the village elders who were
not able to forage or hunt were carving old-fashioned drop
spindles, and the women were keeping them busy all the daylight
hours and long after dark.

And after all these things had been done, there were still tasks,
for Lisabetha was working on her bride-box, though there was
little finery for it save the length of silk and silver thread Ysian had
left her. The thread was enough to begin a deep and complex
border, and she worked on it late hours, while she waited for
Brelian to come in from guard.

"We'll need a count of this," Corlin said. "And a decision,
where it should go."

"That we can work on now. We already know what we need."
Marhan shifted. "The Mothers know we've *talked* it enough!
More beasts, all kinds." He held up a hand, turning fingers down
one at a time. Lisabetha shook herself awake, drew writing
materials to her and began noting items as they were named.
Grewl was in a meeting of his own, with the Chosen, that Jers had
called. He hadn't dared miss it to attend Ylia's council. "Metal for
smelting new weaponry. We've nowhere near enough swords, or
points for arrows and spears. Leather for boots. The game we've
brought in isn't sufficient for that."

"Fruit trees," Golsat took up as the Swordmaster paused.
"We've no seed, no saplings, nothing like that. And grapes. And
salt."

"Paper," Lisabetha said, "ink, fine tips for pens. Wax for
seals."

"Lanterns and lamps, until we have metal to spare from
weaponry, and time to make our own," Levren added. "We're
already running out of proper light *here*. By the time we reach the
valley, we'll have nothing but fire, torches and too hastily made
candles."

Ylia laughed. "And perfumed Osneran soap! We all smell of
smoke and imperfect washing!" And, soberly, "It comes down to
lists, once again, doesn't it? I hope to never hear that word again,
after this year. Speak with people, find out what's needed, things

we can't do without and can't make or grow or fashion substitutes for. We'll see what we can buy through Nar."

They stayed awhile longer, passing the coins around, handling them as though none of them could otherwise believe they were real, talking about what they could do with the sudden wealth, though, if it had been distributed among the people at Aresada, it would have come out to less than a coin each. Put to use in trade, it spelled wealth in a way none of them would have considered a year before: saved lives over the coming winter.

A boat lay at anchor the next morning, an hour past dawn; the Narrans were learning the River and making faster and easier progress against it. And they were working at the route itself: Crews were cutting trees and brush back from the bank in a dozen places to make paths for harnessed horses, two portage trails were already cut, and two of the men who had enlarged their harbor half a dozen summers back were planning the widening of a side branch halfway between Nar and the valley so as to pass by a treacherous rapids.

Kre'Darst had left a shipment on Marckl's new docks: tools and fishing nets. They had brought on three bales of raw wool, bags of meal and salt, two crates of plain, dark cloth for immediate need, a keg of nails for building looms, wire and strong twine for heddles. Plus bundles of clothing and shoes gleaned from their folk for Nedaoan children.

"I've also promise of grains and casks for ale," Kre'Darst said over a hot, if bland, breakfast, "but I held back on that, thinking you'd rather be settled in first."

"Not that we'd mind the ale," Ylia said. "But we'll be better able to spare the women to make it then. At present, everyone is involved in keeping us fed and clad."

"We can get you chickens," the Narran offered. "And geese. The latter make better eating, but for eggs, you'd want the chickens."

"We have a few birds, but not enough," Corlin said. "We'd want both. And those we can keep here, so if you have any the next trip, we'll take them then."

Thank the Mothers for such men as I have. She'd wondered often, when she watched her father share decisions with his council, how he could bear the constant wrangling, the time it took to reach a decision they could all accept. But though there was much she and the Narrans could manage between them, it was so much easier to let someone like Corlin take care of it for her; his experience far surpassed hers, and it would leave her free to maintain cheerful relations with the Narran Captains even when they came to arguing over amounts and qualities, as they might well later on.

"We badly need needles, plenty of them. What few we have are traded back and forth, and half of them are already bent. If many more snap, we'll be in deep trouble."

"Needles," the trader noted on his board. "Chickens, geese. There'll be saplings, coming with Tr'Harsen in another 5-day or so. He got them from Yls. Apple and cherry."

"Good." Ylia scowled at her bowl but dutifully emptied it. Malaeth was watching her closely.

"Now, the other trees you mentioned," Corlin said. "If you truly think they can handle mountain winters, we may as well try them."

"They should do well, Osnera's westlands are plateau, and they grow beautifully there. We got enough for you to test. Your people should like them, and it'll be a good prospect for us as well, since if *you* have peaches and pears we won't need to trade Oversea for brandies. You're easier to bargain with than the Osnerans."

Ylia smiled. "That's worrying; my council won't like it if you get that much the better of me!"

"No chance of that," the Narran grinned, "not with Lord Corry to make the contracts."

"Speaking of contracts," Corlin said, "if you have the cloth ones with you, bring them along, we'll go and look them over."

"Do you need me?" Ylia got the last bite of her breakfast down—it was stone cold, thick and gluey—and let the trader hand her to her feet. Corlin shook his head.

"If we need your signature, we'll find you. But I know you've other things to do this morning. And it'll be awhile," he added, with a sidelong glance at Kre'Darst, who sighed good-naturedly.

"Of course it will, with *you*, sir, it always is!" He reached into an inner waterproofed pocket and brought out a thick sheaf of papers. "Lead on, then, we'd best get started."

To have a home again, a roof instead of stone icicles, to have floors of real wood and dressed stone and cool tiles, rugs instead of dirt and slick, uneven limestone and puddles—real walls with real glass windows, shutters where there was not yet glass, in place of stone and stone again, and drafts and threads of chill air—they are right, who say the most basic of needs can bring also the greatest pleasure. Even though I doubtless could do without such human needs, I found their lack nearly as painful as the Neda-oans did.

18

The weather had taken a turn, as it always did this time of year, North to South and all across the Plain. One 5-day what sun there was was blunted by a spring-chilled wind, or wind drove little squalls of rain before it. There were night fogs and now and again, still, a little frost. And then, suddenly, it was warm and the sky a brilliant blue, cloudless bowl overhead. It would stay that way, almost continuously, until past harvest. Summer had come.

The luck was holding, still: Planting Month had come and gone, with the farmers working all daylight hours and through the night when the moon permitted. The results were heartening: throughout the valley grain was ankle-high and the household gardens were up and growing rapidly. The fruit trees the Narrans brought had been planted near the stream, close to what would eventually be the City walls. All anyone could say for them, so far, was that they hadn't died. But that itself was encouraging.

Three 5-days passed: the Narrans kept busy ferrying Koderrans up-river to the new City, which was just as well, since the folk still at Aresada were growing short-tempered after so much privation, lack of privacy, short rations and uncommonly hard ground for sleeping. Ylia's council debated the matter earnestly, and decided that in order to avoid bloodshed it would be best to begin sending people on to the valley as quickly as possible. Most of them would be of more use there anyway, and the weather was dependable enough that folk could sleep on the grass until they could put roofs over their heads.

More people came in from the South, a draggle of twenty-three young men, several women, a handful of children. The old moutain-hunter Verdren had found them, brought them partway and then sent them on, advising them to keep within the western foothills, to stay out of the mountains until they must head east to the Caves, and to travel with caution. And he'd sent word for her: he'd search the foothill villages south of Yenassa, send her any folk he found. Then he'd search north. She didn't expect him to find anyone; then, too, she hadn't expected this most recent clutch of villagers.

At last, only the weavers—Lossana and Lisabetha among them—and Ylia and her women, her twenty new guardswomen, a number of guardsmen under Golsat, the herds and herders were left at Aresada. The looms had stayed busy, and Lossana was reluctantly allowing them to be dismantled and moved as a length of cloth was finished. Ylia was still elbow deep in lists. She and Lord Corry were working up the contracts with Nar.

She wasn't ready to make the move herself, yet; there was too much that needed finishing where she was. And Erken had asked that she remain until the last. "They've a surprise brewing for you, the folk. Don't disappoint them."

"Surprise?" But he wouldn't be drawn. And she was so busy, the thought of it didn't stay with her long. On top of everything else, there was going to be a Midsummer Fest, a proper, true Fest, with all that implied. And though it might not be so grand as past ones, there would still be sword and bow contests, minstrels and jugglers, games and foot races. The craftsfolk of Koderra had sufficient time and goods from their trading in Yslar to set up booths, and if none were as stocked as they had been, they would at least be there.

This year there would be plenty of Narran traders, and a Narran embassy from the Lord Mayor himself.

This was an important change in status for Nedao. There had always been trade between the lands, but Nar had never installed a permanent ambassador, and now they intended to send the Lord

Ber'Sordes, who had served long years as a Liaison in Osnera. Honor indeed!

The final folk left Aresada a 5-day before Fest opening. The looms were dismantled, the last of the cloth safely aboard Tr'Harsen's *Crayfish*. The weavers and the looms would travel to the nearly-completed docks on Tr'Harsen's boat; the herders, the herds, a guard of Erken's men and several of Ylia's young swordswomen would travel overland.

Ylia and Nisana stood on the bridge and watched them out of sight. Ylia sighed. "I've never worked so hard in my life, cat! I think I could sleep right through Midsummer."

Nisana snorted. 'You couldn't possibly! There'll be enough noise to deafen folk clear out by the River. I,' she added darkly, 'intend to continue my usual custom, and to leave the vicinity for all five days *and* not to return until they've done discussing who won what, and why, and who should have instead.'

"Nice for me," Ylia remarked mildly. Nisana snorted again. 'They'll have you so busy, you'll forget all about me.'

"I doubt *that*."

'Anyway, it's settled. Are we going to stand on this ledge all afternoon, or can we leave now? And *you* bridge, I want to see how you're progressing.'

'Cat, I swear—!'

'Don't. Just bridge.'

Odd, how she'd lost her fear of bridging, that night in the Tehlatt camp. Golsat's near loss had pushed her beyond fear, and it had simply never come back. Odd, too, that it should have been Golsat's peril; it had been a like incident that had won the xenophobic Bowmaster past an irrational fear of his own. She still avoided it when she could. It was exhausting, too demanding, even with Nisana's training. Small use, if she drain herself of Power and could do nothing once she *had* bridged. So far, fortunately, that kind of decision had not come up.

She placed them close to the River but within the trees, so as not to startle anyone who might be near when they just suddenly appeared. They stepped onto the road, and walked out into the open. Ylia stopped and blinked. The road bore straight for the small river, the town, and the Tower looming above all.

Tower—it didn't register until they came into the open, and she could all at once see it clearly. Erken had set the City on the rise she'd chosen, away from the woods. "Cat, look at that, *look* at it!" she whispered.

Nisana's fur rippled, very like a shrug. 'It's nice. They've come on well since I saw it last.' And as Ylia cast her a dark look: 'It wasn't surprise from *me*, you know. It's your folk, your Tower. If they'd consulted *me*,' she added judiciously, 'I'd have said to make it taller, and not so wide, it's proportioned like Koderra and that wasn't properly balanced either.'

'I think that was what they intended, cat.'

'So it was. Are you going to stand and gawk at it all day, or can we view it closer?'

They walked up Marckl's road toward the City. Ylia gazed around her in astonishment: One thing to be told what work was accomplished, another thing entirely to see it, and she hadn't been here since—well, no, not since she'd come back that second day for samples of the soil.

It might have been a different place entirely, save that the mountains had not changed: Where there had been dirt and wiry grey-green grass, there were now huts and fields, some already fenced. There were barns and gardens: recognizable millet knee-high to the man pulling weeds in one near plot. Hard against a hill, not far away, grey-clad Chosen hard worked on a long, low dormitory that would house their kind; others were setting fence and still others were between building and fence, planting and weeding.

There were people busily thatching roofs, people beyond that putting a final side to a cow shed. A small girl with an enormous staff came down the narrow track between two grain-fields, half a dozen brown geese honking and chucking angrily before her. Two old women sat on a doorstep, spinning, and a third stood in the doorway plaiting greens for a luckpiece to fasten to the lintel.

It was active, it was happy; it was home.

They came to a wide, low stone bridge, only rough-finished: planks were still not cut to size and rattled underfoot. Beyond this was a blaze of brilliant pink: the fruit trees were in full, heady bloom. And beyond the orchard, the marketplace.

It was neat and organized, as Koderra's had never been, since that one had grown any-which-way in an already crowded space between the King's Tower and the Gates. This was laid out in three long rows of stalls, a clean-swept square at its end. Houses were set around the market and ranged north of it, stopping just before a series of barracks that would house Erken's and Corlin's unmarried armsmen and those male household armed Ylia took to her personal service. The training and workout grounds were half finished; the armsmen who were not riding guard around the valley were busy nailing the wooden shingles on the last long, low building.

Ylia stepped into the square, turned and stood, gazing astonished at the sight that fronted her. It was, as much as possible under the circumstances, a replica of Koderra's Tower. Not as high, of course, though it rose well above the one-story houses and barracks around it. And it was of plain unfinished wood, not rock, though the outer steps were roughly dressed stone. It blurred as her vision misted; she rubbed tears away with the back of her hand.

"Ah. You like it?" She turned; Erken had materialized silently at her shoulder.

"Like it? *Like* it? I—I can't believe it! Where did they get the time?"

"They took it," the Duke replied gravely. "It was a matter of pride and importance to them, that you have this. You weren't," he added reproachfully, "supposed to have arrived yet. No one is here to meet you except me." He smiled, bowed and ushered her forward. Nisana went off on an exploration of the tall grass beyond the barracks.

It took hours, for though there were only fifteen rooms in all, there was much wonderful hand work in each of them, and she wanted to see everything. The outer doors had been hand-carved around the edges and someone had sacrificed brass plate to make fittings for them. Within, plain Narran tile covered the hall, and benches lined both sides of it. The wide stairs leading up from the hall were uncovered, but polished to a warm glow, as were the banisters. There was a large window of colored glass in the state dining hall—she would use that when the Narrans arrived for Midsummer—and a table of some curiously patterned wood. There was silver-edged plate, and wax tapers in smooth black Nedaoan pottery holders marched down the center of the table.

There was also a small dining chamber, its windows as yet glassless, the shutters unfinished. But Erken assured her this would not remain so for long. He fretted the least flaw, or imagined flaw, as she was certain those who had done the building and supplied the furnishings fretted. Her assurances that it was all beyond any hope she'd ever had were met with pleasure, but did nothing to change his unhappiness over things still not completed.

Down a narrow hall was the guard chamber, a mess for the guard, and beyond that, where odors would not penetrate to the rest of the building, the kitchens. "The open-air kitchens for summer should be finished by Midsummer," Erken said. "We'd not want heavy cooking done inside for such a banquet. But there hasn't been time—"

"It's not a problem, Erken." He shook his head, led her back through the dining halls, across the entry and into the Reception. There were half a dozen long windows running the length of the chamber, a smoothly polished wood floor. And at the far end—a goodly distance away indeed, the room would easily have matched her father's ballroom—was a raised platform, covered in ruby-colored carpets. In its midst stood a high-backed chair, its intricately carved ruff shining with gold leaf. Above it were hangings in pale blue, white and gold: the colors of the House of Ettel. And behind it, a huge royal blue drape bearing her own arms. A shield: argent, a bend azure cottised, bearing a sword unsheathed, all within a double tressure flory and counterflory, or.

She shook her head. "Erken—I don't know what to say."

"Then you have said it," he replied; his color was high. "Now, in that far corner, there'll be a musician's dais. Eventually we hope for a loft but at present it isn't practical."

"Practical," she echoed blankly. Erken laughed quietly.

"Come. You haven't seen the upper floor yet. There's still a lot."

"A lot," she repeated again, but let him wrap an arm around her shoulders and lead her from the Reception. They mounted the stairs, came into a broad hall that was windowed all down its south side, though the glass was only fitted in half of them so far.

"It's been the very pit of the Seventh Hell, getting glass intact up that river," Erken said warmly. "But once the Narrans have their horse-paths cut, we'll have a better way to transport it than water."

"Erken, truly, I don't *need*—"

"Yes, you do," he interrupted her, though mildly indeed for Erken. "Your people say you do."

The rooms were smaller here: A tiny chamber for Malaeth next to her own, a wardrobe beyond that. In this last were hung two gowns, one pale blue and severely finished, the other a deep green with silver embroidery in a wide band around the hips and deeply at the sleeve hems. Ysian's work, the last. *When and where had she found time for that?* Beyond these were a sensibly narrow riding skirt and shirt of dark blue, and the tabard she and Malaeth had argued over: Her house colors ran down the sides and across the hem, her sword was embroidered in gold against the right shoulder. It was well padded and quilted, and would be warm.

These garments hung from pegs. There were three chests in the wardrobe, two new and the large one she had found at Aresada. That still held its cache of arms. The other two were presently empty. The jewel chests stood on a table under a shuttered window in her bed chamber.

There was a real bed, with high posts, though no hangings as yet. Dressed furs covered the mattresses: rag and grass-stuffed wool on a woven rope frame. Nearly as fine as her bed in Koderra, and compared to Aresada's rock with insufficient pine boughs, at least the equal of anything the Sirdar slept on in Yls. Across its foot lay a night robe dyed deep red and woven in the pattern that was Lossana's specialty.

Beyond her bed chamber was a study, two large rooms for her women—a pleasure room for embroidery and sewing, and music; a sleeping chamber with half a dozen beds.

It was going to be a change. A pity: she'd enjoyed the easy camaraderie she'd had with the men, and with Malaeth and Lisabetha when they came north. Even in Aresada, where it was borne upon her more often that she was Queen and not just another of the folk, it had been a relaxed thing: she moved among the people constantly, spoke with them, gave sword training to their daughters, worked occasionally with Marhan or Brelian or Levren and those they taught. Her surroundings, this wonderful present from her folk, would change that, however much she sought to keep the contact between herself and them as it had been. There would be more formality, more separation.

She brought herself back to the moment; Erken was apologizing for the hall flooring, which had been laid in patterns of three kinds of wood but not yet waxed. She finally wrung a promise from him to make no more such apologies when what there was was so excellently and lovingly done.

He stopped outside the next chamber: a small, light and airy room, unmistakably a nursery. Ylia felt her face grow warm. She turned to scowl at Erken, who hastily composed his face. "Long-range planning, of course," he said gravely.

"Long range—indeed," she retorted.

"It's not practical to add them later," he protested innocently, but his eyes gleamed with amusement.

"Damn you, anyway," Ylia said, and started on down the hall. Two last chambers there—guesting rooms, and a long balcony overlooking the market and the orchard completed the upper level. "I'd managed to *forget* that kind of thing!"

"You're not supposed to, Lady Ylia," Erken said formally.

"No, and now I won't be able to, either!" He shook his head, and she sighed. "All right. Give me at *least* through Midsummer Fest, and then bring out your maledictable lists again. We'll work on them, seriously."

"It's for my own protection," Erken said blandly as they withdrew from the balcony and he closed the doors behind them. "If you hadn't named me temporary heir—"

"I know you better than that," she broke in, as blandly. "You'd want me wed and be-heired no matter what."

"Well, you know, you're properly of age. There's no real reason why not," Erken began persuasively, but stopped as she held up a hand.

"There are a lot of reasons why not, and you know it. I've promised you, after Midsummer Fest. *Not* now. Let me adjust to this—all of this—first."

"All right." They stopped outside her chamber doorway. "But you'd better take no more chances like you did against Kaltassa last month! My hair stood on end when I heard about it!"

"I'll keep myself alive," she assured him dryly, but he shook his head.

"That's easy to say, and scarcely guaranteed when you do things like that. Ah well, it's not hard to see where you get it, Brandt was the same way. Stubborn, brave, skilled and reckless all at once. Sheer luck and the Mothers' love kept *him* alive as long as—" He stopped abruptly. "Gods, Lady. I'm sorry. Truly sorry."

"It's all right, Erken." But she'd gone still and small, and freckles stood out clear against a suddenly pale face.

"I—I *am* sorry."

"Don't be. It's true, anyway. You know I want truth from my council on all things."

"It wasn't necessary," he insisted unhappily.

The mood was irretrievably broken. She attempted several conversations, as did he but they fell flat. Finally he bowed deeply, took his leave. "It's near noon-hour, I promised I'd eat with my men and help them with that roof. The women are cooking a noon-meal down in the square for everyone in the City, but I doubt they know you're here. I'll send someone to you."

"No, I'll come out. I may not have many more chances to just wander out and eat where I choose, without fuss." He merely nodded, bowed again, and was gone.

Watching her from my vantage point, where I was able to remain free of the tangle of emotions she fought—fear of the burden, her foreseeing, her dreams, the sword, and the strongest irritation I ever saw anyone bring out in her—it seemed to me she was like one who stubs a toe against a rock: she is fated to stub the same toe again and again, and at least as hard.

19

The mountains were edged with a brilliant dark blue, at least eastward. To the west, the sun was nearing the tops of the ancient cedar grove, and only occasional rays worked through thick trees to touch the clearing, though the rock ledge at its northeast end was warm with afternoon light.

The hunter dropped his bags with a weary sigh. *Damn*, he thought. That rain the last two nights had left everything in this clearing unpleasantly damp. And there wasn't another place to camp, not nearby. Nothing he'd make before dark. And in these wretched mountains, a man of sense didn't walk late; a feeling of being watched, being followed, dogged his steps. He'd done so once or twice, when he was young on the Foessa, and still unwilling to admit there might be things in the world a man couldn't see or touch, things that could still do him harm.

At least his cache was unmolested, unlike the one two camps ago: something had dug down and torn out the triple-wrapped hide food bags. He hadn't gone hungry that night, but he'd eaten at least as much dirt as food.

Fire's going to be difficult. There wasn't any place here to store wood, no cave, no rock ledge overhang—nothing. *Inniva's Warp but I'm tired! This had better work, that's all!* Even if it did, he'd have a bear of a headache to show for it. At times like this, he seriously wondered what had originally seemed so fine about the Foessa, about living alone and by his own wits.

Well, he let the thought trail. Old kettle first. He pulled the ancient, battered thing free of its wrapping: it was blackened, greasy with ash, and the bottom had rotted or been cut from it long since. He dug a little farther, found his knife. Narran, it was a seaman's tool, and more than useful to a mountain-hunter with its double-length and treble thick blade. He located the old place near the center of the meadow, nearer the northern side. The sun had at least dried some of the water, and the dew wouldn't hang on him past sunrise. He squatted down, cut around a chunk of turf four times the size of his kettle. It came away easily, having been cut free numerous times before. The dirt under was black, thick with ash. He dug down, freed the rocks from previous fires that were buried under the ash, edged the pit with them, dug out ash and a mound of dirt until he had a hole as deep as his hand.

He stood, stretched and went in search of wood. *No, not much good wood here,* though some of what he found was surface-wet only. And under a towering fir, he found a few dry needles, twigs, and one hanging branch that might catch if he could get any fire going at all.

Back to the pit then. He spread the leather that had wrapped the bottomless kettle, squatted on that, broke and cut the branch into pieces, dumped the handful into the pit. It wasn't much; he could only hope it would be enough. He stacked the stuff he'd found earlier at his elbow, where he could reach it if the fire did take. The kettle went in next, atop the half-dry bits of fir, and into it went two fists of needles, a crunched-up double handful of twigs. He filled the thing loosely, fished out flint and tinder.

It didn't want to start. Smoke moved for his face with what he swore was intent, set him coughing and burned his eyes. He turned away, caught his breath, rubbed the smoke from his lids, and turned back to try again. It caught, smoldered sluggishly, sent small flames up as he blew on it cautiously, but faded back to a tiny handful of red-edged needles and more smoke. *All right.* And, tiredly, *Damn.* He caught at the rocks on both sides of the pit, fastened his gaze on the kettle and concentrated.

It took time. He was tired and it wasn't easy to focus his thought completely on what he did when he was so worn. And nothing short of total concentration served. And he went totally by instinct here; no one had helped him define what he did, how it worked, how to control it, how to use it without draining himself. *Harder,*

*think harder, there's smoke, black hells, what's wrong with it
tonight?* The edges of his vision went as his concentration
intensified, the ground at his knees, his hands blurred. With a loud
snap, flame spat skyward, the kettle turned dull red, the wood
under it began to crackle. He waited until the metal was nearly as
bright as the sunset had been, gingerly caught at the handle with
his knife and jerked it upward, pulling it free and sending a
cascade of hot clinkers and burning wood onto the waiting stack
below. The fire hesitated, took for good and settled in to burn
properly. He stacked the wet wood close and turned to his second
pack to bring out food.

It took enough of his strength to unnerve him. It always did
that. But it worked. It still caught him by surprise that it did, as
long as he'd done it, as many other odd things as he could do. It
hadn't failed him yet, so long as he was within the mountains,
though it never worked in Nar, and he'd needed it there badly a
time or two. And it hadn't worked to the south either—at least, not
when he went south and west. He no longer traveled south and
east, though he didn't analyze that either. It would have angered
him to have to admit that the southeast of the Foessa scared him.

But it was in the southeast that the Fire-Making had come to
him. Strange things happened to a man near the Lake of the Falls.

It was cool in the tree-shade, not pleasantly so. He stopped to
hold his hands to the fire more than once as he found the skewers,
threaded meat onto them and set them over the fire. It wasn't until
he'd finished he noticed the quiet.

"Odd." He seldom spoke aloud, anymore, and the word
echoed. No birds, not even one. The last time he'd been here,
there'd been families of them, all around; they'd had him awake
an hour before true dawn with their squawking. Bear? But there
weren't that many of them so far north, and even so, they avoided
men. He couldn't sense one, either: sensing bear was simple.

Unbidden, a reminder of the brief, intense fear touched at him,
deep down; the shadow that had darkened more than the ground
and had sent him fleeing back the way he'd come, not long since.
The shadow *she'd* reminded him of. He savagely pressed that
aside.

Check, while it's still light. He set rocks under his skewers,
balancing the meat a little higher above the fire, shoved a good-
sized log into the pit and rose to his feet. One hand sought and
wrapped around his sword hilts.

The trees first. He felt nothing, but the sense wasn't always reliable after he'd pressed it so, starting fire. A man could walk through those woods and see nothing even if it was only six lengths away. Becoming aware of it—aye, but a man liked more warning than six lengths in thick wood, and he couldn't be certain he'd have that, not just yet. In an hour or so—but in an hour or so, it would be dark.

He eyed the rock ledge, calculated. He'd be able to look over the entire area from that height, if there *was* anything to see. And it looked climbable: steep, but not dangerously so. A man was a fool who'd climb something really steep, out alone like he was, a man could fall there and die of starvation, and likely even his bones would never be found.

He shuddered. "Damn, you're like an old woman tonight. What's wrong with ye?" All the same, he tightened his grip on his hilts and drew the sword as he stepped up. His boots scraped across slabbed granite and fallen bits of rock.

Another glance at the ledge towering over him suggested he'd be better not attempting it; it was steep and crumbly. He strode across the slabbed stone. Curious. He'd been here at least ten times and had never before noticed how the ledge dropped down on this northern edge. It was a regular cliff, with a narrow ditch of a gully below it. From the meadow, you'd never notice cliff or depth, more than he had. The far side of the gully reared up in a steep, black fir-covered slope.

He let his gaze sweep the slope, touched at it with what there was of inner sense: nothing. Full sun still smote the slope and the trees were spaced as though it were a park. Nothing could hide there. He glanced over his shoulder. The fire was doing well; it would take just fine, and the wood around the edge would dry. A glance at the sky assured him he'd need to cover none tonight, once he'd dried it. No headache to go with breakfast. The smell of his dinner faintly reached him as a light breeze bent the upper branches and whispered across the low grasses.

And then, suddenly, something else: a sense, a scent, a shiver that caught at the hair on his nape, sent his stomach queasy and dampened his hands. Fear . . .

He whirled, stared into the setting sun; catherine wheels filled his vision and with a curse he shaded his eyes with a shaking hand. His heart was thumping erratically. Fear: it took him by the throat. Twenty small, greyish-white, spiderish creatures were creeping silently from the wood and moved slowly toward him with purpose. They carried knives, short swords, spears. And behind the armed came two more, bearing a stone bowl between them. With his heightened inner sense, its use was all too clear: even across the clearing the reek of blood reached him.

Mothers aid me! He was white under his beard; the hand that brought the sword to guard, the one that drew the dagger from its arm-sheath, were trembling. One of the bowl-holders shouted aloud, the shielding that had almost hidden them was gone, and terror wrapped him in clammy arms. He nearly fell.

They came on, still slowly but with no less deadly intent. *My blood to that dish, my life to their hands*—"Gods and Mothers, your aid to me!" His cry echoed across the rocks.

There was no answer, save that the Mathkkra flung themselves forward. He set his shoulder against stone and waited.

Ylia stood in the place that was already her favorite, of all the places in the Tower: the small southern balcony, where she could gaze out across the flowering trees, across the rough bridge and the broad, shallow river. Beyond them lay the southernmost of the holdings and neatly stone-separated pelts of plowlands to where the river vanished in tall pine forest. A faint, deep gold still reflected off the currents from the sun that had gone beyond her sight moments before: candlelight and hearthlight appeared in open doorways and shutters, the smell of cooking drifted down the City streets. A few men still tended their lands, though most had abandoned them at sunset. Far down the valley, she could hear the high bleat of sheep, the lowing of cattle and the clatter of bells, the calls of the herders as they came to the temporary pens erected near the east base of the bridge. A horseman galloped up the road from the Aresada and clattered across the bridge, rode at a more seemly pace beneath her portal and headed toward the barracks.

Her fingers strayed absently across the sword hilts, and stopped there. It was warm. But it generally was, as though it had a life of its own. *As it does.* The thought gave her no comfort. She pushed it aside; pointless. She'd made her decision when she ignored the warnings that rang through her head in the pit, and taken the sword anyway.

The shield, and the horn, rested in their chest in her chambers, at the foot of her bed. She'd never fought with shield, except one time with Marhan and strictly as an exercise. If the leather lozenge had other use, she didn't know it. And the horn: a day might come when a battle-horn was needed. Like the shield, it might be more than that. She didn't know. The sword: that she could use.

Whatever its other virtues, it was also sword, and none had ever fitted her so well before.

Whatever else it did, at least it did that.

Her hand tingled unpleasantly, she became suddenly aware that *all* of her did. The inner sense came sharply aware: someone or something was calling and for immediate aid. *Nisana?* But she knew even as she sent the thought it wasn't the cat. Nisana was out in the tall grasses behind the Tower, hunting. And who else within Nedao might call?

But that was wrong, too: It was well outside the valley, south of the Aresada and high up the slopes. Need, dire need, that rang through her; terror, disgust, anger at that fear permeated the cry for help. Danger. Someone was near to losing his life.

She closed her eyes, caught at the balcony with her free hand and sent out a search. So intense was that call it brought her around, took the mind-touch and sent it flying south and west. It fastened on its source in less than a breath.

Mathkkra! Mathkkra, sweating and chittering in the light of the last sun, a swarm of them, armed with blades and bloody purpose. They pressed forward to attack. A man faced them, his back hard against stone. His left arm hung useless at his side, a black-stained dagger lay where it had fallen; blood ran down his fingers, from his shoulder.

I know that stone, the Nasath protect me, I know it! Prophecy and true-dream rang her like a bell and she swayed with it, nearly losing the far vision: Her fingers tightened on the hilts, the nails of her free hand dug into the palm. It was the mountain-hunter. He fought like a man exhausted, and without the rock he might have fallen. The set of his face said he knew he wouldn't see the moon rise, but there would be fewer of his enemy to walk away when he fell. *No. No man dies so, not by the hands of these—things!* She drew the sword, pulled the dagger into her left hand and bridged.

She came in behind him and well to the side, fearing to trust her inner sight and the bridging any better than that. She swayed, caught at rock—*It must someday become practical to use, damn the thing!* The hunter pivoted sharply, his breath catching in his throat with a strangled little sound, and he tried to block against whatever was there with his left. He staggered. She willed herself what strength she could, leaped to his side.

The Mathkkra stared at her briefly but pressed the attack as though her presence, and the manner of it, made no difference at all. But the man still stared at her in stunned surprise, and was

nearly run through; she felled three of the creatures as they sprang
for him. At her wordless shout of warning, he pulled his mouth
shut and turned back to fight with a fury that belied his wounds.
The Mathkkra hung on grimly for a long moment and then
scrambled back out of reach, ten fewer than they had been
moments before.

"What are you doing here?" he demanded roughly.

"I came to help you."

"Leave!" he snapped. It was her turn to stare: *What's the
matter with him?* "I ask no man's aid, surely no woman's! Do you
think to tip the balance against so many of those?"

"Why not? Two are twice as many swords as one, or so *I* hear.
But if you prefer death, tell me now and I'll give you a clean one
before I go!"

He laughed. Shook his head. "Funny woman, aren't you?
Who'd want to die, by their hands or any? I've fought here for
near an hour to avoid that fate." He sobered sharply and glared at
her. "But I will not see your death added to my debt to the
Mothers! You came by your magic—go the same way!"

Ylia glared back. "You made it clear enough once you are exile
by choice, but you are still Nedaoan! Take care how you speak to
me!" He muttered something under his breath, turned his head
back to keep a close watch on the Mathkkra. She cast a worried
glance at the sky, another, at least as worried, at her companion.
The sun was already off them. It would be gone shortly and the
Mathkkra would become more bold as night came. And there
might be more of them, more light-shy than these. Or there might
be Thullen.

But with only the two of them, and one clearly unable to leave
the support of the rock, they could not attack. And the Power in
her was near dead still from the drain of bridging.

"Why did you come?" He broke a long silence; his eyes, like
hers, remained on the Mathkkra, who seemed to be discussing
some plan or other. "I asked, you ignored me."

"I answered the rudest of your remarks first; your fault if I
forgot the other," she replied shortly. "I thought I told you. I felt a
call for aid, I saw your need, and I came."

"Call," he snorted, but a chill ran through him. *Gods and
Mothers, was that what I did, when I called upon You for help? I
touched upon AEldra Power?* He was still fighting the strange
reverberations, deep in his own inner resource, that her arrival had
set up. Anger set it thrumming: how *dare* she come here, he

thought, with her sword-marred beauty, her eyes burning a hole in him, her man's breeches and man's weapons so incongruous with such a woman's body and small woman's hands? How dare she shred his concentration so. The white horrors would have him with no effort at all, now, and drain his lifeblood into that stone dish. . . . His stomach twisted and he nearly gagged. "I called no one. Who would answer?"

"Not aloud." He snorted again. "Called. Power to Power," she added, but she herself didn't look like she believed it. He laughed loudly and mockingly. The Mathkkra started, retreated a pace.

"Power to Power. Of course, I forgot, I'm AEldra! Don't I look it?"

"Forget it," she said shortly. *I must have been mistaken, how could a great brainless oaf like this have drawn search, whatever his need?*

"No. I want to know what this gabble is."

"If *I* knew, I'd tell you," she snapped. "It happened, or I couldn't have sensed you all the way from the valley, could I?"

"Why ask me? I don't know about these AEldra things. That's your domain. Look." It took effort, it cost him to set aside anger that was more than half fear for her, terror for himself and the grim certainty of that bowl waiting for him, back there in the shadows. *Get her out of here!* "There is no point to this arguing. Leave now, I have enough blots against my inner being to send me to the Black Well this night. I'd not add your death to that list! I'll take what of these I can with me, to offset. By all the Mothers at once, don't impede me!"

"Impede you!" she shouted in a sudden fury. "Did you think I'd come so far to crouch at your back, you hairy oaf? Did you— 'Ware!" The Mathkkra, white blots in a deep blue gloom, pressed forward. The hunter cast her one last furious look, muttered a blistering oath and braced himself, his right shin scraping against rock. To his intense discomfort, she braced herself hard against his left shoulder and brought up her blades.

Her sword slammed against a short Mathkkra sword, and a clash rang through her head: a shower of blue-white sparks cascaded around her. The breath caught in her throat: *True-dream. By all the gods at once, I don't want it!*

Her companion cried out in sudden terror. The Mathkkra huddled down and away from them, and a patch of inky night sailed down the ledge and across them. "Don't meet its eyes," she

shouted at him. "It'll freeze you!" The creature circled once, high
up, banked over the black fir across the ravine and sailed straight
for them. Mathkkra scrambled down from the rock, screeing fear
of their own. The hunter brought an arm up to shield his eyes. She
threw herself in front of him.

"Shelagn!" Pain ran through her like a shock, the blade flared
and the ledge seemed to shake under her feet. A spiral of silver
smoke shot upward catching the flying horror in its blast; with a
wailing howl that chilled her blood, the thing simply vanished.
She stared at the place it had been, stunned, until the hunter
touched her arm and pointed. The Mathkkra were on their feet
again, beginning a slow stalk.

"By all the Hells at once, what was that, and what did you do to
it?" he whispered. She swallowed hard.

"I don't *know*. Don't ask." He staggered suddenly and fell
against her, nearly taking her down with him. With difficulty, she
helped him back against the rock, back into a niche that would
keep him upright and protect his flanks.

"Leave me." He'd only a whisper left for voice, and only will
kept his fingers around the hilts of his sword. "I won't last another
pass, and you can't aid a dead man!" Silence. "*Please* leave."

"No."

"You—you know, I laughed, when I first saw you, clad like
that. Back in that valley you've taken. But the old Swordmaster
always did teach well. I can see his style in your moves. And you
learned well." His eyes searched her face, though he couldn't see
it at all clearly, for encroaching night and the blur his vision had
become. *What is the matter with me? I can feel her fear, feel her
thought—she's—black hell, she's pitying me, I won't have it!* He
levered himself a little more upright. "Go!"

"No!" *She* wasn't reading *him*, there was too much else
chasing through her thought at the moment: Terror at what the
blade had done, fear for him. He was going to die anyway, more
Mathkkra would come now and even if they fought the creatures
off, he'd die of blood loss before she could do a thing about it. *He
can't! Horrible man that he is, he can't!*

Shelagn's sword: She'd give almost anything not to use it again,
not like that. But—not his life, no human life given to those.
There *were* more Mathkkra. Twice as many at least and with such
reinforcements they were ready to take the humans. And able, for
how could two alone oppose so many? She could feel their

assurance, their certainty—her death. His. Their blood for the stone sacrifice bowl, though the man had already wasted much.

She tore her thought free of them, braced herself and reluctantly brought the sword up again. *The Nasath guard my inner being, and shield it from what I do.* "Shelagn," she whispered.

She couldn't see: the very black of hell came forth with the smoke and hid the Mathkkra. Muted, too, their terrified shrieks. It faded slowly, taking with it her fear, the Fear that was Mathkkra. A faint touch of the second level of sight, all there was in her: two alone remained standing, and they turned to flee. She flung the dagger after one, dropped the sword and brought up her hands to send Baelfyr at the other. It fell, burning, into the ravine.

She knelt, gathered in the sword with fingers that remembered the sharp shock and feared it, but it was again only a blade. With a shudder, she returned it to its sheath and went to retrieve her dagger. She set her teeth against her lower lip, sent a reluctant mind-touch through the bodies of the enemy. None lived.

She turned back, then, and clambered up the rock ledge. The hunter lay in a huddle amid the rock where she'd set him before the last attack. "If he's died," she whispered. His sword lay red and wet across two of his fallen foe.

She knelt, felt his throat for pulse. It took twice-through her mother's calming charm to force her fingers still enough to feel it. There, but fast and much too faint. She caught at his shoulders, pulled him free of the rocks, turned him face up. Probed his wounds with a light mind-touch.

He could die anyway. But that was foolish. She'd healed Brelian once, and after a night twice as arduous as this. If the sword had left her strength enough.

It had. She spied his guttering campfire, and kept protective arms around his shoulders as she bridged them. The distance was so slight, she scarcely felt it, even burdened and worn as she was. She draped her furred cloak over him while she fed the blaze sticks and brought it back to reluctant life. She ate some of the done bits of meat from his skewers, turned the rest to the fire, and went back to him.

He'd lost blood, and he'd received a number of minor cuts. By themselves, those would have healed sooner or later, and if he'd scarred no one would see them. She grinned weakly: if the Mathkkra had marked *his* face from chin to brow, the beard would hide most and who'd see what was left? The grin faded: for some reason, it bothered her, still, the way he looked at her face.

His left arm was broken. It bled still, sluggishly now, from a
deep cut that ran all the way through shoulder muscle. A job,
that's what he'd be. And here, in the dark, alone. She couldn't.
She knew she'd never have the nerve to close her eyes, to close off
all the protective senses to center them on a healing. 'Nisana—
Nisana!'

Long silence. Then: 'What?'

'I need you, come now!'

'I was asleep,' the cat grumbled. 'Can it wait?'

'No.'

The cat grumbled again, but joined and moments later was at
her side. 'Is *this* what you left the walls for? I thought you were
practicing the bridging!'

'I don't. You know that.'

'You should, you know you should—but *this!*' She gazed
around the clearing, took in the fallen Mathkkra, the gravely
wounded mountain-hunter. 'If I were Marhan or Erken, I'd chew
your ears just now. I won't. Explain yourself and this later. I'll
guard, you heal.'

'Thanks, cat.' Now she could close her eyes, close away her
thought, with reasonable confidence. The healing was, as she'd
feared, difficult. But the sword seemed to have taken none of *her*
strength for what it did. Ylia pushed to her feet finally, found the
hunter's pack and covered him with his own blankets, took her
cloak back and wrapped it around chilled shoulders.

'I'll stay,' Nisana offered.

'No. I will. He'll sleep, he'll need a guard. I'll do it.'

Nisana eyed her curiously, bit off a 'Why?' Foolish, all too
often, to ask why humans did things. Frequently they didn't know
themselves. And there were things to do with battle companion-
ship she would never make sense of anyway. Besides, if the man
woke—he couldn't speak with her, and she remembered the looks
he'd given her when they first met. *Worse than that fool of a
Swordmaster, this one. I don't need another such fool.* 'You're
worn, you still overuse for a bridging. Rest if you can, but set a
shielding around you both if you sleep, girl.'

"I will. If there's danger I'll send for you.' She half pulled the
sword from its sheath. 'I need to think. About things—what's
happened here. I'll tell you tomorrow.'' She looked across the fire.
"All right?''

'It has to be, I suppose,' Nisana replied huffily. Mysteries and
turbid riddles. Unlikely in this open child, and momentarily

irritating. She reminded herself Ylia was not the kind who made up mysteries and riddles to give her self importance. *What's chanced here?* But clearly she would get nothing more from Ylia just now, not without simply reading her. And that Nisana would not do, not unless Ylia asked her to. 'I can send Golsat to take your place, if you wish, or Brelian.'

"No. I'll be all right. And I need to *think*."

'I don't like this,' the cat snapped finally. 'But your mind's set, isn't it?' And she vanished. Ylia sighed. Nisana was going to be hard to placate.

The smell of cooking meat brought her back to the moment; she reached for the nearest skewer, cursed as she burned fingers on it, worried meat loose with her dagger and the hunter's Narran knife and tossed it from hand to hand until it cooled enough to eat.

It was with difficulty that she pushed aside all thought save hunger until she'd eaten enough. And then it smote at her from all sides, curdled her stomach and tickled the hair on the back of her neck. *What have I done tonight? And by all the hells of all the gods and demons at once, how did this Nedaoan call to me?*

*If the girl could have seen what I saw of her
thought, beyond what she intended me to see; if
she could have seen the shadings and harmon-
ics of what she thought, I doubt that she would
have been so willing for me to read her. I'd tried,
more than once, to explain even to Scythia why I
preferred not to read human thought. Somehow,
the invasion of privacy must not be as repugnant
to them as it is to those of my kind. Clearly, they
did not realize that I came away each time with a
little more of them entwined with me. Or—
frightening thought indeed—they knew, and did
not care.*

20

"You worry unnecessarily; do not, my friend."

Ylia started, the air going from her in a high-pitched little cry,
and her hand halfway to her blade. It froze there. That voice,
touching inner being as much as ear; that form.

"Eya?" Viewed with normal vision, a being out of Nedaoan
and AEldran myth stood at her side: a dryad, four hands high,
branch-brown and branch-slender, a narrow dark face surrounded
by heavy mosslike hair. Eyes like young willow-leaves gazed out
at her.

Seen with the inner eye, the Dreyz had no true form at all: a line
of light flickered and flared blue-white. Ylia let the Power relax;
she much preferred to see dryad, the light hurt her eyes. The
dryad's voice was resonant, deep, tickled her ear. "I am Eya."
She stepped forward to lay a brittle-fingered hand against a human
arm. "We have kept what watch we could over ye, Nedao's Lady.
This is the first opportunity ye have given us to speak with ye."

That answered her most urgent—and rather resentful—ques-

180

tion. *Where were you when I needed you, you or Bendesevorian? When I found this sword, and when I found what it could do?* "Because of people—" she began. Eya nodded.

"This man will not sleep much longer, so we must be brief. Always you are surrounded by your folk. This is a good thing for your safety, but a difficulty to us. To me." Eya's hand went to the sword hilts. "We were aware, when her bequest betook itself to the Caves, and later, when ye found it. Had it been possible, one of us would have spoken to ye then, for we knew ye were troubled by it." Ylia nodded. *Betook?*

"Betook itself?" she echoed. The dryad nodded.

"What else? Shelagn was never in these northern mountains, and so when it was clear ye would be there a time, they went to you. There was no doubt among us, or in *his* mind, that the time she foresaw had come, and who would be chosen to inherit." Silence. Eya moved a little forward to gaze down at the sleeping mountain-hunter. "It is good that he lives. There are things he will do, that he must do."

"You—you know him?" she asked past a suddenly dry mouth.

"No. That he is Nedaoan, as ye are. More: that he has Power, and that it distresses ye."

"I—it's unheard of, Lady," Ylia whispered. "No one of Nedao has AEldra Power—"

"But it is *not* AEldra," Eya said as the swordswoman hesitated. Ylia stared at her wide-eyed. "Like in certain ways, for the Nasath did not create what they gave your mother's long kin. They took what grew wild in these Foessa, tamed it so that folk could use it safely, and gave them that. What this man has is untouched by Nasath; it is wild."

"Gods and Mothers."

"By all rights," Eya went on, "he should be unable to use it, as ye were, because of the block Plains blood puts upon Power. But this man is resourceful and strong, he has manipulated that block. And so he can do small things with the Power that even he does not think of as sorcery."

"He *called* me." Ylia cast a frightened glance at the unconscious hunter. He suddenly made her very nervous indeed. Another Lyiadd? She knew nothing of him, suspected a thing or two. There was violence in him, a strong temper. If he'd killed, left the Plain because of that—she brought her attention back to the moment with an effort. Eya had stepped back to her side, had a hand on the sword hilts again.

"It was good that ye answered his call."

"You know—?"

"That much. And another thing. The sword is not safe alone. Ye do not understand the things yet as ye finally will. *She* did not, for long. There are three: sword, shield, horn. The sword by itself can be a danger, ye saw that." Ylia nodded. "The shield tempers its strength. Keep them together, that the sword not run wild, that it not take ye with it."

"It would do that?"

Eya shrugged; her hair rustled, and a faint scent of moss and cedar teased Ylia's nostrils. "We do not know. Even she who bore the weapons before Shelagn did not know." And as Ylia cast her a startled glance, "They are old. Older than ye had thought them. Shelagn also thought herself used when she was chosen by the sword. Does that ease your fear? She did not think so for long. Find what ease ye can in that, then." The hunter stirred; the Dreyz shimmered, nearly vanished. He turned his face toward the fire, settled back into sleep. "A last thing. Do not let this man touch the blade."

"I—I don't understand. I wouldn't, I don't trust him. But—not let him touch it?"

"Or let it touch him. What he carries has been building in him for long years, but it lies deep, where he cannot feel it or sense it. If he and that blade touched, it would release that. It might kill him. It would change him."

"He—" Ylia swallowed. "He could become another Lyiadd?"

"Perhaps. He has the strength and the will to pursue any course the Power set before him. It would depend upon him, the kind of man he is. But you know this?"

"I know nothing of him. I fear certain things, though."

"Then by all means, keep the blade from him. Keep the shield with you, learn to use them together. The sword will not be such a burden." The hunter stirred again, spoke aloud; the Dreyz vanished. Ylia cried out, stood and stared around her. The man at her feet rolled onto his shoulder, pulled the blanket snug against his chest and subsided again, but Eya was gone for good.

The hunter stirred again, drawing her attention; she tucked the blankets back around him, her own cloak over all, and settled back down across the fire from him; there was still meat on the skewers, and she picked at it. *Hungry—but I'd better save him some of his own food, he'll wake up hungry as well.* He. Who was he? She hadn't even a name to put to him, nothing save that his accent betrayed the North now and again, and the bow he'd given her at their first meeting was purely Teshmoran. Perhaps not a herder then; he'd held and used that sword, for all his exhaustion, like a trained fighting man. Perhaps one of Corlin's or Erken's, perhaps she'd been right the first time, he'd lost some lady to his stupid temper and left.

It didn't matter. After this, particularly after Eya's warning, she'd stay clear of him and if he got himself cornered by Mathkkra again that was his problem, not hers!

Moonlight cast a chill blue light on the tips of the cedar at the western edge of the clearing, moving slowly down until it cleared the eastern mountains. It glanced off the sword, so that for a brief moment her hands were clad in silver and pearls.

"What have I done?" she whispered. Anger was beginning to edge the thought, pushing earlier fear aside at least a little. "I'm being *used*." Never mind what the Dreyz said, it was still no pleasant thought. "Unfair," she hissed, and drove a fist into the sod.

It was almost funny. Nisana had more than once accused her of Nedaoan fatalism. *Cat, if you only knew!* Deep down, she'd always believed in a way around fate, the right of a man or woman to change the course of an oncoming thing and to so avoid it. But this! This thing cut across belief and sense both. If she believed half of what Eya had told her, a tenth of what she *dreamed*, then she'd been fated to hold this blade from birth. Or perhaps before that. Perhaps it went back to the day Scythia refused Lyiadd and chose instead to marry Brandt, lending an additional weight to Lyiadd's stack of grudges that finally tipped him over the edge and sent him into the Foessa. Perhaps—even before that. She slammed her fist into the ground again, harder. Against such a progression of events as that, how dare she believe herself to control her own fate? And what of Nedao? Would Shelagn's legacy put itself before her first duty to her people?

The mountain-hunter mumbled something, drawing her attention away from black thoughts, and opened his eyes. "Where are we?" He'd seen her, but after that first swift glance he would not look at her.

"At your campsite."

"Not safe."

"Safe enough. But I—"

"Those that attacked me?"

"Dead, all of them."

"You know this for certain?"

"I know it. If there are others, I don't sense them, and they haven't attacked." He cast her a sharp glance, looked away and sat up. "Do you want water?"

"Yes." She handed him the bottle, held out one of his skewers. He took it, tugged meat free, chewed. "It's overdone. How long have I been insensible?"

"By the moon, two hours. It's dry but edible. I've had some."

"Oh." He pulled more meat from the skewer, stuffed it into his cheek. He brought the hand down slowly, moved his fingers with care. "That—my arm was broken, there was a rock, I heard it break." Dark eyes met hers squarely across the fire. "Your doing, isn't it?" He didn't sound much pleased.

"I healed you, yes."

"I thought you dead. It was the last thing I remember thinking," he said harshly. "That was all my last thought, that I'd killed Nedao's Queen. Nice thing for you to do to me."

"Nonsense," she cut in crisply. "You didn't kill me, no one did. My choice. I saw your need, and I came."

He sighed heavily, clearly a man pushed beyond patience. "That's another thing, this about *seeing* my need—"

"I wasn't finished, quiet! I saw your need, but it was *my* decision to come here. I could have left you to the Mathkkra."

"I see." He didn't sound like he saw. "Well, then. So tell me again how I called you here."

"No. Why should I bother? *I* don't understand it, anyway. I told you what happened. At first I thought another AEldra was calling, but obviously not." *Wild Power.* She barely held back a shudder.

"Ridiculous," he snorted. "There's no AEldra in *me!*"

"I can see that for myself, and *stop* interrupting me! That's what happened. Why, I don't know. I don't fully understand AEldra Power, I came to it late. And I don't understand these mountains. But one of those who came north with me has Sight, and for a time she could *hear,* AEldra fashion. Because of the Foessa."

"I told you, I don't have Power," he said stubbornly.

She sighed. "Whatever you say." *You certainly don't have manners!* she thought furiously. "But the Foessa are strange, and strange beings inhabit them. But you must already know that."

Brief silence, as though he wished to emphasize that he was not overriding her speech. Then: "You need not look at *me* when you say that. Strange beings."

She gaped at him, open-mouthed. "I never did!"

He chuckled, and for the moment became quite human. "Got you! All right, I'll grant you that much. These mountains are strange. And my mother had the Sight, so perhaps," he added more to himself than to her, "*that* could explain certain things . . ." He sat considering something for a while. His eyes strayed thoughtfully to the small fire, he held his hands to it. "I am in your debt," he said finally. For some reason, this seemed to make him angry once again. "I owe you blood-price. I will repay the debt."

She shook her head. "If you choose to see it so. The healing was no danger to my life."

"No," he remarked sourly, "and neither were the Mathkkra, were they? Not much!" Another silence. "The matter of the debt is *my* choice, not yours. Even Nedao's Queen cannot gainsay that." Another silence. He moved to push away the blankets, his hand hesitated on the fur-lined cloak. "That's none of mine. Did I also have your covering? Gods and Mothers, woman, but you shame me!"

"I was warm enough, and you needed it. There's no shame in that."

He scowled but finally shrugged, fished some more meat free of the skewers and popped it into his mouth. "What was that creature, the thing that flew?"

"Thullen. They're not known in Nedao—"

"Thank the Mothers for that!"

"—or weren't. We've seen all too many of them since I came north and Village Telean killed two, not long ago." He eyed her, mumbled something she couldn't quite catch. "They did. So much for your 'stodgy' herders."

"That word is going to haunt me," he remarked dryly, and turned aside to spit out a chunk of fat. "What are Thullen?"

"It's a long tale. Come to Midsummer Fest and hear it all then," she said. *And what do you make of that, exiled Plainsman?* If he'd left Nedao for cause, as she half thought— "For now, you know all you need to of them: do not look at them directly, and they die on plain steel." *Not this time,* she thought, and fought a shudder. Did he remember that? She couldn't tell, his face was giving away nothing at all. Save, still, that very faint offensive look, the more active displeasure whenever his eyes met hers or touched on her right cheek, and flinched away from what they saw.

"Midsummer Fest." He caught at the words. "Why?"

She laughed. "Why, to test my blades. You offered once, remember? And I seem to recall you using yours for more than swatting your horse today. That's a proper skill you have!" Silence. "I haven't tripped over my sword in years."

"Yes," he groaned, "hold that against me, too. All my words come back to haunt me tonight!" he considered, finally shrugged. "Perhaps. Why not? If I'm not halfway to Nar instead."

"Good enough. I'm going, then." She rose to her feet. "It'll be my skin if I'm not in my bed before my women come to wake me, and that's with the sun these days."

He stood, shook the blankets to his feet, held out her cloak with a flourish. She pulled it around her shoulders, suddenly grateful for its warmth. A light breeze was bending the grass, soughing through the trees. It ruffled her hair, chilled her exposed ears and nose.

"Well then. My thanks for your aid. I suppose I owe you that, besides blood-debt," he said, suddenly stiff with formality. Nedao's Lady. He could have touched her; at the same time, he couldn't possibly have reached across the gulf that separated such as her and the likes of him. *Black hell,* he thought, savagely. "Next time I call out your name, to come and die at my side, leave me be!" She stared at him. "I'd as soon die alone than take a woman's coddling!"

Her eyes narrowed. "I hope you do! Alone and certainly not missed! You're stubborn and fool enough, too! Just trap yourself against a ledge again, we've twelve-year-old shepherds who have more brain than that!" He drew in a deep breath and started for her, but whatever he bellowed out was lost as she bridged back to the tower.

"Damn!" She slammed the flat of her hand against the door jamb.

'Why?' Nisana pushed through the partly open door and leaped to the flat railing.

"Nevermind," she said grimly. "I'm going to bed."

"Good. I don't like trying to deal with when you're angry and short of sleep both.' But she accompanied the swordswoman down the hall. 'That *was* amusing," she added as Ylia strode into her chamber.

"What was?" She began removing one boot by digging at the

heel with the toe of the other, but stopped abruptly. "You *weren't* watching me!"

'Why not?' Nisana demanded reasonably. 'I was keeping an eye out for more Mathkkra. You should appreciate that. But you know Malaeth would find it most inappropriate, that you were spending long dark hours, unattended, with a stray male."

Ylia shoved the first boot aside with a kick, bent over to drag at the other. Her face was hot. "Why? He'd be the last to attempt my virtue!"

'So I noticed. All the same, there *are* forms. You know that as well as I, and your future mate should be pleased to know we kept you pure.'

"That's quite enough, cat!"

'Curious, too. I would have wondered where did such an uncouth Nedaoan get Power. She answered that.'

That brought Ylia back around, sword belt in hand. 'You saw her too!"

'I was watching you, I told you. For your safety. I have spoken with Eya and others of the Folk, once or twice. She was never able to come to you because you were never alone."

"She said that."

'Yes. It's a pity the hunter is unlikely to return to his folk. I'd like to work with such as that, to see what he could do. Raw Power,' Nisana added thoughtfully. 'Think what someone without *your* narrow attitudes might do with all that Power!'

"If you saw us at all, cat, you know he wouldn't even acknowledge he has it."

'So? You were the same, until recent.' Nisana gazed at her measuringly. 'That was a goodly bridge, the best you've managed so far. Fortunate you thought the matter important enough to do it.'

"Don't rag me, cat," Ylia implored. "You didn't see what passed earlier, when I called on Shelagn and the blade answered. Look. Please!"

Nisana jumped onto the bed, padded to Ylia's side, reluctantly joined. She sat with her eyes closed a long time, pondering. 'Odd,' she said finally. 'Most odd. That the blade should have powers of its own, brought on by *her* name—who would have thought it? Was it forged so, I wonder, or did it come by them later, and at whose hand?'

"I don't care about that." Ylia tossed the cloak across the foot of the bed, tossed the tabard on top of it and began unlacing the mail shirt. "I want to know what it's doing to me, that's all I care about right now."

'You shouldn't let it frighten you. Remember what Eya told you.'

Ylia gazed at her in exasperation. "Nisana, think! Think, how you'd feel to have such a thing in your hands, and not know which of you controlled the other!" She shivered as she dropped the long-sleeved shirt to the floor, untied the drawstring waist of her breeches, loosened the laces that bound them close to her calves. "Malaeth had me a nightshirt yesterday. Where did she put it?"

'Not a thing I'd know,' the cat replied. Ylia sighed, retrieved her shirt and pulled back the bed furs to discover the long, pale blue woolen shift lying across her pillows. Nisana watched as she dragged it down over her head and pulled her hair free. 'I still cannot believe that is a comfortable way to sleep,' she remarked. 'All tangled up in cloth. How do you stand it?'

"It's not as warm as your fur, or as comfortable, but just as essential. I sleep cold, you know that, cat."

'I know. Eya's words should have reassured you. And the Nasath had a hand to that blade. Perhaps they themselves gave it the power of her name. Would they put a blade in your hands that would enslave you?'

"I don't know." Silence. "I know Eya believes otherwise."

'Then trust what she says. Do you think she lies to you?'

Ylia shook her head reluctantly. "No. It's only that—"

'Don't say it. You spoke with *him*, could he have done such a thing to you?'

"You meet with Nesrevera once, and you know this for truth?"

'Hush, silly thing. I've always known it. You know it, or would if your brains weren't mushed with fear.' And, as Ylia pulled back indignantly onto one elbow, 'You've already told me it frightens you. I've *seen* as much. Why deny it, what shame is there in admitted fear, if you deal with it?'

"Cat, you just can't have seen what it did!"

'Of course I saw. It slays with the Power—not the Baelfyr, though it's like. Do you fear the Baelfyr? Well?' Ylia reluctantly shook her head. 'Well, then.' Silence. 'You used it without the shield to dampen its strength. Was *that* anyone's fault but yours?'

"How should I know to carry a shield, Nisana? No one said, there was nothing to tell me I must! I've never fought with a shield, even in practice with Marhan!"

'Well, now you know,' the cat replied shortly. 'I would begin bearing them together, if I were you. At least you'll have no trouble keeping the sword away from the man, will you?'

"Thank all the Mothers at once for that. With luck I'll never see him again."

The words lodged themselves somewhere deep in the cat's inner being, and stuck there uncomfortably. *That's not so—gods grant me no foreseeing for this child!* But it faded even as she could feel the least edge of a sense of some *thing* that would come to pass. Grief and exhaustion was all she could tell, and even that was gone as she tried to make sense of it. *Use what is given to you,* she urged herself tartly. 'Sleep,' she offered Ylia, 'and try not to dream of your gallant hunter,' she added dryly as she curled into Ylia's cloak. 'Erken would not find him at all a suitable addition to his lists.' Ylia levered onto an elbow again and sent her a scorching look, rolled back into the covers. Nisana's humor was a curious and seldom thing, and lead-heavy.

The sun was warm on the courtyard before she came down the next morning. In the square, twenty-five young women were waiting, and the smiths had been busy, for fully half of them now had their own blades. It made a difference. Lisabetha, who had managed grimly with the heavier blade, made astonishing progress with her new one, enough that after a brief break for water, Ylia set her and Eveya to teaching the basic crossings to another group of girls while she explained more advanced maneuvers. Marhan and Golsat, on their way to the docks from the barracks, stopped as they broke a second time.

"Damn me for a fool, they're good, boy," the Swordmaster finally admitted.

"Good enough that you'll finally help me?" Ylia inquired with a grin.

"Why? You have 'em in hand!" The old man replied with obvious glee.

"For now. There are three other groups, four times the number who want to learn, and only one of me."

"I'll aid," Golsat offered. "I spoke for it in council. I'll back that with action."

"Huh." Marhan shook his head. "I've my hands full, anyway, and Golsat knows as much as I do." *Enough for women, anyway.* That hung between them unspoken.

"Probably more," Ylia said sweetly. *Thrust for thrust, you hidebound old man!* "He's younger and can hold to his feet longer."

Marhan chuckled in appreciation. "In fact, unless you need him to get you down to the River, I can use him right now."

"I think I can find the docks alone, brain's all it ever was." With a last dark look at the females gathered around the water buckets, he strode off. Golsat waited prudently until he passed the far end of the bridge before he laughed.

"Gods and Mothers but he's an odd one!"

"I know," Ylia returned.

"He speaks with pride of what you're doing. Don't trust what he says to your face."

"No, I never do. I know him. Thanks for your aid."

"Pleasure. Now, how do you want to divide them?"

"I'll stay with the novices. You can take the more advanced. Lisabetha's among them."

"Good. That leaves you," Golsat eyes them as they spread out again and began the practice sets, "Levren's delightful daughter. Better still!"

"Now, whatever," Ylia laughed, "could you have against sweet Lennett? She's hardly arrived from Yls. What *could* she have done?"

"Sweet," the dark man grunted. "Sweet, she says! I've ridden herd-guard with her three times already. *Sweet,* she says! She'll alienate half the valley before fall with that mouth and that attitude of hers!"

"She's eager, that's all. She wants sword-training, always has, and she's over-anxious to make up what she sees as wasted years."

"Hah. Someone had better tell her to watch herself. Hard to believe she's Lev's child: the man's never said four rude words in his life, and he never takes offense."

"No." *He fears, poor Lev.* But he could control the debilitating fear of foreigners, and when he couldn't control it, he carefully absented himself. Even so, he'd taught some of Tr'Harsen's men bow. Only a few of them realized what it cost him, and the Narrans not at all. Golsat knew; he'd faced the brunt of the Bowmaster's xenophobia until close contact, chance and a Mathkkra sword had nearly separated them for good. And Levren had been there for him.

Lennett—*Dragon of a daughter,* Lev had called her, and now Ylia could see that high-strung edge in the girl that had led him to compare her to Lisabetha. There was a passionate streak in both of them, a cutting edge sharper than most folk had. Ylia wasn't certain she liked the friendship that had sprung up between Lennett and the orphaned Danila, either: Danila had an edge of her own that Lennett would only encourage. Then again, because of Lennett, Dani had given over her determination to remain at all times with the herds and had accepted Levren's and his wife Ilderian's fostering. One more in Lev's lively brood was hardly noticed.

"I see her mother's managed to keep her clad like a girl," Golsat went on. "Lev says she's kept the household upset since her arrival. She wants breeches like yours."

"Poor Lev."

"No, poor Ilderian. She's no control over the girl."

"It's not likely anything Ilderian could have done would change that. Look at me, think of my poor mother." Ylia glanced out across the novice swordswomen: Lennett there, tall and blade-slender, blade-tough. The shirt was loose, the sleeves modestly wrist-length, her riding skirt too full for proper freedom of motion. The girl wasn't letting it slow her at all, and her face was truly fierce with concentration. "If Lennett gets her breeches, she'll have earned them. All right, you first levels! Sets of two, four full patterns, *move* it!" Golsat shook his head and moved to join the waiting advanced girls.

They finished just short of noon-hour. Golsat went back to the barracks for his meal, Ylia returned to the Tower. It was cool in the high-ceilinged hall, pleasant in the small dining chamber where Malaeth brought her a plate with cold meat and bread, with a handful of long-stemmed onions. A jug of wine and one of water stood at her elbow, together with a silver-handled Ylsan glass goblet that had been a gift from one of the Koderran survivors. She ate quickly, and stared out the open window across the river. As far as one could see, there was activity, despite the mid-day heat: Women knelt to weed or plant; others were handing bundles of grasses up to roofers. A steady hammering formed a background of noise, and as she watched, a high-sided, flat-bottomed barge slid by the window, two grey-bearded men poling it down to the Aresada while a third sat in the front with the tiller.

She drained the cup, refilled it with plain water, and read the note Lisabetha had tucked under her knife that morning: Breakfast with the Narrans. Discuss ale. Sword lessoning. Noon-meal. Weavers' barn. Lossana had got the builders to put up a house near the barracks, past the market, and had installed the Aresada looms in it. It was an idea she'd taken from the Koderran crafters, who said it was common in Yslar to group crafters in such buildings. More efficient, perhaps; the grouping of spinners, weavers, dyers at Aresada had certainly made for pleasant work, with so many other women to talk to while the work went on.

Meetings, then: Grewl. She worried about him; she hadn't had much chance to talk to him of late, and she heard all too many rumors about factioning among the Chosen. Even Tr'Harsen had said something, just before they left the Caves: "Watch that man, the pale-eyed one. He expected messages from Osnera, he was pestering me for any that might have come in for him or the old man. He's planning trouble." She couldn't doubt that. Whether she could do anything about it, though—Grewl was reluctant to take control of those buildings out there north of town. Perhaps she should apply pressure, if she could, and see that he did. They couldn't afford upheaval; she couldn't afford Jers setting policy for the Chosen, not now.

After Grewl, Council, which now included the men who had advised her father, newly arrived from Yslar. The table was getting crowded, these days. She'd have to break out a separate, sub-council, one to rapidly deal with things the Koderran councilers didn't yet understand: Marhan, Levren, Erken and Corlin. Those who knew the risks they faced, here deep in the Foessa.

Another meeting, just after, with Levren and Marhan—Queen's Bow and Swordmasters—to keep a finger on the pulse that was all Nedao's armed.

She grimaced. A meeting with certain middle-aged village men; Eveya's father, and all too many like him, who disapproved of swordswomen but had not yet actively forbidden their daughters to learn. They wouldn't dare, of course, not with their Queen as an example. But it made bad feeling all the same. *And how I'm to deal with it, to reassure them and to make it so they don't leave full of resentment at having been manipulated by another young girl—no matter what her station. Ugh!* She dismissed the thought. It was guaranteed to put her off lunch.

After evening meal, yet another meeting: Erken, Corlin. With Midsummer Fest a matter of days away, and with the Narran embassy on its way, there was still planning to be done for both. Contestings: They'd decided, already, that the standard sword and bow crossings would go on as they always had; that was as much a matter of pride to her as to any of them. But they still needed to finalize what contests would be held, how many bouts, where each would be set, what times: things she'd always taken for granted, it amazed her the amount of planning and work that went into them.

She'd decided on her own that the traditional prizes of silver coin and ribbon to the winners would be awarded as usual. The coins would come from the dowry, and she feared Erken would wrangle with her over it. But there wasn't much they could buy with such a small handful of silver, from Nar or anywhere else, nothing that would bring so much happiness. It seemed to her a tiny price to pay for the semblance of normalcy, and the Mothers knew they needed that.

Grewl: She kept coming back to him. The old man still wouldn't take leadership of the Nedaoan Chosen, though it had been offered to him by an enclave of them. He held that he hadn't been yet confirmed as Nedaoan by Osnera. Osnera, in fact, was keeping all too quiet about the situation in Nedao, though Tevvro must have reached his people a time since.

She didn't doubt they'd act. Grewl didn't. And *he* worried, she knew, that they'd try to bring the Nedaon house back to the narrow line held by the Heirocracy, something totally impractical in Nedao, considering the Osneran line against witchery, and Nedao's Queen.

In the meantime, he and Jers watched each other closely, the Chosen watched both.

Was Vess in Osnera now? What, she wondered, would he do there? Was he hoping to come back to Nedao with the support of the Heirocracy and wrest the ruling from her *that* way? *Stay there, cousin. Live longer.* Her hands twitched themselves into fists. *Or don't stay, come back and this time you'll fight me. This time I won't let Brel and Marhan set aside common sense. Come back, and let me repay the debt I owe you. Blood-debt, but your blood.*

And then, a last matter: Erken and his maledictable list. But he wouldn't be put aside any longer. *If he thinks I'll wed and produce offspring while we sit surrounded by danger, he's mad, and I'll tell him so flatly!* How had such as Leffna dealt with such things? Set aside her sword when her body became awkward and only picked it up after the child no longer depended on her? Such few other swordswomen she knew of—Hrusetta, Adiadda, Shelagn—had died young and childless. *I hope,* she thought sourly, *that's no omen,* and warded herself with Golsat's luck gesture as she pushed back from the table.

I shall spare you humans a recitation of what one cat finds attractive about another, or even what an AEldra cat finds to attract him or herself to another of cat-kind, AEldra or not. It certainly is little like human attraction, which seems so often based upon a gown, sight of a beaded slipper under the hem of that gown, loosened hair that has been seen for so long plaited. Fortunate indeed that that is the beginning of human attraction, and not the whole of it, but even as a beginning it is highly amusing to one who knows the proper things to look for in a mate, AND at first meeting.

21

It was with grave misgivings that she prepared for the formal reception of the Narran Embassy. This, more than anything else, brought upon her with unnerving force the fact that she ruled. There was no Brandt, no Scythia, this time, to take obeisance from the Ambassador while she stood scarcely noted at her father's side. She had run over the ritual receiving words with Erken, again and again and was muttering them to herself one last time as the women installed her in a deep green dress that clung smoothly to shoulders and breast—she was acutely aware of them in such thin and close garb—and fell free to the tops of her soft beaded slippers. Her hair was shaken free of its usual plaits, brushed in a dark gold ripple down her back until it shone; half was drawn back over her ears to a high knot and the rest let hang. Two wild roses were twined in the knot, a ring of beaten silver and malachite set at her throat. The hair was topped, then, with the crown that had replaced the gold band Bos had fashioned for her when she arrived at Aresada. This was not large, a delicate tracery of wire and fine-work, its only show the three emeralds above her forehead.

She worried, though she and Nisana both had searched, long and hard, before she changed. And she was angered by that worry. It made everyone happy to have her clad properly for this reception. Truthfully, she felt better about receiving such an important man as Ber'Sordes at least *looking* royal. But—

But. Even with no clear-cut cause for it, she worried. It hadn't helped that Marhan and Erken were both trying to force promises from her that she'd stop fighting. How could she? A Nedaoan ruler fought at the head of the army, not commanding from the rear or from a table safe within the Tower, spending lives while his own hide was safe. Her people knew that, so did she. Erken had been stiff with displeasure when she'd reminded him.

They can't stop me. They should know better than to try. Because I'm Nedao's first Queen in five hundred years doesn't have to mean that everything changes. And it won't. She brought her full attention back to her women, who were exclaiming over their finished product.

She turned, stood in surprise as Lisabetha held the mirror. *Mothers, is that me?* It had been long, seemed longer, since she had worn women's clothing, and the person who stared back at her was a stranger. *I have lost weight.* She eyed herself critically, turned a little. Hair swirled around her shoulders, settled to the small of her back. *And my hair's grown, never trust Malaeth, plaiting's been good for it.* Overall—well, she was clean, at least, and they'd done their best for her. *I'll never look as Mother did, when she received Narrans. I'll do, though.* The Narrans settled back into her stomach in an icy knot.

Lisabetha stowed the precious mirror, came back to tuck a stray hair away and settle the neck ring straight. "I'd forgotten how wonderful you look in green."

"My thanks. *I'd* forgotten how naked one feels in a dress like this, and without a sword." She smiled. The dagger was cool against the inside of her leg; not even Lisabetha knew it was there, and Malaeth had fortunately not sensed it. "I suppose I don't need it for the Narrans."

"No," Lisabetha agreed gravely. "If you're not warm enough, there's the short cloak for this."

"I'm warm enough and there'll be people and probably a fire in the dining hall. You're coming down with me, of course."

"Well, I—"

"Malaeth should, too, but she doesn't care for formal dinners anymore. She says her appetite's not up to them. You can't think to let me go down unattended."

"Brelian and Erken are going to escort you, remember?"

"Unattended," Ylia interrupted dryly, "by another female, of course. You're as bad as I am, forgetting all the rules. It's custom and honor, of course, and you're protecting my virtue." Lisabetha giggled, she laughed. "Let's go, before I lose my nerve."

They walked down the hall to the stairs in a companionable silence. Somewhere below, there was a muted rumble of speech, but in the main hall itself, only two of her door-warders, Erken, and Brelian. She halted briefly. Erken gazed up at her in unconcealed pride; Brelian stared in amazement, became aware he was staring and dropped his eyes. He was red to the ears. *Is this how it happens, that friends and companions suddenly see the gap between my station and theirs, and become titles and stations of lesser placing than my own?* It saddened her to think it, that Brel might see himself henceforth as Queen's Champion and picture a chasm between them. *Not if I can prevent it,* she decided firmly, and went down to meet them.

The tall Anaselan bowed low over her fingers, and she winked across his back at Brelian, who managed one in response, and then, across her shoulder, sent another to his intended. "It's only me, Brel," she said as Erken straightened. "As ever."

"Hardly that!" he protested, but the smile he gave her was real and shorn of awe this time. "You are—well—Nedao's Lady. Our Queen."

"All of that," Erken broke in smoothly as the boy fumbled to an awkward halt. "The Narrans will be pleased, Lady. And all of us proud. You look quite as beautiful as your mother ever did."

"And you, my Duke," she retorted, "speak sweet falsehoods so nicely, a woman might take them for truth. Thank you." The Duke eyed her sidelong, gave a little snort of laughter and held out his arm. She rested her hand on it with grave precision, bit the corners of her mouth to stifle a laugh, and let him lead her into the Grand Reception, Brelian at her other side, Lisabetha just behind her.

Young Menfred, his face at least as solemn as her own, pushed the doors open and stood just inside to call out: "Ylia hra'da Brandt, Queen of Nedao and Aresada, Protector of the People and Chief of its armies!" She swallowed hard. *Father, guide me!* She

hoped that either she was not as red as she felt or that the lighting
was still inadequate in the high-ceilinged Reception.

A number of gaily clad men stood between her and the throne,
and bowed as she passed. Erken led her—a fact for which she was
suddenly grateful—handed her onto the high seat and took his
place at her left shoulder. Brelian stood a step down, also on her
left and a little aside, and Lisabetha stood at her right hand.

A middle-aged man, his near-black hair beginning to grey at the
temples, his face clean-shaven, stepped forward and bowed
deeply. "Queen Ylia. I am Ber'Sordes of Nar, chosen by the Lord
Mayor as Ambassador to you and yours. With me, I have brought
Ang'Har and H'Lod, two young lords attached to my household,
and the captains whose ships brought us up-river to you:
Tr'Harsen and Kre'Darst." He produced a packet of gold-sealed
and red-ribboned papers, which Brelian came down to take.

Her young Champion handed the papers to her with a bow of
his own, returned to his place. His eyes, like Erken's, were all for
the Narrans. For they were fashion-conscious, this wealthy class
of Nar—they did not, as Nedaoans understood it, have nobility—
and the fashion had apparently recently and radically changed.
The Nedaoans had never seen anything like it.

Ber'Sordes, despite his age, was as amazingly clad as any of
them: His tunic was short, ending just below his hips, and over it
he wore a short, brilliantly scarlet cape, lined in black. A stiff
collar framed his face and the curled hair that barely covered his
ears. His legs, still well muscled, were clad in smooth-fitting
black hose. Crimson leather short boots, turned down across the
toes to reveal a pale yellow lining, completed his garb, save for
the gold, silver and copper woven belt that held a ceremonial
dagger to his waist.

H'Lod might have been thirty, though it was difficult for her to
guess age among these men. His face was lined like a sea-man's,
and—unusual for a Narran—he wore a long beard. She learned
later this was part of a vow he'd made, to not shave until he sank a
Sea-Raider and sent its crew to the bottom. He, too, was clad in
the new style, though plainly. His tunic was a rich brown, a thin
line of gold trimming and an embroidered dolphin its only
ornamentation. His hose and boots were brown also, his cloak a
deeper brown lined in cream.

Tr'Harsen and Kre'Darst she had not at first recognized, for she
had seen them recently only in working clothing, often wet and
muddy. Tonight, one dressed in four shades of green, the other in

two shades of blue and gold, they shone nearly as brightly as Ber'Sordes.

But Ang'Har was the one who drew the eye and held it: He was as bright as a tourney banner. The short cape of brilliant blue was made of at least a full circle of fabric, and lined in a rich green, its high collar covered with gold arabesques, its fastenings jeweled. The tunic was green like the cape lining, broidered with gold and silver thread. The full sleeves of the shirt were right blue, left pale green, and the cloth hung in long folds when he bent his arms, falling nearly to his knees. Even his hose were parti-colored: blue on the left leg, pale green on the right, and his low shoes were also reversed, blue and green. The face that topped this astonishment of color was smooth and almost as pretty as a girl's, and only the shrewd eyes gave away that this was a grown man and a Narran trader.

Ylia stirred, hoped that she had not been staring, and brought out her prepared little speech. "We are pleased to welcome you to our halls and gratified that the Lord Mayor has chosen to send us a full embassy. In time, and when we are able, we will reciprocate, and look back upon this time with true pleasure, that it has brought about proper relations between our two peoples.

"We present to you, my Lords, Erken, Duke of Anasela, and Brelian of the House of Bordron, our Champion.

"It is a pleasure to us, that you have come to celebrate Midsummer Fest after the manner of our kind. And now, our doorwarder will escort you to the dining hall, where others of our council await your arrival." She stood, came down the stair and held out her hand. Ber'Sordes bowed gravely over the fingers and turned to follow Merreven. H'Lod tapped Ang'Har on the shoulder to rouse him, and they went out behind the Captains.

Ylia waited until the doors shut behind them and let out a long sigh. Erken laughed. "Come, now, Lady Ylia, that was well and proudly done. All that fuss for no cause, eh? And the worst of it is behind you now!"

She groaned. "Until tomorrow, when it comes around again. And beyond that—" She sighed again. "Forever."

"Bah. Look for no sympathy from me, you were born to it."

"You *like* it," she accused darkly.

"You make it sound terrible," Erken said, "and you managed quite well after all."

"I had no choice. Oh, well. Come, my Lord," she added with a wry smile, "*we* would have an escort to *our* dining hall." Brelian smothered a smile, stepped back to fall in behind them and take Lisabetha's hand.

It was, actually, a very pleasant dinner. Ber'Sordes sat at her right hand, the rest scattered among her council, with Tr'Harsen next to Lord Corlin at the other end of the table. The food, thanks to the Narrans and to redoubled efforts on the part of Golsat and his hunters, some of the fishers with new Narran nets, and the abilities of her staff, was varied, well prepared and pleasing to the eye.

Of her council, only Marckl was absent, for he and his men were putting in long hours to get the road finished. Even Levren was here, carefully set down between Lady Lossana on the one side and Bnolon's Lady on the other, Lisabetha across from him. No one could possibly realize how carefully Ylia had planned her table, so that the Queen's Bowmaster and counciler could take meat with foreigners.

By the time the venison was served, conversation was progressing smoothly: H'Lod was arguing good-naturedly with Ifney and Bnorn over the price of goats, Ang'Har discussing the weft and warp of his tunic with Lossana and offering to obtain the pattern for her if she could not work it out from the garment itself. Far down the table, Corlin and Kre'Darst spoke about the River and various means of making it more negotiable, and Tr'Harsen and Bnolon and Bnolon's Lady were deep in a discussion about ales and the various wines Nedao found most pleasant.

The only jarring moment, to her mind, came when Ber'Sordes leaned near and said in a voice meant to carry no farther than her ear: "A good man, Ang'Har. I'm pleased I could bring him. Already he is an excellent trader and has second command of the *Sea Spray*. Being son to my brother, of course, he is marked for greater things, and could become Lord Mayor in his own right—certainly he might become an Ambassador."

"I am pleased he could be here also, then," she replied with a smile, but inwardly she flinched. *Here it begins, the Peopled Lands send their eligible high-born to seek the hand of the unwed Queen of Nedao. Ugh. Does Erken know this?* If he did, it didn't show on his generally open countenance. Ang'Har, for his part, was deep in conversation with Ifney, but his gaze strayed in her direction all too often for her liking: particularly since he blushed like a boy and hastily turned away every time she caught his eye. *Puppy. If they're all as green as this boy, I'll wed Erken!* She had to bite the corners of her mouth, hard, to keep the smile back. *Why not? He's noble, Nedaoan, certainly capable of fathering princes and princesses*—she hastily abandoned the thought, afraid she'd never be able to look Erken in the eye again if she didn't.

At least it put Ang'Har temporarily out of her mind, and the next time she caught him gawking she took it with a more tolerant humor.

They'd reached the sweet—fresh berries and cream, a fruity Osneran wine to accompany it—when the inner sense caught her by the throat with its warning. 'Damn. Nisana—?'

'I sense him too. It's your beloved mountain-hunter, and he's near.'

'Not mine, damn his thick hide! But it *is* him, isn't it? I swear, cat, if he's in trouble again, he can die of it before I go after him!'

'No argument from me—it's not him, Ylia. *Look.*'

'Nisana—!' But the cat was no longer there. With deepest misgivings, she reached with the inner vision, and whatever Ber'Sordes was saying to her serving woman faded away as she *saw. All the demons of the blackest hell at once, I knew this would happen!* She stared at her wine-cup, thought as fast and hard as she could. That *drawing* was still pulling at her, making it difficult to concentrate; she severed use of the Power entirely.

Mathkkra; they'd set upon Marckl's road crew, near one hundred of them, against twenty tired men and a handful of bored guard. There was chaos and fighting out there, and where was that cursed hunter? She hadn't seen him anywhere.

But that was scarcely important at the moment. Speed was. "Erken, my Lord Duke, I must see you, outside. Immediately. Corlin, if you'd be so kind as to take my place?" She rose, motioned the Narrans and her council back into their seats and strode from the hall. Erken was at her side to hold the door and shut it behind them. "Marckl's attacked. Mathkkra."

"How many?" Thank all the Mothers at once, he didn't question her vision.

"A hundred, or more. Gather what men you can, get to him." She started as the door opened, but it was only Brelian, not the half-dozen curious Narrans she half expected.

"They worry in there. What's to do?"

"Mathkkra. They've beset the road."

"Gods and Mothers. Marckl?"

"Tell the Narrans there's no danger here. We'll have more news for them shortly. Come right back, though, I need you."

Erken had started for the outer doors but he caught her last word and turned back as Brelian stepped back into the dining room. "You can't!"

"Erken, by the Black Well, *don't* waste time arguing with me! Therea," she shouted as one of her women appeared at the head of the stairs, her attention caught by the shouting, "get my sword, quickly! Go, Erken, it will take you time to get men and reach the end of the road. Brelian and I can get there at once."

"And do what, die with them? You can't—!"

"Can't I? That's an order. Blast you, man, this once do as I say!" Erken flushed angrily, but he set his mouth in a tight line, turned on his heel and left the hall at a dead run. Brelian came back into the hall as Therea ran across the landing, but Malaeth was ahead of her. Ylia cast her eyes heavenward.

"What is this?" Malaeth's voice was shrill with fury. "Have you lost your mind, girl? You are *not* going out like that!"

"Malaeth, whom do you think you're arguing with? I don't have *time* for this stupidity! Every minute you waste is another man dead! Therea, throw me that sword!" The woman hesitated as Malaeth turned an awful glare in her direction. She moved then, leaned across the railing and dropped it into Brelian's waiting hands. Ylia buckled it at her waist, tore the crown from her hair, scattering pins across the tiled floor, and pressed it into Malaeth's hands. "Here, do something useful. Hold this for me! And don't look at me like that, I'll be back for it!" She held out a hand and caught Brelian's arm; he drew his sword as she closed her eyes and bridged them away.

It had been few minutes, actual time, since the inner sense had wakened her to the danger, but matters were considerably worse: the ground was littered with the spidery grey-white bodies but several of Marckl's men were down, and she could not see Marckl among those still standing. She caught Brelian's shoulder. "Get among the men, get them bunched. Away from the creatures. I dare not use the Baelfyr if it may go against our own." He nodded, slid behind an enormous fir bole and began working his way toward the River.

It seemed forever; it took only the length of five deep breaths before she heard him cry: "Erken rides to your aid, to me! Get close together, the Lady Ylia brings her own weapons to the

fight!" A ragged cheer went up. It was some moments before
Brelian could group them, though, and several of the men were
unable at first to fight free of Mathkkra.

She stood where she'd bridged, irresolute. Still dangerous to
use the Baelfyr, and the sword—that terrified her. But Brelian was
making headway, finally. She caught at the hilts, hesitated, pushed
the blade back firmly into its sheath. The dress caught around her
legs as she strode forward; with a blistering oath she reached to
drag it free, tucked the loose fabric through her sword belt. She
brought up her hands as small white shapes hurtled down the road
for her: Baelfyr lit the trees, the road; five fell dead. Beyond them
a man cried out in sudden fear.

"Draw *back*, I *told* ye, get away from the foul creatures and
stay together, that's your Lady with the fire, but it'll burn ye as
well, if you're to hand!" Brelian's Northern accent, normally
unnoticeable, came out under stress. Ylia turned as motion to her
left caught her eye, and killed three more.

There was a stretch of time, then, where she was moving
continuously—now down the road, now across it and back again.
Baelfyr flared and flared again. She was tiring. A harsh cry and a
splash—Brelian's curse—another of Marckl's men was down.

The filmy green stuff was slithering free of the belt again; she
caught her heel on fabric and fell. Three Mathkkra, near enough to
be ready for such a chance, leaped on her before she could rise,
but not before she had the dagger out of its leg sheath and in her
hand. Two died on it, the third turned to flee, vanished in a ball of
flame before it had gone five paces. She rolled to her knees but
another flung itself out of tree-shadow and onto her back. She
parried the knife that sought her throat with her own blade, two-
handed, fell over hard. It landed on the bottom, wind driven from
its body; her dagger pinned it to the dirt.

She eyed the area warily indeed this time before she attempted
to stand, but for now she was alone. She stood, dropped flat half a
breath later as an arrow whined past and buried itself with a nasty
twang in the tree just behind her. " 'Ware, you blasted archers,
I'm over here!" she bellowed.

"S-sorry!" someone shouted back.

She dragged the dress from under her knees, rose again and this
time made her feet. The Mathkkra had turned, suddenly as they
always did, and were fleeing toward the Aresada. Brelian was
exhorting those with him to follow, and behind, she could hear

horses coming from the City. They passed her without seeing her and vanished down the road after Brelian and the Cave-folk.

She sighed, wiped sweat from her forehead, ran the length of skirt through her fingers before tucking it back, more firmly this time, through the belt. Not torn, good: Malaeth wouldn't have forgiven her *that*. But it was gritty with dust. She made a wry face, anticipating the scene to follow. 'Cat! Your aid here, we've wounded!'

'Later.' Nisana's touch was more distant than it should be, if she was in the Tower. 'The herds were attacked, I went to aid. There are two guards dead, two hurt, and one of the children wounded. Three sheep are dead and three missing, and the girl Danila hysterical. Unfortunate I can't heal, but the others are doing what they can.'

So that was where she'd gone. 'I'll come as soon as I can. Is anyone in danger?'

'Of dying? No. If you must have my aid, call. Otherwise, I'm needed here.'

Gods and Mothers, what caused this? And why tonight? A moan nearby roused her: One of Marckl's boys sat just off the road. A knife lay in the dirt near his hand; blood soaked his shirt. Beyond him, three more she could see, and one of them did not move. She healed the boy, and another—an older man she knew by sight though not by name. The third man was still unconscious, an ugly knot behind his ear where a thrown rock had caught him.

Brush crackled behind her. She leaped to her feet, sword and dagger both out. "Who?" Foolish, for who but Mathkkra would sneak up on her like that? And they would not answer save by fighting. But the sense of him was already strong: mountain-hunter.

He came out from heavy tree-shade, stepped onto the road, arms well away from his sides. "Again you have the better of me. Though you'll get no insult this time, Lady."

"You. What are you doing here?"

"You invited me, remember? Though I don't recall you asked me to such a fight as this. There are enough swordsmen down by the Aresada to deal with three times the enemy they've trapped. I thought *you* could use my aid."

"I'll be glad of it, just now, here." She tore strips of cloth from her underskirts, "Help me find the wounded, bind any you find bleeding, and mark for me where they are."

"I'll do that." He took the handful of soft fabric and started off.

"Wait. Do you know the northern Lord Marckl by sight?"

He started. "I know Marckl of Broad Heath, is he here?"

"Somewhere. I fear he's dead. If you find him, call me."

"I will." He turned and strode off down the road, turned toward the River and vanished among the trees. Ylia turned back to the wounded.

After the brief battle was over (and the damage already done), I touched the child Danila's thought, so as to calm her, for that is my particular skill. And I found a thing there that was disquieting: revenge, anger, hatred, and so strong for such a baby. Or so I thought—I, who should have known better, having laid my thought against hers. But like the humans, who only saw her tears and heard her impassioned vows, I thought: "This is a human child, young in years, and such children forget quickly." As though children felt less strongly because they are young! But it was that child, with her total devotion to duty, who succeeded where others one and all failed; who set in motion events of great benefit to Nedao. And, of course, to her beloved—stupid—sheep.

22

She stumbled through the woods in search of survivors, healed three more men of painful cuts, and another man of concussion from a thrown rock. There were four beyond her healing or anyone else's. The hunter's voice rang out suddenly from near the River: "I've found him, come quickly!"

The Lord of Broad Heath lay face down in the sand and gravel of the bank. The handle of a broad-bladed throwing knife was barely visible against the black of his cloak; the blade was buried to the hilts high between his shoulders. The hunter squatted beside him.

"I think he was breathing when I first touched him, but I don't

205

know now. He's lost too much blood. I'm afraid to touch him at all."

She knelt, felt the fallen man with a light mind-touch. There was a faint, slow pulse, but it wouldn't be there long. She was at the edge of her strength. And there were the herds still. The man next to her radiated worry. She could sense his presence almost as clearly as she'd sense Nisana's—*Nisana's. Gods and Mothers both.* She glanced up to find anxious eyes studying her. *Two to heal, one for the additional strength. It need not be an AEldra, the Mothers know I wasn't*—her sudden jubilation faded into nothing. No, she hadn't been properly AEldra when she'd aided her mother. And Gors, 'Betha's brother, had died.

But Marckl had nothing to lose, as Gors hadn't had, if they tried. If this stubborn hunter would cooperate—"You spoke of blood-debt, not long ago. If you could repay it, now, would you?"

He eyed her warily now. "How?"

"An odd way. I intend to try to heal him, as I did you. But he's further gone than you were. I'm already worn, I doubt if there's enough in me to save him. But if you aid me, if I can draw on *your* strength and not only my own—will you?"

He swallowed surprise, and something he would not call fear. "He's a good man. You need all your good men. What must I do?"

No hesitation, though she'd expected that, if not argument. She held out a hand. He took it, rather cautiously.

"Just be there. Keep hold of my hand, and let your other rest on his back, near the blade. If this works, you may feel yourself growing weak. I don't know. Don't let go my hand, don't take your hand from Marckl's back. And when I say, join that hand with my free one. I will clasp the knife. Do *not* resist, stay with me, follow my lead. If the blade is withdrawn too quickly, he'll bleed to death before I can do anything to save him." Silence. They looked at each over the fallen Lord Holder. "You're certain."

"Yes. Go."

The Nasath give me strength—and him too!

It was hard, worse than she had feared: Marckl's inner being was sunken into itself so far that it was reluctant to return to life; it flinched from pain and awareness of the knife, sullenly ignored her, avoided the healing. The nearness of death permeated him, sending bile to her mouth. She swallowed hard. Her legs were trembling, a shudder was threatening her entire body. The hunter made no sound, no move, though she was aware the strength she used was not all hers, terribly aware in this AEldra bond of the latent Power in him.

'Don't die, Marckl, by all the Mothers at once, you can't die, Nedao needs you, I need you, Ifney needs you, your household needs you, you can't die!' She was mumbling to herself, to him, trying to drag at him that way where the healing itself was falling short. Nothing. 'Blast and damn you, man, you haven't finished that road yet!' The mountain-hunter started, cast her an astonished look. *He didn't hear that, what's the matter with him?* Her concentration wavered, was pulled sharply back to the wounded Marckl: Suddenly, beyond hope, he drew one deep, shuddering breath and a faint agonized cry went out on it.

"Now!" Her voice was a rough whisper, it was all she had left. Two hands moved slowly, surely and as she healed cut muscle, torn veins, erased damage and pain both, the knife came out. Marckl lay flat on his stomach, face turned toward her; he was breathing normally. She freed her hands, felt him cautiously, but that had been his only injury—and it was gone. She caught the hunter's limp hand, gripped his shoulder as he swayed, and willed him back what strength she could spare.

He stirred. There was a sick look to his eyes, a set to his mouth as though he'd held back retching by will alone, as she had. "Was that—was that what you did for me?"

"No. Nothing so difficult, nothing so horrid. You were hurt, but not lost in the inner silences. You'd just lost blood. The Guardians grant I never need to do anything like that again." She stared at him blankly. "You *did* feel it, didn't you?" Silence. "You felt that."

"I—I don't know." He scowled at hands that still tended to tremble, clasped them under his knees. "*You* said I might feel weak when you used my strength."

"I didn't know. How could I know? I also said I hadn't done it before, didn't I?"

"No," he replied shortly. And, reluctantly: "It was—that was terrible. As though I were *inside* his body." His gaze went through her; he was staring off a great distance indeed, speaking to himself. "It was going cold and dark all around me. I never thought death would feel like *that*." He shook himself. "I saw what you did, how his body healed when the knife came out." He brought his hands out level, transferred his gaze to them. They still trembled, but not as much. "I saw that, I felt it. Unless my mind's going." He smiled faintly. Shrugged. "Too many years in the Foessa, a man talks to himself. First step toward Foessa madness."

"You're not mad."

"Kind of you to say so."

"No kindness on my part. It's the truth. Not in what you felt." She met his eyes briefly, looked away from that intense, close gaze. "I told you, the Foessa did strange things to one of us, coming north. She could hear AEldran mind-speech. For a time. She can't now, not much, but we've been among Nedaoans, protected from the—well, the odder parts of the mountains."

"Ah." He shrugged. "Perhaps. If you came tonight because of my call, I suppose I can't call it impossible, can I?"

"I—you did that? On purpose?"

"Of course on purpose, what did you think? I was on my way up from those new docks, and I heard fighting. The men were badly outnumbered. With me alone and on foot, I didn't have much choice: I could leave 'em and run for aid, or die with 'em." He shrugged, turned to stare out into the trees. "Thought I'd try the other way: the one *you* said worked."

"You—you pulled me from dinner with the Narran Embassy," she said finally. She tugged the hems free of her belt and dropped them over her exposed leg.

"Almost didn't recognize you, all woman-clad. Hadn't been for that fire of yours, maybe I wouldn't have at all." He cast her a flash of teeth that was probably meant for a smile. "That's nice, I like it."

"Thank you." The words threatened to stick in her throat; she wasn't certain what to think of him mannered. It made her wonder what he was up to; at least when he sneered and shouted, she knew what he was honestly thinking.

"Didn't look very sensible out there."

"It wasn't. I could have used help, where I was." *Or couldn't you see that? Or were you having too much fun watching?*

He grinned. "Not likely I'd come up on anybody tossing fire about as casually as all that! Besides, you looked as though you could take care of yourself. There were some here who couldn't."

She laughed faintly. "Tell that to my Swordmaster. He'll have my head for this."

"No doubt, if he's still Marhan. Good man, but touchy."

"Mmm. Marhan. And he's gone touchier with age. Though I'd have to agree with him, this is nothing to fight in."

Silence. She stood, brushed dirt from her skirts, fidgeted with the sword-belt. He was spilling pebbles from his fingers, one at a time. More silence. She cleared her throat. "Have you seen the valley yet?"

He threw the rest of the rocks; several cracked against trees. "From a distance, across the Aresada and higher up. You've civilized the poor old thing, haven't you? And in such a short time. But I like your City, it has good form. What building fresh does for them, I suppose."

"Thank you. Is that why you're here, to look it over?"

"Partially. I was curious. And I thought I might be able to catch one of those Narran boats down the sea. I've a stack of good pelts to get rid of, and there are things I need."

"Ah." Ylia watched as he picked up another handful of pebbles, began tossing them into the brush. "There are Narrans all over the City just now, you know. They're absolutely panting for trade. You'd do at least as well here and save yourself the cost of passage. We could probably supply you as well as they could, if you're only after salt and meal and the like."

"Well—"

"And Nedao could quite frankly use your coin."

He tilted back his head and laughed. "The woman bargains like a Narran! I'll come away poor!"

"Not if you've been dealing in Nar," She replied dryly.

"Well." He tossed the last of his pebbles, vaulted to his feet. "I'll think on it. Are you safe here? Fool question, you're safer than I am, coming and going like that. And your men are on their way back. I'd better grab what arrows I can and go now."

"What, before you're seen?" she laughed. But he stopped short, as though she'd struck a sore point, scowled at her.

"Perhaps." And, challengingly: "What cause to you?"

"None, why? I don't care if you did murder wherever you came from. It's nothing to *me* so long as you don't attempt it again here and now. I don't really care why you're exiled at all. Is that good enough for you?"

"Sorry," he mumbled grudgingly. "Well, then. A better night to you than you've had, thus far."

She held out a hand. "My thanks for your help."

He touched it with his own. "Mmmm." He turned away, melted back into the trees.

He was barely out of sight when she heard the horses coming back from the Aresada. She moved back into the middle of the road to wait for them.

Erken's face was cut and scratched from riding through brush and his eyes were still hot as he dismounted and came to meet her. "We killed most, but a number escaped up-river. It was too hard for us to follow and we lost them."

"You did what you could," she replied, no less stiffly. "The creatures are crafty beyond what we might expect, seeing them and knowing what they are. And they are not hampered by size and mounts."

Marhan slid from the saddle and stormed toward her. "By all the gods I ever heard of, look at you! Do you think yourself blade-proof? Where's your sense?"

"Sense!" she laughed sourly. "If either of you dares mention sense! I *warned* you, I warned Malaeth, and still nothing would do but that I dress for the Ambassador!"

"No one sent you here," Erken said flatly, "but your own stubborn self. Forgive my saying so, Lady, but it's truth."

"Black hells, Erken, it was *my* aid and Brel's that brought heart to Marckl's men, they would all have been dead before you reached him! Marckl would be dead, he was breathing his last when I found him!" Brelian, still afoot, slid past Erken's horse, stood beside her. "Brel, there's men scattered all over out there, the badly wounded are healed but there are still some to be tended. Marckl's near the river, right on the bank. He'll sleep a full day or more. Ten men dead, Erken. Ten men, Marhan. Because Brelian and I were here, they aren't *all* dead."

"Even so—" Marhan began furiously.

"Even so?" she overrode him. "Will you both, *now*, free yourselves of this absolutely stupid notion that I do not intend to rule as my father did? I follow Nedao's way! The Narrans will simply have to adjust to my breeches and armor, as the people have. And by the Mothers, you had both better do the same!" She turned on her heel and walked off.

"Where are you going?" Marhan was subdued, but not totally without words.

She shouted over her shoulder, "Back to change, and then I'm bridging to the herds. They were attacked also; there are dead and wounded there!"

"There's—*what?*" Erken shouted after her.

"You heard me! We lost guards and sheep tonight. The Mathkkra came at us from both sides! Send men out there when you get back!"

'You ought not to alienate him,' Nisana commented over the distance as Ylia bridged back to the second-floor balcony.

'Hah. He'd better quit pushing me, then, or he'll *think* alienated. I'll have the ears off the man! Is everything under control where you are, cat? I won't be long now.'

'Not good, but all right. I'll wait.'

Ylia slipped into her chambers without meeting anyone. Down the stairs, she could hear a muted murmur of voices: Malaeth and the rest of her women there, waiting for news. She undid the sword belt, unlaced the dress—with difficulty since the ties were between the shoulder blades and hard to reach alone—and let it fall to the floor. She gazed at it a moment, made a face, picked it up and crossed to the open window, shook it vigorously. Dirt flew. It wasn't torn, but it would need a good wash, after this.

The breeches and shirt were in the chest at the foot of the bed. She dressed quickly, pulled on her boots and strapped the dagger sheath to her calf, rebuckled the sword over all. It took a moment in the half-dark to find a leather tie for her hair; she ran her fingers through it to dislodge the few remaining pins, knotted the thong at the base of her neck.

A riot of questions met her at the foot of the stair. "Marckl's men were attacked by Mathkkra, the creatures are gone, Marckl's alive. Erken will have the rest of the news for you shortly, he was on his way back here when I left. Menfred, bring Lord Corry out here, will you? Malaeth, don't fuss, please, I'm still whole and so's the dress. I hope the green's a good dye, though."

"The dress will wash and mend. *You* might not!" The old woman snapped in reply, and turned to start back up the stairs, taking the other women with her. It was suddenly, blessedly quiet in the hall, though she could hear the same kind of excited babble in the dining hall when Corlin slipped out.

"Lady Ylia?"

"Corlin, apologize to the Narrans, will you? I've just come from Marckl's road. Erken will tell you about that when he gets here. He's on his way. I'm going out to the herds. Mathkkra, both times."

"Two raids, across the valley, at the same time?" He frowned. "I don't like the sound of that."

"Nor I. Ten of Marckl's men are dead and two of Erken's out with the herds, plus three of the sheep. And Erken's in a filthy mood. There's wounded out there with the herds still, so I'm needed. If you would, get some more men out there, we'll need help getting the beasts in."

"All right. I'll tell Ber'Sordes where you are, and I can handle Erken."

"Good. I'm glad *one* of us can."

The wind was a summer one: low, light and warm, and the moon was down. Sheep bleated anxiously, cattle milled, and the herders and guards were keeping them all in a tight knot, lest they bolt again. Three Mathkkra lay face down on the hillside not far away: more beyond them. The two dead Nedaoans were nearer to hand, dark bundles under cloaks.

Momentary panic when she came so suddenly into sight. 'More trouble, cat?'

'No. Everyone's nervous.'

'Understandably.' Aloud, she added, "I've come to aid the hurt, and there will be more armed here shortly. Lord Corry's sending help."

Nisana sat on Danila's lap, letting the girl stroke her fur. Nold sat next to the girl, a protective arm around her shoulders. Danila was no longer hysterical but there was a grim determination about her that sat oddly on a child of so few years. *But she must have nearly twelve summers. When I was her age, I was ready to begin sword lessoning, and taking ill anyone who'd hold me from it. Not so odd after all, perhaps.*

Ylia moved among them, setting injuries right. Fortunately, considering how tired she was, there were none serious. Even with Nisana's help, she was still trembling with exhaustion when she finished. Nold stirred as Ylia came back to Danila, tried to struggle to his feet until she laid a hand on his arm and shook her head. He subsided gratefully, he looked as worn as she felt. "Are you all right, Danila?"

"It's been hard on her," Nold said. Worry for and pride in the girl stood out all over him. "But she killed four herself. You have skill, Danna," he added with a smile and an encouraging shake.

The girl's small face remained grave. "I wish I had killed them all!" And, as Nold patted her shoulder awkwardly, "Don't do that! I wish I'd killed them all, because they killed sheep! Killed three and that—that thing carried off another!" Her eyes brimmed over; she sniffed. "I'm sorry, Lady!"

"Don't be. You did better than some grown men." But to Danila, this was obviously not enough.

"Really, Danna," Nold snapped, "the Lady never *said* to hold them with your own hands! Or to get yourself killed protecting them! The loss wasn't your fault, after all!" The girl scowled at him, and he rolled his eyes. "There's always herd loss, girl! Always has been! Wolves, eagles, poachers—and sheep are stupid, don't you know that by now? One of my father's sheep fell into the pond, tripped and drowned in a puddle that wouldn't have covered its belly, standing! You can't keep such stupid things safe against everything!" He glared at her again. "Especially not those!" One hand shot out to indicate the Mathkkra. Danila's yellow-fletched arrows were still in two of them.

"It's all right, Danna," Ylia soothed. "And don't berate her, Nold. She takes the task seriously for one so young. That's praiseworthy."

"If sheep are so stupid," Danila's voice went high and quavered, "then all the more reason to guard them close. We cannot afford to lose them as we once could." She glared at the other herders. "If we all had good aim, they might not have got away! Instead of just twelve dead, it might have been all of them and no one hurt, and the sheep not gone! And Usenna's father dead!" Her voice broke. "These are the last of the herds, if they all get stolen or killed, where will we get more?" Nold laid a placating hand on her arm but she shook it off angrily. "Not all of us have warding-families yet. What work will be found for those who haven't homes when the herds are all—all gone?" She dissolved into tears again. Nisana leaned against her hard, butted her small hard head into the girl's arm. It came out to wrap around her; the girl buried her face in dark fur. Ylia caught Nold's eye and drew him aside.

"She'll be all right. When she's calm again, let her know how proud I am of all of you. The road was ambushed, too, but Marckl's men fared worse than you did. The Mathkkra thought the herds an easy mark and found otherwise. Now," she went on, "Lord Corry's men will be here shortly. See that the herds are got back to the pens. We won't try to overnight them in the fields for a while. Make certain the two dead sheep are brought in. We can't afford to waste them."

"Yes, Ma'am."

"And Nold, will you see personally that Danila gets back to the Bowmaster's house?"

"Of course I will."

"Good." 'Nisana, are you staying with her?'
'Awhile, not long. I'll come back as soon as I'm able.'

She watched from the main upper balcony, over the reception, as the herds were driven into the pens; watched, too, as the children and their guards came on past the Tower. Danila's small head drooped, and Nold was practically carrying her. Ylia smiled. The girl would sleep tonight—that at least. And Lev would be good for her, he'd help her sort out her misery. Ilderian—well, Ilderian had a good heart. Though the Mothers knew she hid it well enough. *Go easy on the child, Ilderian, she's fragile, and may crack.*

Actually, I frequently spent some time at Nedao's Midsummer Fest, for there were often good things to eat—and enough soft-hearted children or women to see I got a taste of them. And as one so completely removed from all possibility of sword use, I found it intriguing, and after so many years of living in Nedao, came to enjoy the formal crossings, the tests of skill. Of course, I would never have let Ylia know that—any more than the old Swordmaster would have told her she was the most important thing in his life.

23

First-morn of the Midsummer Fest dawned cool and bright, cloudless and with little hint of the heat to come later. Already folk were crowding into the City, dressed in what finery they had, and those who had stalls were busily setting out food and wares. The smell of *yushas*—long strips of spiced meat, strung on wooden skewers and cooked over an open fire till they crackled—mixed oddly with that of fresh breads, corn pats and a variety of teas.

Ylia staggered out not long after sunrise, not readily but well aware of her duty to the Fest. Malaeth brought her bread and fruit, dressed her hair in plaits without comment and brought out the blue breeches and shirt, the silver-thread edged tabard. "The rest of 'em are dressed bright, so should you be. And it washes, same as the green." Ylia cast her a guilty look, but the old woman was past anger. "*And,*" she added, "it's a good color for you, make the Narrans take note."

"Malaeth, you *haven't* espoused young Ang'Har's cause, have you? Because if you have, I swear—!"

"Which one's he, the baby with the pretty clothes? Wonder which of ours will be first to copy *him?*"

"That's easy. Erken, of course. Followed, if she bullies her mother far enough, by Lennett. I'll warrant you didn't know Lennett's worn Ilderian down to the point of breeches for the crossings tomorrow."

"Of course I knew it," Malaeth replied huffily, "and you should be ashamed, giving the girl such an example. Little flibbertygibbet! Breaking her poor mother's heart, that's what." She sighed. "Ilderian should have taken a harder line with the girl and her father both, I suppose. Her own fault if the girl's beyond her now."

Ylia laughed. "Look at me and say that, do you?"

"*You,*" the old woman said accusingly. "As much your fault as anyone's. Nevermind, I'm not arguing with you today, and that's flat! Now." She snatched the thin band of gold out of Ylia's fingers. "You wear the more visible one today. That circlet isn't suitable for Fest. Nor Narrans."

"Malaeth, it'll fall off and break."

"No, it won't, not if you behave yourself like Nedao's Lady and don't join in the wrestling!" Malaeth fastened the plain gold crown in place with a handful of pins, slapping Ylia's hand away impatiently when one scraped her scalp. "Hold still, you're as bad as when you were a child!"

"You're worse," Ylia grumbled, but resigned herself and closed her eyes. Malaeth shoved four more pins into place and stepped back.

"There. The plaits are *not* seemly, to my way of thinking, and certainly no way to deal with those Narran nobles, but it's useless to argue with you."

"Good, I'm glad you don't intend to." She stood, brushed crumbs from her lap. "You'll be down later, of course."

"Haven't missed one yet, have I?"

There were people everywhere and the square was four-deep already for the ceremony to begin the sword crossings. Most of the folk disbursed immediately after she spoke the greeting and stepped back onto the covered dais, since the first day was given over to preliminary bouts and the first morning to novice class. Only relatives and instructors stayed for the novice crossings, there was too much else going on to spend the time on them.

Ber'Sordes and his household remained, though. She sent one of her warders to offer them a seat in the shade.

"Lady. This is a genuine pleasure, it grows warm out there."

"Just wait," she said. "They'll be toasting *yushas* on the rocks here by late afternoon." He cast her a startled glance, smiled appreciation of the joke as he caught it and turned back to watch the fight in progress. Several of his men withdrew on errands of their own, leaving finally only the ambassador and his nephew and three of the household.

Be nice to the child, she reminded herself, *he's part of the embassy, and maybe he'll dissuade.*

"Two of my men," Ber'Sordes said, "have signed for your competition. They'll be up this afternoon, early."

"Good. Our men need competition more their own size, and friendly for a change."

"Yes, I'd think so. Tell me," the older man said, "if you will, of these creatures your Lord Corry calls Mathkkra. I've never heard of them before."

She paused a moment to watch the two boys backing each other around the square and to collect her thoughts. *Corlin obviously told him little. Don't add the wrong things to that.* "They were Plains-dwellers when our kind first left the Isles and came north. We thought them all dead if they'd ever really been," she said finally. "Unfortunately we ran across them, my companions and I, when we came through the mountains after Koderra fell. Since then, we've seen them off and on. They avoid daylight, and they prefer odds balanced heavily in their favor. They're not brave or good fighters, but they can overwhelm by sheer number."

"So Lord Corry said. He also said," Ber'Sordes added curiously, "that they are blood drinkers, and that they nearly sent you to join your ancestors."

"Damn," she laughed ruefully. "He was *not* supposed to spread that around."

"He's not the only one, Lady," Ang'Har said diffidently. "Your Champion told me how you saved his life, last night." His face was a mixture of the previous night's awe, astonishment, a certain degree of uncertainty as to whether he'd been ragged—and something else: she could almost hear his thought. *Ladies do not wear swords and men's pants, and ladies are gentle creatures to make songs of, and ladies must be protected and sheltered from evil and even bad thought, but . . .* It was absolutely painful to watch him carefully meet her eyes, and not look at her marred cheek.

Suddenly, she could almost feel sorry for him, irritating as his adoring gaze had become. It had to be hard on a boy, brought up to chivalrous behavior as he'd been, to come up-river to meet Nedao's young Queen—someone who should be all things a chivalrous gentleman could wish—and to realize she was nothing of the sort. Particularly after his first sight of her, in that feminine bit of green. *Poor child. He'll learn, if he stays here long enough.*

"Well, yes, I did. But he saved mine a few times, too. We all pretty much took care of each other that way. We didn't keep track after a while—*I* didn't. Don't," she laughed, "take all Brelian says straightly, not about me. He'll tease you."

"Ah." Ber'Sordes clearly didn't believe her, and Ang'Har wasn't certain. She stood.

"Stay here if you like, I'll return. I have to speak with Duke Erken." *Ugh.* The thing couldn't be put off any further. She owed him an apology for making him look small before his men, if nothing else.

It was awhile before she found him: The small City was full of happy people, the narrow streets crowded, and it was difficult for her to see far. She finally ran him down in front of the barracks.

He sat on a bench in the shade of the northern wall, talking with three of his young sword-sworn who were scheduled to fight before noon-meal. He looked up as she approached, motioned the three to leave and stood, rather stiffly. Ylia dropped down to the bench, patted the place next to her where he'd been. "Come on, man, I'm not going to hurt my neck staring up at you. Sit!"

"As you please, Lady Ylia." And he sat, a proscribed distance from her. His expression was aloof.

"Erken—all right, I'm *sorry.* Don't look at me like that! I'm trying to apologize! I had no right to speak to you in such a way, certainly not before your men and Marhan's. I was upset. It wasn't entirely your fault."

"All right. I was angry myself," Erken said evenly. "Mostly because I feared *you* would be among the losses, Lady."

She bit back anger. That wouldn't solve anything. "I understand that. I'm grateful for your concern. But remember what I said last night. I'm not backing down from that, either. You'll have to accept that I'm Father's heir. I'm Nedao's Queen, and Nedao's rulers have *always* fought at the fore of their armed."

"It's not necessary for you to do that. You have armed, you can use them."

"It *is.* Erken, if my brother had lived to take the ruling, you'd *never* have said that to him!"

"That isn't so."

"You know better! At least be honest with me, Erken." They gazed at each other for a long minute. "Think about it. I've sword skill, I've my mother's magic, and by that, I've twice the protection Leffna had when *she* led Nedao against the Llhaza and the Tehlatt, and when she fought the pirates and their Ragnolian allies." She paused; he just looked at her, his face unreadable. "I'd wager anything she faced the same arguments you're giving me. She *still* led from the fore. Just as Father did. Just as I do. And will." Still silence. "That's how it is, Erken, and I'm not going to argue about it with you, not now, not later, because it's simple fact. Nothing you or Marhan or anyone else says is changing that." His mouth twitched. "I'm sorry I lost my temper last night, sorry I shouted at you. That's all I came to say. Father would never have done that." Silence again. "Dammit man, say something!"

Erken shook his head, laughed quietly. "By the Black Well, you're Brandt's equal for stubborn! All right, no more argument. For all the grey hairs you've given us, I notice you're still alive and unharmed. So far."

"I'll stay that way," she assured him seriously. "I've already taken my novice marks."

Mothers. She'd had to remind him of that, hadn't she? He seldom noticed her face these days. He was used to it and tan was hiding what was left of that faint line. *Thank all the gods at once she brings enough prestige in name and land to overshadow that scar. If she were merely noble, she'd likely die husbandless. And thank the gods also that Brandt didn't live to see it,* he thought. He drew a deep breath, expelled it in a rush. "I'm sorry also. Friends?" He held out a lean, sunbrowned hand; she met it halfway.

"Friends." She eyed his three boys, who were trying to run another set of crossing patterns. "You'd better get back to them. They need your help."

He groaned. "I try to remember that boys all start rough. It doesn't always help." He stood, handed her up; there was a gleam in his dark eyes. "And speaking of rough, when do your women compete?"

"Just after boys' novice class. I decided on fifteen of them, finally. Fewer than the boys. I thought I'd save everyone such long-drawn agony."

Erken laughed, motioned his three back to his side. "Equal honors on that one, Lady."

"Equal indeed. I got you under the ribs and you know it! I'd better get back to the Narrans, speaking of boys' novice crossings, I left poor Ber'Sordes watching them."

"Ah. Well, watch out for the pretty one, then," the Duke grinned cheerfully. Ylia groaned.

"Gods and Mothers, is it as obvious as all that? Tell me you haven't added him to your lists!" she implored.

"What? That puppy? You're supposed to *have* children, not wed 'em!"

Ylia laughed. "Don't worry, my friend. He's undergone a bit of a change since I hung the sword from my belt again. This morning he looked like he'd bit an apple and found a worm in it."

"Huh. Puppy," Erken muttered to himself. "Are the Narrans serious?"

"I'd never try to second-guess a Narran. But now you know how *I* feel," Ylia said, and left him.

She purchased—though the good woman tending the stall would have given them to her—a mug of fruited wine, a stick of well-toasted venison bits, and wandered back to the square. Two of Ifney's youngest and greenest were there now, and Ber'Sordes and his personal servant alone occupied the shaded dais. Behind them and down near the River a horrid clangor was rising, as a pair of smiths began a race to cast and finish a complex harness clip. There was an enormous crowd around them, apparently undetered by the full sun and the heat rising from the forges: she could see wavering farms and fields behind it. She had passed the honor of presenting that prize to Corlin.

She slid into her seat, brushed damp hair off her brow and sipped her wine. It had been cooled in buckets of river water and so had the fruit, to the point it was almost too cold to drink.

"This is highly amusing," Ber'Sordes commented. "We have nothing like it in Nar, and the Ylsans seldom indulge either."

"Well, it's primitive, or so I'm told. But not as primitive as others—"

"I've heard from your man Golsat how his mother's folk celebrate the day. You dare not call this primitive," Ber'Sordes protested with a smile. "From things he's said, I wonder anyone is yet alive here."

"They've been filling your ear, haven't they?" Ber'Sordes smiled again.

"Narran curiosity."

"Well, you can't trust Golsat, either," she replied with a smile

of her own. There was a flurry of applause as one of the two
boys—more by chance than skill—disarmed the other and made
his touch.

"Perhaps not. He tells a good tale, though."

There was a council meeting with noon-meal: short in honor of
the Fest, absolutely essential in light of the attacks. Marckl, of
course, still slept, though his wife sent word that he seemed
otherwise well. Brelian could not be found at all, and even
Lisabetha had no idea where he might be.

"Well, it's clear to *me* there's a hold of the little nasties right
close!" Ifney snapped. Marckl's near-death sat hard with him.
"Now, whether they were somewheres about first, or saw us
coming and took us for easy prey isn't important. Fact is, they're
here and what do we intend to do about 'em?"

"There's something wrong, though," Erken said. "As many of
us as there are, and so many of us armed. *That* is not what the tales
say of Mathkkra."

"You're forgetting Lyiadd," Marhan said.

Erken shook his head. "Even so, even changed: they can hide
themselves with magic, they're more aggressive, they have the
Fear. There were only a handful of us in the valley for several 5-
days running, and we saw nothing of Mathkkra. This *must* have
been a band that set upon us as a test, and having failed it, they
will not come back. Doubtless they are ten leagues away by now,
and still running."

"Do you believe that, we may all be dead by Harvest," Marhan
growled.

"Lyiadd may not be dead," Levren said in the deadly silence
that followed the Swordmaster's words. "If he is not, he would
send Mathkkra to harry us." He glanced at Ylia, but she was
staying out of it for the moment. *Sensible. Stay still, let us bring
Ifney and Erken around,* he thought.

"Remember, too," Marhan added sourly, "that even five
hundred years ago, Mathkkra were fond of Nedaoan sheep! If
your mind balks at the greater horrors, Duke, then remember that.
The sight of so many sheep could bring Mathkkra."

Erken shook his head stubbornly. "I was not arguing that we
fail in vigil, or in preparation. I merely state what no one else
considers at all, that with or without this Lyiadd and his female,
these may have been attracted by a few men away from their
weapons, attracted by sheep and only a handful of guards and

children with them. That's all. If we're to consider all pos-
sibilities, then consider, I beg you, that this is also one!''

"All right." Ifney, surprisingly, came to Erken's side and held
out both hands for silence. "The Duke's right. We have to
consider that, even though we stand prepared for the worst! I say,"
he added, "that we begin a search. If they are nearby, let us find
the nest of them as Merreven did, and wipe them out."

Ylia cleared her throat. "Useless. Remember what else I told
you? In the Foessa, none of us were aware of them until too late.
Nisana and I had searched intensely with the Power only a short
time before, and they hid from us. They can shield from the
Power. More, though, we had Golsat, Marhan and Levren
watching for danger. They're among the best trackers we have."
Ifney favored her with a sour look but refrained from comment
and resumed his seat. "If you want to search, though, by all
means, let's do it. There are plenty of young armed who could use
the experience, riding circuit on the valley. Golsat, if you have the
time, teach some of them tracking. We don't have enough who can
do that."

"We can get more distance-glasses from the Narrans," Erken
said. The prospect of something to do took the hard lines from his
face. "Bnorn, you still have horns among your guard, haven't
you? We could use them to sound alarm, if there's another
attack."

"That's a good idea," Ifney, too, looked pleased at the thought
of some kind of action. "We can use mirrors, too. My herders
used them to talk across the hills. Just small rounds of polished
steel. Something to fit on a sleeve or in a belt-bag. There are
signals. A lot of us know them; we can devise any new ones we
need."

"Fine." Ylia pushed back from the table. "We lost twelve men
last night. We can't afford to do that again.

Levren held up a hand. "Another thing we should begin to
consider, now. If there is a true hold of Mathkkra and Thullen, if
Lyiadd has sent them against us, we will need to fight them. That
will take serious preparation; the last time we fought as a people
was three hundred years ago."

"The Plain—" Ifney began, stopped as Levren shook his head.

"No. Fought as an armed people, not a folk with its back to the
wall, trying to save anything it could. We need to train our armed
anyway; this merely pressures us to do it now, instead of next year.
Or the year after. Maneuvers. Strategy. Tactics."

Erken opened his mouth, closed it again, Corlin leaned on his hands, gazed at them in turn. "Lev's right. We're few armed, and we've insufficient weapons, insufficient men—and yes, women— to protect us. The Mothers know it's not been long enough since we came alive from the Plain. It seems unfair indeed that we should not be left awhile in peace. But the time and the means aren't left to us to choose. They seldom are. We dare not be unprepared. I will begin training my own in battle maneuvers. Directly after Fest." He held out a hand. "Erken?"

Erken clasped it. "You know I'll aid. Let's think on what's needed. We can meet after Fest." He glanced up as one of his men came in, tapped the back of his hand and nodded toward the square. "They're beginning the afternoon crossings. I'm wanted for judging."

Outside it was clear and hot, and the street was thick with dust. The Narrans—Ber'Sordes still, Ang'Har and H'Lod once again— had moved from the dais and now sat in a patch of shade with Erken, Golsat and Marhan. Those three were judging, and Golsat was indicating the finer points of swordplay to the ambassador. Ylia arrived in time to see Ifney's boy from the morning passes flailing nervously against Bnorn's grandson. The crossing didn't last long, and the boy shrugged ruefully in Ifney's direction as he left the floor. Ifney waited until he vanished into the crowd, rolled his eyes and shook his head.

A cry went up from the end of the bridge as the first of the afternoon footraces began. Ber'Sordes's minstrel, who had been wandering around the square, shook his head at the noise and moved off in the direction of the barracks, where it was quieter. An appreciative crowd followed him.

There was a lull after the second round men's crossings. The square was empty, the women's competition would not begin for another hour, not until the sun was off the square. Marhan leaned over to speak to Erken, who shrugged, and then to Levren. Ylia couldn't hear his question, but the Bowmaster's response reached her: "Don't know. He hasn't been around all day."

"He was supposed to be here after the—well, he's here somewhere. Blast! I'd better start." Marhan rose to his feet and strode to the center of the floor.

"The third men's passes will be at first hour tomorrow, and the women's first passes today after the last footrace. In the meantime," he raised his voice to cut through the babble, "in honor of our guests, who have sat patiently through the sword exercises so far—*and*," he added as many laughed, "I grant you, now and

again seen good work and often good promise—I would like to
offer an exhibition of sword and dagger fighting as it should and
can be! To that end, I, Marhan, Swordmaster to the House of
Ettel, hereby lay challenge to any who will come against me." He
swept his hat from his head and bowed. There were cheers, a
splatter of pleased applause—but no takers. Marhan laughed.
"What! D'ye mean let me stand here and look foolish? This is not
even to first blood, only a disarming! A contest!" That brought
him more cheers and applause, yet still no opponent.

"Erken, what is he doing?" Ylia leaned down to whisper. The
Duke shrugged.

"Brelian and he set it up between them," Levren said. "But I
think it was too much for Brel. Fest. Remember last year, who
took the whole of the sword contestings!"

"Brendan," she whispered. "Poor Brel!" *Mothers guard you,
my Bren, as you now guard my father.* She swallowed hard. *Do
something, don't weep here and now, fool!* Marhan was still
standing unchallenged in the center of the square, jibing with
those watching. "Why don't one of you take him?"

"Not up to it," Levren said. "My skill is with the bow. I'm no
fancy swordsman. But why don't *you*, my Lady?" He cast a
meaningful glance at the brightly clad young man on Ber'Sordes's
far side. "Give him a chance to look at you properly!"

"Levren," Erken warned. So far Ber'Sordes had proven to
have keen ears indeed.

Levren just grinned at Ylia. "Well?"

"Corlin could take him, I'd wager," she began, but her hand
was edging toward her dagger.

Levren laughed. "He's not given to display like you and the
Duke here are. Go on, this should be fun!"

"Certainly," she retorted. "Since you get to sit in the shade and
watch!" Levren laughed again, jumped to his feet.

"Accepted!" he shouted, and Marhan turned.

"Bowmaster?"

"No, the Lady herself!" Levren gave her a shove and
applauded loudly as he resumed his seat. There was momentary
silence, broken by a rush of excited whispering, and a few
nervous laughs. Not that many had ever seen her fight. They'd
seen Marhan. Though he was old, his skill was still renowned.

The Swordmaster himself bowed gravely. "A privilege and an
honor, my Lady," he said aloud, and in an undertone, "This was
not what I intended, boy!"

"So?" she said with an impudent grin. "Angry with me? Work it off here and now, why don't you?"

"That's—!"

"Sorry. Joke. I'll let you stand out here alone, if you prefer. But wouldn't you like to help me quash the Narran puppy? He won't even think about becoming the Nedaoan consort after *this*. Particularly when I win."

"I don't care who you are or why you took the bout," Marhan grumbled. "I will *not* give you the contest!"

"You won't have to, old man," she laughed, drew her blades, held them high for first touch. "I'm about to take it." Marhan matched her gesture, and the crowd went silent.

She hadn't taken a formal crossing in nearly a year, except in the Foessa with Brelian, the once. She had never attempted one against any as experienced as Marhan. Oh, they had played at it when he taught her, but this was the real thing, totally different from a practice.

It was fun, for all that. He *was* good, as good as anyone had ever said, as much fun to duel as her father had been, and they played each other brilliantly, outrageously. She leaped high as he cut at her boots, reached as he spun clear on one heel, back and out of reach; she lunged, would have touched his shoulder but his sword was already there, protecting his back. Nor could she find any opening when she finally began to seriously try. Not at first.

The sun was hot, beating at her eyes. Suddenly, she knew she'd have to try to take him. She couldn't stay out in the open much longer. And for all his age, Marhan seemed to be bearing up better than she.

Somehow, somewhere, she found enough energy to come across the square after him, and Brendan's high-wristed maneuver sent his sword flying. Half a breath later, her own blade spun high and landed at Levren's feet. They stepped apart, Marhan held out a hand. "Draw, I think, M'Lady?"

"Draw. If you don't finish me, the sun will!" She gripped his fingers.

"A good trick. Who taught ye *that*, boy?" he murmured against her ear.

"Trick?" she replied sweetly. "Accident, old man, I assure you!"

Marhan snorted, went to retrieve his sword. Levren gave her hers back.

"Well done," Erken whispered. Ylia winked at him as she started for the Tower: the Ambassador's nephew was gone.

It happens often enough; harsh words, thoughtlessly spoken, alienate the closest of kin, or dearest of friends, and accompanying pride forbids that the words be set aside, until the breach is insurmountable. Nor is this strictly a human failing, for there are those in my own vast family separated forever by a sudden, stupid explosion of temper and unrecallable words. Or so those exiled from each other see it, that the gulf between them cannot be crossed. Stupid and short-sighted: Often it takes nothing more than emotion as strong in another direction entirely—surprise, joy, relief, a sudden surge of love, one alone or all together—to dispel such feuds as though they never were. I know, for I have seen it happen.

24

By midmorning, second day of Fest, there were six men left for finals the third day, eight women for semi-finals in the afternoon. The square was thereafter taken up, alternately, by archers and knife-throwers.

It had not surprised Ylia at all that Lisabetha was among the eight women; she fully expected the contest to go between 'Betha and Eveya at the last, and beyond that—well, Eveya was undoubtedly stronger, but Lisabetha was skilled and determined, and she practiced furiously the past 5-day, stealing whatever time she could from weaving and the work on her bride-box to fence with Brelian.

Brelian, his face grey and somber, had appeared the previous afternoon to cheer her. He was still haggard, and abnormally quiet where he sat judging the archers with Levren and Corlin.

The real surprise of the first day had been Lossana. There was dead, astonished silence when she stepped into the square, her grey-touched hair plaited back and tied down with a band, her legs clad in a modified pair of riding breeches that afforded her both modesty and ease of movement. She'd lost to Marckl's daughter, but not by much.

Ylia, freed from judging for the morning, wandered among the stalls, watching the crafters trading with Narrans, bartering with the farmers and fishers. There were three minstrels strolling through the crowd: Bnorn's, a girl 'prenticed to him and Ber'Sordes's man. There were jugglers and a City man who'd thrilled her as a child on his high stilts. He'd found time and materials to construct the stilts, if not the long skirts that he normally wore over them, and walked on the outskirts of the throng. There were races and contests of various sorts for the children, judged according to age and paid in toys and trinkets.

She took noon-meal in the tower with the Narran Ambassador, the two ship captains and Lord Corlin, partly to set the contracts for ale going out, wine coming in, horses to be brought up-river and Nedaoan plow-harness to go down. Ber'Sordes was excited about carvings he'd found, and eager to deal for them, willing to exchange coin or the rare swirl-grained chalcedonwood from the south for it. He, Tr'Harsen and Kre'Karst left finally to go scour the stalls again and speak directly with the crafters. Corlin, who had the judging of the afternoon archers along with Levren and Brelian, left moments later.

Ylia drained her cup, refilled it with water and drank that. "Mothers, it's hot!"

'So? If you had sense, you'd stay inside and nap, as I do.'

"And offend everyone in sight, cat!" She rubbed lightly behind the dark ears as Nisana leaped to her lap, then to the table. "Nothing there you'd like, I don't think."

'I ate earlier, and it's too hot, now. Someone's coming,' she added, and sat, curling her tail across her feet.

"I don't hear anybody." But just then the door opened and Marckl stepped inside.

"They told me you might still be here. Lady." He bowed very low indeed.

"My Lord," she matched his formality. "I'm glad to see you on your feet again."

"They say I wouldn't have been, but for your aid," he replied, bluntly and much more like himself. "My men told me this morning. My wife wouldn't. I remember nothing of it, you know," he added candidly. "I must have been the first to fall. I don't even remember the creatures coming at us. Serdiv tells me there was a knife and I cried out and fell and he thought me dead. Before he could do anything, they were surrounded. Serdiv says he gave himself up for dead right then. He told me, too, that it was you and the boy, Brelian, who turned matters. I owe you blood-debt."

"If you see it so, I accept," she replied. "But all you've done on the road, everything you and your people have done to help with rebuilding more than pays any debt—"

"Anyone would have done that," he replied impatiently. "There's others have done as much or more." He scowled at his hands. "Erken tells me you believe the two raids by a single tribe with single intent. That this Lyiadd you spoke of set them against us. Do you still think it?"

"I—yes. That's only my opinion, though."

"Good enough for me," he said bluntly. "There'll be no more work done on the road for a few days. My men are unnerved, and I can't blame them. Ten of my sword-sworn dead! These Mathkkra owe *me* blood price!" He glared at the far wall. "After Fest is over, me and mine would like your permission to search for them."

"If you want it. We've guard around the valley, but we can always use more. Remember what I told you, though! They're woodcrafty beyond hope of our matching them, and they can hide themselves, from true sight or that I command."

"Oh, they're good," he agreed grimly. "But we'll find 'em. We will indeed!" And, with a brief and abstracted bow, he turned and strode from the chamber.

'He makes me hot, just to watch him,' Nisana remarked sourly.

'Hush, cat. His heart's in a good place.'

'So it is,' she conceded grudgingly. 'But can't he slow down and relax?'

'No.'

'All right, silly question. I'm going to find a cool place out in the woods. Call if you need me, but mind it's important!' Nisana leaped to the window ledge, teetered there a moment, vanished outside.

Ylia swallowed more water, picked up the bit of bread left on her plate, and the last slice of orange on the serving tray before her and ate them. *Real bread that doesn't taste of other things. Who'd have thought it such a wonder?* A shout went up under the window and horses clattered by in yet another of the races. Dust drifted in through one of the open windows at the far end. She made a face, got up to shut it.

"Lady." Menfred called from the door. "There's a man out here who'd speak with you, but he won't give his name, and he doesn't have the look of—"

A loud voice overrode him. "Look of *what*, by all the Mothers at once?" The door was pulled from Menfred's grasp and slammed against the wall. The mountain-hunter clapped the boy across the back; Menfred gasped as the air was driven from his chest, the hunter propelled him back toward the hall. But the boy dug in his heels and caught at the sills with both hands.

Momentary impasse; the hunter was larger and undeniably stronger, but Menfred was determined and was well braced. "There's no danger here," the hunter's laugh echoed through the room. "I'm not going to assassinate *her*. She's better than I am, and anyway, I don't want to." Menfred shook his head. "Lel-'San's spindle, tell him, will you?"

"It's all right, Menfred." She came up the length of the room. "I'm done with my meal. We can talk in the outer hall." She pushed past them both, and walked into the hall.

The hunter laughed again as he followed. "This is public enough, isn't it? What, do you doubt me after all?"

"Why should I? You've had a chance or two for my blood before this. You've forgotten *appearances*," she added shortly.

"Appearances? What's that mean?" he demanded.

"I can't stay in that room with you, alone. Don't you know that?" Realization widened his eyes and sent a flush up his neck and across his cheeks.

"Never intended *that* either, dammit," he finally managed.

Ylia laughed. "I never said you did. I said appearances. You've been a long time away from civilized men and women, haven't you?"

"Now you mention it," he replied with a sudden grin. His color was still unaturally high. "But you've made me forget, speak of appearances," and he went onto one knee. "Majesty. By your leave."

"Yours. Stand." And, as he remained kneeling, head averted,

"What are you doing? If this is a joke, it's heavier than your first. I said get up."

"No joke. I've come to pledge to my Lady and again be a man of Nedao."

"You—you *what?*" She stared down at him. "Bless the man, will you stand up so I can look at you properly? I said to, didn't I?" He stood, she scowled up at him. "My word ought to be enough for you."

"There is a debt between us. I acknowledged it, you accepted it, and I've come to repay it. It goes against my grain to owe, anyone, in any coin."

"You don't owe me anything, remember? You helped me save Marckl."

"Then that is between me and Marckl. *You* saved *my* life. That happens to be a matter of reasonable importance to me. And that is between us."

"Well, then. Tell me what you're fitted for, what you do. I'll find a use for you."

"Use. Mmmm. Hadn't thought of that. Well." He rubbed his chin. "I hunt, of course. But from the look of things hereabouts, you won't depend on hunting for your meat much longer."

"We hope not. We can still use hunters. Golsat—one of my companions from the King's city, you may not know him—is over-extended. He could use a skilled hunter."

"I know Golsat. He was Teshmoran for many years. I didn't know he'd become a King's man, but I'm not at all surprised. Man's good. Well." He turned away from her, paced across the hall, back again. "I have some arms skills."

"I've seen you fight."

"So you have. Corlin of Planthe could have vouched for me. I was one of his armsmen, for a while."

"He probably still can, if he can recognize your face under that beard," she said. He clapped his hands together, tilted his head back and roared.

"So Lord Corry cheated the Tehlatt of his hair! Hah! I wonder how many women he widowed in *his* escape?"

"You'd better ask Corlin. He and I haven't talked about that." Silence. Outside there was a clatter of horses, a loud cheer as the horse race finished just outside the Tower. "Well. If you were a guardsman once, you can be a guardsman again. We haven't enough men with your abilities."

"You haven't—"

"I fought with you, remember? So there's only one small matter remaining. Your name. I don't know it. I need it before I can give you the oath."

"I—oh." He considered this gravely and silently for some moments. Finally shrugged. "It's no great matter, I suppose. It's just that—" His voice trailed off; he roused himself with a visible effort. "I just haven't— Well. No great matter, is it?"

"Not much." she retorted. "Spit it out, man! How awful can it be?"

"I—well. It's Galdan."

She stared. "Galdan? *Galdan?*"

He sighed. "Of course *you'd* know it, wouldn't you?"

"I would? All Nedao knows it! It's not exactly a common name, you know. Just Erken's only son, no wonder you've been so shy of naming yourself!" Silence. "I'd never have guessed by looking at you. You don't look at all like him."

"Father? No." He shrugged. "My looks were more Mother's than his, I got his temper instead." He eyed her resignedly. "Well. Now you know. Speak the words, will you? Before," he smiled weakly, "before I lose my nerve."

"Impossible. You haven't any," she said. "Kneel, then, Galdan Erkenson, of the Third House, and speak the oath after me." *If I remember it!*

His face was grave as he repeated the words that re-bound him to Nedao: "I, Galden, son of Erken, son of Irdann, swear by my good sword arm and by my dagger, by the strength that is in me and by the Mothers who gave me life and so shaped it that I walk in this place and time, and by that of me which lives after this life, that I shall uphold the House of Ettel, its Queen and its Honor, to do well the deeds commanded me and to protect the folk of Nedao. All this do I swear." He kissed the copper-hilted dagger she held out to him, the fingers that held it and, holding to them, rose as she drew him up.

"Rise, Galdan. Your service do we take and cherish, and in return for it, your care and protection we take upon ourselves." He started, gazed at her blankly, wide-eyed, for the words she now spoke were the House-oath, used in creating a knight of Queen's personal guard. He stood dazed as she finished. She tugged at his arm; he inclined his head so she could place the kiss on his brow that sealed the oath—she could not reach his forehead at all otherwise. "Be then Lord Galdan, Baron of the Third House, and armsman to Nedao's Lady."

"I—I shall." He shook his head. "You didn't have to—I didn't give you my name so you'd—"

"Don't be foolish. Did you think I thought that? Or did you hope to stay unknown behind that beard for long? Keep if you like, by the way," she added, "but for appearance sake, I'd trim it."

"And so I shall," he replied faintly. The fight had momentarily gone out of him. "But that you'd name me House knight—I hadn't thought—"

"Well, what *did* you think? I've seen you fight, you're good. And now knowing who you are, I know where you're needed. You can help us teach new swordsmen. I've fenced with men who learned from you."

"Brendan. Bren, wasn't it? That *is* his dagger then!" She nodded, momentarily unable to speak as it again caught her by the throat and held her hard. He reached with sudden concern at the look on her face, pulled his hand back again as she closed her eyes. Her face had gone carefully expressionless. "He didn't make it, did he?"

"No."

"I'm sorry. He was a good friend of mine. But I didn't know—"

"I—it's all right."

It wasn't. *Black hell, what have I said? But a man can see it, her and Bren. Handsome together: they'd be that. Gods and Mothers, the look of her. Say something.* He opened his mouth, closed it again. What could he say?

She swallowed hard and shook free of the mood with a hard effort. "It's all right, nevermind. We all lost." And, with an even greater effort: "Who did you think would have your service? Marckl of Broad Heath? If you like, I'll send you to him. You can help watch the sheep, late at night." He laughed, and the laugh broke the stiffness that had risen between them. "Good, that's settled. I'll have someone escort you to the barracks. I can't even provide you with a change of clothing, let alone my household colors. But you'll have a roof overhead and decent food."

"More than I've been able to count on in a long time." He knelt. "Thank you, Lady."

"First thing you'd better learn, is that none of those around me do *that*. I'm Lady or Lady Ylia, and if you do more than bend your head, I'll have your ears for mocking me. This isn't Koderra, I'm not Father, and we haven't time for such things just now. And

you'd better save that, anyway, until you've been here awhile!
You may wish yourself gone again.''

"Make a wager on that?" He stood, grinned at her cheerfully.
She laughed.

"No, you're rock-headed enough to hold out from sheer
stubbornness. If you ask me—"

"Which I didn't—" he began. He started, turned to look over
his shoulder as the outer doors swung open with a crash and Erken
strode into the hall. He turned back, gazed across her shoulder and
up the staircase with fierce concentration.

Erken stopped just short of them. "Lady Ylia, we need your
aid. One of Ifney's boys was baiting Corlin's daughter and she
jumped him. I'm afraid she's going to be hurt!"

With a great effort, Ylia wrenched her gaze from Galdan, who
was staring past her as though his life depended on it. He'd gone
pale, and his hands were trembling. The sense of the Duke's
words penetrated, then, and she laughed. "One of Ifney's boys?
Erken, if anyone's hurt, it won't be Lisabetha!"

The Duke sighed and cast his eyes up. "This is *not* the time
to—great Inniva." He was suddenly aware they were not alone,
That back, the set of those shoulders. His heart hammered hard
against his ribs, the blood sang in his ears; he took one hesitant
step forward. "Galdan?" *My son's face, under all that beard*.

Galdan turned. "Father?" His voice had gone husky. "Oh,
Gods and Mothers, is it you?" He moved then, caught at the older
man's hands and buried his face in Erken's shoulder.

"Son." Erken's voice was a scarcely audible whisper. There
might never have been a quarrel; he wrapped long arms around
Galdan's shoulders and gripped him hard.

"Father. I thought you dead, I thought—everything I said to
you that night, and no chance to take it back—"

"Everything we *both* said," Erken corrected him. Galdan
stepped back a pace, dashed a hand across his eyes and laughed,
rather shakily.

"Still arguing with me, aren't you?"

Erken shook his head. "Starting already, are you?"

"Not just yet, I swear it." But the smile widened. "So the old
man cheated the Tehlatt of *his* hair, too! How did you—?"

"Where," Erken asked at the same time, "did you come
from?" They both stopped, laughed. "Corlin wanted the best of
the glory for himself. He chased me and mine out just as the gates
fell. I can tell you that later, where were you?"

"Oh, about," Galdan replied with a grin. "Learning to stand on my own feet. By the way," he added with a sudden mock gravity belied by the gleam in his eyes, "it is my duty, my solemn duty, to present you to my Lady. Queen Ylia, my revered and honored father, Lord Erken, the thrice-worthy, Duke of Anasela and—"

"Irreverent monster," Erken laughed and cuffed his ear affectionately. "How did you come by this ragamuffin, Lady Ylia?"

"We found each other, once or twice," she laughed. "You yourself might have said who *you* were, Galdan of the Third House," she added pointedly.

"Why?" he demanded. "Besides," he grinned cheerfully, "it isn't the kind of information you pass on in the middle of hot battle, is it?"

"Or argument," she said. "Which reminds me, Erken, I'll take care of this small war on the fencing ground. If Lisabetha hasn't already spitted the boy, that is. Find this son of yours something to wear. He's one of my household now; he needs my arms on his shirt."

"Speaking of things one isn't told," Erken began indignantly, but he broke off laughing. "I'll see what I can do."

The crowd was thick around the square but people stepped back to let her through. The fight was over anyway; Brelian and two of Ifney's older men had stepped between Lisabetha and Molver, but it was as Ylia had thought: Molver was on the ground, his sword a full length away, and Lisabetha, both blades still in her hands, glared at him. "You take back the insult you gave the Lady, or by the Black Well, we'll finish this!" she snapped.

Molver shrugged sullenly. "I meant no insult to the Lady, you know that. And I take back what I said, that you'd falter in a real fight. Is that enough?"

"Yes. Thank you."

Molver's companions aided him to his feet, handed him his blade and the three of them vanished into the crowd. Lisabetha's hands were trembling; she stuffed them under the edges of her tunic. "Brelian, was I wrong? He insulted me—all us swordswo-men, saying we were pretending to be men but that we had no real nerve or skill, and that we'd flee like children if a real enemy came against us."

"Well—no, you weren't wrong." Brelian shook his head. "I suppose it's hard enough for you women, just now. *I'd* not have backed down from such words, so it's as well you didn't. And he's a good boy, Molver. When he's done feeling the sting to his pride, he'll be an ally. But I hope this kind of thing doesn't arise again," he added gravely. "I'd greatly rather, if my wife chooses to use sword, that she not carry it to blood."

Lisabetha laughed and drew his arm around her shoulder. Ylia slipped unnoticed back into the crowd.

25

The black ship rode dark waves, her bow turning to cut through them as the *Fury* encountered a fierce and unseasonably late storm. The decks, the men who swore and fought sails, rigging, tiller and wheel, were one and all thoroughly soaked. Down in the Captain's cabin, water pooled at the edge of the door, slid down from an imperfectly fitted port shutter. The air was cool, unpleasantly damp.

Neither Captain Mal Brit Arren nor his young companion paid much heed to the moist chill, the occasional shudder as even the *Fury* met waves she could not conquer: Brit Arren was well on his way to properly drunk; Jon Bri Madden, his youngest crew and cabin boy, was sipping gingerly at his first mug. Brit Arren had asked him to sit, ordered him to drink, and Jon was much too nervous at this sudden change in his usually brusque and abusive master to notice anything, storm and chill alike, just now. Anything, that is, that wasn't Mal Brit Arren. Rumor had it he'd killed the boy, three before Jon. So one or two of the younger men said: it was possible they ragged him. But word also had it Mal Brit Arren was no man to cross when he'd been drinking, and that Jon knew for absolute, painful truth.

"What did ye think of her?" the Captain demanded abruptly. Young Bri Madden started, nearly overturning his cup. Brit Arren made an impatient gesture, then checked it. For whatever reason, he was practicing patience at the moment.

"Her? That—the Lady?" Jon fumbled finally.

"Lady. Hah." Brit Arren laughed into his empty mug; the sound echoed. He set it down silently, shoved it across the table. Jon filled it, shoved it back. Brit Arren's eyes brooded on the large, unadorned pewter goblet. "Like the Sea-serpent's mother is a Lady, so she is!" He grumbled to himself, picked up the cup and drank down half its contents. "Witch, that's what. You mark that, Jon, and never forget it, she's AEldra witch and then some. Something even worse, I don't know what. But I'll tell you, Jon, if they were all like *her*, I'd never board another Ylsan ship, Jon, and that's fact!"

"Sir." Jon could only agree with him, nothing else was safe or conducive to long life. Privately, he'd thought her beautiful, used

as he was to women of his own kind, who always smelled of the
sea and had harsh, shrill voices like gulls. Or Ragnolan dock-
women: dark, oddly scented, falling out of their brightly colored
gowns, most of them. This one: She was almost as tall as he, her
eyes were a blue you could get lost in, her hair golden, her whole
look chaste and sweet, her dress demure—but he remembered the
look in those gloriously blue eyes as she'd stood on the shore,
challenging them to take her out to the ships. Not just the ships,
either; she'd pointed out Bri H'Larn's *Vitra* with absolutely no
hesitation at all. *Witch*. Not what she seemed, how she looked:
She'd eat a man's soul out, like the cicalea were said to, they who
lived at the southernmost edge of the sea, uttering their sweet,
wailing cries to lure ships near—and destroy them on the waiting
rocks.

"Witch," Mal Brit Arren still brooded. "What does Nod Bri
H'Larn think he plans? That woman is death, death on tiny
slippered feet. And the man with her—" He shuddered, drained
his cup. "Gods!"

"Captain, your leave, he's not likely to live, not on the Isles.
Did you *see* him? There's no mind left there, just a great hulk of
swordsman and a child's thought!"

"So he *seems*." Brit Arren shuddered again. "So he appears. I
saw him; I saw his eyes, too. There's a thing about him, a thing
deep in his eyes, where he himself may have forgotten it but it
conjures up smoke and fog and blood, all mixed. Death. I was
glad, Jon, *glad* I tell you, when *Vitra* set them ashore, when Bri
H'Lod went south and let us come back north, for my sleep has
been undisturbed since we parted company!"

The boy's breath hissed in between clenched teeth. He could
face anything, *anything!* Storm, armsmen, beasts and sea-beasts
were nothing. But this that his Captain mumbled sent shivers
running up and down his back and he became aware of the *Fury*
slipping up and down under his feet, all reality going from under
them. Caution was forgotten: he took down the contents of his cup
in two deep swallows and poured himself more. Brit Arren shook
himself, smiled at the boy.

"That's good, isn't it?"

"Sir." Jon nodded.

"Bah, all this *sir* business! Here, this cabin, these walls—I'm
Mal to you. Same as you're Jon."

"I—Mal," the boy whispered.

Brit Arren laughed, a low chuckle that shook his shoulders and brought tears to his eyes. "Bless the lad, it's not at all what you think! They don't tell tales of *that* sort about me, do they?" Silence. Jon eyed him in confusion. "That I warm my sheets with cabin boys? Don't look like that. I don't. No." He emptied his cup again, set it aside. "I need someone to speak to. The crew is a good one. They'd never split on the old man, not to Bri H'Larn or that woman or anyone else. But there's no need to speak my thoughts around, until it's time. One man, that's all I need."

Silence. Jon Bri Madden stirred, fingered the faint, soft bit of moustache that touched the corners of his mouth. "S—Mal, I don't know things, not to help you. I mean," he added desperately as Brit Arren slumped back in his chair to gaze flatly across the table at him, "if you need someone to set plans with you, if you—" He faltered to an uncertain stop.

"I don't. I need someone to back me, someone loyal. You're that, or so you seem to me, and I know men, if nothing else. You're a good fighter, any weapon I've seen you use. You're even-tempered. I need that, too. And once you come from under the surprise of my asking, I think you'll be the man I truly need: someone to hold me back when the time's not yet right. You've caution and sense, Jon. That's two things I've never had." His blue eyes, near black in the uncertain, wavering lantern, brooded on a spot midway between them.

"I'll try, if that's what you want." *The gods curse me for a wet fool, refuse him and I might die. This way I'm certain to!*

"Good." Mal Brit Arren shifted his weight, traced a line along the scarred tabletop. "I challenge Nod Bri H'Larn when we come to port, tomorrow. You'll be my back-guard." He looked up sharply. "You'll do that for me, Jon?"

"I can do that, Mal." The moment had passed; he found himself surprisingly calm, as though death had touched his face and moved on without him.

"And then," Brit Arren said grimly, "we'll feed that golden witch to the fishes."

I would have it known before all that I liked and admired the old Chosen, Grewl. I am not as set in the ways of my beliefs as their kind generally are, and he was not only open in his thought, and intelligent, but willing to accept the unusual—such as myself—and that at his age, too. But many of the others were not so open, and there were a few I most carefully avoided, lest I find the need to choose between harm to a Chosen or to myself at Chosen hands.

And this Jers: There was something the first time I saw him. He could have been a wielder of Power, had it been in him, for he had the strength of will for it, and something else—how to name it?—that spark that must be present for Power to take root. Since that was closed to him, by his blood and his religion, he found another way to another kind of power, or so he thought. Political manipulations, plots and plans within plots and plans. And such allies as he had! Easy to see how he might have thought the matter in his hands, the way he wished it to be.

Perhaps he was half mad to begin, and it was that I sensed that made me uneasy in his presence. Perhaps being thwarted in his desires pushed him down the path of madness.

I was not greatly surprised, then, when the matter came to a head and Ylia told me how it fell out.

239

26

The Fest drew to a close on the hottest day yet: Fortunately for the participants in the final sword-crossings, there were few of those and early in the day. As Ylia had expected, Lisabetha took the coin and ribbon for the women, though she barely beat out her nearest competitor, and one of Erken's men—not yet of age to grow a beard—won the men's competition. There were half a dozen prizes to be distributed among the archers, since there had been so many. When young Danila received the coin and ribbon for her age group from the Bowmaster, she smiled for the first time in days: the matter of the sheep still weighed heavily on her.

There was a fest within the Midsummer Fest with Galdan's return: He had been well known in the North and very well liked.

Ylia called him into the reception the last day of Fest, and gave him a small, hurriedly embroidered patch with her house arms. "For your sleeve. When there's cloth and opportunity, you'll have full colors." She dropped down on the top step, gestured him to sit. He did, taking a place two steps down from her at what he clearly considered a proscribed distance away.

He shrugged. "What I have won't wear out before spring."

"No, but your father considers it unsuitable, and he's not the only one." Galdan made a face and she laughed. "All right, I happen to agree with you! But it's not only my say, and certainly not yours."

"You're *supposed* to rule Nedao!"

"Yes, but even so, the people want certain forms to be followed. I told you, I don't particularly like it, but when Erken says they want things just so, I listen. He's usually right, you know."

Galdan sighed. "I know it. Damn, anyway!"

"My words exactly. Keep your leathers, by all means. You'll be out hunting and tracking and you'll want them for that."

"Too kind of you—"

"We are *not*," she overrode him ominously, "going to argue the matter, in any fashion, *if* you don't mind! New clothing, and soon. So prepare yourself for it. But that wasn't all I wanted to tell you. Since you're once again Erken's heir and since he's mine—"

"Is he?" The Duke's son let his head fall back and laughed

240

loudly. "No wonder he's so cautious of you!" He sobered abruptly, eyed her narrowly. "That had better not make *me* next in line after Father!"

She shrugged. "His choice. If you're dead against it, tell *him*."

"I wouldn't dare, we'd kill each other arguing it. Why?"

"Why what? Erken? I told him, who better? Except Corlin, who was still thought dead when I named Erken. When we found him, he wouldn't allow the change."

"But Corlin's Second House—"

"And as stubborn as you *or* Erken. Don't interrupt me. It's not proper," she added tartly. He shook his head, laughed again. "Anyway, until I have an heir myself, he's it."

"You mean, until you marry some foreign noble or another and present Nedao with babies," Galdan replied bluntly. "Hardly a safe thing to do at a time like this, is it? Since you follow King's rules and fight with your armsmen. Then again," he mused, "if *I'm* so near the succession as all that, perhaps I'd prefer if you—"

"Never*mind*," she broke in sharply. It irritated her, the whole matter did. "We're getting far afield again. Dammit, listen to me and *then* answer, all right? Erken's part of my council, you know that. As his son and his heir, I'd like you to be part of it also." Silence. He gazed at a spot on the top of the step of the dais, clearly surprised by her request. "You know the mountains from here to Nar and here to Yls. We can use that."

"I—" He considered the matter for several long moments. *Sometimes I think she doesn't like me at all, or care for my presence, and then she makes me her knight, takes me to her council, and why? Ah, well. Since it's her, and no fancy court lady, it's all for the reasons she names, no doubt,* he concluded gloomily. He eyed her covertly from under his lashes, looked away as he realized she was watching him. *That I have weapon skill and that I'm Father's heir. Well, if it's what I have to give her, at least I have that much. At least I have it to offer, and—and at least she asks it.* He finally nodded. "As you choose. If you wish it."

"I do. Thank you." With his beard trimmed up, and his hair pulled back in proper Nedaoan fashion, he looked a different man: younger, more handsome, and though neither as tall nor as broad of shoulder as his father, he was a near match for Erken. He'd gone polite on her, too, which was an odd change—at least, sometimes he was. She preferred when he forgot protocol and manners both, as he frequently did, and argued with her as though

she were simply other people and not a title and a figurehead. Few
enough people did that, anymore. "That's settled. Brel tells me
you, he and Golsat have a hunt planned. When?"

"We thought so, if there's no objection. We could still use the
meat, and the shoemakers need the skins. And since Nar sends
more horses, we'll need harness. They can't supply the kind we
use."

"No. They've offered more leather, but yes, we could still use
the meat and we'll need all the hides we can get together, for boots
for the winter. When do you leave?"

"Day after next."

"Have an eye out for Mathkkra—but you'd do that anyway."

"Well, yes, now you mention it." Mildly spoken indeed for
Galdan. "Anything else—Lady?" he added, as though just
recalling his manners. She laughed, shook her head. "By your
leave, then. I'm helping Golsat with the young swords this
morning."

"Brave man," she replied gravely. He grinned briefly, strode
rapidly from the hall.

Matters settled slowly back to normal: The Narrans installed
their embassy in the small house provided for them on the square
and went back down-river with a load of goods. More wool came
to Marckl's new docks and went to the work house, where twelve
long looms were set up, and steam rose continuously from the
color vats at the open far end. More looms were built, large-wheel
spindles constructed, and looms and spindles were never empty,
seldom untended. Lossana spent most of her daylight hours in the
cool shed, overseeing the dye pots, weaving her own complex
pattern into dark blue cloth, helping the older women to teach girls
how to spin.

Lisabetha, too, was spending long hours at the looms, and she
had become Malaeth's chief gatherer of dye plants. Evenings she
spent in the women's chamber in the Tower; she now had more
silver thread for her wedding dress, and she and the other
household ladies were hard at work on the embroidery. Brelian
had somehow found the time to construct her bride-box, as was
his right and obligation, and with the wedding set for the Tenth of
Fruiting, Lisabetha labored long hours to make certain it was
properly filled by then.

New paper came with the wool, and Ylia delivered that
personally to the Chosen. She enjoyed Grewl's company; now that

he no longer had time to scribe for her and her father's man had taken over that position, she missed him.

The commune was flourishing: their crops were high and weedless, their sheep fat, and there were new twin kids. Within the walls, the Chosen women had their own looms going to turn out cloth for themselves and for trade, and Grewl had begun to reorganize the scholars to the painful task of reconstructing the histories lost when the Tehlatt razed the Citadel. He received the cloth-wrapped bale with a good deal of pleasure.

He took tea with her in the large open hall, where several others were already eating a small afternoon meal or drinking a cup of chilled, watered wine before returning to late tasks.

"Do you know, there's an idea I have I'd like to put before ye," he said once they were settled. His Nedaoan was surprisingly unaccented, save for the touch of Northern in it that told who'd taught him.

"As you wish. I have no say here, though. You know that."

He smiled, sipped the clear red, tart tea. She took a taste of her own: odd combination of herbs, and what, she wondered, contributed that bright color to it? *Remember to ask.* "No say— well, perhaps not. I would not say that we live here on sufferance, certainly. But we are a foreign order residing on land granted us by you. But," he forestalled her, "that was not my need, to have your permission for the task as Nedao's Queen." He sipped again. "Do you like that?" She nodded. "It's an Osneran tisane, modified for what grows here. I'll see you get a bag of the dry to take with you."

"Thank you." *Sage—there's definitely that. Wild rose hip for the tartness, but that doesn't account for the color—*

"No. It occurs to many of us that history isn't all ancient days. And we've folk here who can tell us the tales we had copied before. They'll hold, so as to speak. We've begun recording the fall of the Plain. And with your permission, I'd like the right to set down the tale of your own escape from the King's City, and your coming to Aresada." She stared at him over the rim of her cup, surprised. Grewl spread his hands. "Of course, if you'd rather not—"

"No." She stirred. "No, I'd—I'd like that. I'd prefer it were you."

A movement at her elbow brought her around. "The Lady prefers—but I interrupt. I hope nothing of too private a nature?" Jers stood beside her, his body inclined to a proper bow, his face set in a servile smirk. His eyes were pale blue, cold and hard as ice. Ylia opened her mouth, closed it again and to her anger felt red wash her face.

"The Lady and I were speaking of the histories and my copying of them," Grewl said placidly. If he saw her sudden flush, he ignored it. "It is not forbidden us to welcome outsiders and to give them refreshment, Jers."

"Not under old rule, no, it is not."

Grewl eyed him with mild curiosity. "Under *current* rule, unless I am gravely behind on my understanding of such things. The Lady brought our paper, it will be possible for us to begin the writing once more."

"I am glad," Jers smiled, and it was a chill smile that matched his eyes, "that you will have occupations for your failing years, should you choose to remain here." Something crackled; his hand had tightened convulsively on a roll of thin Osneran decree-paper. Ribbon quivered across the backs of his fingers.

"Should I—? Oh, yes. I think I shall do that. These are good people, and the histories well worth the copying. And the Lady tells me there will be children to teach their letters this winter."

"Perhaps so. They will not be taught by you." He unrolled the crumpled paper, shoved it forward so it nearly touched the older man's nose. Grewl caught at the edge of it, gave Ylia a look across the other edge that said *caution and silence* as clearly as if he'd been AEldra. He held the paper steady—Jers was apparently incapable of it—and read. "The Heirocracy has set full seals to the bottom, see that, old man! There will be no trifling with such a ruling, not on your part!"

"No?" The old man eyed him mildly indeed, but Ylia let out a held breath. Whatever was happened here, this young fanatic was not simply going to walk over the elderly scribe: There was a core of hard metal in Grewl.

"Read it again!" Jers shouted. There was a murmur among those scattered about the room, annoyed looks from several; two women looked in through the archway that led to the weaving room, then disappeared. But they were back moments later, with the rest of the weavers filling the hallway behind them. She doubted Jers saw them; he had eyes only for Grewl. "A ruling—an *order!*—from the Heirocracy! You are mentioned only insofar as you are given the right to remain here, if you so choose, to direct the scribes' chamber and to oversee the work undertaken there. See?" A trembling hand shot out and stabbed at the paper.

"That is all it says of you, old man! Beyond that, read for yourself! See how the Heirocracy has decreed for us here!" He stood back, folded his arms across his narrow chest and stared balefully down the length of his nose at the older man.

Grewl took the document unhurriedly, and perused it. He looked up finally. The hall was becoming crowded, as more and more Chosen came from the fields, from the hen-coop, from the kitchens. Jers had eyes only for Grewl, and Grewl turned to Ylia as though he was aware of no one occupying the hall at all but the two of them. "This isn't pleasant news, Lady, I daresay you won't care much for what the Heirocracy orders."

"She won't—!" Jers exploded. "This witch has no say—!"

"Ah, brother?" Grewl leaned forward and tapped his arm. "If you recall, there are lands where such a remark against a crowned ruler would cost you your tongue, if not your entire head. It *has* happened, and I doubt, Jers, that you're ready for martyrdom. Are you?" Silence. Astonished silence. "As I was saying. They intend that the house here take again a firm line against—"

"Against witchery in all its forms?" Ylia put in as he paused.

"Even so. They suggest that young children can be taught better than elders, and that therefore an emphasis is to be placed upon schools for the young, to bring Nedao eventually to the true way. No overt move is to be made against the House—Jers, you wished to say something? No? I do not think he intended I read this to *you*, but perhaps Jers is learning a lesson of his own, today."

"You cannot—!" Jers made a grab for the paper; Grewl shifted his weight so his back and shoulder caught the younger man's body. He held the paper just out of reach. "That ruling gives me control of the Order in Nedao! I am Father now, and I tell you to give that back to me!" Silence. Grewl met Jers' furious glare with a mildly quizzical look of his own. Jers drew a deep breath, let it out hard and fast. "Destroying that will not change matters, Grewl. Give it to me."

"But I have not yet finished reading it," Grewl replied reasonably, and turned away to bring his attention back to the document in his hand. "I'll tell you what I sense here, Lady," he went on.

"I'd—appreciate that." Ylia spoke past a dry throat. This was not the kind of situation she could handle, and even if any of her own that could were here—Corlin, Erken, Joffen who'd been her father's man in charge of delicate negotiations—even they couldn't help with this! She felt acutely uncomfortable and definitely in the way. And Jers had transferred that chill gaze to her now. *He hates me for how I was born, what I had from my mother, for something I can't control! How can he think like that?* She swallowed, sending a sudden wave of anger down: Manipulate children! Well, Jers would be good at *that*, wouldn't he? Look what he'd done to Lisabetha, who'd been schooled by him as a child to hate AEldra, and all that it implied. To hate and fear her own foreseeing which she could not help!

Not her fight. No. But now she knew all too well what Marhan had felt, when she'd pushed him away from Vess.

Grewl drew her attention again, but not before she noticed the hall was quite filled with silent, intent Chosen, and that a number of these stood behind Grewl. "What I think is, our young friend Tevvro managed to reach Osnera, and perhaps spent some of his father's coin—and your cousin's, if he still had any—to buy what he could there—"

"You *dare* suggest," Jers spluttered, "that the Heirocracy would accept *bribes?*"

"I've seen it, and the results of it, and so have you, young brother," Grewl replied evenly. "Unless your eyes are too blinded by ardent belief to see that the members of the Heirocracy are also men?" Silence. "No, that is what I see. Now, either the coin was not sufficient, or the Heirocracy has greater plans, and a depth to them that will not reveal itself for a time to come. Else Tevvro himself had been here, with full papers and an escort of inner house guard to see that the changes in policy were properly adopted. To send a paper, stating such outrageous things as it does—"

"Outrageous? *Outrageous?*"

"—well, that simply asks for trouble. As well we know. To attempt such a policy, in such times, and with the ruling house headed by one who wields the Power—"

"He was right; she has besotted you," Jers hissed. One of his own followers caught at his arm and whispered against his ear; Jers shook him off in a fury. The man retreated a few paces to confer worriedly with three of his fellows.

"He?" For the anger that was twisting her gut, she managed to hold her voice steady. "My cousin Vess, you mean."

"Your cousin," Grewl agreed, forestalling whatever remark Jers intended. The younger man attempted to override the older, then subsided momentarily. "Now, as I see it, they are driving us into a box from which there is only one exit: Surely they do not believe Jers will have the free assent of a majority of the house here. Tevvro would have had a better grasp of numbers and leanings when he left than that! No. He sees that one of us—I fear he thinks me, and I fear he is correct in that—will take Jers' right from him and give him choice, to remain under the new order or to leave for good. Then, when Tevvro and your cousin have consolidated their gains, and when Nedao again flourishes, they will return. And this time, the Heirocrat will send full guard."

"They—they can't do that!" Her voice *did* tremble, this time.

"It won't stop them trying, of course," the old man said unhappily. "And I resent being pushed into this position, knowing that is what they are doing. I am not a piece on a board game, to be moved—but then, board pieces do not have wit. I hope I have. My friends!" he raised his voice as he stood, and turned slowly to take in all the crowded chamber. "I have spoken with a goodly many of you, and doubtless you know what has passed here, and what this paper contains!" A worried murmur of conversation buzzed through the hall. "We can deal with this at evening-meal if you choose. But I would greatly prefer that we do so now, at once, in the Lady's presence. She has granted us this place to live, and at expense to her folk, both in land and grain, men to help us roof, beasts and paper. I personally would prefer, very much so, that she not go back to her own halls worrying how much of the Order in this document will be carried out!"

A man nearly Grewl's age pushed forward; he climbed to the bench at the scholar's side, held onto his shoulder for balance. He waved his free arm for silence and got it. "Brother Jers. We have discussed this matter before. We know you have adherents. Brother Grewl has adherents among us also. It has always been the case that in distant lands, the Heirocracy may command, but the Order itself had final say as to its actions, since the Heirocracy and its members may not fully understand the political situation under which the House exists. Or other such matters as can only be understood by those living in that foreign House."

"This is *not* such a matter," Jers shouted. Twenty other voices drowned him out.

"Silence!" the old man on the bench bellowed. He got it. "We are not children, fighting over a toy here. We will discuss this as reasonable men and women! This land is ruled by a woman who uses sorcery among her weapons. I personally do not believe as Grewl does, that there is no harm at all to this, but that is *not* my business, to see to the ordering of Nedao's ruling House! Nor to subjugate its children. Many of the Nedaoan women have the Sight. Would you cleanse that from them?''

"I have," Jers began defiantly. He faltered to a halt as Ylia cast him a scorching look and the elder on the bench waved an impatient hand at him.

"And the creatures—these Mathkkra? I saw the bodies. I heard from one of the parentless children about them. *They* are magic. Will you cleanse them also?" Silence. Jers dropped his gaze but his eyes were still furious. "Or the things that fly? I think we should be grateful for all such protections as we have against evil beings such as those. I oppose the Heirocracy's Order. This is not the time or the place to hold to strict Osneran policy."

"I agree." Grewl, his face full of misgivings, got to his feet. "We have tasks here. We have those among the Nedaoans who came to us freely and who share our beliefs. If we attempt to take the line Osnera dictates, we will find ourselves all boarding ships for home, for even if this Lady remains kind to us, her council will throw us out. We have only one real choice: to remain on good terms with these folk, and to set aside the Heirocracy's order—or to leave. It is not for us to dictate Nedaoan policy, or to dictate to Nedao's Queen. That is what that Order intends." Silence. "Though I warn you. If we attempt what is asked of us, we leave Nedao. If we do as I have said, as Hadriad here urges, as many have agreed with us that we must, then we must eventually face charge of schism from Osnera."

"If we're driven from Nedao," one of the younger women spoke up, "they won't treat us much better than if we *had* created schism. Would they?"

"Well," Grewl smiled faintly. "To imprison us for spreading false doctrine, they would have to have us in hand first, wouldn't they?"

"This is all wrong!" Jers shouted over a worried murmur of conversation. "What you do here, Grewl—" he rounded on Ylia so suddenly she recoiled from him. "*She* is the cause of this, she has cast spells upon you, and turned your thought!"

"That's not true or right." Sata—one of the Chosen women Ylia and her companions had rescued along with Grewl, deep in the Foessa—pushed forward, confronted the young Chosen. "If that was so, *I'd* say what Grewl does! Well, I don't feel as he does at all, I'm not best pleased about this AEldra magic and that's honest truth! Never was! But I agree with him that whatever we believe, we're *here,* and the people support her. For us to try and subvert children, to undermine her popularity—we haven't the right, and we wouldn't be here long if we tried it!"

"Osneran line was never that hard against magic until lately, anyway," someone else deep in the crowd said. "In my grandsire's time, it was accepted and the Heirocrat himself had dreams and truth-knowledge."

"But—!"

"Silence, Jers. I put it to vote!" Sata shouted. There was a shifting of bodies; Jers was pulled back by four of his own and this time he went away quietly enough and stayed with them. "Those who support Jers and would see him Father, would accept the Order!" A few muttered responses to that, but the spirit had gone out of Jers' supporters. Sata looked around at Grewl, who stared at his hands in resignation. She smiled tightly. "Those who would see Grewl Father, and follow the path of common sense!"

"There's no sense to schism," someone muttered, but he was shouted down by an overwhelming "Aye!" Sata touched Grewl's shoulder lightly, and nodded as he looked up.

He sighed, stood. "Either way, we might well lose. This way, at least we've gained time. Brother Jers—"

"You dare not call *me* brother, old fool," Jers hissed.

"I would call even a full AEldran brother, if I chose. Brother Jers, you have a 5-day for your decision. I hope your brothers who care for you will help you make it. I know the One will, if you ask His aid. But there will be no further schism in *this* house, if I am to serve as its Father. Either you accept my policy in this time and place—and bide your own, if you will, but in seeming and proper behavior. Or you may leave to join your friends in Osnera."

"There is no choice," Jers said flatly. "I will not remain in a land where sorcery is condoned as it is here! There is a Narran boat down at the River, I will be on it when it sails." *And give a full report on you, in person, as soon as I can,* his look added. He turned on his heel; two of his supporters went with him. The others looked at each other, at the stiff, retreating back, shook their heads and vanished into the crowd.

Grewl dropped back to his seat; a few of the Chosen came forward to speak with him briefly, but Sata and several of the other women got the room cleared. Ylia started to stand; Grewl touched her arm, and shook his head. "We weren't done speaking, if I recall correctly."

"I—" She laughed shakily. "I don't remember. I'm sorry."

"Ah. Your own story. I fear I'll be busy a 5-day or so, unfortunately, but thereafter I should be able to begin work on that. I hope you're not worried by all of this," he added.

She shook her head. "Not by you, by those here, no. Vess, though—I should have known he'd be up to such a thing!"

"Well, it won't do him much good. He and Tevvro both have much to learn if they intend to use the Heirocracy as a stepboard to control of Nedao. The Heirocrat hasn't half the power he thinks or wishes he had, outside the Order. It was different, two hundred years ago, but even then only west of the sea. Then many lands rose or fell by the Order's decisions. So they still make their secret deals and policies, and believe that such things matter."

"But, if they declare schism—"

Grewl sighed. "Well, yes. That might be serious. But mainly if any of us ever wished to return home." He stirred, finished his tea. "We've bought time, a year or two of it. I greatly doubt your cousin will stir from Osnera between now and then, particularly if he truly thinks they can aid him." He set the empty cup aside. "I'm again reminded, speaking of tales, I had never heard that sweet story of your Nisana's before. Does she know any others?"

"Dozens; she used to tell them to me long after bedhour, when Malaeth thought me alseep."

"I'd greatly appreciate it if you'd get me another."

Ylia laughed. "I'll try, but she's not always nearby these days! Mice!" She made a face. "You'd think intelligence like hers would keep her from eating mice, but it doesn't."

"If she runs short where you are," Grewl replied gravely, as she made ready to leave, "ask her if she'd come here. We've no cat or dog of our own and we've mice rampant in the feed."

*The Nedaoan Mothers bless me for lack of wit:
I understand that humans have tempers. All
beings of a certain level of intelligence have
them. Even I have the reputation for one, though
I hold that I am more even of disposition than
most folk; certainly more so than most of my
own kind. But why is it human temper invariably
shows itself in raised voices? Which are I must
add, less than pleasant to more sensitive ears.*

27

Marckl had been as good as his word; he and his armsmen
combed the ridges for a full 5-day after Fest end. They found
potential summer pastures, a number of shallow (empty) caves,
several hides'-worth of open meadow thick with mushrooms,
breathtaking panoramas, slides and sheer drop-offs, and four hot
pools that could be used as cures. Plus numerous additional
valleys that—like the high pasturage—would, in better times, be
excellent lands for Erken, Marckl, Ifney and the other nobles
when they took lands of their own once more.

They found no trace, footprint, or scent of Mathkkra.

Ylia and Nisana made their own searches and found much the
same—nothing. It didn't help either, that that was all they found.
"They're out there, cat. You know it and I know it. They're
waiting for us to relax guard again, that's all."

'No argument on *that* from me, girl. I'm not your brainless
Duke!' The cat paced the length of the council table, then back
again. Ylia slumped in her high-backed, cushioned chair, exhausted from the hot council meeting that had just ended, and the
search she and the cat had just concluded. The lamp before her
guttered, went out. Nisana paced halfway back down the table
then sat. Her tail twitched. 'There must be a way to find them.

251

We've had fools' luck that they've not attacked since, and against those more vulnerable even than the herds and herders.'

"I know it. But if there's a way I can't figure it. Erken's men, Marckl's and Ifney's, Bnorn's—mine, both of them—they're all ready to follow the creatures next time there's attack." She sighed heavily. "Why am I telling you this? *You* were here tonight, you know how much squabbling *that* took!"

'Spare me a reiteration,' the cat snapped. 'My ears still hurt. Why must men *shout* so? But you and I know how fast Mathkkra run, and how well they move through close trees and brush, when horsemen must either slow pace or be knocked from the saddle!'

She nodded, and closed her eyes, rubbing at them absently. "It was easier to go along with them than to argue with Erken and Galdan both. Have you tried that lately?"

'Why should I? It's more amusing to watch you at it, and to watch you and Galdan so carefully avoiding each other's eyes.'

"Nisana, that's not funny." She sighed heavily and the cat snorted a laugh. "I don't even think he likes me much."

'Oh, no. He just came back to Nedao because he enjoys squabbling with his father, and ogling the peasant girls,' the cat retorted. 'But never mind, you'll argue with me next, and I'm *bored* with arguing.'

The guard on the herds was redoubled, but they were kept out at pasture—there'd been too much damage to crops, driving the beasts back and forth every day, and with so many to feed it was becoming impractical, particularly now with all the lambs, calves and kids. And there wasn't enough feed to keep them penned constantly near the bridge. The council took most of the children off guard. Only Danila refused to be counted among those, and even Levren could not dissuade her. He compromised by making certain Nold was on watch with her.

Three 5-days after Midsummer Fest, the hiatus was broken: on a black night when thick cloud covered the moon, the Citadel was attacked, two Chosen badly injured, one of their sheep killed and two lambs taken. The border guard had come upon the uneven fight almost immediately and driven the creatures back into the woods. The Chosen were given warning horns in case of another such raid, the border guard given an extra two turns per night past their low buildings. The Mathkkra were tracked at first light, but the trail vanished almost immediately on rock.

And now it seemed the creatures chose to make up lost time,

and while there was only one death over the next two 5-days, there were raids and ambushes every night, sometimes as many as four at a time. The sword-sworn of the minor lords, the Northern Baron, and Erken and Corlin rode in long shifts, out of saddle only to sleep and eat. Ylia overrode her council, then, and sent some of her young women out on border guard, the rest to inner guard, hoping they could be of use there.

They were. Folk who had complained loudly over the clash of femininity and weaponry were effectively silenced when they found themselves defended by their daughters on their own doorsteps. Many young women who had held back at Aresada came forward eagerly for training.

But still the creatures' retreat remained hidden. Though two hundred had fallen to Nedaoan bow and sword, the numbers that came against them never lessened.

"To me, that still indicates a single stronghold," Marckl insisted at a particularly tense meeting.

"It doesn't *matter!*" Ylia shouted down the uproar that followed this remark. She jumped to her feet, pounded on the table and finally got silence. "We *know* they're out there, they've proven that to us! We *know* there's enough of them, and so long as we finally find and destroy them, I cannot see what it possibly matters if they all occupy one burrow, or if they have twenty!"

"Exactly so," Galdan spoke up before any of his fellows could voice a harsher remark. "And we could use the time here in a better manner than to simply argue this thing over. After all, we've decided we must find them and destroy them. We're all agreed on that still?" Marckl rolled his eyes and mumbled something to Ifney. "So why don't we go on to something a little more pleasant, like the wine the Narrans plan on sending us? Is there still a problem with barrels for the ale? Because if so, I'll pick men and go for the wood myself."

"My son—" Erken began, quietly for him. Galdan clapped him on the shoulder.

"A jest, Father. It's been so long since you've heard one at this table, you forget how they sound." It was Erken's turn to roll his eyes. Galdan clapped his shoulder again. "Seriously, if there's a problem—"

"No problem," Marckl mumbled. "There's still a lot of downed wood beside the road—"

"Not pine, you know—"

"—of *course* I know," the older man snapped. "Most of

Teshmor's ale came from my estates, you know! Wasn't aware there was a problem. We can drag what's needed out as far as the cooper needs it. All the way in to the City, if he likes."

"Fine, Marckl, you deal with that," Ylia put in hastily. "And my thanks. There's a shipment of wine due in a day or so, Ber'Sordes ordered it and Tr'Harsen's bringing it. They said it's on account. Corlin knows all about *that,* if any of you needs detail, why not ask him later. Because frankly, I'm tired, and you all look as tired as I feel."

"If there's anything else, we can chew on it tomorrow night," Bnorn said as he rose to his feet. "I'm tired, too, and my head aches. I think we'll have rain tonight or tomorrow, by the feel of the air."

"Wonderful," Ifney said as he pushed his chair back. "The grain won't like that."

"It won't hurt, if there's no more to follow for a few days," Marckl reminded him.

"True." Ifney smothered a yawn. "Bnorn's right, the air's oppressive and I'm tired and I ache. It's been years since I've spent so much time horsed."

"Huh, how d'ye think *I* feel?" the Swordmaster demanded from the doorway.

They straggled out of the council room, still grumbling and complaining, but there was an undercurrent of relief in even Marhan's peevish last remark.

"Lady? Are you all right?" She opened her eyes—odd, she hadn't remembered shutting them. Galdan hovered uncertainly over her. She smiled tiredly. "Shall I send for your women?"

"No." She held out a hand. "Just help me up. I'm too tired to move." Warm fingers caught at hers, pulled her upright.

"Pushing yourself, aren't you?" he asked.

She shrugged. "Some. Not as much as others I could name who've hunted mountain sheep, Mathkkra and still found time to fight four duels in the barracks."

"Now, how you heard about *that,*" he exclaimed in exasperation. "Father's been talking again, old gabbler!"

She laughed. "You wrong him. Golsat and Brel and I are good friends. And arms-mates, remember? But I could have heard about that last fight from anyone housed down there!"

"Not my fault," he began, all injured virtue. "They forget I was barracked in Teshmor when some of them were still growing second teeth, and they insist on setting upon me in—"

"—in time-honored tradition," she finished for him. She was still laughing. "Forgetting, of course, that you three have sworn brothering and anyone who fights one of you comes against all three."

"They haven't forgotten that," he reminded her. "The last two brought comrades. If you heard anything you must have heard it all."

"I had. You haven't helped them, poor babies, by your sudden change from those old hides, you know." She cast him a meaningful look as they emerged into the hall. He moved a correct—she couldn't possibly call it mockery, for all the exquisite care he put into it—pace away from her. "It simply begs trouble."

"What, this?" All innocent surprise now, he indicated with a sweep of his hand the short, dark blue half-circular cape lined in paler blue, the dark blue tunic with his token of service stitched to the shoulder, the full sleeved bleached shirt with its blue cuffs and the plain black hose. Like many others, like his father, he'd been first amused and then taken by the new Narran fashion, but even Erken had not been able to obtain the garb as quickly as Galdan and Brelian had: they'd bargained it away from the traders. Golsat, always plain-clad, looked plain indeed between the two of them. "I merely thought to save you the trouble and expense of dressing me."

"I—see." She personally was torn: It was odd, and a little uncomfortable, seeing so much of a man's legs. Perhaps not that different from her own breeches, or so Lisabetha had told her: at first one didn't know where to look.

But since these two and now Erken had adopted the style, there'd be more to follow, and likely there'd come a day when baggy breeches laced from knee to ankle and a loose jerkin over would be worn by the few and would then be the thing that looked odd.

"If you'd rather," Galdan said, breaking in to her thoughts embarrassingly near the mark, "I can always change back."

"Whatever for?" she demanded sweetly. "I rather enjoy looking at your legs." And as he turned red, she laughed, but she was as crimson as he was.

As suddenly as they'd begun, the raids ceased. In one night, two separate clutches of Mathkkra were completely wiped out, and they were the last. Council meetings became even hotter as those at the long table argued the same point back and forth that the commons argued: The creatures had finally given up. No, they had done no such thing, they waited to make certain the foolish humans thought it, and would then come against them to find them unprepared and easy pickings. Ifney and Erken nearly came to blows over it. Ylia finally set the meetings to every fourth night since they were becoming nothing but a battleground. Trade was progressing well on its own. The grain harvest was doing well. And she was heartily tired of argument every night.

She'd offered Grewl temporary quarters in the City, where the Chosen could be guaranteed protection. He'd thanked her but said they needed time to finish their halls before winter. Marckl, though one of the most outspoken of the council against the outland religion, sent several of his men to help the commune with its stone outer walls.

These were men who'd been part of the herd-guard; Ylia's young women replaced them. Most of the men were riding border guard and Erken had admitted frankly that his own young men found herd-duty tedious and boring. It was, under ordinary circumstances.

But if the herds were attacked again, it was no assignment for the ill-trained, and when Ylia took it for her swordswomen she made that clear to the council. *They won't look upon them as lesser because they're women, not if I can help it. Lesser because they're not much trained yet—that's a different thing. So long as they recognize the difference.*

Her women made no objection when the task was set before them: *They* were bored, they had some training, certain skills, and since the raids had ceased, they'd mostly returned to their households. Farm chores were boring indeed, compared to the exposure they'd had so far to fighting.

And Levren was pleased: His Lennett was one of those assigned to herd-guard. A little routine, he reasoned, might give the girl a dose of patience, and teach her that being swordswoman had its disciplines besides just the heart-speeding pleasures of learning crossing patterns and fighting. And she'd be there to help Nold keep an eye on Danila.

28

It was a vast hall, its ceiling higher than the greatest hall Vess had ever seen in his life. Gold shone dully among the beams, touched the edges of occasional tables, benches set here and there along the chill marble-floored length of it. There were fires at either end; he avoided these and the clutter of men who surrounded them. All they did was discuss their problems: what chances they had the Heirocracy would meet with them, hear what they had to say, give them what they sought. *I do not lay my soul bare for any man, any woman, let alone these.* Two months of kicking his heels in the enormous lobby had erased whatever respect he'd once had for Chosen: the men, the organization, the religion itself. *To the Black Well with them all,* he'd think savagely—behind a blandly polite smile of his own—as yet another grey-robed individual passed him, smiled pleasantly and moved on.

He hadn't seen Tevvro in three days: the Chosen had finally been summoned into a clerk's room, after seven petitions and three purses of his father's gold, judiciously spread among those who saw petitioners. From there—well, he couldn't guess. And he certainly would *not* ask those pale, snotty clerks, any of the gossipy, whispering clans of grey robes leaning close to the fires. For all *he* knew, Tevvro might be laying in a head-foreshortened coffin—rumor had it they'd once executed their own, if they felt the failing great enough. Perhaps they still did.

Then again, such an absence, combined with the more speculative glances of those sharing the vast hall with him, the more frequent attempts to draw him into conversation: Perhaps Tevvro was even now meeting with the Osneran Great Father and his council; maybe . . .

There had been the one moment his heart had risen, just that one moment, when Tevvro had spoken to a Chosen clad for long travel and learned of the Ruling that was on its way to Nedao. It had shattered around him as Tevvro explained in cold, ruthless detail why the plan would fail, why this was good, why it suited them.

It doesn't suit me! A smile turned the corners of his mouth as yet another grey-robed man bobbed his head and passed. *To wait—*

here, of all the Mother-forsaken places on earth!—to wait two years or more? "He imagines I'll forget the bargain I made with the *Vitra's* captain," he whispered. "But I'll return to set that bargain into force sooner than he thinks."

Because there was the other thing: the thing about which Tevvro knew nothing. Nor, if Vess could help it, would he. The odd message pinned to the inside of his door by a plain silver dagger. His mother's dagger had looked like that, unadorned save for the hilts that looked like twisted rope—until you looked closely and saw it was a serpent, eyes and mouth hidden beneath the cross-grip. Hers had been smaller, a lady's nail tool shaped to match her Lord's. Save that Nala had never had a proper Lord.

Impossible to locate the deliverer of the note and its rather unusual pin; in a maze like this, anyone could have slipped into an unlocked chamber to leave it. He wouldn't ask.

He fished the message out of his belt-pouch, devoured it once again though he knew its contents by heart already. One hand traced the rough, poorly healed scar that ran from temple to jaw as he read: "There will be a ship leaving Osnera, a five-day from the day this reaches you. It is called the *Vanity*, it is Holthan. Take it. A 5-day out from Osneran soil, another will come to take you from the Holthan ship. You will know it by its shape and color. You will know its captain by his eyes." Unbidden, a man stood in his thoughts: Captain of the *Fury*, Mal Brit Arren, eyes like northern snow and ice in a frozen dawn. "He will bring you to a place of sanctuary. What you want will be yours: Nedao. Nar. Power."

His hand moved down to touch the edge, where the signature had smeared. He couldn't make out the name at all. The two words under that were hardly any clearer, but they'd leaped off the page at him, catching in his throat, threatening balance and vision both so he fell, weak-legged, onto the bed the first time he saw them. They still dragged at his breath with little clawed hands. "Your father."

"Father," he whispered, as he had that first night: a testing of the word. It vibrated his whole body, filling him with a hunger he'd never known, never realized he *could* know. And how strange it felt: not *your* father, *his* father, *anyone's* father, no. "*My* father."

He'd tried since then, tried hard to remember everything she'd said about him, the few words she'd written in the diary he'd found after she'd gone to the Citadel. He was tall, very tall. There was more he couldn't remember, perhaps later he would. He folded the note with grave care, restored it to the belt-pouch.

Movement, chatter and the click of a latch brought him around: Tevvro came through an open door surrounded by clerks and other Chosen. He was red-faced, grim. It was some time before those around him disbursed and Vess could reach him, but the look of the man was enough.

Tevvro confirmed that as they walked back to the small room they'd shared the past long days, and longer nights. "They won't listen to me! Father did what he could, but it was only enough to get me in the door, not to pay anyone to listen. They made up their minds. We'll get nothing further until Jers fails and Nedao is more settled. They'll let us return, then."

Bribes. One thinks of them as holy because they are the Fathers of these religious. They're men, just like any men. He'd known that of Tevvro for some time, of course: he'd spent too much time too close to the young Chosen not to be aware of *his* desires, his all-too-human attributes. Tevvro was ambitious, greedy, and he'd taken this less physically chancy way to his goals.

And: *They'll let us! I am a Prince of Nedao, no common grey-clad Chosen! I do what I choose, none of their desire!*

It took effort for Vess to compose his face to sympathetic listening, to distress at the final blow to their hopes as Tevvro spoke. Deep down, he was assessing the Chosen, finding him wanting indeed. Just behind that sympathetic face, there was a man impatient to wind up the loose ends of this fool's mission and be gone. *But with care. He's a piece of low value, but he may still come to use. The groundsman travels the circuit, weaves the marks, becomes Duke. A groundsman is no use on my board: a Duke might be. Do not waste him.*

It took everything in him not to draw a great relieved breath, as though from where he stood he could smell the sea and freedom.

So often that summer, I found myself grateful that such young as I bore have long since grown and left me. Young are a burden. That feeling was particularly strong when I came inadvertently against that hoyden Lennett. Had she been one of my own she would have felt the touch of my claws against her ears, I can assure you.

29

The sun dropped into ominous black mountains of cloud; the air was thick and wet. An occasional flash lightened the cloud front from within; thunder rumbled across the valley. The Month of Storm-Clouds looked ready to live up to its name.

The landsmen hurried tied sheaves of grain into carts and barrows, bundled it into shelter. The market was already deserted. Canopies fluttered and snapped in a rising wind; a yellow-grey light filtered into the upper chambers of the Tower. Women ran to close windows, to pull shutters over openings as yet un-glassed. Marckl and his road crew cut short the celebration of the last of their work and pelted back to the City. The Narran ship tied at the dock was brought around into shelter and re-tied, more securely and at both ends.

Nisana, whose fur had been crackling for two days, sought shelter in an inner corner of the main dining hall and determinedly willed herself to sleep. She hated storms.

Rain slammed into the valley, bending trees under a shrieking wind, lighting it from end to end. The thunder was immediate and deafening. But as quickly as it came, it was gone, rolling rapidly toward the Plain, leaving behind soaked wash, flattened gardens, enormous puddles, and a much lighter atmosphere. People emerged from their houses and barns and set about their remaining chores. The sun came out briefly, dipped behind the horizon moments later.

"Well, that should make tonight's council meeting more pleasant." Lisabetha pushed the enormous shutters open, returned to Ylia's sitting area where they'd been sewing: the girl on her pale green silk, Ylia mending her spare dagger belt.

"I hope so, it's certainly lightened *my* mood." She stood, fastened the dagger back below her knee. "I think that should hold. It still slips down my calf, though."

"Put guides for the belt on the breeches themselves," Lisabetha suggested. She set aside her own work. "Someone's coming—fast."

"I hear them." Boots; someone was taking the stairs two at a time. Merreven and Eveya slammed into the door jamb together. "Lady—," they began, stopped. Eveya pushed past the doorwarder. "Lady, the herds—"

"By all the black hells at once, tell me you weren't jumped in the storm!"

"They caught us by surprise, we were on the way back to the new pens, thought we'd have time—"

"Tell me, we'll bridge back to them. Did you ride?"

The girl shook her head; blood splattered in drops from a cut high up in her hairline. "No, I had to run it; the horses scattered first thing." She plaited her fingers unhappily, watching from the door as Ylia caught at her cloak, brought down her sword, pulled on her boots. "We were out where four of the back grain-fields come together, you know it?" Ylia nodded. "The sky just opened, there was lightning practically on top of us."

"And so, sensibly, you had everyone bunch the animals and get down off the horses, so as not to attract it. Don't look so upset, girl, it's the first thing any of us learn about storms, isn't it? And as soon as you did, there they were."

"We never even saw them coming," Eveya said flatly.

"Any killed? Here, let me heal that, it won't take half a moment and it must hurt you."

"My fault I have it," the young swordswoman began angrily. Ylia shook her head.

"Don't argue, hold still! There. Now, take hold of my arm, you'll feel like you're falling but it won't last long. 'Betha, you or Merreven, get Erken—get *someone* out there, fast!"

• • •

The grass was soaked and it was growing dark. One of the women lay flat, another braced herself upright against a stone fence, nursing an ankle. Nold sat on the grass next to her, his back to the fence, his right arm cradled in his left. The sheep bleated and tried to bolt as she and Eveya came in, but the rest of the swordswomen and the herders had them well bunched.

They'd come off well, considering: one bad concussion from a flying rock. Another woman had tripped over a small white body and twisted her ankle in the fall. Embarrassing but not serious. Ylia put both quickly to rights. Nold's wrist was badly sprained, not broken. He flexed it, took the first deep breath he'd had since the storm broke. And then, as he stood: "Oh, no."

"What?" There was nothing she could see wrong, except that the boy's color had gone, and she had to catch at his arm to keep him from falling.

"Danna—she's gone. *They* have her."

"No." Eveya had caught his last words. "No, I watched them go! They had no prisoners, boy!"

"The One protect," Nold whispered, and touched his lips with his left hand, "Lennett's gone, too. They've gone after the Mathkkra, Lady."

"They wouldn't dare!" Eveya began, but Nold shook his head so vehemently she stopped.

"Danna would. And Lennett—she'd dare anything, you know that!" the boy said flatly. "Lady, *you* know how Danila felt, you saw her last time, when they killed the sheep."

"I thought she'd forget," Ylia said.

"Well, I did, too." Nold was walking in a nervous little circle, peering out across the valley, though it was still too black with clouds to see far. "She didn't. She wouldn't have anyway, but Lennett—she and Lennett—they've been full of plans, all this time." He shrugged, scowled westward. "I don't know what they were, not for certain, Danna wouldn't tell me, and Lennett—she wouldn't—well, nevermind."

"I know Lennett, it's all right." Maybe Lev wouldn't discipline the girl, maybe Ilderian couldn't, but Ylia had words stored to heap on a swordswoman who'd look upon a boy like Nold as inferior. *If she's done this, taken that child into such danger, given this decent lad such a scare—given me such a scare!—I'll have the hide off her!*

"They were at it again this afternoon, though," the boy finished. His eyes were still hunting, but without hope.

"This is my fault," Eveya said grimly. "You gave me the task of caring for the flocks, and I failed at it."

"You did all anyone could have done to protect them and the herders," Ylia said sharply. "Better than any of us have met their match in Mathkkra before this! How did you intend to manage against a grandfather of a storm, a skylarking fool of a swordswoman and a stubborn, unforgiving child, all at once. Answer me that!" Eveya shrugged unhappily, turned away. "Well, then! Think on it. Use sense! We intended to track the Mathkkra. We'll have to track Mathkkra *and* the girls."

"I'm going with you," Nold said, and his young face was set. Ylia nodded.

"You have that right. We need horses, though." It was some few minutes before riders approached in the now near-total dark. Torches spluttered to life as they came to a halt. Galdan jumped from his horse, handed the reins to Brelian and came to meet them.

"Merreven said the herds were attacked."

"No loss to the flocks, minor injury, all dealt with. But—"

"We came prepared to track now, before they can destroy the trail."

"We have to track them anyway. Danila and Lennett are both missing. We think they went after the Mathkkra."

"That girl! If it isn't one thing with her, it's ten," Galdan replied feelingly. "All right. I brought extra horses. Your boy said the guards' were scattered."

"We need two: I'm coming, so is Nold."

"If you—"

"You don't intend to argue with me, I hope," she began sharply. Galdan shook his head, lowered his voice so Nold couldn't hear him.

"Not my intention. But to follow the Mathkkra! Are you certain they aren't prisoner?"

Ylia moved closer to him as Nold started toward them. "Eveya says they had no prisoners. Her eyes are good, and Nold says it's what Danila wanted to do."

"What Lennett convinced her she wanted, more like." He expelled air in a noisy gust. "I just thought. You can track them, can't you? Nedaoan girls out there? Even if the Mathkkra can hide themselves, the girls can't." Ylia nodded. "So I'd be twice a fool to argue you're going with us. We'd better start now, we're nearly out of light. Eveya, do you want extra guard?"

The swordswoman shook her head. "I *think* we can manage from here," she said sourly.

"Don't misread my words, girl!" he snapped. "We've all been knocked down when we least expected it, one time or another. We brought half a dozen spare mounts. Lady, choose for the boy, your own's among them, and let's *go!*"

"Right." They moved swiftly, but it was still full dark by the time they started into the foothills.

The trail led into a grove of aspen, across a muddy little creek heavy with runoff and up a ravine. They climbed, crossed the creek several times, came out onto a bare ridge. The trail, still clear, dropped down again and into pine forest, and for a few minutes they lost it on thick needles. Golsat leaned low on his horse's neck, finally found where they'd gone through brush. Branches were pushed west, and hadn't yet completely snapped back into place. Not far from this, he found a yellow-fletched arrow, set on a low branch.

"Lennett's, I think. They use similar. Not stupid, not totally," he said as he passed it back. "They're setting a trail for us." He slid it into his own arrow pouch.

For some distance, they moved through the open-floored forest, and again there was conscientiously good sign: broken branches, footprints in the mud at the edge of a rill, stacked rock when they suddenly emerged from woods and onto a deep, boulder-strewn, dry stream-bed.

But it was still slow going, even with that much aid. It was middle night and they had covered less than two leagues when the Mathkkra trail vanished completely. Now there was only Lennett's and Danila's.

Mind-touch was tenuous: Ylia could not sense the Mathkkra any longer when they shielded, and somehow the girls following that path were partially shielded also. She had enough sense of their direction to keep after them. That alone saved them twice, when there was no marker and the ground was too hard to give normal clue.

The moon rode high, slid in and out of cloud, sank toward the horizon and was gone. They came out onto a crumbling ledge far above the valley into near total darkness. The torches were wearing down, and one or two had gone out. They dismounted, led the horses up a steep bank, through a muddy cleft and onto higher ground. Westward, the ground sloped down to trees and brush. The ledge dropped off sharply east and west, widened here and there to a furlong or so.

There was a line of mountains to the east, an ominous, dark red line of cloud outlining them. "All right." Galdan scowled at the guttering torch, ground it out in the sandy rock underfoot. "There's nothing here for us to see, unless Golsat's better than even I think him."

"Nothing," Golsat said and turned to Ylia. "It's your search, now."

"Don't give it up," she replied. "If they've been caught," she lowered her voice, cast an anxious eye after Nold, who'd moved on down the ledge on his own, "then I've lost them, too. And I may alert them to our presence, be aware of that." She sighed; so long on horse, she'd never ridden all night before. "It's not always the answer, Golsat, you know that."

"I know. But sometimes it is." He held her horse steady as she closed her eyes, sent out yet another mind-search. Galdan eyed her briefly, decided she wasn't quite ready to topple from the saddle, turned to break his men into groups of two and three to search down the ledge and beyond it as soon as it grew light.

The girls had to be ahead of them. The last sign had pointed this way. Ylia opened her eyes, scanned the terrain around them with the second level of sight. If they came up here, there were only two ways down. Unless they had doubled back. *Doubled back.* "Golsat! That cut—" She pointed. "Not the one we just came up, the one right behind it. Check that." He nodded, hurried off. She dismounted, followed him and sent out another search. *South* of the ledge, unexpected. Therefore to be expected in these.

And that was what they'd done. Even as Golsat waved an urgent hand, Ylia's touch closed around another thought: exhausted, shredded and riddled with terror and determination, equally mixed. Danila and Lennett, beyond doubt. The sight confirmed it.

"I have them!" It was light enough for Galdan to catch her gesture as she remounted and he was back on his own horse and at her side, the rest of the men close behind. "They doubled back."

"You sense them? Mathkkra?"

"No, the girls. Danila's safe, Nold," she added as the boy caught up with her at the base of the cut. "A league or so. There's a cliff, green-stone like Aresada, pocked with small caves. The girls are just short of that. I can see them. We'll find them now."

They were backed into a water-hollowed hole in the rock, scarcely visible for the brush covering. As the rescue party came into sight, Danila scrambled out and waved them on. Ylia leaped down, caught at the girl, held her close; she clutched Ylia's shirt-front and shook. Golsat and Brelian had Lennett between them; the young armswoman could barely stand.

"I won't tell you just now how foolish you were," Ylia began sternly.

Lennett's voice—a whisper unlike her usual sharp, strong voice—reached her. "You don't have to. I know."

Danila nodded from deep within Ylia's cloak. "I was so scared, even with Len to protect me. But we did what no one else could," she added defiantly. She leaned back to meet Ylia's gaze squarely. Her face was dead white, exhausted, her eyes all pupil. "I found them, I said I would, if I had the chance, and I did."

"Yes. I saw that."

"We were careful to leave sign. Lennett did that, she knows how because her father taught her. I knew we'd be missed right away and you'd come after us."

"Great Mothers, you knew that, did you? Well," Ylia gave her a little shake, "I may tell you, you weren't missed for nearly an hour!"

"You might have got yourself killed," Nold caught at Danila's shoulders and pulled her around. His face was as pale as hers. "Danna, every sheep in the valley isn't worth your life in trade!"

"You're not *listening*, Nold, I found—"

"You found them, I know that. But *you're* not listening," Nold overrode her, and he punctuated his words with a hard shake. "You might have died. Danna, they could have turned back and caught you, and what then?" She shrugged. He closed his eyes, let his hands drop, turned and walked away. Danila gazed after him.

"He was worried for you," Galdan said. He wrapped an arm around her shoulder. "So, tell us about this finding, Danna, and we'll have another tale for Ber'Sordes's minstrel, to go with the one about the Tanea-a-Les, won't we?" The herder-girl smiled doubtfully. Lennett, her face still drawn but her eyes coming to life, laughed and clapped her hands together in delight. Ylia sighed.

"You're encouraging them, Galdan. Don't do that!"

"Why not? They succeeded, didn't they? Copying *you*, I'd wager, particularly in *one* case." Lennett blushed. Somehow, the girl could never find the words to come back at Galdan, though she usually had a ready retort for anyone else who teased her. "Tell me." He dropped down on a fallen log, pulled Danila down beside him. Lennett moved away from Brelian's supporting arm, dropped down on Galdan's other side. Ylia eyed them tiredly.

"Well," Danila said, "they ran fast, but I always could run."

"*I* couldn't, but I've learned," Lennett said. "Anyway, for a while, it wasn't too hard to keep up. And then later, we could still hear them even when we couldn't see them too well.

"They stopped a few times, that was when Len set better markers. We knew you'd be close behind."

"You *knew*, did you?" Galdan eyed them in turn.

Danila met his gaze with a level one of her own. "Well, the Lady always comes like that, by her magic, when there's trouble, and *you* know the guard is always somewhere near, now. So I'd thought it out, back before Fest, that if I had a chance, I'd just follow them."

"Now, you'll notice," Galdan said, gravely indeed, "that your Lady always has another sword with her. That's sense."

"Well, yes. I had Lennett. She's good."

"Not against a hoard of Mathkkra, though, do you think?" Galdan asked reasonably. Danila shook her head.

"Of course not. We weren't intending to fight them, only track them. And if I'd asked Nold or someone, he'd just have stopped me."

"Well answered!" Galdan laughed. Ylia threw up her hands and went back to her horse. "So you came on, the two of you, because you had no choice."

"Well." She eyed him doubtfully, suspicious that he was laughing *at* her, but his face reassured her. "Well—"

"Well, look what we did," Lennett urged him. She was sounding more and more like herself. "We found them. I'll wager you lost them way down the hill, didn't you?"

"A little beside the point, considering your orders, wasn't that?" Galdan inquired gently, but there was steel under the ease of manner. Lennett flushed again, turned away. "Guard the herds, I think that was what you were to do. Wasn't it?"

"I was *doing* that," Lennett muttered. "And when Danila was going to go anyway, even without me—well, I was *still* guarding a herder, wasn't I?" But she no longer sounded as confident of herself. Galdan turned back to Danila.

"It seemed forever, but the moon was barely down, when we came up to the top of that big bald ridge, and then we were just far enough behind we nearly lost them. We caught up again only because it was starting to get light."

"Where are they?"

Lennett turned back to point farther on. "We saw them scrambling down into a hole in the ground. There's rock ledges on three sides, with trees in between and heavy woods behind, and so much rock on the ground, you wouldn't see the opening, only going by. When they'd all gone in, I looked hard and I could see it hardly at all."

"Well." Galdan considered in silence for a few moments. "Brel. Golsat. I haven't your kind of experience with Mathkkra. Do we go on now and check? Is it safe? Or even worth the effort?"

"Won't do us any good," Golsat said. "This is Ylia's task." He smiled faintly as she came back from her horse. "One I'll cheerfully leave to her."

"Good enough, Golsat," Ylia said. "I'll search first. Once the sun comes up, it'll be safe to approach. You can go look it over; take Brel and Galdan with you. See if you can estimate numbers, scout the ground carefully. We'll need to present a coherent picture to the council." She suppressed a yawn. "Both of you girls, next time I'd suggest serious thought on the consequences before you attempt anything so rash. You had luck and skill to your side, but that doesn't always serve, and you know how Mathkkra treat prisoners." The girls nodded in unison, both suddenly rather subdued. "And Lennett, I'm afraid there'll be repercussions for you. Eveya will have to hold an inquiry on your interpretation of your orders. That still doesn't lessen what you both did here. It was something none of the rest of us could. I'm pleased about that, but you did break orders." Lennett inclined her head; Ylia couldn't decide if she was taking her censure seriously or not. Between them, Levren and Eveya would see she did.

Galdan waived one of the armsmen forward. "You girls needn't stay. You're both tired. Lennett, you can ride with Peryan. Per, give her a hand up. And Nold, wipe that scowl from your face. Your girl's in one piece and if the rest of us can forgive her for such a night, you'd better not hold back! You can ride her double easier than the rest of us. You two start on back and we'll catch up to you. Now," he added mildly but with real authority. The boy brought up a smile and held a hand down. Galdan boosted Danila up behind him.

"Don't be so touchy, Lady Ylia," he grinned at her as they started up the cleft. "You set the pattern yourself, after all. Lennett's out to be your mirror image. You should be proud of her."

"I refuse to argue with you," Ylia said repressively, "and be quiet, can't you? I'm trying to search again."

I hated the fighting, all of it, always. Not swordplay, the real fighting. But for me, this time, it was far worse. To enter not only the tunnels, but the minds of the Mathkkra—for that was what I did, at any rate, when I came so near them. I doubt that Ylia felt anything like I did, for her sake I hope not. The man: who can say what a Rogue might feel? Whatever it was, he never told either of us.

30

Two days and near sleepless nights of furious planning followed the discovery of the Mathkkra-hold. It was late afternoon of the tenth of Storm-Clouds before they were ready to ride out.

There'd been the furious arguments, blown tempers—but this time with true cause, mostly over the number of armed who would ride, the number to be left behind. Scouts and spies left where they could keep an eye to the Mathkkra-hold were widely divided in their opinion as to how many were burrowed there: estimates ran from two hundred to more than seven. Against these, Erken had wanted to send out no more than two hundred armsmen, Marckl insisted upon five times that number, and every other member of the council had a strong opinion on some number between.

On only one thing had Marckl, Marhan, Levren and Erken been able to agree—that none of the women should ride with them. Ylia had argued that with them long and hard. With her own backers—Galdan, Golsat, Brelian, and Eveya, the captain of her women—the others were overruled. In the interest of peace with Erken and Marhan, Ylia had compromised, leaving most of her women with the border guard, taking only these—like Eveya— who had skill, who had fought Mathkkra before and who would not give in sooner than any of Marhan's green boys did.

There'd been no argument over whether Ylia was riding with them; at least, she thought grimly, she'd heard the last of *that!* She and Nisana were necessary anyway, for they were to set Baelfyr within the tunnels and drive the Mathkkra from their safety.

They finally compromised on the number of riders: five hundred to go, the rest to keep close watch around the valley, lest the Mathkkra descend in their absence on the helpless—or in case those who thought the hold to be one of several were right.

Late afternoon, tenth of Storm-Clouds. It was blazingly hot, the sky a dark shimmering bowl overhead. The merest edge of black cloud hovered behind the northern peaks, promising relief from the heat and himidity, but also warning of storm that would likely hit just as they reached the ridges. Ylia stood on the top step before the Tower, near dizzy with pride as Nedao's army rode through a cheering crowd: There, at its head, Erken, Duke of Anasela, clad in dark blue and silver, fifty men at his back and his standard—a stag at gaze on a field of green—fluttering limply over his head. Just behind him, with another one hundred men, rode Corlin, Lord of Teshmor. Lossana had stitched his banner, finishing it moments before he took to his horse: Or, a wyvern vert. His men, like Erken's—like the rest of the armsmen—were clad as best they could manage, for none of the lords could yet afford proper colors for those who served them. Levren rode at Corlin's side with twenty additional bowmen.

Marhan rode after, at Ifney's side and with his men—many of these were still green indeed, and he felt their need for his presence greatest. Marckl followed close behind. Lastly came her own household: Galdan, Brelian, Golsat. Eveya and twenty hand-picked women. Five men of Galdan's choosing. Nold rode at their head, the Queen's colors fastened to the tall pole and that to his saddle. Galdan dismounted, held her stirrup and fell into his place behind her. The crowd roared out a great cheer as she touched the horse's flanks and spurred to the head of the line. She raised her sword on high to acknowledge the cheer. The shield caught on her belt as they moved at the brisk canter across the bridge. She shifted it, but it wasn't much better. Awkward.

"You're committed to this." Erken came up behind her. "I wish you wouldn't, you know."

She sighed. "We *can't* have it out again at this point, Erken! You *know* the alternative."

"We've volunteers enough—"

"Also known as dead men," she interrupted crisply. "I've been in a Mathkkra hold, remember? I *know* what they're like. No. There's no danger this way, not to me, to Nisana, to any of ours. You're an experienced armsman. You know damned well you use what works. If you doubt that it works—well, don't."

He rubbed his chin. "I don't like it. That's all. That we depend on—such things."

"Magic. I *know*, Erken. You and Marhan," she couldn't help adding. "It can't be helped, not without unnecessary loss of life. Foolish exchange."

"Perhaps." He shrugged, but dropped back.

"What was all that?" Galdan came up on her other side. "Is Father still grumbling?"

"When doesn't he? He and Marhan, I'll swear—!"

"I can't think why they worry, after all, *I'm* here to protect you. Well, they can look at it so, can't they?" he added with a grin as she cast him a dark look.

"I see. And they needn't know it's the other way around," she said dryly. He laughed.

"Hah. You said yourself we fight well together."

"When did I say anything so foolish?"

"I think you did—you meant to," he added with another grin. "The odds are more ours this time, too." He dropped back as she shifted her weight so the grey mare could start the steep climb up the first ravine.

They rode rapidly where they could, hoping to beat the storm. The entire northern sky was black and a wind was rising, moaning through the trees, hissing across bare rock. They reached the saddle without interference. Most of their number—Erken, Marckl, Ifney, Corlin and their men—went on by foot, taking a wide circle around the rotting cliff and rubble. The horses were picketed, and a guard left with them.

Nisana bridged from the Tower as Ylia and her picked guard started down the ledge, the last of the fighters to work into position. Eveya and the women under her branched off a few paces to the right, Brelian, Golsat and the others moved way to the left a little farther on. Galdan stayed at her side. Unlike Erken, she hadn't been able to dissuade him; at the moment she rather welcomed his solid presence. *Mathkkra—hundreds of them. And we're provoking them to attack.* She wiped damp palms on her breeches.

She stared at the rough-faced rock, the clutter of boulders and brush, and across them to heavy forest. Five hundred men hidden there and how many would return? Nisana leaped to her shoulder, turned neatly in place and nudged at her face.

"Tell me when you're ready," Galdan breathed against her ear.

"Take a count of a hundred, to make certain everyone's settled over there," she whispered. "But stay by me, I'm going closer in now." He merely nodded. She skirted dry brush, set her feet down with silent care, making no more noise than Nisana would—than her companion did. Galdan cast her a brief, admiring glance; her concentration on the hold before them was such she wasn't aware of it. Three lengths from the hole, in plain sight of it, she stopped. Held up a hand. He nodded again, drew his sword. Something was tickling the hair at the back of his neck, touching his stomach with evil little fingers. Somewhere, not far away, there was a scent of blood, fresh blood and old death. But he knew it wasn't his nose that was scenting it.

'Ready, cat?'

'No.' Nisana's fur was hackled, her eyes black, her body vibrating with the horror of what she sensed of them through the shielding. Ylia eyed her worriedly. *She* knew they were there, but only because she could see the entrance to the hold from where she stood. 'I never will be, not against that. Begin!' Ylia reached up to press the cat's ribs, held her close to her face and joined.

They passed through the barrier and the Fear was suddenly about them, coming hard from all sides. *Are they aware of us? They can't not be!* Silence, still. They searched, mind-touch moving down low-roofed crumbly passages, through a maze of chambers. 'There!' the cat snapped suddenly. 'The sacrifice chamber, the first place, set it there!' They both jumped as lightning blazed a blue-white path across the sky and a crashing roar followed on its heels. 'Set it now!' Ylia staggered, scarcely aware as a strong hand caught at her arm and steadied her, unnoticing, also, as Nisana's claws dug for a better hold against the mail shirt, pierced skin and drew blood. Baelfyr roared through the chamber, out and into the corridors. She forced herself on, went deeper yet, set it twice more.

A howl topped the thunder; Galdan yanked Ylia back. Nisana flung herself out and away. One of Erken's men was suddenly visible in a blare of lightning, hands tight on hilts, his face set. With the suddenness of nightmare, a hoard of Mathkkra burst from the ground and spilled across the clearing.

'Nisana, get out of here!'

'No! I can—'

'Get killed by accident, get back to the horses, *go!*' Galdan stared briefly as the cat vanished; his fingers tightened on Ylia's shoulder and he pointed. She drew sword and dagger as some of the creatures broke free and came straight across the clearing for them. They shield caught again, and threw her off-balance. *I can't do this, despite Eya's words. It'll kill me. I'll be careful. That's all.* She crouched down, dropped the dagger and dragged the shield free, tossed it behind her into the rocks. Movement back there: her armed and Erken's backup coming around to block the gap. Somewhere across the clearing she could hear Marhan shouting above the storm.

She caught up the dagger, leaped to her feet and held the sword high, an extension of her arm to bring her household armed forward, cried aloud: "Nedao!" "Nedao!" came the cry from half a hundred throats behind them: it echoed across the boulder-strewn clearing. "Nedao!" Galdan roared in reply, and as he set himself to her left, struck his blade against hers.

Lightning lit both blades as they touched, lit two upturned astonished faces: Silver flame crackled from the points. Ylia cried out in sudden pain as heat washed through her in a red-hot wave; Galdan shouted something, she never knew what, and staggered away from her. Only the rock saved him from a fall. The Mathkkra halted uncertainly, turned, fled into the trees in the other direction, and were cut down.

Gods, I'm killed! Galdan thought, dazedly. But he could move, could see again. Could see and feel all too clearly: the Mathkkra were a bloody horror as they had never been on that ledge where *she'd* saved him. He was dimly aware, through the roil of pain/overly sharpened senses/more pain/tingling nerves of a hand reaching for him; Golsat had come diving out over cover to help him back to his feet. And then his vision was clear, his nerve steady, he was again his own man. *Or am I?*

Mathkkra had swerved away from Ylia's deadly silver blade, from the shower of ghastly radiance she and Galdan had triggered, onto Eveya's swords. But more came, and again more, until it seemed the hold was bottomless. The line to the south disintegrated, the fighting became one on one. The Mathkkra drove hard to the east, pressed men back into the trees, but Marckl and his men swept around behind from the north and kept them from breaking through. North, Erken and Corlin were hard beset but their lines had held hard, and in the worst place, for many of the men were strung three deep across the base of cliffs, with only rock to protect them and not always enough of that.

"To me! Hold!" Levren's voice rose above the storm as a winged form detached itself from the northern cliff and floated downward. The men around him held their ground—greatly to their credit, for many of them were young and the death-stench of the thing was heavy. It trumpeted deafeningly then and spiraled to earth, half a dozen arrows in its belly. "Look sharp!" Levren shouted. "Avoid their gaze, shoot them down! And come with me!" He turned and moved south behind Ifney's lines so he and his bowmen could have a better view of the cliff face.

The storm was nearly overhead: lightning and thunder mixed, Ylia's ears rang with the noise. The rain still held off. Pale bodies littered the ground, blue in the lightning. But there were more still, and more again: and now they fought frantically, seeking only escape. Three Thullen lay in the clearing, two more among the trees. Another had escaped, bearing off the shrieking lad who'd gone too far into the open for safety and had looked too high to sight his arrow.

Her sword arm cramped, she staggered, swore as her toe stubbed into rock. Galdan tugged at her shoulder. "Come back here, out of the front lines, rest!" And as she shook her head, he glared at her. "Even your father did that, you know! You're too tired to be safe out there. You'll get someone else killed besides yourself, you fool!"

"All right, let go of me!" she shouted back. Galdan called over his shoulder; Golsat and two others pressed past them and to the fore. "I never fought for so long before," she said as they moved back and he found her a flattish rock.

"So? It's nothing to be ashamed of."

"I'm *not* ashamed—!"

"Your face says otherwise. Rest. Sit, have some water, take a good look at your armed. See who needs backing up, moving around. Part of your job also, you know. Father and Corlin can't see clearly enough what's needed, from where they are." She cast him a dark look. "Don't look at me like that. It's not *my* fault the King never sent you on maneuvers."

"We never *had* any, not lately," she said defensively. The water was warm and tasted of the skin holding it; she rinsed her mouth and spit most of it out.

"No one did, remember? Well, Father and Corlin—once or

twice since I came of age. So I'm up on you, but only by that much. Drink that, nevermind the taste, you need it."

"I—" She fought irritation. He was trying to aid her and he was right, she'd no experience at this kind of fighting. She took a decent mouthful of water, got it down. "Thank you."

"Part of my duty," he said stiffly, but when she looked at him, he grinned. "How's your sword arm? Tight? Here, I can do it better for you." He rubbed the long muscles in her forearm, pressed circulation back into her shoulders and neck. She leaned forward, pulled the shield free of the boulders where it had caught. "Can't think why you sported that thing in the first place. It's not sense."

"Sense *you'll* never understand." she muttered in reply.

"If you say so. Now. Have a better idea of what's out there?" He drank, made a face at the bottle but swallowed.

"Mmmm. Ifney and Marckl are spread too thin. And Marhan's gone—I haven't seen him since I sat, have you?"

"He was in the trees a moment or so ago. I heard him. He's holding a second line just behind Ifney, in case anyone gets through. Corlin and Father could perhaps spare a few men for that west line, though."

"Fine. Get somebody over there to tell them so." She rubbed her palms and her fingers while he found two men to work back uphill and around to the northern rock ledges, then stood as he came back. "All right?"

"Fine. Or—" He glanced around, shrugged. "Fine as it gets, just now."

"If you're ready, then, let's go."

"At your side, my Lady." She cast him another dark look, but if he was attempting his usual heavy humor his face gave no sign of it.

They were finally beginning to turn the odds; the Nedaoan army was pressing slowly in toward the clearing, and even Marhan's second line of westward defense was clearly visible through the brush and first trees. No Mathkkra had escaped, so far, and for the first time it seemed as though their numbers might be dwindling.

"'Ware!" Galdan shouted suddenly. "Thullen!"

It banked high, swerved to avoid a shower of arrows. Three protruded from a long, leathery wing as it turned again and came east. Two more sailed down from the cliff and followed it. One of the women screamed. Some of those behind her simply turned and ran: Ylia could hear Golsat bellowing after them, could hear

Brelian gathering her remaining armed together to stand against
the tri-fold attack.

*Bendesevorian, your aid to me; I fear the blade and what it
does. Eya, that I dare trust your words.* Her hands shook as she
reluctantly brought the sword up; the lead Thullen was heading
straight for her, its mouth open wide so even the rows of tiny
rasping teeth were clearly visible in the nearly constant lightning,
the black eye-pits questing for her eyes. Galdan glanced at her,
saw her intention in her stance and braced her hard with his
shoulder. "Shelagn!" And the sword came to life.

Silver fire swirled outward: With a terrible, terrified cry, the
Thullen tried to turn aside, too late; flame enveloped it. A cloud of
silver smoke hid it from view as the cries grew fainter, smoke and
fire compressed—it was gone. The two behind it came on, veering
wide around the smoky ball that had been their leader. One was
knocked back half a dozen lengths by the force of a dozen arrows
and the bolt of Baelfyr that struck it. It slammed into the cliff face,
burning fiercely. Men scrambled frantically away as it rolled down
the rock.

She pivoted as the reassuring pressure at her side vanished: the
third was flying in low and Galdan was ready for it. His blade
sheared through wing and bone and tore into the massive head,
and caught there. The great wings flapped, it gained altitude;
Galdan, with a startled cry, was pulled off his feet.

"Let *go* of it!" she shouted above the storm and pelted after
him, but the Thullen was down again, still thrashing. Galdan
staggered away from the rocks where he'd been thrown. Eveya
was already there; her sword cut deep through the brown-furred
neck and the creature went still. She fought Galdan's sword free,
brought it to him. Ylia caught at his free arm. "You all right?"

"Uh. Wind knocked out." He sounded it; there was a scrape
across his cheek, his eyes were blurred. "I'll live."

"You'd better!" she snapped back.

"How about you?" he demanded.

"I'm fine, don't worry about me. You sit. Eveya can hold my
hand for a while. That was good work, Eveya!" Galdan shrugged,
winced as pain knifed through his head and shoulder, and sat
gingerly. He was seeing at least two of everything at the moment,
the back of his head hurt, and his legs had twisted when he came
down. And the *sense* of that thing, as his blade had touched it!
*Gods and Mothers, have I lost my mind? Or gained something
else, when that blade and mine touched?* he wondered.

"Lady—look!" Eveya caught at Ylia's left shoulder as they moved forward, pointing with her sword. The Mathkkra were bolting. Levren's voice rose above storm, the cries of wounded, and the shrieking of the enemy: "Keep the lines, do not let them escape!" Then with a final flare and crack that left the senses reeling, the storm broke and rain fell in thick grey sheets.

"Hold the lines!" Brelian, not far away to Ylia's right, brought her armed in close, but there was no need: The Mathkkra saw only the trees to the west. Corlin's men came around wide to help box them in and Brelian and Golsat moved out with her household. Ylia sighed wearily, sheathed sword and dagger.

"Galdan, how are you feeling?"

"Fine," he mumbled.

"Fine," she mimicked harshly. "It's not polite to lie like that. I can see you're hurting. I need your help, and you can't give it if your eyes aren't tracking and your ankle's the size of a gourd." He sighed. "Nevermind, I'll mend it, just—sit still, will you?"

He sighed again, but with relief this time, as she withdrew her hands from his forehead. "Thank you." And, with a rare genuine smile, "You look much better when there's only one of you."

"Next time," she replied tersely, "don't stay with it for the ride." But she smiled in spite of herself.

"If that's your order," he grinned.

"All right, let's not. There's too much to do here yet."

"You're worn—" He stopped as she turned an exasperated face to him.

"I have your father to give me lectures. You're *not* going to suggest I desert the wounded, are you?"

"All right, *all right!*" He threw up his hands. "Then I'll help you! Is *that* all right?" She nodded shortly; Nisana, who had been keeping an eye on the battle from the horse pickets, bridged to her.

The fighting had receded downhill, leaving only her and Galdan, half her household as a guard, and the cat. A few of Erken's men were beginning to drag aside slain enemy, to mark their wounded, to move as many as possible to what dry ground there was against the southern ledges. There were wounded everywhere.

Galdan was silent as she worked, providing strength when she asked it, otherwise watching only. No, he hadn't imagined it, even without touching her, he could now tell what she did, how she healed. It stirred something deep down in his own inner being, something he could sense, couldn't quite reach. *I could—I think I could do that*. It frightened him: He was a Plainsman, no AEldra wizard, he'd never even had his mother's Sight! And he was acutely aware of Nisana's thoughtful gaze, her rising curiosity. He wondered if she could bespeak him, as she did Ylia; if she could hear his thought. But somehow he knew she'd make no effort to read him, that she would respect his privacy of thought. He was intensely grateful for that. Whatever was there, he didn't want anyone to know. Didn't want to know himself. *What has it done to me, that hells' blade of hers?*

Sprain, a cut, another sprain. Broken arm, a bad cut that had nearly stopped bleeding. A terrible cut to the upper leg, bad loss of blood: He'd known she'd need his aid for that one before she asked it, startled her by taking her hand before she could reach for his. Another broken arm. One dead. And then another; fighting had been intense here. He had to help her to her feet now, each time, had to hold her arms so she didn't fall over. The cat was clinging to her shoulder, even *she* looked exhausted. Ylia was beyond that, but he'd done *his* share of trying to reason with her. Sooner or later, she'd simply pass out and that would be an end to it.

For now: One of Erken's boys moaned, not far ahead, deep in tree-shadow. There were two of them close together, one dead, the other near it. Ylia blinked to focus her vision, reached for the boy with a hand that wanted to tremble. *I haven't much left, Mothers aid me there's no more seriously injured, I can't save them if it's so*. She'd have sent Nisana back to the horses, but the cat was past bridging, and certainly past aiding her. Galdan still stayed with her, his hand strong, dry and hard as ever, reassuring in its constancy.

Something different— she couldn't waste the effort to try and understand it. Something different about his strength. About him.

Three of Ifney's lads lay in a heap, in the middle of the way the fleeing Mathkkra had taken; only one was still alive, but he was scarcely hurt at all, most of the blood on him that of his friends.

Ylia leaned into Galdan this time as she stood, the only admission she'd make of how worn she was. He looked around them, hoping he'd see no others, so he could presuade her to return to the City and her bed. "One more," she whispered. "There." She pointed.

Oh, no. He knew, even before she did, and he would have held her back if he'd dared. She saw only someone needing her aid, one final man who'd tried to stop the fleeing Mathkkra—single-handed, because the boys with him had fled or fallen, because there was no one left to back him, no one to guard his dagger side.

Ylia walked unsteadily through the trees, dropped heavily to the turf. Her hand touched the bare skin of an arm, came away redly wet. She felt for pulse at the throat; her fingers stopped. Froze against harsh beard, old skin, the soft leather bag Marhan always wore around his neck. "Marhan?" She was shaking, her voice trembled. She couldn't sense him: There was no Marhan left there to sense. 'Oh no, oh no, oh no.' Nisana struggled alert, leaped down from her shoulder to touch at the old man's arm. She leaned against Ylia's hand, wet as it was with the Swordmaster's blood. "Marhan! *Marhan!*" Ylia's voice broke; she caught at his jerkin, buried her face against his shoulder and burst into tears.

Galdan knelt beside her, finally wrapped an arm around her to pull her away. She tore free of him, staggered to her feet. Levren, who'd come running when he heard her outcry, caught her close, held her while she wept. Over her head, his eyes met Galdan's. Galdan shook his head. Levren closed his eyes on his own pain, leaned down to whisper against Ylia's ear. She shook her head violently, tried to pull away from him. She was trying to say something neither man could understand.

But Galdan knew, knew as surely as he'd known it was Marhan and known the old man was dead. Ylia's beloved Swordmaster had bled to death while she healed cuts and bruises; he'd died before she found him, and this time she'd call the fault all to herself.

A great pity for her and for the old man enfolded him, nearly pulling him down with it. An idea touched him: *Try. She tried with Marckl, when she couldn't have hurt him, trying. You can't hurt either of them. Try.* And, as his hands took hold of the old man's, as he brought the lolling head onto his knees: *Inniva aid me, I have no right to ask this, what I seek here is for no mortal man, but she's grieving herself ill for him, and I can't bear to see it.*

Somewhere, deep inside, things were moving that hadn't moved before. He knew what *she* used to heal; if it was in him, he couldn't use it. Well; he had strength of will; he caught that up, brought it forward, focused it. 'Marhan. Marhan, come back.' No response, just as he'd feared—*No! Never think that way, the fire only catches if you know it will!* 'Marhan. Swordmaster!' He opened his eyes, stared down at the limp, unresponsive body. And, suddenly compelled, across the now moonlit glade.

Someone was standing there. He blinked, tried to focus.

Marhan stood there, staring blankly into the distance. Moon shone through him. "Marhan?" Galdan whispered.

The old man seemed to suddenly take in his surroundings. Dark eyes peered near-sightedly to both sides of him. *"Marhan!"* Galdan wrenched at the source of his will, put everything there was in him into that name.

"Galdan?" The faintest of whispers, the sound of it only touched the younger man's thought.

"Marhan, come back," Galdan's whisper was as faint. Levren, a pace away, still stroked Ylia's hair, her shaking shoulders, and apparently heard and saw nothing else. "Come back to us, Marhan."

"I—" Silence. So long a silence, Galdan thought he'd failed after all; he fought away that dark certainty, pushed it from his thought with an effort that left him momentarily blind. "I was—" Marhan made a gasping little sound. "It hurt—ah, pain!"

"No, don't think on it. Come back, Marhan, we need you. She needs you," Galdan repeated. Marhan took a step forward, a second. Squinted at the man crouched on the ground before him, at what he held.

He shook his head. "I can't. Enough. I'm old and tired, lad, I can't face it anymore. Any of it. Leave me alone."

"We're all of us tired, just now, Swordmaster. Come back." The uncertainty was gone; he'd win, he *had* to. Behind him, Ylia still sobbed as though her heart was broken. As it was. "We'll rest, it won't be so bad tomorrow."

"Easy for you to say," Marhan responded peevishly, and with the first hint of life to his voice. "You don't have to carry seventy-eight winters on your back! Leave me be, I've overstayed."

"No. Don't leave, Marhan. She needs you."

Marhan scowled, sucked at his moustaches. "She'll forget me."

Galdan's fingers tightened angrily on unresponsive shoulders. 'You can't believe that, *look* at her!' his thought railed. The old man recoiled a pace from his fury. He darted a glance in Ylia's direction, turned back to fasten a doubtful look on what was before him. 'You're a father to her,' Galdan argued, 'she's lost Brandt, will you deprive her of her other?'

'I'm not—!'

'No? You and she are like my father and I were, when I was a boy. Brandt never gave her that kind of love, for all he loved her. He loved her like a daughter, you've loved her like a son. You know what that's meant to her.' Silence. Marhan just stared at him. 'You know what she's feeling just now, don't you?''

'No!' The old man turned away, covered his ears, but the inner voice assailed him.

'She lost Brendan, just that way. He bled to death before she could save him.' Something deep down quailed from that; he'd known, Golsat had told him. He'd never *known* it like he did now, and it cut into his concentration; the old man seemed, briefly, to shimmer.

A sudden warmth pressed against his leg, a furred presence; he glanced down, startled. Nisana. Dark, wide green eyes gazed up at him as Nisana fed him what little strength she had left.

"She can't face that, Marhan." The form steadied as he spoke. "That you should die, here and like that: it'll drive her mad, it'll kill her. You can't die like Brendan did. You can't do that to her."

"I know." The faintest of whispers again, touching only the inner ear. Marhan had lived through the pain of her loss; his own rage at being unable to prevent either Brendan's death or his beloved Ylia's hurt. He hesitated. Turned back and took a hesitant step toward Galdan. "I—I don't know the way. I can't."

'You can. We can.'

'The pain,' Marhan whispered. 'There was so much of it. I can't face it, not again.'

'You won't, Marhan. I swear it.' The shirt was clinging to him, back and front, sweat prickled his eyelids, beaded his lip. Marhan cast Ylia another glance, this time so full of love and pity it brought tears to Galdan's eyes. Nisana nudged against his leg again; he shifted his grip on the Swordmaster's body, rubbed his eyes left-handed and closed them.

Warmth spiraled through him; he couldn't hear the cat the way he knew *she* could, but he could sense what she was trying to tell him. It wouldn't work that way, though; he could tell. He shut her out, finally, burrowed down into the very innermost of himself and sought strength. His ears were humming, his entire body vibrating with this strange new thing. There was enough awareness left to him that he would hear Ylia's choking, dry sobs, Levren's soothing whisper.

Warmth moved through him, coursed through his hands. He couldn't think, there was nothing left to think with, there was only this, only here and now. It seemed forever, it seemed no time at all. He started as strong old fingers twitched against his arm, and the old man's body moved abruptly as Marhan drew in a deep breath.

There are those who have suggested since, many times, that it was my notion, my thought he took when he restored the old man to life; at the very least, that it was my Power that aided him. Nothing of the sort. Seldom have I been so frustrated in my attempts to communicate with anyone; never have I so urgently—and with so little success—wished a link between myself and a human.

In the end, of course, he did not need my aid at all, though I think he was glad of my presence. For he was as resourceful with his odd gift as he was strong and stubborn. Fortunate that he was so stubborn. I doubt anyone else could have argued that obstinate old man back to us.

31

It was nearly noon-hour when Ylia woke, dazed, stiff and miserable, uncertain why she was any of those things at first. She lay still a long while, trying to remember: the battle, a daze of lightning, blood, shrieking, a confusion of bodies and sudden black dark, heavy shadows from overhead as Thullen swooped across them. And gods guard them all. Galdan's sword hard against her own. Her body jolted with the remembered shock of that touch. Everything rain and mud and puddles as the Mathkkra fled, and then the healing, moving from one man to another until she could have wept from the ache in her knees, standing and kneeling again. The blur her vision became, until she could barely see where the next fallen lay, could hear little of the muted cries of pain through the ringing in her ears.

He'd stayed with her that entire time, he'd been with her when she'd found Marhan. Tears tightened her throat painfully; she fought them back. It was confused, it had been then, it still was. Because Marhan was dead, he *had* been. She'd never, ever get over the touch of his hand: limp, chill beyond the chill of human flesh, unresponsive. Levren had held her, she'd only been dimly aware of Power somewhere.

Then Nisana teetering on her shoulder—the cat was nearly as worn as she was, insisting she pay attention, the feline mental shout reverberating through her agonized thought that the Swordmaster was not dead, that she'd misread him because she was too worn. Galdan's hand on her shoulder, he and Levren leading her back to where the old man lay. Marhan's fingers warm, moving against hers, his breath a garlic-flavored mist against her cheek.

'He's sleeping still,' Nisana's thought touched her. The cat was curled on the blankets, halfway down the bed. 'Worn, that's all. The man's too old for such sport.'

"Nisana. Don't lie to me, he wasn't just unconscious. I didn't imagine it, he was dead."

'Don't start again or I'll send you back to sleep,' Nisana warned. 'He *wasn't*. Because if he had been, who could have healed him?' Ylia opened her mouth, closed it again. 'I can't heal at all, and you were past helping anyone just then.' Silence. 'Well? That leaves no one. You made a misjudgment. Fortunately not a serious one. But you wore yourself silly with weeping for no cause.'

"Cat, you're not telling me everything. I *know* you, I can tell."

'Nonsense. If you'd been in control of yourself, you'd have found pulse. It was there.'

Ylia sighed, closed her eyes. She didn't believe a word of it. Nisana gazed at her with mild irritation. *I tried, man of the Foessa. It wasn't likely to work anyway, was it?*

She brought her attention back to Ylia: she was staring up at the ceiling now, talking as much to herself as to the cat. "That sword. It's been responsible for too much."

'Now what has it done? You said something last night, but made no sense. No more than you're making now.' Ylia told her; Nisana digested the knowledge in silence for some moments. 'Ah. I knew something had changed in him, I couldn't understand how. You should have had the shield with you, as Eya told you,' the cat added accusingly. 'No one's fault but yours if he touched the blade and its strength was free to work on him. The shield's at the foot of your bed, back in its chest; Brelian found it and returned it. Fortunately for you. Learn to use it! You could have avoided some of this, if not all.'

Ylia sighed. "She said not to let him *touch* the sword! When did I ever let him near it? And would you have had me carry that awkward bit of wood and metal for the first time in a real battle?"

'I'd have you practice either its use or practice carrying it out of your way, that's what I'd have.' Nisana grumbled. 'You needed it, you didn't have it. Don't blame the blade or the Folk. You can't say you weren't warned.'

Silence. "No, I suppose not. It did something to him. Did you feel it?"

'I had other things to worry.'

"Even later?"

Nisana stretched hard, sat up. 'I wouldn't chew at it so, girl. He's not worried about it, not like you think.'

"How would *you* know?" Ylia demanded irritably.

'You need more sleep,' Nisana commented. Ylia sighed. 'Because he was down in the square an hour ago, he, Brelian and Golsat. They were making certain the Ambassador's minstrel gets a straight version of the tale of Queen Ylia leading Nedao into battle!' Ylia groaned. 'So if he's chewing at a worry, he hides it better than most men.'

"They'll all three think worry," Ylia said, momentarily distracted, "if they sell Grievan another exaggeration like last time." She pushed covers aside, padded across the cool floor in search of a clean shirt and breeches.

'I like that song,' Nisana replied. 'The Narran has talent, and he leaves out the high notes that hurt my ears. He says very good things about *me*. And it served your purpose, afer all. That Narran boy no longer pursues you, does he?'

"He probably has nightmares about the Tanea-a-Les," Ylia retorted, "but that's not the point. It's embarrassing, listening to all that, as though I actually—"

'—actually went openly into a Tehlatt war camp, stole their prisoners, fired their tents, battled and slew their chief,' the cat broke in calmly. 'All of which you did. So?'

Ylia shrugged into her shirt, tucked it into the breeches. "It's embarrassing," she repeated firmly. 'Especially with everyone sitting there *smiling* at me. Try it!"

'I was there also, remember? I didn't see what the fuss was, but then, people always stare at me. It doesn't bother me anymore.'

She jumped down from the bed, stretched and bounded into the hall. Ylia scowled after her, sat back on the bed to lace her breeches down.

"Are you—you are awake, good." Lisabetha paused uncertainly in the doorway, came in with a tray. "Malaeth thought you might be up, or that you should be, and sent me with food. Tr'Harsen's back, he has fresh oranges."

"Good. I forgot I was hungry, until just now." She settled down with her meal. Lisabetha caught up the comb and went to work on her hair. "Ouch."

"Don't pull away, the comb's caught—sorry." She replaited one side, began loosening the other, picking out snags as she went.

"What's wrong, 'Betha?" Something was; the girl was radiating worry in all directions.

"Nothing."

She caught at the comb, the hand that held it. "Not nothing. Tell me."

Lisabetha stood silent for some moments. "I dreamed last night. I couldn't sleep, I was worried. Most of us were. We didn't know what would happen. But then, I was—just there, in a large, round room. I thought I could see water beyond a window, but it was smeared with rain and the glass was warped, as though it had been poorly made. There were tapestries on the walls, rich carpets on the floor. I thought I saw a fine Southern one among them, one of those the Ragnolers weave with the dark colors and curious patterns they take from smoke dreams.

"And then *he* was there. Lyiadd. He and Marrita stood before a brazier, the smoke was dark red, and it seemed to me they were waiting for someone." She finished the second plait in silence. "It was *dream*, the true kind. *He* waited, and whatever he was waiting for, he wanted it very much. She stood by him, aided him, but I knew she was not pleased. That whatever Lyiadd sought, she did not want it."

Ylia closed her eyes. The cold truth of the girl's words shivered through her. "We knew he lived. I knew, even when I denied it most. But if I had it to do again," she added bitterly, "I'd make certain of *both* of them, and let them try to fight their way back up the walls of the Black Well! Not my fault, he said," she added, even more bitterly. "If he knew!"

"He?" Lisabetha touched her arm.

"Someone I spoke to, once. A little while since. About Lyiadd.

Nevermind. But I *should* have killed him. When I had the chance. Should have killed them both."

"You thought you had. There was no time to be certain," Lisabetha urged. "And Marrita: I cannot believe you would have killed a woman unarmed."

"Perhaps not. Though Marrita is scarcely unarmed! I didn't, that's all that matters now." She roused herself. "There'll be council tonight. We'd better tell them."

Lisabetha looked even more unhappy. "Must we?"

"We'd better. No one will look oddly at you, that you dream, remember that; not my council, not with me for comparison! But not at you. 'Betha, they ought to be told what you've seen. Perhaps not all of them will believe—"

"Marckl," Lisabetha said feelingly.

"*And* Erken," Ylia said, "who should know better since his wife had Sight. But now we've destroyed the Mathkkra, people will want to think us safe and relax vigil. If Lyiadd lives, we dare not." She picked up the orange—it was pale green around the stem, soft and juicy as she bit through the rind. Lisabetha took up the comb and finished her plaits in silence. Ylia rose, pulled on her boots and started for the door. "It'll čome out all right. Don't worry it, 'Betha."

"I won't." Lisabetha's smile faded as soon as Ylia was gone. The other she'd seen—the one she couldn't bring herself to name. The one she *thought* she'd seen, and in such circumstance? What if she'd held back vital information, not telling all of the dream? "I did it to keep her from worry, that's all," she whispered to the empty chamber. That was at least partly true. Then again: What if she was wrong? But—what if she wasn't?

Ylia had a long search for Erken—partly because the man himself had just been seen almost everywhere but was none of the places where he'd just been seen, mostly because she was too tired to move energetically after him. She finally ran him down at the far end of the bridge, where he was speaking to the prior night's herd guard. He was muddy, rumpled, his hair and beard tangled and his eyes heavy. He confirmed what she could see: he hadn't yet slept, had remained behind with a contingent of his men to see to the burning of the Mathkkra slain, had ridden back to the stream to see if any had recrossed it, had helped seal the main entrance to the tunnels. He hadn't left the high ridge until an hour past daylight.

"We can safely consider that hold wiped out." Pride vied with exhaustion. "I will *not* wager as to whether there are more of them, however."

"No. I doubt anyone would, after this."

"I was proud of our forces." Erken ran a hand through his hair, scowled at it in distaste. They walked slowly back across the bridge. The river was heavy with runoff; a number of men were down by the supports, dragging trees and snags free. "Considering how young and how green-trained many of them are, we still lost only fifteen all told."

"Did you get a count when it got light?"

"I lost it at eight-fifty. Marckl thinks a thousand, though I myself doubt that."

"Gods and Mothers, if we'd known that—" She stared at him, shocked. "It goes against everything *I* know of them. They do not live so many to a den. Erken, they *must* have been set against us!"

Erken bit back a yawn. Shrugged. "I know little that's real save what I've seen in these mountains. It's not sense, though: Those who subsist on meat alone do not live in large tribes, it leads to famine." He smiled faintly. "That's plain logic."

"It's sense, either way," she replied. She added, as they stopped mid-bridge to let wagons by, "You should see yourself, Erken, you're near to falling where you are. Get some sleep, man, you're no use to yourself or any of us if you're that tired."

"I'd thought to—"

"No. Whatever it is. Do it later, or pass it on to someone else if it won't wait."

"I suppose," he yawned, stifled it neatly with the back of his hand. "Your pardon. I suppose that's sense too. I'm too tired to think whether I should go sleep now, or wait until tonight."

"I know what you'd tell any of *us,*" Galdan's voice came from behind them. "Revered Father, you've saved Nedao for the moment, go rest on your honors." Erken cast his son an exasperated look. Galdan clapped him on the back and gave him a hard shove. "Go ahead, you'll feel foolish indeed, being carried to your blankets! We'll manage somehow in your absence." Erken sighed and threw up his hands in surrender.

"All right, I'm outnumbered, boy. Though I'd like to see you carry me anywhere, considering how I still outsize you."

"Old bones don't weigh as much," Galdan retorted with a wide grin. "There's council tonight, blessed and honored parent. I'll see you're wakened for it."

"You'd better!" Erken started off.

Galdan shouted cheerfully after him. "I'll have you up for a bath and meat beforehand so you're fit company! You're testy when you have to think on an empty belly!" Erken merely waved a hand and kept going. Galdan laughed, turned to prop his elbows on the rail; gazed down the River. "It's come up. There may be flooding this spring if it's so changeable."

"It was a particularly bad storm last night—but you're right. Your father had men out this morning, he and Marckl, to take note of any spillover from the banks." She leaned on the upper rail, too, but she had to stretch to get her elbows comfortably set. She finally hunched her shoulders, since Malaeth couldn't see her, and rested her chin on the smoothed wood.

"I should have known," Galdan said ruefully. "That he wasn't out making up to his women as soon as he came back." And, as Ylia cast him a sharp glance, he grinned. "Come now, that was a jest, and you know it! Father's not looked at any woman but you since Mother died—and it's not," he added hastily, "at all the same kind of look." Momentary silence. "If you thought I meant that."

"I should hope not," she replied stiffly, but he winked at her and she laughed. "He's a good man, Erken. I'd be lost without him."

"He knows things—one or two of them." Galdan nodded. The smile slipped from his face; he brought it back with an effort she missed; her gaze was on the workers who were dragging the wreckage of a flat-bottomed boat back up the west bank. "Did you sleep well?"

"I must have, I remember nothing. Nisana brought me home— I *think* I remember that. I could have ridden."

"There wasn't any point to it, and I don't think *she* wanted to ride with a group of smelly humans." Ylia cast him a sharp glance; his attention was all for the water. Or perhaps he was looking through it.

She swallowed. Opened her mouth to speak, closed it again. Shifted her weight and swallowed again. "I remember before Nisana took charge of me, though." The high, strangled voice scarcely sounded like hers.

"Do you." Spoken so softly she could barely hear him above the noise of the river. Silence. Armsmen walked past them, clattering on the boards, a group of giggling children tore across the other direction. Galdan turned his head, gazed at her profile for some moments. Turned back to his contemplation of the water.

"I *was* tired," Ylia whispered, more to herself than to him. "And that kind of tired—physical and inner—can distort what one sees and feels. But not—not that much." Another, even longer silence. This one stretched uncomfortably. "I wasn't wrong, was I?" She stared out across the trees, watching as a hawk soared from pine to pine and vanished in the direction of the Aresada. She felt rather than saw his shoulders slump, the faint shake of his head. "*You* did that?" And now she looked full at him.

He'd gone pale; sweat beaded his upper lip. Ylia touched his arm; he jumped. "I did that," he finally whispered in reply.

"Lel'san's threads, *how?*"

"I don't know. I—can we not talk about it?" He made an attempt at a smile that only served to intensify the frightened look in his eyes. Moved by a sudden impulse, she caught his hand, held it.

"I'm sorry."

"You're sorry?" He shook his head. "Why?"

"I can see what it's done to you, a little. I know I'd be upset by it, and I've always had the Power, if not so much of it as I now have." Silence. "And I'm sorry because it's partly my fault."

"Not yours. Your blade."

"Mine. She warned me, not to let you touch it—"

"She? Nisana?"

She hesitated. "Another time. Who is not important. What is important is that I should have warned you, should have been more careful with it."

"And your Swordmaster would be dead," Galdan said bluntly. Ylia closed her eyes. Tears welled up under the lashes, coursed down her cheeks. He reached, gently brushed them away.

"I'm sorry," she said finally.

"Don't say it, you needn't be sorry—with me or for me. All right?"

"I—it was just—when Brendan died—"

"I know. Brelian and Golsat told me, awhile since. Well, Marhan's not. Because I had a sudden urge to cross blades with you for luck," he laughed shortly and with little humor, "and came into something that's—something *you* can explain to me," he finished abruptly. He turned back to the river. "Someone has to. I feel like I'm going mad."

"I—"

"Don't say you understand it," he overrode her sharply. His shoulders sagged again. "Sorry."

"I wasn't going to. I can't. I've told you before about 'Betha. How coming north through the mountains, for a while she could *hear* Nisana or me."

"So?" He cast her an irritated glance.

"She was only in our small company and in the mountains for a few 5-days. She didn't spend year after year in the Foessa, like you have." Silence. "There was something about you almost the first time I saw you. The call for aid that reached me: An ordinary Plainsman could never have reached my thought like that. You wouldn't acknowledge it, though, and I didn't have the right to look for it."

"I never *thought* of it as Power," Galdan said plaintively. "It was just something useful I could do, finding my horse or starting a fire when the wood was wet." He shrugged. "When one day blends into the next and you begin to judge time by seasons, you don't think much about things like that, you just do them. I certainly didn't think of it as something like yours or Queen Scythia's."

"It's not. Not exactly. Ours was granted by the Nasath—"

"—for aid in battle, I've heard the tales."

"Yours is native. Wild Power." He stared at her. "The Foessa have been bleeding it into you. The Mothers only know what my sword set free."

He stared at his hands, turned them palm up. Moved his fingers thoughtfully. "I couldn't hear Nisana last night. I know she was trying to say something, I could feel it all around me, the effort of what she was doing. I couldn't hear her. I—I don't think I could hear you."

"Try, if you like," she said. He closed his eyes, rested his forehead on his hands. Shook his head finally. "That doesn't mean much. It's there. What it does, how much you can make of it, what things you can do—I'm sorry, I don't know. It's not enough like AEldra that even Nisana can tell. I know less than she does about it. I can tell you, though, that I was blocked until partway through the mountains. Because I wasn't full AEldra. You're not even half AEldra." She sighed faintly. "Under normal circumstance, I'd say it was nearly impossible for you to use Power at all, except that you have. You do. She said you were clever and resourceful, that you could work around the barriers to use it." He shook his head, confused. "I could barely muster the far vision, back in Koderra. I could use at most a spark of Baelfyr. I couldn't find a way around it. You have a block that won't let you do things even a half-AEldra can, but you've manipulated it.''

"I start campfires, avoid bears and track my horse over rock," he said faintly. She nodded. He let his head fall back onto his hands. "I could tell what you did, last night. When you healed," he whispered. "I could tell who needed you the worst, when you would need my strength." He swallowed, brought his head up and stared across the fields. His eyes were noticeably wet. "I knew before you did that—that was Marhan."

"Gods and Mothers."

"I knew how it hurt you, because I could *feel* it, and I couldn't bear it. I—'' He stared down at his hands. "So I tried." He made a tremendous effort, managed to dredge up a smile. "It's changed. My safe little odd thing that let me eat hot meat on damp nights, suddenly it's not safe anymore. Suddenly it scares me green, and I don't know what to do about it.''

"I wish I knew what to tell you." She walked along by the railing, turned down the path to the River's edge. Galdan followed. "If I were Nisana, I'd say learn how to use your Power, to bring it out, to hone it. Study what it does, how far it goes, so that you're in control. But that's how Nisana thinks. I resented her bullying for too many years to offer you that course. And if you don't want it—''

"I don't *know.*" He picked up a handful of pebbles, tossed them into the roiled, muddy water, one at a time. "But not wanting it doesn't matter, not if it's mine. Even so, to do what I did last night—'' He threw the rest of the pebbles. "No man has the right to do that. I'm—if I did that, who's to say what else I could do? And whether it would be good? If I could save a life, then maybe I could kill." He clasped his hands together to stop them shaking. "Maybe I'd—''

"Maybe anything," she said flatly. "Power is. I used to think, like most AEldra do, that there's good Power and evil. I don't believe that anymore, I've seen too much of it, too many wielders of too many varied kinds. Power is. It's good or bad only because of the person using it: It can be something to delight the eye and fill the inner being with joy. It can heal, it can protect. It can kill. It can save a friend or—I almost had to kill one, once, to save him a worse death.''

"Brendan?" The name came out flatly. She gave him a startled look.

"Bren? No. I never had a chance to do anything for him, anything at all. I wish that wasn't what I had to remember him by, because it hurts." She drew a deep breath, let it out in a rush. "It was Brel's friend, Faric. When we hauled Corlin out of the fire, the Tehlatt had him. That was nearly all the choice he had."

"You would have—"

"I'd have loathed myself, Galdan, but I'd have done it. It's a two-edged blade, the Power. You never forget that, once you have it. Anything you do with it could dangerously drain your strength."

"I know. I've seen you."

"Not just things like the healing. Even something like seeing in the dark, sensing things around you, using mind-speech. Even *that* can be a burden. Almost anything you do with it can be turned against someone or something." She swallowed. "Another thing, something I've only just found. The bond you form with the Power, it does something to you. When I healed Marckl—I carry something of the man in me now, because of that bond." *Something of you,* she thought uncomfortably.

"I know that. I know things about Marhan nobody should know. Except Marhan." He shook himself, forced a smile. "You're making me sorrier for myself than I was. You can stop listing drawbacks, please."

He turned back to the River; she watched his back for some moments. "You're not going to become another Lyiadd," Ylia said finally. "If that's what you fear."

"You don't know that."

"I know you."

"*Do* you?"

"I think I do. Well enough." She managed a faint smile. *Better than Marckl, in some ways.* "Besides, you can't. Erken wouldn't stand for it."

That broke the tension. Galdan let his head fall back and he laughed. "So he wouldn't, and he's no man to cross, my father! Do you know," he added with an almost normal smile, "I've always wondered how Queen Scythia balanced all those colored balls, the time she came north for Mid-Winter. I still remember that! Show me that, will you?"

"Mother's trick? I *think* I can do that, I haven't tried for a long time. But—" She concentrated briefly. "Ah. On demand." Four large iridescent bubbles hovered just above her fingers. Galdan reached gingerly. One of them transferred to his hand. And a second. "Light touch," she warned, "or they'll break. It's largely will, once you create them." Galdan gazed at the fragile things. As he stared at them, they quivered, burst in a shower of colors.

"Too hard. Next time, perhaps—" He stooped to gather another handful of pebbles, began tossing them into the water. "I have to think about this. So I'd like your leave, if you'll give it."

"Yours." She wasn't really surprised. She'd expected him to go before this. But his next words did surprise her.

"We need someone to ride a wide circuit around the valley. I can do that, be useful while I'm trying to put my mind back in order again."

"You'd—return then?"

He nodded. "I took House Oath, didn't I? As I recall, that's good until I die, and I plan to put that off awhile yet, Lady. And I'm one of Brelian's two supports for when Lisabetha claims him, tenth of Fruiting."

"I didn't know. I should have."

"You've had other things to think of. So you don't get rid of me so easily as *that*, Lady." He stood back to let her climb up to the bridge before him, sketched her a salute and strode back toward the town. She stood where he left her and watched him out of sight.

Humans have the oddest habits, but none are more curious than the rituals they create to sanctify mating. As though the public display can intensify or alter what is in the heart and mind! As though the gods might bless them in no other way!

32

The rest of Storm Clouds passed uneventfully: There were no more raids. The border guard remained strong, the guard on the herds remained heavy, and the council passed a mandate that all children of ten summers and above learn bow. There was no resistance, and for the first time girl-children took their places at the marks next to their brothers.

Golsat and Ylia met with Grewl, and not long after most of the outland Chosen began bow lessons. Levren was too busy training young armsmen and women—even if he had been able to withstand the strain of being surrounded by so many foreigners. But Golsat's status among the Chosen—indeed among the Nedaoans as a whole—was no less than the Bowmaster's.

The Women's Elite Guard, under the Queen's tutelage and banner, doubled by summer's end.

The second grain crop was harvested, the valley was thick with smoke from the field burning for several days, and casks of unaged ale were sent down-river. Wine and spices came back in exchange. Ber'Sordes brought an offer of raw flax for cloth and plants; the Koderran Council—Brandt's men, Corlin, Marckl and Ifney, Lisabetha and Lossana—wrangled for three nights running over whether the unpleasant-smelling stuff could be worked into cloth anyone would wear. Lossana finally made up a pattern piece of it and overrode them all, proclaiming it an odd fiber but a tough cloth, and one they could use. The Narrans examined her swatch, exclaimed over her color and pattern, and offered to buy all she had to spare.

Ylia sat on the southern balcony, where she could catch both the last rays of a late afternoon sun and the first cooling breeze from the River. It was blessedly quiet down here: even though the City Council was meeting and all the windows were open, she couldn't hear the shouting. Occasionally she could catch the sound of Lisabetha and Annes giggling down in their rooms, one of the other women singing, noises from below, the last of the market-stalls closing for the evening, and the guard riding out.

Compared to the session with her council earlier, it was quiet indeed on the southern balcony.

And from here she could see the road. *She* knew full well why her eyes strayed that direction so often. Galdan—damn the man, she missed him. Odd, since he irritated her more often than not when he was around. Well, she missed his cooling presence at the council table, too: Levren and Golsat were good at it, but Galdan was better.

She drew her dagger from its forearm sheath, stared absently at the copper ship, the copper wrapping. Ran her finger lightly over the guard. *Brendan. Bren.* She didn't think about him much, of late, and when she did it was with an odd sense of guilt. *But I haven't forgotten him.* If he hadn't died like that. If there had been more time. *It might have been that by now, we'd be friends, armsmates. Nothing else. It happens to people.* If Lyiadd hadn't known how best to hurt her, by taking what she loved most. . . .

She restored the dagger to its sheath, turned back to her study of the River, the fields beyond them, the heavy stand of forest with the road vanishing into its shadow. She could almost see the high ranks of the Foessa through the trees: they'd be snow-tipped already, those to the south. *I wonder where he is, and what he's thinking.*

Erken had questioned her, the night Galdan left, and she hadn't known what to say, since Galdan had clearly not told him much. Erken was visibly unhappy—*he thinks something he said or did, and he worries*—though he asked nothing else. But as the days passed, he, too, spent considerable time gazing off to the south or west, and she knew his thought was the same as hers.

Marhan—to all outward appearance, his ordeal hadn't affected him at all, but now and again she wondered. Something about the

look of him. People didn't remember a healing, but *this*—
Whatever he knew, remembered, felt, he kept very much to
himself, and Ylia knew better than to ask.

The Month of Fruiting came with its crisp mornings, hot days
and chill nights, and Lisabetha and Brelian's wedding drew near.
Tension was high in Lord Corry's house, and 'Betha was strung
tight, for Galdan and Golsat were to stand for Brelian in place of
his parents, to speak for him at the joining. "If it goes wrong, if he
doesn't come, I'll die, I'll just die!"

"He'll come," Brelian assured her. But he didn't look as
certain as he sounded. Golsat finally went in search, but returned
on the sixth, late, and alone.

"If anyone could track him," he grumbled, "*I* should be able
to! There's no trace of him, anywhere nearby. The man's half
bear."

Ylia finally attempted a search of her own, but with no better
luck. Whether he shielded himself consciously or unconsciously,
she was able to find trace of him—but not Galdan himself. She
was more relieved than not: If she'd found him, what would she
have done, dragged him back unwilling? He'd promised. She
doubted he'd let his friend down.

And so she was not particularly surprised when, on the evening
of the eighth, he wandered into the council meeting as though he'd
never been gone, save that he'd a new change of the Narran
fashion. But he would not meet her eyes or his father's, and he,
Golsat and Brelian strode arm in arm from the chamber immediately upon adjournment.

Ylia swore under her breath, started as Erken chuckled in her
ear. "I didn't know you knew such words! Tch, Lady! But you
speak for me. I think he's been visiting young Ang'Har's tailor,
did you ever see such colors?"

"Hah. Peacock," she huffed.

"No, I saw one of those once, they're blue and green. This, if
my eyes still work, was red and gold, right down to the legs. Of
course," Erken went on, "he has got the legs for such frippery."

"A plague on him *and* his parti-colored hose."

"I think," Erken grinned, "I'll go find him, and see what he's
up to. I know that look and I don't like it much."

"*Two* plagues on him," Ylia replied shortly and dropped back
into her chair as Erken left.

• • •

Tenth of Fruiting: At Lisabetha's insistence, they were reviving the ancient custom of Sword Swearing, adding it to the Chosen ceremony. Ylia stood with her and Brel in the middle of a high platform that had been set up in the center of the Square. The couple were resplendent in silver and white, the platform itself was covered in cloth of sky blue, hemmed in gold. Ylia held their two swords—a little awkwardly, for the hilts were bound with silver ribbon and white blossoms. While most of Nedao stood and watched, Lisabetha took her blade and extended it hilts first to Brelian. He took it, and in a voice that quavered slightly—he forgot the words once, and Golsat had to prompt him—he swore aid, protection and fealty to her. He then held his sword to her, while she repeated the oath. Ylia bound the blades together with blue and gold ribbons. People cheered.

Then Grewl spoke the Chosen rites: Corlin and Lossana came forward to stand with their daughter, Galdan and Golsat with their friend.

Ylia was finding it hard to keep her eyes off the two men behind the radiantly happy Brelian: Galdan wore blue and white with gold—Queen's colors—in the Narran fashion, down to the parti-colored hose. Her House arms were worked prominently on the cloak. And Golsat! She had never seen Golsat in anything but common armsman's brown. And there he stood, resplendent in full Narran garb, deep green touched with yellow. Conservative, by standards such as Galdan's, but astonishing on Golsat.

The Chosen ceremony was short; she dutifully inclined her head as Grewl turned to the people and invoked the blessing of the One, and then it was over. Grewl turned back to set Lisabetha's hand in Brelian's; Galdan moved forward to hug them both, hard, planted a kiss on Lisabetha's face and jumped down into the crowd. Golsat caught them both by the arm, smiled and followed.

"Lady Ylia," Erken touched her arm. "If you'd like down from here, you're rapidly being deserted and you don't look dressed to go clambering on platforms today."

"So I'm not. Thank you." She let him catch at her waist, lift her down. "That's new, I like it."

Erken held out his arms, resettled the short plum-colored cape over his left arm. He looked extremely pleased. "D'ye think so? I liked the look all along, but I couldn't see the cost. Though frankly," he laughed, "there was the matter of color, and how a man was to decide which he wanted. Now, I'm a man of simple taste—"

Ylia laughed. "You always were, of course!"

"Well—perhaps not. My son claims he sold his skins at a good price. I have to presume that he did."

"Galdan! I should have known. His, yours. And have you seen Golsat?"

"I confess astonishment. He'll be sorry he let my son lead him into such silliness, though."

"You think? He looks—well, I'd never thought of Golsat like that before, but he looks—"

"Exactly so," Erken put in as she sought the right word. "Every maiden in Koderra has marked him down this morning, you watch!" He gazed out across the crowd. "There. I think I shall go and see what he's up to. I haven't seen the boy so clean and neat since his mother was still dressing him." And he slid through the people and was gone.

She wandered back toward the Tower, found Golsat, walked through the market with him. "I like that, you've good taste."

"I feel half undressed, if you want the truth," Golsat said bluntly. "But it's not as bad as when I first put it on, so I suppose one adjusts. And it's for Brel and 'Betha, after all."

"For whatever cause, I like it."

"Thank Galdan, then, he chose the colors and had it done for me."

"Oh." She stopped, purchased a cup of cold fruited wine for both of them. "How is he?"

Golsat shrugged, raised his cup in toast. "To Brel and 'Betha. They're a good match, they'll be happy. How's—? Ah. Galdan. He's well enough. Pleased with himself, just now, but that's the trading, he struck a hard deal with Kre'Darst and came off to the better."

"Ah. He told *me* he'd be searching for Mathkkra."

"Oh, he did that, but with no result. Said it was all dull enough stuff, it could wait until after today. He brought back trinkets for Brelian and Lisabetha. I hope I'm nearby when he gives them. Silver-bound, matching daggers."

"That must have been *quite* a bargain."

"He had the better part of a season's catch with him, and furs are fashionable in Osnera just now. Kre'Darst didn't come off poor by the trade."

"No, he wouldn't." Golsat left her with Corlin and Lossana and went in search of his friends. The minstrels were playing down by the bridge: some of the younger folk had taken it over for dancing. Ylia took a cup of the summer wine and a piece of soft yellow cheese, went back through the square and the market with Lossana.

There was a feast late in the afternoon, then more music and the square was cleared for more dancing as Ber'Sordes's new household musicians came out.

The square was crowded: The music was good, and dancing a favorite pastime among the Plainsfolk. Erken danced once with Lossana, once with her—she wasn't as comfortable as most at it, but her mother had taught her until she was at least competent. She danced once then with Corlin, took a formal set with Ber'Sordes and Ang'Har after that, and was glad to sit for a while.

She saw Golsat once, when he was dancing with his sister—one of her newest swordswomen—. *Mothers, if Erken wasn't right.* Girls who had never paid heed to her dark armsman before stared after him now. Golsat seemed blissfully unaware of the havoc he was creating. She thought fleetingly of Ysian, and wondered what she would think of the change in Golsat.

A form came between her and the dancers; startled she looked up as Galdan bowed, gravely correct. "If no one has claimed the next dance of you, my Lady, I would be honored to take it."

"No one has, and you may have it, First Knight of my House." If he could be ridiculously formal, so could she. "The honor is mine." He inclined his head, stood just behind her chair to wait for the music.

He danced well, which should not have surprised her. Erken's son would never have been permitted to trip over his feet or his partner's, not if Erken had the say. He remained gravely correct, a little aloof, spoke not at all, led her back to the dais when the music ended and vanished into the crowd. She gazed after him briefly, a frown creasing her brow. But Ber'Sordes was at her elbow, offering her another cup of Narran summerwine. This was the dark vintage they grew and fermented high on their main island; it retained the flavor of grapes, reminded her of the juices Malaeth had made for her when she was a child.

The musicians took an hour to rest, people milled around the square. Down one of the market aisles, Brelian and Lisabetha must have turned up, because someone had started one of the more raucous songs made for the honor of the newly married. She could feel the blood in her cheeks, hoped none of the Narrans would ask her for a translation.

Galdan and Golsat wandered past just as the musicians began to play again. She winced. *More tradition, Mothers help us all, one we could have done well without.* Both were loudly, joyously drunk. As they vanished into the crowd, they broke into another wedding-night song. This one was fortunately not as specific as the last, for she was certain the Ambassador couldn't fail to hear them.

Nor did he. "That's an interesting tune," Ber'Sordes smiled. "What does it mean?"

"Um. The usual things, happiness to the new couple, all that." Ber'Sordes looked disconcerted indeed. "Oh."

"No, not *that!*" she laughingly assured him. "But I think it would be better if either of them could sing!"

"Well, perhaps they can," the Ambassador ventured. "Sober, that is."

The music started up again, livelier tunes and now mostly the younger boys and their girls danced. The older folk stayed to the outside, enjoying the music, clapping in time to it, trading comments about those who danced, noting who danced with whom, gossiping over which might be the next wedding. Lisabetha and Brelian led out the first two dances, then vanished for good.

Ber'Sordes gave her another cup of the heavy red wine. It tasted good as it was, even better fruited. The Ambassador was telling her dry little tales of his service as a Liaison in Osnera, keeping her laughing. Even Ang'Har, now that he no longer looked at her as though she were the light of a full moon dazzling his eyes, proved to be likeable, able to tell a good tale. He collected them too, along with the sillier of Nedaoan folk songs.

"Ang'Har, you *don't!*"

"Truly," he replied earnestly. "You've the best of the kind I've ever heard, and I've heard a lot of them."

"You can't! No one does that! Except me."

"You?" His mouth fell open.

She laughed. "Swear it! But—I don't believe this, you actually have gone in search of people to teach you those songs? I'm surprised you found anyone who knows them—or would admit to knowing them."

"I like them," he insisted. "I particularly like the way people groan when you start singing, but they always laugh at the end."

"So they do. D'you know 'The Five Tinkers'?"

"That's the one with the green dye, and they—no, that's another one."

"The green dye is 'The Soldier's Strange Brew.'"

He laughed. "Of course! The Soldier's Strange—oh." He cast her a dubious glance. "A Lady shouldn't know *that* one!"

"It's borderline," she admitted. "I never sang it for my mother, and I wouldn't sing it here and now. But I know it, and I laugh at the last verses. Thank you," she added as Ber'Sordes filled her cup again and handed it back to her.

"Well, *my* favorite, so far," Ang'Har said, "is 'The Lady and the Dragon.'"

"Oh, *no*. It's mine, too. Especially—"

"—What I like best—"

"—and he's just so smug, so caught up in how wonderful he is, and—"

"—and then he tries to rescue her from the dragon before it eats her and he offers to marry her and—"

"—'and I'll be yours forever, you lucky wench'—"

"—those aren't the words *I* got, but—and then *she* says—" and, together, and near enough to key, they both sang: "'Pardon me, sir, if it's all the same, but I'd rather have the dragon.'" Ylia collapsed back in her chair, giggling weakly. Ang'Har laughed, and the Ambassador applauded them both.

"It's *terrible*," Ylia said finally, but she broke up again when Ang'Har met her eye and winked.

"Of course it is, they all are. That's the point, isn't it?"

"My position prohibits me to say so. Accident, no doubt. Not deliberate intent." She managed the words without a stumble, but it took care. 'You're drunk,' Nisana's thought intruded suddenly, accusingly. 'I am *not*, cat. I'm—'

'Drunk,' the cat finished for her as she paused to seek a better word. 'You'll have a head like a melon in the morning, and you're getting silly.'

'Silly. Hah.' But she set the half-filled cup aside and pushed to her feet: steadily, or so she hoped. "My Lords, by your leave. It's been a long day, and—that's a sneaking wine you have, Lord Ambassador."

"So it is." Ber'Sordes inclined his head gravely. "So much so," he added, "that I hope you will not take offense if I do not rise. I think I must save my strength for the return to my quarters." She laughed, shook her head. Ang'Har stood to hand her down from the platform, and he walked her around the Square.

Eyes; someone was glaring at her. She glanced off to both sides—no one. The feeling persisted. Ang'Har stopped at the first step when they reached the Tower, bowed low over her fingers and was gone. She gazed out over the Square, the dancers, sighed deeply and happily, and turned to climb the steps. It was, suddenly, a task to take all her concentration indeed.

She reached the door, caught at it, turned as footsteps thudded up behind her. Galdan stood before her. "My Lady." He opened both doors for her, closed them behind him.

It was shadowy in the hall, the ceiling was lost in gloom and the stairs were dark; only two candles burned in the glass enclosures on either side of the doors and one on the ledge at the head of the steps. "My Lady." She turned. He closed the distance between them. He was steady on his feet but the words came out oddly.

"Lord Galdan." This formality was something new with him tonight, and she found it irritating: was he mocking her? Laughing at her? There was something under his words, under his constant 'my Lady' that dug at her. "You're in your cups tonight, aren't you?"

"It's expected," he replied cheerfully. "I was celebrating. I'm not drunk."

"Kind of you to assure me so." Silence. "You're between me and the stair, and I'm tired. If you don't mind, I'd like to get by you."

"And if I do?" he demanded suddenly. "If I do mind?"

She sighed. "Are we back to fighting? All around the circle and back to its joining. If you want to argue, fine, do so. But not with me, not tonight. I'm tired, and you're drunk."

"Hah." She stepped to one side, stopped as he moved to again stand between her and the stair. *"I'm* drunk. Not so drunk that I do not remember my duty to my Queen *and* my arms-mate. You gave me that duty, if you remember."

"If you—"

"Hush, woman, let me speak, this once!" He caught at her shoulders, punctuated his words with a gentle shake. She felt his fingers hard against muscle. "Ang'Har the Young. He's on Father's lists, I'll just wager he is! He's noble, as Narrans figure it, and he's pretty with his baby's face. He'd look fair on Nedao's throne." She opened her mouth, shut it as he cast her a searing look. "He'd never lead the armies, but that's all right, the ruling is yours by birth and *you* do that anyway! Of course, you could keep him as consort and deny him the throne, but Nar might take that hard—" The wine had gone from his voice as he spoke and anger seeped into it. It curdled in her stomach.

"You can't talk to me like that!"

"No? As a member of your council, as your arms-mate, as your Household armsman? But someone should tell you such things, before you make a fool of yourself!"

"I make a fool of myself? You must be drunk indeed to stand there and say that to me as though you mean it!"

"I have sworn to your service for all my life," he said flatly, and punctuated his words with another shake. "And I would swear to more, did I ever hope to see assent in your eyes, Lady." He pulled her close, kissed her hard and let her go; she stumbled, caught at the banister for balance. Before she could say anything at all, he was gone.

"Ylia?" Malaeth and two of the older women came in moments later to find her standing in the hall, staring past the doors. "Are you—you've been drinking, girl!" the old woman accused. "Did you eat enough tonight?"

"I don't remember. I think I did."

"You'll know in the morning," Malaeth warned. "And whatever are you doing here in the hall? It's late and you'll catch a chill down here. It's gone cold."

"Has it?" Ylia asked vaguely, but allowed herself to be led upstairs. Malaeth hung the red and gold dress on a peg, checked it over briefly.

"You wore that all day and kept it clean and untorn. I'm astonished, girl!"

'She danced in it, too,' Nisana put in sleepily from the bed. 'That's usually good for a ripped hem or two. Are you ill, girl?'

'No—fine.'

'Huh. If you've taken a fever—' But she tucked her head back down under one paw and went back to sleep.

Ylia let the old woman install her in the sleep shirt, sat quietly as Malaeth brushed her hair down and tied it in the single plait for night, then slid under the blankets. Malaeth tucked them around her chin, closed the long shutters and took the light away with her.

There was the sea: she'd the smell of it, suddenly, and the whispery sound of it hitting sand, pulling away. She couldn't see it, because the tower filled all her vision, blocking everything else, including light. She pushed through a rotting canvas curtain. Steps: They wound around the outside of the tower, inside a thick rock wall. She could sense how thick. There were no windows, no openings. *I'll smother,* and for a moment, she couldn't remember how to breathe. Her feet went on climbing, her knees were beginning to ache with it and there was a catch in her side.

An odd smell to the air: scented smoke. And, with a sinking feeling in the pit of her stomach, she realized she *could* see, because there was the outline of a door ahead of her. And the light that outlined it was deep, darkly red. The red of dried blood.

The door was closed, perhaps latched. She passed beyond it, was in the next moment beyond the still closed door and in a round room. It was at the top of the tower: the walls were stone, but the roof was wood and high-gabled. Tapestries covered the walls, holding back the damp and cold of the rock; there were deep carpets under her feet. A fire in a wide pit had smoldered down to red; smoke trailed from it to a hole in the roof far above. Two braziers, capped, stood just beyond it. *Lisabetha saw it first, now me*. It came as no surprise when she turned and saw the two who occupied the table at the room's center.

They were unaware of her: Marrita stood behind a heavy, ornately carved chair, her hand resting on Lyiadd's shoulder. There were lines at her eyes that hadn't been there before: something had exacted a price from her. Whatever had taken, though, had given also, for there was something about her—a sense, a scent, a feeling. Power to twist and rend, to destroy. The Lammior's Power.

And the man: creature in man's form, she'd thought him, on first sight. He was that and more. His hands rested on the edges of a dark bowl; red smoke trailed over its edges to slide in curls about the tabletop. Those hands had nearly killed her once, but with steel, he'd used steel, threats, an AEldra strength—warped but still knowably AEldra. His face came up: there was a curious blankness to his smoke-colored eyes, as though something of him had been lost, not yet found.

But his hands: They terrified her. They could kill with a touch, could tear flesh, burn and blacken it, rend the inner being—less than a touch, with the thought of a touch.

It took an effort that left her ill to tear her eyes from those fingers where they rested against the lip of the bowl. A map on the table beyond him—*look at that instead*, she urged herself. *Map*— the Peopled Lands were sectioned off into three parcels, light-colored hatchings dividing them. As she stared at the map, it seemed to crisp at the edges, red crept around it and it burst into flame. Her eyes were seared, she stumbled back. Horror gripped her suddenly, her legs refused to work, she could not breath. And Lyiadd's eyes came up, Marrita's did, and sought hers—

She screamed, threw herself to one side, and suddenly woke. Nisana, every hair standing on end, leaped for the pillow. 'A dream, that's all! Here—calm yourself—' She rubbed against an unresponsive hand, butted Ylia's face with her head. Ylia panted, became aware she was panting, brought her breathing under control. "Not dead," she whispered. "Not dead."

'No. It's all right, don't fret it.'

"It's not all right. Not—did I cry aloud?"

'No, you woke no one, just me.'

"Good." She turned onto her side, pulled the furs close about her throat. "I dreamed—"

'Tomorrow,' Nisana broke in. 'Don't think on it, sleep again. Come, close your eyes—'

'I can't, I'm afraid—'

'You can. I'm here. Trust me, girl. I'll guard you—'

"Against that—"

'I can. You know I can, and I will. Trust. Sleep.' It took time, took enough time to worry her. The girl finally slept. *She never dreamed before, not like this. Poor girl—she has enough to fret, without fretting things she can't yet reach. And she'll worry it. Is that why the dream came to her, to worry her and wear her down?* Nisana resettled herself hard against Ylia's shoulder. *It won't, not if I can prevent.*

It was a warm morning, sunny like the day before had been. A number of City folk were cleaning up the Square and there was a crowd down by the River awaiting the launch of a new cargo barge. She rode by, waved and smiled at those who greeted her, but she had Marckl's road to herself, and the docks were empty: Kre'Darst had gone back down-river at first light, and the goods he'd brought had long since been stored or forwarded up to the City. She tied the grey to a tree, walked out the wooden platform, dangled her feet over the water and stared at the trees on the far bank.

"Black hells," she whispered. Lyiadd! Where was he? Had she seen things happening or what might? She shook that aside, Nisana was right. She couldn't be rid of him by worrying the matter, and there were other things to chew down at present.

Such as—? She flinched away from it, then came back to it several times. What was the matter with the man? For that matter, what was wrong with her? "Just as I think we're friends, he goes off, or goes distant, and I begin to wonder if he has any regard for me at all! Perhaps he's still offended by—'' One hand came up reluctantly to trace the faint line running down her right cheek. No. That *had* bothered him badly, she'd seen it in his face whenever he looked at her, at first. For a long time now, though, she'd swear he hadn't even noticed it, save as being part of her.

And yet, last night—. He *was* drunk. *I'd have sworn he hadn't even wanted to speak to me, let alone touch me. Madmen and nightmares, I'll never drink Narran wine again!*

Nisana appeared suddenly at her side, and sat regarding her. There was an amused gleam in her eye.

'You've thought yourself in a circle ten times this morning, girl. Obviously you and this man are intended for each other and neither of you wants to admit it first. Personally, I prefer the direct ways of cat-kind.'

'Nisana!'

'I always knew where I stood with my mates, there was none of this silliness. Though I admit it's amusing to watch, in a way.'

'Nisana, you can't just—!'

'Are you safe here alone?' Nisana inquired dryly. Before Ylia could respond, she added thoughtfully, 'I *think* I prefer cat's ways, it's been a long time since I've even thought of it, one way or the other.'

'Cat, I swear—!'

'He's coming,' Nisana broke in sharply. 'Don't speak with your pride, girl! Watch your words, say nothing you'll regret.' And the cat was gone. Ylia scrambled to her feet as Galdan came out of the woods and onto the sunlit dock.

He was dressed in his skins, and didn't seem surprised to see her. *Sensed me. Like a bear, no doubt.* He came up, knelt before her formally. ''Lady.'' His voice was low and it trembled, she scarcely caught the word; he was subdued indeed.

''Galdan? What is this?''

''A favor. For both of us. I want release from my oath.''

''You want to return to the mountains.'' He nodded. She stared down at him, caught off guard and at a loss for words.

''I've paid my debt to you, the blood-debt that brought me here. I think it might be better if I leave now.''

What game is this? Haven't I enough to worry without this? ''Don't talk nonsense!'' she snapped. His head jerked, startled eyes met hers briefly. He turned them resolutely back to the rough board before his knees.

"It's not, you know," he began flatly, much more like his normal argumentative self. He stopped abruptly.

"You look ridiculous down there, and I don't believe you. You stand up, look me in the eye and say all that." Silence. "Well?"

"That's not proper—"

"It's never stopped you before, has it?" And as he stayed where he was, she added in exasperation, "All right, if you're going to be like that, so can I." She dropped down cross-legged on the dock so he must look at her or turn away. "There. Now, if *you* sit, we can possibly reason this out." He shook his head, eyed her cautiously and looked away again.

What is the matter with the man? But quite suddenly she knew. What he felt, what he truly wanted. What she wanted.

By all the Mothers at once. Fool, Ylia, to not have seen it before. Different, entirely different, from the thing she and Brendan had begun. Stronger, in some way, less ethereal. But Nisana was right: *Choose your words carefully.* She could find years to regret the wrong ones. He was proud, like his father—like her. He'd want nothing of her, if he thought she offered pity or charity. *How can he doubt?* she wondered hotly. But that wasn't fair; when she hadn't known herself. But now she did know, she wasn't about to let him out of reach.

"You can't leave," she said finally. "You're needed here. Your father needs you. And what about Golsat? Brel's gone with Lisabetha, you'll leave poor Golsat to face the barracks alone. That's not the act of a true friend."

"I—" He cast her another little look, turned his face away. "Father and I argue. Your council meetings will be a lot better without both of us at one table."

"That's a poor reason for depriving Nedao of a councer with your knowledge."

"Perhaps. You've Golsat for that, though, and he has other things besides me to occupy his time."

"Things substitute poorly for friends. Don't you know that?" He shrugged. "Well, *I* know it. But it doesn't matter, because I won't release you."

"You—?"

"Absolutely not."

"But I—"

"No. And be quiet." She moved to her knees, gripped his shoulders hard. "Just listen to me, Galdan Erkenson. You swore to my service, you pledged to my aid, you're the First of my Household armed and my arms-mate."

"But—"

"Will you *stop* interrupting me? It really doesn't match this servile posture you're trying to hold." She punctuated the words with a shake; it moved her as much as it did him. He caught her eye, bit his lip but the laugh broke through.

"By all the hells at once, you're a stubborn creature! I—well, I just didn't want you to have the embarrassment of looking at me every day, after what I did last night. Is that so bad?"

"I don't know. Were you *trying* to insult me? Besides, do I look embarrassed?" she demanded. He eyed her critically.

"Well! Now you mention it, you've gone rather red—you do that nicely, by the way, I like it—"

"Quiet. I don't know why I talk to you. Maybe you should leave after all."

"No, you said I couldn't and I do honestly try to follow my Lady's orders." He grinned cheerfully. "It helps when they're consistent."

She cast an imploring glance upward. "You're incorrigible."

"Well, then." He jumped to his feet, held out a hand. "Does that mean you intend to take me as I am?"

She laughed, caught at his fingers. "I suppose it does. That's a straight trade, after all."

"So it is," Galdan caught her up in his arms and smiled at her. "So it is. Well, then, Lady mine, what next?"

"You put me down," she began severely.

"Not a chance, now that I've got hold of you! Next suggestion?"

She shook her head, laughed. "All right, then! You come back to Koderra, right now, and get out of these hides. They smell."

"Ah." He sniffed cautiously. "So they do—unless that's—no, of course it's not you. And?"

"And," Ylia said with a smile to match his, "we find your Father's lists and put a new name at the top."

"Now, with *that,* I wholly agree." He kissed her lightly, set her on her feet, and held out a hand.

Epilogue

He stood in the shelter of the stone lintel, where he could gaze out over the sea, the harbor, and watch the incoming ships. *Soon.* He'd sensed it during the night: It had colored his dreams, ruined his sleep. *If he hates me—men have hated other men for that much; for less than that.* But, no; he'd have known, if the boy had come for vengeance. *Boy? He's no boy, he's grown. What boy he was —I lost that, long since.*

His hands clenched. *They had no right to exile him, damn them all to an endless night! As, so help me, I shall!*

The dawn had come, gone, and the sky was clouded over again. Wind blew chill across the water, ruffling his sandy red hair, bringing with it the smell of the dead shellfish and greyish weed that littered the high tide mark. He drew the furred cloak closer, stepped back farther into shelter.

Alone. She wouldn't have waited anyway, not here: Not her way. It bothered him, though, that he'd been made aware of it. She had no right to make her dislike so clear to him, none. Whatever she meant to him, whatever he owed her. Oh, she'd aided him, helped him find the one he sought—he still, *still* couldn't do it alone! Only when she knew for certain he wouldn't foreswear it if she didn't.

He stared down at his hands. Black flame licked at his nails, faded as he willed it. *Mine.* Though it hadn't been for long, and there wasn't much else he had, just now. Even memory was a chancy and sometime thing. There was still much he couldn't remember. The dagger: He remembered that dagger. Remembered, from somewhere deep in a flame-wrapped hellish dream, two women's voices: 'I wish you joy of your lord, Marrita. Such as I left, you are welcome to!' Marrita's reply, so broken with weeping it was scarcely understandable, fading by the moment: 'I will have your death for this!' The Lammior's Power: *Thanks to women—to both of them—I have it. I will have it. Not that the*

*other will have gratitude at my hands, in the end. No. She'll pay:
for that dagger, for my pain. For his pain. For all of it.*

Movement out to sea caught his eye as an approaching thought
touched against his inner senses: A ship, black sail bellied with the
wind, tacked across the harbor entrance, back again, and crew ran
to bring the ebony fabric under control. As it came into calm
water, he could make out individuals. The captain—his close-
cropped red hair a beacon, even in such grey light—stood in the
bows, shouting orders back to his men. *Serve me well, Brit Arren.
There's reserve in your service to me, though you think you keep it
hidden. Retain your Raider's pride, your doubts, the odd thing
even you dare not call conscience. Lock them in the holds of your
mind—and serve me.*

His thought was broken as the *Fury* came around and the
anchors went down: A boat was lowered on the far side, came into
view. Two common seamen rowed it, the captain himself—his
back stiff with disapproval—steered. And in the bow, still facing
to sea—Lyiadd caught his breath. Clenched his fists, hard, to
break the moment. *Mine. Is it possible? And will he accept me,
after so long a time?* It was a boyishly slender figure, a straight
back and light brown hair with none of his red to it. *Hers was that
color—Nala's. A little darker, perhaps. I've forgotten, it's been so
long.*

He pushed free of the doorway, walked down the paved path
and out onto the dock as the boat came near. The seamen leaped
out, held it against the dock. The passenger stepped up, the
seamen stepped down; the boat went swiftly back to the *Fury*.

Vess set his feet cautiously against the unmoving dock, brought
his head up as footsteps thudded on the planking. Stopped. He
stared at the man five paces away from him.

*Father..He's tall, just as Mother said. But I remember the other
thing now: the strength of him. He radiated it, that was what she
said. Like a god, she said. His throat hurt.*

*There's no hate in him, not for me, not for his father. I'd know.
But he's been hurt, hurt badly. Blade-hurt, heart-hurt.* His breath
caught as his eyes fixed on the long, rough scar running down his
son's face. *Like hers. I marked her, just that way. I remember that.*

Vess reached down to the sheath strapped to his boot, drew the
silver dagger, held it out, hilts first. He swallowed hard. Brought
up a smile. "Father?"

Lyiadd smiled in reply, took the remaining steps to bring them
together, took the knife and Vess's other hand in his own. "My
son."